"It's only one kiss, Ian."

Not quite pressed against him, she stood close enough that her skirts absorbed his body heat through his trousers. "You've wanted to kiss me since you cornered me in the alcove. Deny it."

He slid the pad of his thumb against her bottom lip, sending tiny shivers through her nerves.

Three years ago, he'd walked away from her. But in the surrounding sunlight pressing against them, three years was a lifetime ago, and she no longer cared what had gone before.

What she did care about suddenly seemed more urgent, more perilous and infinitely more satisfying.

"I could kiss you," he said, lowering his voice and his mouth toward hers. "If I thought you knew how."

Other **AVON ROMANCES**

Coming Soon

And Don't Miss These
ROMANTIC TREASURES
from Avon Books

Melody Thomas

Sin And Scandal In England

AVON

An Imprint of HarperCollinsPublishers

AVON BOOKS
An Imprint of HarperCollins*Publishers*
10 East 53rd Street
New York, New York 10022-5299

Copyright © 2007 by Laura Renken
ISBN: 978-0-06-112960-5
ISBN-10: 0-06-112960-7
www.avonromance.com

First Avon Books paperback printing: October 2007

Avon Trademark Reg. U.S. Pat. Off. and in Other Countries, Marca Registrada, Hecho en U.S.A.
HarperCollins® is registered trademark of HarperCollins Publishers.

Printed in the U.S.A.

10 9 8 7 6 5 4 3 2 1

I want to give a special thank you to Kate Hauk for coming through with much valuable research and for being such a great friend. Your enthusiasm inspires me.
And to my oldest son, Brent, a huge influence in my life. I love you.

Chapter 1

England

For Bethany Munro, gaiety and frivolity ended the moment Ian Rockwell walked through the arched doorway.

As if the winter snowstorm outside had swept into the glittering ballroom, a stir of cool, speculative whispers reached those finding respite at the sumptuous buffet table in the back of the crowded room. A scandal in black, his broad shoulders shaped by an elegantly cut evening jacket, he walked with physical grace, a quick dimpled smile, and that promise of sin prevalent in his eyes—a gaze reserved solely for the woman on his arm.

Champagne flute arrested against her lips, Bethany found her breathing constricted by a tightly laced corset. Since venturing from secluded country life two years ago, she had learned quickly enough the world was rife with temptation. It surrounded her, taunted her. Yet she had never been tempted, for the carnal fantasy of only one man haunted her from the past and seemed to frame her future.

But now here he was, with the beautiful widowed

Countess Dermott draped on his arm, the one man who had ruined all other men for her, cordially greeting their host, casually stepping back into her life even as he did not know it yet. She watched as he moved with a smooth urbanity, stopping occasionally to speak with people as he worked his way across the room, a man comfortable amidst the aristocratic glamour of such wealthy surroundings.

Bethany had not seen Ian in three years, and she had never expected to see him again. Her blond hair was upswept and perfectly coiffed; her blue azure silk-and-tulle gown nothing more than another jewel amidst a sea of rainbow-colored attire. She wondered if he would recognize her in the crowd, then her growing apprehension usurped the initial flutter she'd felt—because he *was* really here at Whitley Court, a very dangerous place for them both, and the last place in the world she wanted to encounter him.

Her awareness of him became so palpable that it seemed to stretch taut across the distance separating them. Her heartbeat raced. She suddenly wanted to slip from the ballroom. Did she dare? But as she considered the question, he suddenly looked across the ballroom directly at her.

She froze as rigid as the naked mermaid ice sculptures to her left and right. His eyes touched and held her, only the merest hesitation in his sensual features, his face dark and intent. Then the woman on his arm spoke to him and, just that quickly, the contact shattered.

He bent his leonine head to listen, his mouth widening into an easy smile, his handsome face taking on a boyish cast in the warm glow of lamplight reflected in the golden tissue-draped walls and ceiling of the ballroom—all as if the last ten seconds had not occurred, as if Bethany had only imagined the touch of green fire in his eyes when they'd fallen on her.

Ian Rockwell had barely noticed she was alive.

Bethany felt a stab in her chest, yet despite herself, she made herself stand straight and tall and wrapped herself in cool composure as if she had never laid her heart at his feet and he had walked away.

Charlene giggled close to her ear. The tip of her crimson lace fan strategically placed at her chin shut Bethany's mouth. "Don't bother lusting after him, oh friend of mine," she whispered. Bethany and Charlene Dubois, her host's daughter, had met at England's Academic Conservatory for Young Ladies two years ago. "As you can see, my Aunt Serena has taken Sir Ian off the market."

Bethany was astounded by an unfamiliar timidity and the growing tightness in her chest. Had he been a "Sir" when she had known him? "I have no idea of whom you are speaking," she replied, snapping open her own fan.

As the orchestra opened another waltz, the final set for the evening, Ian escorted the exotic Countess Dermott onto the floor. He seemed to tower over the dark-haired beauty. She was not tall, so perhaps every man around her looked that much taller.

"Yes, you do." Charlene laughed, the action setting fire to the diamond necklace that lay atop the pale shelf of her ample bosom. "He is quite wealthy, rich as Croesus they say," she added coyly. "My aunt met him a few months ago at the home of a mutual acquaintance. It would be a coup for Papa if Sir Ian should decide to join our organization. The Rockwells are an established family."

"Are they?"

Charlene giggled, as if Bethany should already be privy to such local details when, in reality, she'd only arrived at Charlene's home from the conservatory two weeks ago. "His family has resided in these parts since the Vikings dominated this countryside. He is a bachelor again. His wife passed away a few years ago."

Wife? Bethany's heartbeat stumbled. "He was married? When?"

"Three or four years ago." Charlene waved her plump hand dismissively as she turned her focus to the banquet table. "Some whirlwind courtship and wedding that ended tragically. No one really knows what happened." She examined the creamed salmon and cucumber hors d'oeuvres with the eye of a connoisseur. "Do you want one?"

Bethany shook her head, a sudden queasiness overtaking her. She wasn't feeling her best.

Charlene plopped the cucumber wedge between her lips. "Sir Ian wasn't married long enough for him to bring his wife home. In fact, the prodigal son only just returned this fall. He has been somewhat reclusive. Papa must have included him at the last moment. He isn't on the guest list." Charlene turned the topic to the group of Italian gentlemen currently approaching from the other end of the buffet table.

Outside the large windows, huge snowflakes had begun to crystallize against the glass as the storm sweeping off the North Sea began to blanket the provincial estate in white. But inside, the air was clement, nearly hot. Drink and food were liberally proffered to guests. Couples filled the dance floor. Bethany sighed. Ian had been married and widowed since she'd fallen in love with him those years ago.

As a handsome Italian count requested her hand in the waltz, she forced a smile, accepting his invitation to dance as if she were an actress stepping into the part of a grand play. She danced with an exuberance and passion that extended to every corner of her life. Indeed, she never did anything halfway. The world was her oyster and she was its pearl, she'd always told herself, many times, as if saying it often enough would make her believe it was true. Perhaps that had been her greatest fault. She put too much of herself into the *act* of living. People were always telling her she worked too hard at making others see her, and now, when all she wanted was to disappear into the tiny cracks in the floor, she felt as if a huge ball of light were shining down on her, revealing her most embarrassing flaws.

"You are here for the next two weeks?" her partner asked, sweeping her in a majestic circle to the flowing strains of music.

The fragrance of his flowery cologne surrounded her in an altogether unpleasant way, but she presented him with a distracted smile. "Yes. And you?" She asked, despite knowing he was. She'd seen the exclusive invitation list and knew exactly who was invited to this event, which was why Ian's presence caught her off her guard.

The count followed with a chat about the weather and other mundane topics that did not require her full attention and enabled her to catch glimpses of Ian and the countess. "Yellow," the man said after another turn.

Yellow? She pulled herself out of her thoughts.

"I have seen you in London recently," he said. "Some

weeks ago, I believe. You were wearing yellow."

Something in his tone cooled her. "I haven't been to London in months."

"No?" He leaned back and considered her. "I am sure I saw you there. But I cannot put my finger on where."

She threw herself into the waltz, a fact noted by her partner for he pulled her nearer.

"And as I said, sir. You are mistaken. Miss Dubois and I were still at the conservatory until the break two weeks ago."

"You are good friends with Lord Whitley's daughter?"

"We attend university together. Her father sponsors the science curriculum at the conservatory."

"Ah, an enlightened woman," he said, his dark eyes intent on her face. "It is odd to me that I should find a woman with your, um, assets . . . unmarried."

"My assets?" She feigned ignorance. "I am hardly wealthy. Certainly not as you are, sir."

Pleased with her flattery, he tightened his hold. "You are very beautiful, Signorina Munro."

Bethany traveled alone with her maid, and some men erroneously considered her easy pickings. She spent the rest of the dance fending off the loquacious count, as he seemed bent on seducing her. She suddenly wanted out of this room. She stepped on the man's polished shoes, nearly causing him to trip, her usual glib riposte hidden in her apologetic smile. *Oaf*, she thought, and couldn't care less if this foreign lothario considered her ungainly and gauche.

The music concluded in a resounding crash of cymbals. The man, limping, escorted Bethany off the floor, back to the buffet table, with a flourish typical of every

Italian she had ever met, then he bowed over her gloved hand and quickly made his escape. Snapping open her fan, she watched him move into the crush exiting the floor. Her eyes suddenly froze on the couple standing just at the edge of the dance floor. Her pulse halted.

Bethany had stopped searching for Ian. Now, without any effort at all, she stood less than thirty feet from him, his tall form easily recognizable in the crowd. Her gaze rose from the white-gloved hand intimately splayed on the woman's small waist . . . and collided with his eyes.

Her breath shuddered to a complete halt. Ian was watching her over Countess Dermott's diamond-sprinkled hair, his expression now devoid of its polite mask as he raised a champagne flute to his lips and sipped.

Bethany did not imagine the touch of green fire in his gaze, assessing her, closing the distance between them, melting the years as if they were no longer part of the past. She felt that touch deep within her like a bruise on bone.

They each looked away from the other at the same time. And, despite the initial shock and illogic of her response, she felt something else, something familiar and very much alive. Something that made her a little afraid. He not only knew who she was, but he was not pleased to see her—any more than she had been to see him.

She relaxed a little as another man stepped forward to claim her hand for the next waltz, until she saw who it was.

Lord Whitley's secretary and bodyguard, Sir John Howard, stood in front of her. If there was any man present tonight that made her sick to her stomach, this was he.

Dressed much as Ian was in a formal jacket with tails, he might have been dashing if Bethany had a penchant for older, slippery men who took advantage of younger women. "Miss Munro," he said, "I believe I am on your dance card."

She had no dance card and didn't pretend to be polite. He'd been watching her, she realized, and not in the way one watches a woman he wishes to seduce. "My feet ache, Sir John. I have finished waltzing for the night."

She sidestepped him but he moved to block her exit, casually reaching across her for a chocolate strawberry on the table. "I see you have taken note of the countess's latest lover." He bit into the sweet fruit.

It was never a good sign to come under Sir John's scrutiny, and, while his words bore a hint of indifference, his eyes continued to study her. His conversation bothered her. Not because the exchange was highly inappropriate, but because he had discovered her uncertainty with such ease and would make her the insect in his petri dish.

"You believe they are not?" he asked.

She fixed her gaze on Sir John's face. "Why would I take note of anyone Countess Dermott considers her lover?"

Why would it matter to him what she thought?

"I see I have made you uncomfortable," he conceded.

She smiled. "Not at all, Sir John."

Uncomfortable was too mild a response for a man she suspected of being a cold-blooded murderer. Without excusing herself, she swept past him and let herself vanish into the crowd.

* * *

Ian had not expected to see Bethany Munro at this gathering, had not planned for the fortuitous possibility that he would confront someone who knew his past, least of all the winsome sprite whose life he had once been charged to protect. He had been watching her for some time now and had observed her conversation with Sir John Howard.

For a moment, he lost her in the throng. Then she emerged from the eddy of silks, satins, and velvets near the doorway, a vision wrapped in a blue April sky, a brilliant counterpoint to the swirling snow outside. How the bloody hell could he have been at Whitley Court for two days and been completely unaware of her presence?

His eyes narrowing slightly over a flute of champagne, he listened absently as the countess talked to the man who had arrived to claim her for a waltz.

The countess leaned nearer and whispered a seductive invitation in his ear. Her scent of jasmine touched his nostrils. "You will not go far? The treasure hunt begins at midnight. I insist we be partners."

Ian smiled down at her with his normal nonchalance, opting to ignore the imperious tenor of the command. "And which treasure will we be hunting tonight, dove?"

Serena stepped back in a rustle of amber silk, her hazel eyes promising the kind of wealth a man could only find between satin sheets. Ian looked at the foppish gent beside her and recognized him as the youngest son of a neighbor.

"Sir Ian." The man formally bowed his head, "How is your mother? She could not be present?"

The orchestra launched into another boisterous rendition of Strauss, and Ian found himself restless and no longer caring to smile and talk over trivialities. His mind's eye continued to follow Bethany. "My mother is well," he replied shortly.

Serena tapped the man on the arm with her fan. "Truly, our dance will be at an end 'ere we even waltz."

"You do not mind, old chap, that I borrow your countess?"

Despite the powerful incentive to throw himself into the part of Serena's jealous lover and suitor, Ian handed the countess over to the young lord. He raised his glass to his lips and watched indolently as the other man led her onto the dance floor. Though he had not at first been inclined to be any woman's gentleman suitor, Serena was beautiful and amenable, reason alone to have accepted her invitation to this country retreat. Yet it was not feelings for the dark-haired beauty that Ian fostered, but thoughts of a fairer damsel now crowding into his head and distracting him.

The crowd continued to thin as couples changed partners and returned to the floor. He raised his eyes to the place he'd most recently seen Bethany; his height offering an advantage when it came to spying on the actions of others. He finally found her at the exit, waylaid by their host.

He brought the champagne glass to his lips and leaned a shoulder against a nearby marble pillar. His gaze settled on Bethany's luminous fair hair, bereft of adornment, then moved to her shapely silhouette limned by shadows and light wavering over the fringes of the room. The last he'd heard, she was in residence at the Academic Conservatory for Young Ladies.

So why is she present at a country retreat hosted by

the sitting head of the most deadly anarchist movement in England?

Ian's mood was growing less charitable as Lord Whitley spoke to her, smiling at something she had said, and Ian watched the viscount's study of her departure.

Bethany Munro was clearly no longer the starry-eyed seventeen-year-old who had once slipped her arms around him and whispered in a voice he still remembered that she loved him.

No indeed, she was not.

He pushed off from the pillar and, navigating through the crowd, discreetly followed her out of the room.

Chapter 2

Ian watched two flanking footmen nod to Bethany as she strode past them into the corridor. The moment the reveling crowd in the ballroom could no longer see him, he picked up his pace, his footfall silent on the crimson and ivory Aubusson carpet. Her path took him through the ceremonial hallway, and he was beginning to wonder where she was headed so far from the ballroom. The Elizabethan stone house was built with two newer quadrangles that connected to the older part of the house in the center, in the way of a grand palace. They were entering Lord Whitley's private wing. There were no guest rooms in this part of the house.

Getting lost in these corridors would be easy. Clearly, she knew her way around.

He walked past an alcove, stopped suddenly, and slowly turned. He didn't know what made him turn, the exotic scent in the air perhaps. She'd stepped inside, partially revealed by sconce light, and stood with her back against the wall next to the tall window, draped in black velvet. Eyes of clear blue challenged him.

"Ian," she calmly said as if three years had not passed since she'd last seen him. "How are you?"

"Bethany Ann," he acknowledged.

He came to a stop in front of her, and even after all this time, she still felt familiar to him, perhaps not as comfortable as an old pair of leather boots, but to him she would forever be the barefooted wild child who loved horses and fat black cats. She didn't belong here; and her unexpected presence was already proving complicated, if only because he'd chased her down.

"No polite banalities?" he said with an underlying edge. "No flirting, pleading, or batting the eyelashes in an effort to explain what you are doing here?" he asked as if he held some masculine prerogative over her being. "Hell, for that matter *why* are you consorting with Whitley's crowd? Who brought you here?"

"It is a wonder I forgot how domineering, stoic, and perfectly capable you are of minding my business."

"Appreciate my restraint thus far," he softly warned. "Finding you here at Whitley Court is . . . how does one say? An—"

"Inconvenient coincidence?" She observed him coolly. "Forgive my assumption. But aren't you at Whitley Court as well?"

He knew Whitley's reputation among the upper reaches of the ton. He knew other things as well. What he didn't know was where Bethany's loyalties lay.

Leaning against the wall, he set his mouth in a straight line. His jacket opened to reveal an embroidered silk waistcoat. He didn't ask her about the Italian count with whom she'd danced, an arms manufacturer out of Milan. Or how well she knew Sir John Howard.

He folded his arms, straining his superfine formal attire. "I'm with the countess. I no longer work in my old job in any capacity."

He didn't elaborate. But it was the truth. His tone now conveyed it was her turn.

She tucked a wayward strand of hair behind her ear. "Viscount Whitley is Charlene's father and a benefactor of our school, for which I have been hired on as a temporary science instructor for next season while I finish my studies," she said. "There is nothing untoward about my being here either. I came with Charlene."

He cocked a brow. A blush heightened the color on her cheeks. "Then it looks as if we are both here for two weeks of relaxation and pleasure. There is nothing quite like a hot toddy in front of a roaring fire as the wind and ice are pounding on the windows."

"You presume too much, Ian. Just because you know my guardian and were once acquainted with me—a very long time ago, I might add—does not give you leave to exert control over me now, especially since you were the one who disappeared without so much as a by-your-leave, no less. I don't need anyone's permission to do as I please.

His shoulder remained against the wall. "As I recall, that independent-minded declaration of yours is nearly verbatim what you told me three years ago in the barn at your home."

His gentle tone softened her defenses. "What do you remember about anything I might have said?"

"I remember that much about you," he said in a quiet voice, and when she looked into his eyes, she knew as well that he remembered her kiss. He had left her that day without saying goodbye.

She suddenly looked away. He brought her face back around with the edge of his hand. Golden light from the sconce sifted through her hair, drawing out a glimpse of flaxen among the darker strands—light against shadows—the source of the scent he'd smelled on her when he'd passed the alcove and turned. Frankincense, perhaps or myrrh, like Queen Bathsheba from the land of sand and sickle moons.

"Tell me why you left the ballroom tonight," he asked.

"Tell me why you followed me?"

His expression politely blank, he fastened his gaze on her face touching briefly on the faint flutter at her throat. "Perhaps there is just something intriguing about a woman with something to hide," he said.

"Are you sleeping with Charlene's aunt?"

His brows lowered ominously. "Do you even know what that means?"

She laughed. "Would you prefer the scaled-down proper interpretation between lovers who share the same bed? Or perhaps the more graphic one visible in the congested slums and rookeries just east of Charing Cross in London? Neither of which pertains to the actual act of sleeping."

Ian continued to study her, half amused, his contemplative gaze direct, but she did not look away. "I'm glad to see you're all grown up, Bethany."

She glimpsed the indentation of a ring on his finger beneath his glove, and he was suddenly conscious of the need to curl his fingers into his palm. She looked up and found him watching her.

Vaguely listening to the faint strains of a waltz coming from the other end of the house, he realized he'd been standing there in the alcove with her far too long.

"Charlene said you were a widower. Why didn't you ever tell me you were married?"

His face did not change expression. "I didn't tell you because my personal life had—still has—nothing to do with you."

She brushed off her sleeves. "You've danced around my questions, lied about your reasons for being at Whitley Court, and now you would dismiss my questions as irrelevant. Truly, you consider me a dunce." With a smile that did not reach her eyes, she tapped her fan hard on his arm. "But it is nice to understand now why all those years ago you didn't take my virginity."

"Jesus . . ." He laughed on a suffocated breath. "Is that the manner of talk they teach young ladies at that fancy conservatory you attend?"

Clearly, Bethany liked that she had shocked him. Though she clearly preferred to smack him across the head with her fan, so he should consider himself fortunate. "I'm no longer seventeen years old, Ian Rockwell. Nor am I so gullible. You *might* want to note that before you tell me any more lies."

She started to walk past him but his hand shot out against the wall and blocked her. Her body responded with an indrawn gasp, her eyes chasing up to his. No more studied nonchalance. His half-lidded gaze was as far from paternal as she would ever glimpse in a man.

A charged second passed, then two, where Bethany seemed unable to draw in breath. "You're behaving rudely, Ian."

They stood inches apart, Ian holding her trapped between his body and the window, the fabric of her dress shaped against his legs. "Am I?"

"You know you are."

On edge, as restless as she, he raised his gaze from her lips to her eyes. A frown tugged at his brow. "I don't think you are gullible."

"You aren't just here because you and the countess wish to entertain one another in bed, Ian. Every guest has made a substantial contribution to Lord Whitley's workhouse reform fund. It was a requirement for an invitation. You could not have gotten here without doing so. Since when have you cared for the beleaguered masses?"

"If donating to the cause is a requirement to be at this country retreat, then why are you at Whitley Court? The last I heard, you had no money. What did *you* donate to get yourself invited?"

"That isn't fair, Ian," she whispered.

He stopped short of laughing outright and shook his head. "Fair?" Even to his ears, the single word sounded proprietary. He lowered his arm. "I remember once you told me you wanted to be a physician," he said. "What happened to you?"

"It wasn't feasible to follow in my grandfather's footsteps." She lifted a shoulder in a shrug. "Women are too frail and simpleminded to be doctors."

A part of his mind not engaged solely in battle with her picked up voices drifting into the alcove from down the corridor. It took several seconds for him to recognize the orchestra no longer played, and another few seconds to note Bethany had also discerned that fact. And yet, he was not inclined to pull away.

"You? Simpleminded?"

"The treasure hunt has started," she pointed out. "Unless you wish to explain your presence alone with me, I suggest we not be seen together."

The voices grew louder. In the charged silence, neither moved.

Finally, he stood aside to let her pass. "Good night, Bethany."

She brushed her palms down her skirt and a fragrant swish of blue silk escaped as she stepped out into the hallway, reaching the staircase as a gaily dressed couple suddenly emerged from another corridor. Too intoxicated to note Bethany's presence, the pair laughed and stumbled up the stairs.

Then the stairway swelled with people as more couples joined the first, reading scraps of paper in their hands, laughing over possible clues handed out in the ballroom after the final waltz for the night. Oblivious to discovery, Ian moved nearer to the paneled wall, just out of the light but not quite in the shadows. Bethany had paused, put her hand on the newel post. Then, as if sensing his stare, she turned her head. And something stirred in his depths. Something dark and unwelcome. Something unpleasant he'd put to bed long ago.

In her room, Bethany sat at her desk, copying papers, the scratch of her pencil the only noise in the silence. She still wore her gown from that evening's activities but not her satin slippers, having kicked them off near the door when she'd returned to her room a few hours ago.

Drunken laughter erupted somewhere outside her window. She stole a glance at the ivory and glass clock on the marble mantel across the room. It was well after midnight. Charlene would wonder why she had not been present at the treasure hunt tonight.

She turned in her chair and pulled aside the heavy draperies. A momentary lull in the snowstorm left the world a pristine white. Treasure hunters had ventured into the enclosed courtyard, rooting around the fountain and throwing snowballs at each other, much to their own amusement. The colored globe lamps strung on posts winked in the breeze. Normally Bethany would have joined them in their revelry.

But she had stopped caring about the festivities. She felt restless. After the conversation with Ian tonight, emotions had bubbled to the surface. She told herself she didn't care with whom he spent his time. For three years, he'd been spending his time as he'd seen fit and Bethany had survived well enough.

But mostly, she felt angry with herself for allowing her flirtation tonight. Then for not allowing it to go far enough.

Glaring at the ceiling, she knew she would do better if she embraced larceny and deceit with a wider grasp.

"Mum?"

Bethany's gaze swung toward the center of the room. Her young maid stood just past the circle of light. Bethany folded the papers on her desk, shoved them back into their protective casing, and edged them into her pocket.

"I was gone longer than I expected." Mary carried a steaming mug and brought it forward as Bethany stood. "But I made you your special chocolate. Will you be returning downstairs?"

Bethany accepted the drink from Mary's hands.

"Thank you, Mary. Not tonight. Did you find out where Sir Ian's room is?"

"Yes, mum." Mary walked to the window and pointed across the courtyard. "There. The room at the end."

Bethany stared across the courtyard. The curtains were closed. But light pressed against the glass from a crack in the draperies.

"If you should like, I could tell Miss Dubois you are suffering a megrim and that the toddy put you to sleep," Mary said.

Bethany turned away from the window. She inhaled the thick gooey aroma from the mug Mary had brought her and then sipped. She could taste the brandy. Normally she didn't drink, but tonight drinking seemed just the thing. "A megrim isn't too far from the truth."

"Are you not feeling well, mum?"

Even Bethany's special face powder did not entirely conceal the circles under her eyes. A little bit of clay and iron oxides worked miracles on a complexion, but Mary was right. This evening, she looked pale. It was one thing to have a milky white complexion to add to one's beauty arsenal, but another thing entirely to look dead.

"It's nothing to worry about, Mary." She set down the drink and let Mary unbutton her gown and help her undress for bed.

"Did you know that Napoleon was poisoned?" Mary said with growing drama in her voice. "Some believe it was arsenic. A tasteless—"

"I know what arsenic is," Bethany replied, her voice muffled behind the flannel of her nightdress. She poked out her head and drew on her sleeves. "I've not been poisoned with arsenic."

"Napoleon didn't believe he was either."

Mary was like a giant sea sponge. But instead of absorbing seawater into her pores, she absorbed information, whether it be from books at school or her surroundings. Last month Mary had read about Napoleon's life and death in one of the history books Bethany had given her. Now she viewed everything as a conspiracy. Before that, the story of Robin Hood had caught her imagination, and she feared taking the roads through Epping Forest, lest they be robbed by men wearing pointy hats and green hose.

Yet Bethany would rather spend time in Mary's company than anywhere downstairs tonight. She felt comfortable around the younger woman who found so much in life to enjoy. They had known each other since the days they discovered one another in a crowded Brighton train depot. Mary had been booted off the train to London as a stowaway. Bethany literally collided with her as the girl tried to pick her pocket. But instead of having the little minx arrested, Bethany bought her a London-bound ticket. Mary had refused to leave her side since and was more friend than personal servant.

As Mary helped Bethany button up the nightdress, she chatted about the servants of those attending the ball and about those who would be remaining until the end of this country retreat. Bethany learned there were four Italian noblemen, three Frenchmen, and two Russians from the consulate present, none who interested her.

"What did you find out about Sir Ian?"

Mary had returned to check on Bethany an hour ago and Bethany had sent her out for all the much-needed gossip. Mary began removing the pins from Bethany's thick hair. "He is more handsome than you told me he would be."

Bethany met Mary's gaze in the glass. "I didn't tell you he was handsome. I told you he was tall."

"He's wealthy, too. His family owns an estate north of here, a vineyard in France, and a sugar plantation in Jamaica." Mary began to turn down Bethany's bed. "Countess Dermott was quite put off that Sir Ian did not appear for the treasure hunt until it was nearly well over. In fact she was angry, mum."

Sitting at the vanity, Bethany set down the hairbrush. "He didn't appear?" Where had he gone when he'd left the alcove?

"Sir Ian was later found with a group of laggard treasure hunters sipping brandy and playing billiards."

Mary came over, picked up the brush, and began combing out Bethany's long hair. "This *is* rather exciting. I feel like a spy."

Bethany took Mary's hands and wanted to shake the dreamy look from her face. What she was doing could be dangerous. "You are never to let on to anyone that you actually care about what is said belowstairs. You understand that, don't you?"

"I know that, mum."

Bethany knew Mary was a social butterfly. She was nice and bubbly like a glass of champagne, and sometimes she talked too much. "Promise me you will not get comfortable around anyone here."

Mary's brown eyes widened. "I promise, mum."

Bethany relaxed a little. "You've been given enough blankets to sleep warmly?"

"Yes, mum. I'll be as snug as a bedbug."

She walked Mary to the door. "Good night, then. To-morrow comes early. I want you to go to bed."

Bethany shut the door and turned the key in the lock. She leaned with her back to the solid oaken panel and looked around her. A lamp brightened the chilly confines of her room, which, unlike the castellated grandeur of the rest of the manse, was decorated in soft lavender eyelet and primrose velvet, her favorite colors. She had not really noticed that before.

Anyone who had been in her room at school would know that she loved both colors. Charlene, knowing her penchant for all things violet, had probably told her father to put her in this room to make her feel more comfortable. Only she was not comfortable.

Bethany wasn't the first from the conservatory to be invited to Whitley Court. Some months before, her science instructor, Mrs. Langley, also active in Lord Whitley's close circle, made a similar trek. Shortly afterward, the board at the conservatory had hired Bethany to temporarily replace her. Bethany later heard the instructor had resigned and moved to France, where she'd married. That gossip was a lie. Mrs. Langley had been her mentor and her friend; she would never have left England without telling her, and the only man Mrs. Langley had been seeing before her disappearance had been Sir John. He had brought Mrs. Langley to Whitley Court, where she and her maid had simply vanished.

Bethany had tried to go to the authorities. But no one had cared about a penniless teacher rumored to have eloped when there were *real* crimes to investigate. No one would even make an inquiry. And going to Lord Whitley with her suspicions about Sir John without proof would have been akin to accusing Charlene's father of complicity in murder. After all, Mrs. Langley had been at Whitley Court with Sir John just before she'd disappeared. Over the past few months, Bethany had started collecting information on Sir John. But what had started as a murder investigation was turning into something equally nefarious as she'd begun to learn more about Sir John and his activities in Lord Whitley's organization.

She withdrew the sheath of papers from the casing in her pocket she'd placed there earlier when Mary came into her room. Inhaling a slow breath, Bethany knelt beside her travel trunk set at the end of her canopy bed. She unlatched the lock. Feeling beneath the satin-lined lid, she revealed a special compartment. With an audible metallic click, she slid out the drawer. She'd taken the papers from Sir John's private study, made copies of them, and would have to get them back before they were discovered missing. After replacing the compartment, she walked to the window. Huge snowflakes had begun to fall again. No one was outside now, but she could see the tracks left from their play in the frozen courtyard.

She started to turn away and stopped. As if her mind had the magical power to conjure him up out of ice and imagination, she suddenly saw Ian. He stood at the window across the courtyard.

She could see that he was in white shirtsleeves. She leaned nearer to the glass but otherwise didn't move. Not even to breathe.

It was definitely Ian, his hands in his pockets, an unmistakable edge to his stance. Restless did not describe what he made her feel. Looking at something off to the left, he had not seen her. Not yet. Then from across the courtyard, she felt it when he turned his head and found her in the window. Her back straightened. In her mind, she imagined his did as well, as if coming to attention when the queen walked into the room. His eyes held hers, imprinting themselves on her senses, and for a woman who prided herself on her instinct, she knew he felt it, too.

After a moment, she reached up and pulled the draperies shut, not because she *wanted* to shut him out, but because she *could* not. She sank into the plush chair away from the surrounding light and closed her eyes, letting her mind venture backward to a time that still held sway over memories.

Ian had been a friend to her once when she'd had no one else. Few people actually knew of the hours they'd shared in the dead of night when he'd found her alone in the barn with her horses. With her grandfather ill and the surrounding events that threatened her family at the time, he'd protected her life when she'd been in danger, even from herself.

She now recognized why he had not allowed her youthful flirtation all those years ago, and understanding his reasons helped her know the kind of man he was. That he had conducted himself with the highest professional and personal standards made his importance in her mind grow all the more. Even if he had not been charged with protecting her life, he didn't forget he was a married man.

Certainly he had been in love with his wife, she realized, wondering what manner of woman could command the heart of such a man. For Ian didn't strike Bethany as a man who would marry for anything less than an all-consuming love.

Suddenly the emotions evoked by that uncomfortable sensation in her stomach became something infinitely harsher than the memory of their one unfinished kiss.

Bethany may no longer be seventeen or his charge, but she still did not walk in his same circle. He remained in a stratosphere above her in terms of experience, while she was as young and green as she'd always been. That thought annoyed her.

Chapter 3

"**T**ruthfully, sir, I have no idea what you see in these people," Ian's valet grumbled from the dressing room doorway. Behind him, gray light filtered into the chambers. "The cook dared complain when I asked for a pot of coffee this morning. He complains every morning. You'd think I was asking him to hunt down a boar and roast the thing for breakfast for all the trouble it would take to put water in a pot and boil it."

Ian swished his razor in a porcelain basin of water and raised his chin to the glass. He could see the clock on the dresser behind him. It was nearly ten. "I'll survive without coffee, Samuel."

Samuel heaved an enormous sigh and went back to attending to his duties. "Will you be bringing the countess home to your mother soon?"

Ian barely missed slicing his throat. He scraped the blade across his chin and again swished the razor. "It is doubtful she is interested in meeting my mother," he said without bluntly telling Samuel exactly what did interest the countess.

"It's been three years since you were married, sir." Samuel returned to the doorway of the dressing room, unusually chatty for any time of the day or night. "No one expects you to continue mourning as you do. Your mother wants to see her grandchildren before she dies."

"Mother has grandchildren. My sister has given her three."

"Your sister is not you."

Ian finally peered at the steward over the edge of the towel. "This isn't the place to discuss my future, such as it is, Samuel."

"Women are a confusing, contrary lot," Samuel commiserated, clearly missing the hint that this was not a topic Ian wished to discuss. "It is no wonder I am content to be a bachelor. Unfortunately, you are not I. Then again, perhaps it is possible you have not yet met the right woman to bring home to your mother."

Ian wiped the shaving soap from his face as Samuel began talking about other women present at Lord Whitley's grand retreat. In three days since their arrival, and as one privy to gossip belowstairs, Samuel could detail names and character references and the latest gossip detailing Lord Whitley's guests. This little country retreat on the outside seemed just like any other rout or ball or assembly he'd ever attended minus the pinch-mouthed matrons who kept an eye over their young charges. No one kept that kind of eye over anyone here.

Samuel Briscoe III was a well-meaning, white-haired old man, the last of the Northumberland Briscoes who had served four generations of the Rockwell family, and Ian thought of him as a father.

Samuel had picked Ian off the ground too many times to count in the nearly thirty-one years of their acquaintance. He'd rapped Ian's knuckles when he didn't study hard enough, dusted off his backside when Ian fell off a horse, and given him and his siblings some semblance of a childhood in a world that did not seem to stretch from the walls of his family's massive estate. Samuel had been with the family when they'd buried Ian's father and again when his mother buried her eldest son. Samuel Briscoe figured he'd earned the right to speak his mind on any topic.

And Ian allowed him to prattle on and on because it was simpler to listen to the older man talk than it was to think about women.

He'd missed most of the treasure hunt. He might have felt guilt for abandoning Serena if she had not played the bitch to the hilt when she'd finally found him shooting billiards with the Italian count Bethany had danced with.

Even as he'd returned Serena to her chambers he'd still been dwelling on Bethany. A response that had surprised him the most and pleased him the least, like a punch from a Billingsgate stevedore that held enough power behind the blow to lay him out flat.

Until last night in the alcove, he had thought himself dead when it came to feeling anything beyond a base sexual need for a woman. But something had happened to him in his response to her and he'd learned enough from his past to tread with caution when in doubt. Especially around an irritating imp who still possessed the power to warm his blood.

Bethany was part of a past he'd worked too hard these last years to erase, a small part perhaps, but she was from a time in his life he had no interest in revisiting. Her unexpected presence here had already complicated matters.

But whatever reason had brought her to Whitley Court, he wouldn't believe it was because she'd become like the passionate disciples recruited by Whitley and men of his ilk to help spread their message and do their bidding. Whitley was dangerous. Bethany might be young—certainly she was idealistic—and at times had shown a great deal of naivety, but she wasn't stupid. In fact, she was sharp as a tack, all grown up with a woman's body that had filled out her blue gown in a way that gave a man pause.

Whatever Bethany's purpose here was, she had no idea the kind of people with whom she was dealing. He, on the other hand, did.

So why had he been lying in bed most of the night, staring at the underside of the canopy, dwelling on her comment about her virginity or lack thereof, thinking about her life, and wondering if she had been happy? He had never thought of her being with another man before. And now something that had never crossed his mind suddenly became a focal point for his thoughts.

A tap at the door saved him from further contemplation.

Ian threw down the towel. "I'll get it." He grabbed a shirt from the rack on his way out of the dressing room and shoved his hands into the sleeves. "Finish brushing out that jacket, Samuel."

Ian wore his trousers loose around his hips with his braces slapping at his thighs. He buttoned the shirt and tucked it into his waistband. The knock sounded again just before he opened the door. A tall man with a shock of black hair stood in the corridor, his hand raised to knock again. The first thing Ian noticed was the man's half missing index finger. Dressed in a black jacket with a crisp white shirt, he looked to be two score. Ian knew him as Meacham, Sir John's steward.

The man cleared his throat. "I hope I am not disturbing you." He handed Ian a note.

"I was told to give you this. Is ten o'clock suitable?"

Ian unfolded the slip of paper and read it. His presence was requested in his Lordship's private library. The bold signature of Lord Whitley's private secretary, Sir John Howard, was scrawled beneath.

With no change in expression, Ian glanced at the clock on the mantel behind him. Nine-forty. The day was getting better by the hour. Sir John Howard, no less. Whitley's watchdog, and the very man Ian had followed to Whitley Court. Sir John was on his game. This summons had come earlier than anticipated.

"The time suits."

"Very well, sir. He will see you in the library in twenty minutes."

Ian watched the man turn away before shutting the door. Samuel was standing in the dressing room doorway with Ian's jacket in hand. Ian shook his head. Raising a finger to his lips to shush Samuel, he waited a moment and opened the door. He found the hallway empty. Since his arrival, he had scoured every corner of his room for passageways or peepholes that might be present. Except for the passageway, which he'd blocked off, the room was remarkably free of any remnants of clandestine activities from decades past.

"Is everything all right, sir?" Samuel asked as he held the jacket and Ian slipped his arms into the sleeves.

"Maybe."

Whatever Sir John wanted, Ian hoped it was not to attempt to put a bullet through his head.

Finished dressing, he braced his foot on a chair, bent over his knee, and strapped a stiletto to one calf. He shook out his pants leg to cover the weapon and straightened to find Samuel watching him.

"Rats," Ian said to Samuel's silent inquiry.

The very worst kind.

The sound of laughter waylaid Ian in the corridor. His hand froze in the midst of a knock against the library door, transforming the tension inside him to something far less identifiable. The musical sound had come from near the stairway, just past the alcove where he and Bethany had stood last night.

He lowered his arm, and like the pied piper of Hamelin, the gaiety in Bethany's voice broke him away from the serious business of the day and led him up the corridor. Who wouldn't have noticed the sound of her laughter followed by that of a child's voice sprinkled within the emptiness of the corridor, especially when most of the houseguests were still abed? He continued past the library and toward the grand entryway.

Bethany suddenly rounded the corner and they smacked into each other, the top of her head cracking against his chin. He reeled backward two steps before he caught himself and her in his arms. She was warm and velvety soft. Her gleaming hair was braided in a coronet around her head beneath a pert hat. All this he registered as he watched her sky blue eyes widen. With a startled gasp, she stepped out of his arms, leaving behind a faint scent of white soap and something else he could not quite discern, but which indulged his senses in a way the countess with all of her expensive French perfumes never had.

"Ian . . ."

The tall window behind her provided scant illumination, yet all there was seemed to pool around her. She wore bright yellow, an absurdly cheerful and warm color on this frigid morn, and it seemed as if the room had warmed ten degrees with her presence.

He placed the back of his hand against his lip and frowned slightly. "Kindly warn me when you decide to trot out of a room so I will at least have the providence to move."

"Oh, my." She leaned forward to examine his mouth. "I've injured you. I apologize most sincerely. Have you a handkerchief?"

She didn't sound too heartfelt, and he probably shouldn't have snapped at her. Her eyes captured his and held them prisoner, and it was with much effort that he forced himself to look down at his hand and inspect it for blood. She pressed a white frilly handkerchief against his palm. "Keep it," she offered. A quirt dangled from her wrist. "I shall not prevail upon you to return it."

"You are awake so early?" he said, wondering where the hell his mind had hied off to that he suddenly found it difficult to talk.

"It's hardly early, Ian." She took a step backward half-turned, and he stopped himself from staying her with his hand. "I've been awake for hours. Adam was downstairs—"

"Adam?" He realized he was following her retreat. Their steps made no sound on the plush red carpet.

"Lord Whitley's young son. I just returned from riding."

"Do you not sleep, then?"

"I sleep very well, thank you. Most of the time." She tapped his chest lightly with the quirt handle. "When I'm in a comfortable bed that is. And you? Did you sleep well?" Innuendo flavored the tenor in her query. "I understand you missed the treasure hunt. It must have been disappointing."

So far they had held little back from one another. He saw no reason to do so now. "Are you asking if I slept alone, Bethany Ann?" His words had the effect of halting her retreat. Her face colored prettily in mortification. She presented a fetching picture, tightly cinched in serge.

"I most certainly am not asking that. As if I would care."

Like the steps of a waltz, their dance had somehow brought them back to the same alcove where they'd stood last night. "Then what were you asking?"

Bethany pitched her chin up and looked him in the eyes. "Truly, I expected more from you than such an insinuation in so innocent a question, Ian."

He leaned a palm against the wall at her back and felt the strangest compulsion to breathe in the scent of her hair. "Never expect anything from anyone. That way you will never be disappointed."

"What a terrible thing."

"What is terrible? That you choose not to let yourself be disappointed or that I may not have slept alone?"

"Trust me, Ian Rockwell, your affairs bore me to tears."

Laughing ruefully, he wished he could say the same

about hers. Her involvement with Whitley and his organization interested him very much.

Although it was very heroic of her to stand her ground, she must have known the sensible thing to do was walk away from this conversation. "If you don't mind, I need to change for breakfast," she said.

Ian lazed a shoulder against the wall, a smile lifting the corners of his mouth as he observed her departure. Her bustle swayed nicely with her agitated gait. He'd shocked her. It served her right, he thought. She had no business flirting with him. He brought her handkerchief to his nose.

His gaze suddenly drawn to the frilly slip of fabric in his hand, he opened his palm and turned the square edge of lace over. He touched the handkerchief again to his nose, and recognized the pleasant scent as the same one she had worn last night. How long had it been since he'd felt a visceral response to any woman? Even if he still did not quite think of little Bethany Munro as a woman—his body was having difficulty discerning the disparity in his mind.

How long had it been since he'd felt anything at all?

Bethany didn't stop until she reached the sanctuary of her bedroom and shut the door. She leaned her head back against the solid oak portal and shut her eyes, fighting for breath. He was so bloody arrogant!

Mary appeared in the dressing room doorway carrying a rose-colored lacey gown over her arms. Bethany pushed off the door. "I want to wear the velvet." She had planned to wear the cornflower velvet at brunch Thursday, but she would wear it this morning. Good fortune had given her a bosom and small waist and the gown displayed her assets with just the right amount of prudence and daring.

Removing her gloves, Bethany walked across the room and dropped them on the bed. Her quirt followed. She slid the pins from her hat and eased it off her head. She could talk about her virginity to Ian's face and not blush, but let him counter with equal remarks about sleeping with another woman, and she's mortified. She walked to the window and leaned her forehead against the cooling glass. What on earth was the matter with her?

She started to move away when a snowball hit the glass. Bethany whirled. Another snowball exploded on the pane. She opened the window and leaned over the edge, her breath steaming in the icy air. Little Adam bounced up and down in the courtyard laughing and waving at her. Wrapped in ermine, Charlene stood behind her brother. The cold had brought the apples to their cheeks. "You have been caught out, dear friend," Charlene said. "I've been looking everywhere for you. I'm taking Adam back to the nursery. Will you be down to breakfast?"

"I'm changing now."

A hedge three feet high grew below the window. For a moment as she watched brother and sister move past the fountain and a wind-tortured tree, Bethany felt her smile falter. She and Charlene had been best friends for two years when they'd ended up boarding together as students at the conservatory. Their alliance became sealed forever that first month when they escaped being hauled away in a paddy wagon after a suffragist march gone awry and they ended up in Haymarket only to be mistaken for prostitutes. They spent all night trying to get back to the conservatory before the head mistress discovered them absent. That night had been one of the most memorable of Bethany's entire life. Bethany wished she could return to those days when everything had been simpler.

"Mum," Mary said from behind her.

She helped Bethany change. When Mary had fastened up the tiny buttons in back, Bethany sat on the bench in front of the vanity. Mary placed a cloth over Bethany's shoulders and began to repair her hair.

"Have you ever kissed a man?" Bethany asked.

"Cor, mum." She giggled. "I'm seventeen years old. I've kissed plenty."

"You have?"

"There be Alfie, the stableboy, and his brother, the cobbler's son and the baker. But kissin' is all I do. I'm savin' myself for marriage."

Bethany gave Mary a look of laughing severity. "Truly, I'm glad to hear you've maintained standards."

Mary continued chatting about her vast experience with men, most no more than boys. Certainly Alfie the stableboy and his brother weren't yet twenty. It only made Bethany oddly estranged by her own lack of worldliness. She'd kissed her horse and her cat. She'd kissed her younger brother and her grandfather's gristly cheek. She'd kissed Ian once.

Bethany opened her jar of powder and an unpleasant but brief odor wafted up to her before disappearing in the other sundry of scents spilling from various dainty bottles lined up on the vanity. Bringing her nose closer, she wondered if she had imagined the odor. She'd noticed the same faint smell the first time she'd opened the jar just before the ball last night. Clearly, something wasn't right with this last batch of powders she'd made.

"Do you want me to help you with the powder, mum?"

Bethany set the lid back on the jar, slid it to the side, and reached for her favorite cologne bottle instead. "Did Charlene bring the powder I made for her at the conservatory before we left?"

"I don't know, mum. I can find out. Will you be wearing powder today?"

Bethany had made the powder herself just before she'd gone to Whitley Court. It was something she and Charlene often did as a lesson in basic science for some of the newer students. Maybe something had gotten into the powder. It wouldn't be the first time. Though the conservatory kept no toxins in the laboratory, they did use carbolic acid, an ingredient used in disinfectant, to clean the cutting board. Bethany could scrub down every countertop and mortar and pestle in the lab, and that still didn't always prevent the surface from holding residual contamination.

"No, I won't be wearing powder today."

She stood and readjusted her bodice, shimmying slightly with the movement as she arranged her gown, ignoring the tremor of nervousness. Everything she owned fit within the bounds of proper fashion. But what woman didn't encourage nature a bit?

She smiled at Mary in the glass. After all, virtue and beauty were assets that went hand in hand in a room filled with men. "How do I look?"

Mary crossed her arms, studied Bethany, then worked her own magic on the gown. "If it's yer bosoms you want to put on display, you best pull the cloth a might lower."

"I don't wish to be on *display,* Mary."

She just wanted Ian to notice her.

Chapter 4

Ian nodded to Sir John Howard's steward who had escorted him into the library. Sir John lounged in one of two chairs across from the hearth where a rolling fire burned. A silver carafe sat on the breakfront next to a plate of hot rolls.

"Would you care for coffee or tea, Sir Ian?" Sir John asked.

"I'll save it for breakfast," Ian answered, remaining in the center of the room where the steward had left him.

"I'll have the tea, Meacham," Howard told the steward.

Ian scanned the room with its comfortable appointments and floor-to-ceiling bookshelves. Despite the large stone hearth, a dearth of warmth prevailed in the room. He found that amusing, if only because being summoned here like a criminal brought to mind pitchforks and all sundry of torture devices used in interrogations. He expected the room to be hot.

"Is something amusing you?" Howard asked.

Ian scraped a palm across his jaw as he surveyed the other man. "Does Lord Whitley make it a point to have you interview his guests for him? Or am I special?"

"You are a curiosity."

"Not to the point where I'm going to get a knife in my back, I hope."

"I could take exception to your implication, Rockwell."

"Call me cautious, Howard."

All pleasantries aside, they'd dropped the formality of their names and titles. Howard twisted the silver signet ring on his pinky, his gaze fixed on Ian. "Men like us usually are cautious, are we not? But unlike you, I don't allow those whom I've been charged to protect get themselves killed."

Ian didn't move, didn't even draw breath.

"Since the Home Secretary's death," Howard continued, "it seems you have been relieved of your official capacity with the Crown and banished to the frigid North Sea coast while our government carries on its own little investigation."

Ian's jaw clenched only slightly, but he didn't look away, nor would he give Howard the satisfaction of asking how the hell he obtained that kind of information. Ian already knew. "Why I chose to return to my home is none of your business."

"Quite the contrary. It's my job to know Lord Whitley's guests. I take my responsibilities seriously. That includes getting to know Lady Dermott's paramours and friends. The countess is his lordship's precious sister."

Ian took the chair that gave him a view of the massive hearth, a fact that did not escape Howard. Ian sat back and relaxed. "I'll take a cup of that tea," he told the steward.

Howard seemed pleased that he'd gained some ground on Ian. He crossed his ankle over his knee and accepted a cup of tea from the steward. "We are businessmen at heart, after all, are we not? Both of us doing jobs that we are paid to do? I have not brought you here to condemn you for past mistakes," Howard said. "I am not the English government or the police."

This time Ian smiled, though he was far from pleased. He braced his elbows on the chair arm, studying the illustrious Sir John Howard. The man was in his early forties, probably not more than ten years older than Ian. His hair was black in the shadows, his eyes gray and as warm as a North Atlantic ice flow. "You're very good, Howard. I'm impressed you found all that out in"—he mentally calculated the time since he'd been seeing Countess Dermott—"four months?"

"Some believe the Home Secretary's assassination was an inside job. What do you think?"

"I think the coroner's jury doesn't know what the devil it's doing. But then what does it matter what I think? I didn't come home to rehash my feelings on the matter of my dismissal."

"How is it that a man who comes from a family such as yours is in the business of guarding some of the most influential people in this country, Rockwell?"

"It is precisely *because* of the family I come from that I did what I did."

"You must feel betrayed by your government? Who would not after what they did to you?"

The steward offered Ian a cup of tea. From the corner of his eye, Ian had watched him prepare and pour the tea. Satisfied the brew had not been doctored, he sat forward and accepted the cup. "Isn't my government your government, Howard?"

Howard smiled over the rim of his cup. "It was merely an expression of my own discontent. Given the controversy that surrounds some of the organizations Lord Whitley supports, there are political factions that would do him harm. You understand, for his sake, I must be cautious. You don't seem concerned that you have been ostracized from your people. Unlike I would be, were I in your position."

Ian schooled a bland expression, regarding Howard silently. "What I am is someone who is bored very easily, Howard. Is there a reason I am here?"

"Someone in your area of expertise would have intimate details of the lives he is served to protect. Would that be correct?"

"Someone in my position does not kiss and tell, Howard." Ian leaned forward on his elbow. "Not even for money."

"Are you guilty of a conspiracy to kill the Home Secretary?"

Ian frowned, his feelings on the matter more intimate than he cared to explore. "What do *you* think?"

Howard returned his teacup to its saucer and smiled. "I think it is a shame your people threw you away like scraps to dogs." He set the saucer on the tray. "I also think you are not my informant."

Ian would have choked had he been drinking tea. "Informant?" He raised both brows. "I am relieved."

Howard smiled tightly. "I am amused that you find my assertions outrageous. Unfortunately, I am currently managing just such a problem. There is at least one person present at this retreat who thinks he will leave here with a list of those attending this function, along with other valuable papers stolen last night. I had to make sure you were not he. I am confirming that as we speak."

Bloody hell. Ian leaned forward. "And while I am sitting here chatting over tea, you have been searching my chambers?" He shook his head and laughed. "Quaint, Howard." Ian was annoyed by the amateurish subterfuge as he was angered by the trespass. "If you'd warned me, I could have tidied up my room a bit."

"There are certain political factions who would rather make Lord Whitley a scapegoat for this government's inadequacies rather than find a solution to fix problems. He has many political enemies."

Ian set down the teacup. "Everyone in power has enemies."

Someone spoke from behind Ian. "Yes. Everyone has enemies." Ian turned to see Lord Whitley shut the door. "Which is why I am careful."

No doubt Whitley had planned this morning's encounter to a script. Ian burned with irritation, but he shouldn't have been surprised. He rose to his feet as much out of surprise as out of etiquette.

His lordship walked to where he stood. "Do relax, Sir Ian," Whitley said. "Will you not sit?"

To hell with niceties. He didn't particularly cherish having his chambers searched and his personal life dissected. The viscount had accessed government files only those with the highest authorization could retrieve. "I'd prefer to remain standing," Ian said

He had spent the last decade of his life doing more than guarding the lives of diplomats, industrialists, and on occasion a notorious criminal or two placed in hiding while waiting to give testimony in a government tribunal.

Once he'd even guarded the life of a pretty, blond

seventeen-year-old girl put in harm's way when her family had been used as bait to lure one of the most dangerous criminals Ian had ever known. But no one had ever died on his watch—until last fall.

With a polite forbearance not indicative of his station, Whitley asked the steward to leave the room, then proceeded to pour his own cup of coffee from the pot on the breakfront. "Sir Ian, it was not my intent to offend. But we have become aware that you have certain talents that are of interest to us."

Ian awaited Whitley's point.

"My sister's less than biddable disposition toward you has forced me to approach you sooner rather than later. I will be the first to admit your invitation to Whitley Court is because I wanted to meet you."

Sipping his coffee, he peered at Ian over the rim as if coming to a decision. "I have no interest in my sister's romantic interests. She will do exactly what she chooses with the men in her life. However, no one comes into this house without my knowledge of whom and what he or she is. I know a man's political leaning, his assets, and usually most of his past. You have special talents of interest to me. Like Sir John here. You deal in certain delicate aspects of security.

"The fact that you may not agree with my political beliefs is not important. You understand security and protocol. You are a man of integrity, the manner of individual I am looking for to join me.

Whatever Ian had expected of this meeting, that statement was not part of it.

Lord Whitley laughed. His eyes were friendly and surprisingly without guile. "Perhaps you thought my purpose for asking you here more nefarious."

Whitley walked around the chair to where Ian stood. Whitley was as tall as Ian, standing over six feet, with a peppering of gray in his hair, charismatic and dangerous. His lordship was a larger-than-life folk hero to some, an anarchist to others. Yet, he bore the austere lines of one who'd labored in the political trenches his entire life. Ian might not like his politics, but there was something about Whitley's demeanor that made Ian stand up and take notice.

"Your presence would add a certain degree of respectability to this organization," Lord Whitley said. "In return, perhaps I can give you something you don't have. A better vision of the world."

"With all due respect, my lord." Howard sat forward. "I don't think you should be offering—"

"Sir Ian is not responsible for the missing guest list," Whitley interjected, and to Ian said, "I believe Howard is more overset by the fact someone took the list from beneath his nose."

Ian watched the color darken in Howard's cheeks. "It was not beneath my nose, my lord. It was in a safe along with . . . some of your accounting ledgers."

"In Sir John's defense, he understands that certain people who attend my functions do not want their names bandied about in public," Whitley said. "In my defense, I assure you we will find the culprit. We do not take lightly those who would betray us."

Because of Lord Whitley's vast unpopularity with the current Prime Minister, Ian understood why some people would not want their names connected to one of Lord Whitley's private functions. And Ian could count on all ten fingers who would be interested in this event's exclusive guest list, starting with his own government. That list would be worth a fortune to the right people.

"Eventually all rooms and servant's quarters will be searched, discreetly of course," Lord Whitley said. "The culprit will not get away."

Ian studied Howard. "It must be difficult for you to have something that important stolen on your watch."

Howard rose to his feet.

"Enough." Whitley held up his hand. "His room has been searched." His eyes on Ian, he asked, "Would you consent to a search of your person if I should ask?"

"If you should ask, my lord. I have nothing to hide."

"We all have something to hide, Sir Ian. But I do not believe you are responsible for the missing items. Now it is finished and concluded to my satisfaction, Howard."

He spoke to Ian. "I need men I trust to protect me and my interests from those who would destroy what I am trying to do. It is no simple task, as Sir John will attest. You would work with Sir John, of course. Eventually you might come to do more."

Howard didn't seem happy about Whitley's last statement but was wise enough to remain silent. He needn't have worried. Ian would have been a fool to jump at the offer. For one thing, jumping on Whitley's bandwagon too quickly would only make Howard more suspicious than he was, maybe even Whitley as well. For another, Ian didn't trust Whitley. "I am somewhat without words," Ian said.

"But you do not accept."

"I'm not currently for hire, my lord."

"I don't expect you to come to any decision today, Sir Ian," Whitley said. "In fact I would be suspicious of your commitment to me if you did. People who come to work for me need a higher level of dedication than one might find in other quarters. This is not a job any can take lightly."

"Your politics require a vigilant security force."

"My politics are not popular," he said, "and people have tried to blame me or my philanthropies for everything from promoting moral vice among the laboring classes, to threatening the very caste structure of England, to carrying out assassinations. But do not consider me weak. I may look at the doctrine of forgiving one's enemies with skepticism, but I am no anarchist." Whitley's mouth turned up at one corner. "I suspect you wondered, Sir Ian."

"You associate yourself with known arms dealers. It *had* crossed my mind."

"The Italian family you are referring to also owns the textile mill in Wapping and employs a thousand people. You didn't know that?"

Ian blinked. This time, he was the one caught off guard. "No, my lord."

"Despite the perception men like Count Verástegui may bring to my circle of supporters, I am not in the business of cutting off my nose to spite my face, Sir Ian."

Whitley clapped a hand on his shoulder. "Think about all I have said. If you are interested, I encourage you to visit my stables and view the grounds. Enjoy your time here. You may yet find yourself bored with your new life as a gentleman and decide you want to join me." He pulled out his watch and flipped open the lid. "If you will excuse me. Breakfast is currently being served in my private dining room. Sir John will escort you." It was not a request but a command. "I will talk with you again later, Sir Ian. Enjoy the rest of your day."

After Whitley left, Ian let his gaze go over the bookcases and the two sensual Rubens paintings. He couldn't keep from looking for the peephole in the wall. Now a missing guest list put a new twist in his uncomplicated cynical approach to life. Someone else was putting a finger in his pie.

"His Lordship trusts too easily," Howard said in the silence that followed.

Without expression, Ian turned back to Howard.

"I do not, Rockwell."

Ian did not respond to the subtle threat in the man's voice. Sir John Howard's mistake was that he considered himself invulnerable, a mistake that would eventually kill him.

"I'm retired, Howard." Ian kept his tone mild, with just enough boredom to be a non-threat to a man whose arrogance outweighed his judgment. "And I'm hungry. Shall we dine?"

Conversation in the Whitley private dining salon was lively and loud, punctuated by the bark of a small dog when Ian entered the room. Bethany looked up from her poached egg as he stepped beneath the entry door arch and stopped.

Sitting next to Bethany, Viscount Whitley's daughter rose to her feet in a swish of pink candy-stripe flounces, a curly-haired miniature poodle in her arms. "Sir John.

Sir Ian," Miss Dubois said prettily. "Do help yourself, Sir Ian." She motioned to the steaming silver platters filled with eggs, sliced ham, and bread laid out on the breakfront.

Nine other guests most Ian recognized congregated around the table. The men had come to their feet, but whether it was out of good breeding or because Sir John had walked into the room behind Ian, he didn't know. People feared the little bastard. "Countess Dermott is not present?" Sir John asked.

"My errant aunt never arises this early," Miss Dubois said as if in explanation to Ian. "So I hope you will content yourself with our charming company instead." She introduced Bethany to Ian.

He finally turned his gaze on her. "Miss Munro," he said, his voice temperate, though his manner was less so as his gaze grazed hers. She had changed her clothes from that morning. He'd liked her in yellow, but blue was her color. The fact that she was staring at him with gemstone eyes that seemed to cut caused him a good deal of wry amusement. Yet in the midst of it all, he found himself admiring her beauty, discomfited that she could paralyze his thoughts with such effortlessness.

He forced himself to look past her and greet the others who stood around the table, his manner a hallmark of ease among the inner circle of Lord Whitley's guests because no one expected any less. Miss Dubois waved Ian to the breakfront. Sir John was already serving himself. "Please serve yourself," she said. "It is nearly noon to be sure. Most of us have finished supping."

Conversation had started up again. Somehow, Ian managed to keep his eyes from returning to Bethany. She returned her concentration to the single poached egg in front of her, busily tapping at the shell with the dull edge of a knife as if she were mining for ore. Ian set his plate directly across the table from her, absurdly pleased that he'd startled her, and caught the slight narrowing of her eyes. His lip was still bruised from where she'd knocked him silly earlier, and the touch of her eyes had the adverse affect of reminding him of that wound. A liveried footman approached. Ian asked for coffee—not tea. The entire world thrived on East India tea. But give him a cup of hot Jamaican java to help him make peace with the day.

"Are you enjoying your stay with us, Sir Ian?" Miss Dubois spooned sweet cream over her strawberries.

From over his coffee cup, Ian's glance touched Sir John, though his gaze did not linger overlong. "My stay thus far has been pleasant enough."

"If you are overset because Papa ordered Sir John to interrogate you this morning, please know that he does that with every man for whom Aunt Serena and I have affection. You are at this table, which means Papa approves of you."

Ian set the cup on the saucer. "I am at this table because I am hungry. Famished." He buttered a steaming croissant. "The set of your table is as diverse and delightful as its hostess. Thank you."

The girl seemed to blossom like a rose at the silly compliment, and Ian wondered if she was so starved for approval that something so small would make her so happy. "This may be my first bout as Papa's hostess, but you can thank Miss Munro as well. She and I planned the menus together. We've been working on this country retreat for months."

Ian touched the corner of a serviette to his mouth, and he looked over at Bethany, her unexpected abashment bringing the color high into her face. "Well done of you, Miss Munro."

"And now you will all have the rest of the afternoon to enjoy yourselves at your leisure before our grand supper tonight. Except for Sir John, of course." Miss Dubois gave her full attention to her father's secretary. "Unfortunately he hasn't the same time for leisurely pursuits. He will be in meetings all day."

Sir John's hands froze on his cup. Miss Dubois cooed to her poodle and fed it a strawberry. "But then Papa pays him well to be at his beck and call." She smiled for the benefit of all. "Work, work, work. True gentlemen should have more important things to think about."

Color mottled Howard's face like two raspberry stains. Ian saw Bethany lower her fork and look oddly at her friend. But just that fast, the topic changed, and Miss Dubois began chatting about the treasure hunt in which neither he nor Bethany had taken part, sweeping away the chill in the air like a zephyr blowing across the wintry sky. Ian leaned back in his chair, his elbow on the table as his hand cradled a coffee cup and he considered Charlene Dubois and Bethany's friendship.

A part of him remained aware of the conversation, but the better part of his thoughts dwelled on the mystery that had quickly become Bethany Munro. He had not dismissed the fact that he'd found Bethany in Lord Whitley's private wing of the house last night before the treasure hunt, and now there was the issue of a missing guest list.

"Did anyone get lost in the tunnels this time?" he heard someone ask, followed by a round of conjectures and laughter as if getting lost in the tunnels snaking through Whitley Court were some great joke.

"Last fall two people went into the passageways and vanished for an entire night," the lanky man sitting next to Ian said, the casual comment passing over those at the table. "That science teacher at the conservatory. What was her name?"

"Langley, I believe was her name." Someone else laughed as if in memory. "A prim piece of baggage."

Howard speared the last morsel of ham on his plate. "All skinny arms and legs and a laugh like an ill-tuned pianoforte. She eloped with the poor chap a week later. Quite the amusing tale so I'd heard."

A bout of laughter followed, and if Ian hadn't been looking at Bethany just then, he would not have seen the hatred flare in her eyes, emotions that briefly flashed before she'd grabbed them back.

"Miss Munro was her assistant at the conservatory, Sir John," Miss Dubois said. "Mrs. Langley left without saying goodbye to her students. A sore point to some of us who were her friends."

"And she did have friends," Bethany quietly said, her words falling like a boulder into the center of the table.

Sir John leaned forward to better glimpse Bethany. The hard lines of his face briefly eclipsed by speculation. *"Amore."* He chuckled dispassionately. "It does peculiar things to a woman's mind. Even intelligent women, I'm sure."

"Mrs. Langley was a widow," Bethany said, "not someone in the first blush of love."

Sir John dabbed at his lips with a napkin. "Then her elopement must have been all the more surprising to be sure. Have you ever been in love, Miss Munro?" he queried.

Bethany knew Ian was watching her. Sipping his coffee, he'd crossed his feet at the ankles and clearly waited for her to reply—as did everyone else, it seemed. But unlike everyone else, Ian was not watching and waiting for her answer. He was watching *her*.

"I've been in love," she replied.

Charlene was the first to respond. "You have?"

"He was a noble naval hero killed off the southwest coast of Spain between Cadiz and the Strait of Gibraltar."

"Trafalgar?" Ian said, drawing her gaze, and her expression briefly warmed at the amusement she saw in his eyes.

"You loved someone who died at Trafalgar?" Charlene asked.

"She's referring to Lord Admiral Horatio Nelson's death at Trafalgar seventy years ago, Charlene," Sir John said, clearly dismissing them both as quixotic harebrains.

"I happen to admire the man, Sir John, as well as Hannibal, George Washington, Wellington." Bethany proceeded to name off four more influential military leaders who had stood up to tyranny to shape the course of history. "And Zeus."

Sir John's brows arched. "The Greek god?"

"Her black cat," Charlene supplied behind a snort of laughter.

"He's a male." Stirring more cream into her tea, Bethany raised the cup to her lips and looked directly at Sir John. "Doesn't that count?"

His darkened expression came back at her. Looking away, she allowed her lashes to fall over her eyes, an act of submission as false as it was well timed. She hated him. It was almost more than she could silently bear to remain at this table. But remain she would. From the corner of her eye she could see Ian idly moving his long fingers up and down the smooth porcelain coffee cup. Her heart still raced as if she were running from some fire. Sir John was a dangerous man to make a fool of in front of a group of people, and Bethany knew she had done just that. Yet she could not summon the good sense to care. She wished the ground would swallow Sir John Howard and drop him in hell.

The discussion moved from Zeus the cat to the weather, but Bethany had stopped listening. Sir John dropped the serviette on the table and rose to his feet. "If you will excuse me, Miss Dubois." He politely bowed over her hand and said charmingly, "But as you know, I've meetings to attend, letters to sort, orders to execute. I leave you in fine company."

Charlene's smile faltered. Others had also begun to move away from the table. Breakfast was over. "But the first meetings do not begin for an hour."

"Then your father will think me none other than prompt." He looked at Ian who had yet to remove himself from the table and looked in no hurry to do so. Then strode from the room.

Slowly Bethany shifted her gaze and looked into a pair of stormy green eyes that somehow held the light in the room when everything else screamed colorless and gray. Something surged and crackled between them, before he uncurled from his chair and stood. She thought he was leaving, but he only ambled to the breakfront, no part of the man who had made her blush earlier that morning visible in the one she now saw.

Charlene sighed, reaching across the table for the last of the strawberries. "Well, this has certainly been an interesting morning."

Bethany studied her friend's flushed face and tight mouth. "What was all of that about between you and Sir John?"

Charlene stirred her berries. "Let me throw that question back at you with your divine sense of the absurd. Horatio Nelson?"

Bethany didn't know why Charlene was suddenly miffed. She'd certainly added her part. "It was meant as a joke."

"Why do you dislike Sir John so?"

"I never trust people who smile for all the wrong reasons."

Charlene set down the spoon with a *clank*.

The servants began to clear away the dishes. Charlene babbled something about the chill in the air. The little sweater on the poodle was not nearly enough to keep it warmed, and she excused herself.

Not forgetting for one moment that Ian stood somewhere behind her, Bethany forced her concentration back to her egg. She felt his nearness like the heat of a candle flame. Realizing she was strangely dizzy, she pressed a finger to her temple. She'd only had tea and had left her egg mostly uneaten. Her loss of temper with Sir John, Charlene's strange behavior, Ian . . . always Ian somewhere in her thoughts like weighted ballast balls, left her feeling just a little bit muddled.

His voice came from behind her. "Any more time passes, that egg will hatch into a full-grown chicken."

A bowl of steaming porridge appeared in front of her and she gazed up at him in surprise. He took the seat Charlene vacated, warming Bethany with his presence in the way a wolf warms a fat woolly sheep. He stretched out his long legs and indulged in a sip of hot coffee. "Watching you try to eat that thing has been painful," he said as if his kindness should require an explanation.

She caught a note of something in his voice. Something she didn't know if she should trust. But it was almost as if he *cared*.

Unless he was just buttering her up for an interrogation, in which case she'd enjoy the porridge anyway and let him talk his ears blue. "Thank you. I'm usually a horse when it comes to my appetite."

"Aren't young ladies *supposed* to eat like birds?"

"Heavens." She laughed. "Do I look like a young lady?" The words had come out all wrong and ended on a cough. "I mean . . . I'm hardly young."

A smile almost lifted one corner of his mouth. "Tell me about Mrs. Langley," he said after a moment. "I thought you were the science instructor at the conservatory?"

"I was hired shortly after her . . . disappearance. My position is temporary while I finish my studies." She swallowed past the sudden tightness in her throat, then quickly spoke past it. "They oughtn't have said the things they did."

From across the room a log settled in the hearth with a hiss and a spark and she jumped. The mood slowly changed between them as if the sparks from the fire warmed the air a hundred degrees. In spite of her hard-won control, she felt as if she'd just gulped down a glass of champagne and something swelled in her chest so that she could barely breathe.

She glanced down at herself hoping she wasn't spilling provocatively from her gown, while a wild, wicked part of her hoped she was.

To her horror, Ian intercepted her glance. Amusement laced his expression as if telling her that some things never changed.

She could dance a naked jig on the tabletop and have no affect on him. "You are *such* a bore, Ian."

Unfazed by her indictment of his character, he remained with his hands wrapped around the fragile porcelain cup, his eyes almost warmed by the chandelier light. But it could have been a trick of the light that played her false for she sensed he was not amused at all. He finished his coffee. The chair creaked when it gave up his weight and he stood.

He'd said no more; yet she had the sickening feeling that somehow he had just read her deepest, darkest secrets.

Chapter 5

Bethany's deepest darkest secret took her back through the servant's passageway two days later, the same path she had taken the night of the ball to Sir John's chamber. She swiped at a trail of web and held up the lamp in her hand, illuminating the dark corridor. Downstairs the hum of distant music vibrated beneath her feet.

The original estate had been built on a sea-swept cliff centuries before. Most of the tunnels she'd encountered in this wing were dangerous and no longer in use. Many had been sealed. It had taken her a week to determine the correct passageway that would lead her to Sir John's chambers. But she could only get there from Lord Whitley's private wing. She'd mixed India ink with a vial of rosewater and made a smear at intervals like breadcrumbs to mark her way. The shine from her lamp picked up each blot and helped guide the way. A person could get lost in these tunnels and never see the light of day again. There were still a hundred places she hadn't gone, especially in the other wings, nor did she have a desire to do so. This house frightened her.

She had never considered herself clever. Luck always had more to do with her success at any given task than any bout of cunning or intelligence. She'd been to Sir John's chambers twice, and, in her experience, the old adage "three's a charm" seemed more a portent of doom than any good fortune headed her way.

She dimmed the lamp and left it hanging on a metal peg in the wall. A dank, musty odor wafted to her from the surrounding darkness. She looked around her and shuddered, aware of the draft creeping through the gray stonework and around her ankles. This part of the corridor opened up into a small dusty chamber that had once been an old dressing room, perhaps of the original lord of the manor before renovations sealed off the room a hundred years ago. A pair of rodent-eaten chairs and an old brocade settee were all that remained.

Bethany withdrew the various legers she'd copied from her pockets and walked to the panel door. She had to stand on her toes to put her eye to the Judas hole. "Bloody, bloody hell," she murmured.

No one was supposed to be in the room. Yet, she could see Sir John standing in the bedchamber speaking with someone.

Bethany was a firm believer that every disaster is defined and shaped by the smallest of actions preceding that event. She had taken something from the safe a few days ago that deep down she knew she should not have. It seemed in the past few months Bethany's simple investigation into Sir John had inadvertently led to discovering information involving secret money accounts Sir John held and signs that he was embezzling from Lord

Whitley's organization. Bethany didn't know what she'd stumbled upon, but instinct told her it was huge.

She'd worried the last few days over the perplexing exchange between Charlene and Sir John. Charlene's last words in the dining salon hurt Bethany as much as the possibility that her friend might hold a real *tendre* for her father's secretary and bodyguard. Bethany had recognized an evasive feint when she saw one. But Charlene could be as flighty as a flock of blackbirds sometimes, and more often than not required only a diligent shake to make her see a thing straight.

And just that fast, Bethany's busy thoughts butted against Ian— for he remained uppermost on her mind even if she had successfully avoided him the last few days. It was as if the very air warmed with his presence. She hadn't seen Ian in three years and now suddenly she couldn't escape him.

She didn't want to admit to herself that he'd disappointed her thus far. She'd wasted Thursday afternoon's tea gown on a perfectly absurd attempt to make an impression on a man who would find an old weathered tree stump more uplifting. And he still had a way with those sultry eyes that could look at a person as if he could see through them, and still make her feel like a bumbling beatlehead around him. Oh yes indeed, bad things came in threes, she decided, which was why she had been cautious as she'd approached Sir John's door.

She'd seen Sir John's itinerary. He should not be up here having secret meetings. If she had a listening tube, she might be able to discern their words. Instead, she pulled away. "Bloody, bloody hell," she murmured again because the words encapsulated the moment.

She wanted to wait but knew she couldn't. She turned. And nearly died a thousand deaths.

Ian stood behind her.

She startled and almost dropped everything in her hands.

Leaning with his arms folded and his back against one of the walls, he stood unmoving, pinning her with only the touch of his eyes. The starched white collar of his shirt lay loose against his neck. His jacket hung open, the lazy grace of his stance a lie. "Isn't this just plain awkward?" he said in a low voice that sent shivers over her.

A thick rushing sounded in her ears and she felt a burst of panic. She sucked in a breath. He stepped away from the wall, everything about him appearing dangerous.

"Why am I not surprised?" His voice came soft and menacing.

She took an evasive step sideways. "Don't you dare come near me."

"You've been at that door for ten minutes. Whatever it is you want in there must be bloody valuable for you to risk sneaking here."

She clasped the ledgers closer to her chest. Had he been in this chamber the entire time? Had she walked directly past him? "Y-you should have let me know you were here," she whispered in a furious voice.

Finally, the ramifications of his presence caught up to her addlepated brain. What had he said exactly the night of the ball? *I'm with the countess. That is as far as it goes. I no longer work in my old job in any capacity.* He was a complete and total liar. A charlatan, pretender, and con artist!

But then she'd also been less than honest. Conscious of the stolen ledgers in her hands, she brought them closer to her chest as if he would pounce upon her and steal them.

"Clearly, you and I need to talk," he said.

She suspected what that would entail. She'd be doing all the talking, then he'd find a way to have her removed from Whitley Court. He caught up to her when she reached the lamp.

"I imagine you are not often found in someone else's room," she said, returning his whisper. "Especially a man's." She wasn't going to share information until she knew his intentions. She stepped around him, but he was suddenly standing in front of her lamp, blocking her exit. "Get out of my way, Ian."

His face remained calm and expressionless except for his eyes. In the pale light filtering into the open space surrounding them, they burned with fury. "I eat little girls like you for breakfast, Bethany Ann."

"Truly?" Her eyes narrowed. "I thought you preferred more seasoned women."

She started past him again only to have his arm block her, his face only inches away. "The game's up, Bethany." His voice vibrated against her hair. "You and I both know I'll drag you out of here over my shoulder if I have to. I'm making no idle threat. I can assure you whatever game you are about, I've been playing at it longer. And I'm a lot better at it than you are." He caught her jaw with two fingers and turned her face until she was looking up at him with wet eyes. "You are going to talk to me. In my room or yours. At this point, I don't particularly care about propriety."

She tried to retreat. He wraped his hand around her arm. She felt the heat of his palm burning through the velvet of her sleeve all the way to her bone. It took her a moment to realize he'd stopped. Voices filtered to them from down the corridor. They stood like two ensnared deer.

Then he doused the lamp. He pulled her around and she was dragged along by the force of his will as much as by his physical strength. She stared down at the hand, invisible in the darkness but feeling so large and sure, and she suddenly found herself wedged between a rough layer of stone and his chest in the same place he'd been standing when she'd passed him. She raised her palms to his shoulders to push him away, but her hands found purchase instead, as if she were catching herself from falling.

The servants walked by them a few moments later and into Sir John's room.

A shaft of light filled the small chamber and she suddenly found herself pinned by Ian's eyes. His jacket had fallen open around her. Awareness threaded like electricity through the air between them. She felt the hard muscles of his chest and his breath against her cheek. She was cognizant of the heavy thudding of his heart, while her own raced in a maddened flight. All of this she noted in the seconds before the panel door shut, descending the corridor into darkness.

Her hand studied a pearl button at eye-level just beneath his opened collar. Somehow, she'd reached beneath Ian's jacket and splayed her hands across his chest to the warmth beyond the fine cambric cloth of his shirt. Her head barely reached his shoulder, and his height suddenly made her feel vulnerable. There was no refuge to be found in retreat as she waited for him to move.

Neither of them spoke.

Then he lowered his mouth so close, his words disturbed strands of her hair to her ear. "Your room or mine, m'lady?"

"I propose, Bethany, that you and I can have an exchange of intelligence," Ian said. They'd reached her chambers. He dropped his gaze to the ledgers in her hands, then swerved back to her face, in no mood to play the part of a gallant. Deliberately, he'd kept to shadows near the panel door and leaned against the wall. "You answer my questions and I'll answer yours. I meant my earlier threat to see you removed from this place."

"You wouldn't dare stoop so low."

"Then you don't know me as well as you think you do. I have my own purpose for being here and I won't have you interfering. I want to know what you are doing at Whitley court."

"Go home, Ian," she whispered.

Her rebuke surprised him. More so because the words sounded more like a warning than a command.

"Why?"

She held his gaze with purpose. "You overset me, Ian. Do you know that?"

"Then allow me to reciprocate the feeling."

Bethany turned her profile to him, the light from her lamp illuminating her hands as she set the ledgers in a compartment inside her trunk.

At last she turned around. She stood in the center of

the Turkish carpet, her skirts whispering a sound that was both velvet and rusty, as if she were hesitant to face him. He had caught her out but something else had happened while he'd had her pinned against the wall.

A tense silence filled the room. It thrummed like a battle drum in his blood. He'd chosen to come to her room because he didn't trust who might be watching his. Now he could see he'd made a mistake. This room smelled like her.

He shoved off the paneled door, walked toward her, then past her, leaving her to stare at his back. A matching silver hand mirror, hairbrush, and clothes brush lay on her vanity, next to an enameled box containing dainty bottles of creams, rouges, and comfits to sweeten breath. Despite himself, he picked up a delicate cut-glass scent bottle. Ian had a sister. Feminine accoutrements were not new to him. But touching bits and pieces of Bethany's belongings felt intimate, like sliding his palm across the corseted curves of a woman's body, not quite touching flesh but feeling the shape of her beneath his palms.

She snatched the perfume vial from his hands. "That's mine. And I would appreciate it if you would not handle my things."

"How did you get into Sir John's private study?"

"Picking locks is not so difficult if one has the correct hairpin."

"Quaint, Bethany."

He reached around her shoulder, found another perfume vial and held it to the light as if it were Bethany Munro all grown up and mysterious, and he could see past the pretty colors that cloaked her. "You still love girlish, romantic things. Somehow I'm not surprised. Yet *methinks* it might all be a show, an illusion, like the turn of a magician's hand." His eyes narrowed on her lovely face as he was reminded of her conversation in the dining room with some amusement. "You are in love with Horatio Nelson? Who pays attention to a dreamy harebrain after all?"

She removed the second vial from his hand and lifted a haughty brow. "Clearly, you do. But I don't want you in my affairs, Ian. So go away and leave me alone. If you interfere with me, I swear I will never forgive you."

"Is that right?"

She pivoted on her heel. His fingers closed around her wrist. He could feel the furious beat of her pulse against his palm, her flesh warm in his hand. "If you knew me better you would know I never make pointless observations about people. I don't know what manner of mischief you are into here, but I can assure you, it will end in no good for you. Lord Whitley will be inclined to resent the presence of anyone whom he might suspect of being an informant."

"How dare you accuse me of that!"

Her reaction surprised him. "Forgive my assumption. After all, your attempt to get back into Sir John's chambers was purely an accident on your part. You were lost after all."

"As lost as you were to be sure."

"Did you take the guest list?"

She sucked in a sharp breath. But she did not answer him.

He frowned briefly, for he was an expert at getting his way with people through means other than outwardly engaging in power struggles. Yet Bethany had pricked him faster than anyone alive.

He could snap her wrist, and suddenly feeling that much power over her, over anyone, made him pull back. He detested bullies and tyrants, people who used power to control others into doing their bidding. She was afraid, not only of him, but of something else, and it wasn't Whitley. He let go of her wrist.

"You demand answers from me," he said quietly, "but I'm not positive you are willing to hear them, or be trusted with them." He didn't want to be angry. In truth, what he felt at this moment was as far from anger as water was from fire. "Do you know what an anarchist is?"

The answer flashed in her eyes. She not only knew what an anarchist was, but he held the sickening feeling that she might be one. "An anarchist is a person who believes in or advocates anarchism by flouting or ignoring rules or accepted standards of conduct," she said.

"Your well-rehearsed answer is straight from the politico dictionary."

"Are you angry because I know what an anarchist is?"

"An anarchist is a seditionist. Does treason ring any warning bells in your pretty head?" He harbored no charity in his heart for anyone who was an anarchist and would do what was necessary to see this organization destroyed. Bethany would have to know that. "How much exactly do you know about Lord Whitley?"

"You believe Charlene's father is an anarchist? How do you come by that accusation?"

Ian tamped down the rising emotion. "Last fall, the Home Secretary was assassinated," he said, electing to reach her through the truth, at least as much as he could tell her. "The broadsheets called the fire that killed Lord Densmore a tragic accident. What the public doesn't know is that the coroner's jury deemed an incendiary explosion caused that fire."

"I do not understand. How do you know that?"

"I was the bloody man in charge of the detail served to protect Lord Densmore. After his death, I took a hiatus and returned home. By chance, I met Countess Dermott at a function given between mutual acquaintances. Later at an event she hosted, I overheard snippets of conversation about the assassination, things no one but the Minister of Foreign Affairs or the perpetrator of the crime would know."

He considered his next words but realized she needed to be told as much of the truth as he could tell her. "The man I overheard talking was Whitley's private secretary, Sir John Howard."

Her brows drew together. She swung away, walked two steps, then turned, the corners of her mouth crinkled into a frown. "I have no fondness for Sir John," she said, "but I've been attending meetings for a year. We may have rallies that make the government unhappy, but we do not discuss assassinations."

"Do you trust me, Bethany?"

She reached up and tucked a wisp of hair behind her ears. "Charlene is my friend. Her father sits at the head of the Board of Governors for the conservatory. Hundreds of women across the classes benefit from his contributions. If someone here is involved with treasonous activities . . . it isn't Lord Whitley. It's Sir John."

"Can you prove that?" She looked away and he homed

in on her defenses like an arrow. "You can't, can you?"

"That's why you are here," she said. "You're looking for proof against Lord Whitley. You believe he might be linked to the Home Secretary's murder?"

"We already have a link. Just no proof."

"Is Countess Dermott part of such a conspiracy?"

"As far as any investigation pans out, no."

She turned away. The swish of her skirts touched the empty silence. She sat on the edge of her bed and laid her head in her hands.

He suddenly pictured himself crossing the room and turning her to face him. He pictured his arms going around her in comfort, or maybe he saw himself just shaking her until her teeth rattled. But always with her, something held him back, strange protective feelings he didn't want to feel or deal with. Despite her attempt at worldliness, there was still innocence inside her.

Perhaps it was for that reason he went to her, not touching her, but standing close enough to feel her skirts press against his knee. "What happened to you, Bethany?"

She regarded him from solemn eyes.

"Tell me why you took the guest list?"

"I don't know why I took the list. It was there, in his papers locked in the safe, and looked important," she said.

His mouth frowned slightly at the edges. "Since when have you become a safecracker, too?"

Bethany did not consider herself a safecracker.

Two weeks ago, when she and Charlene had just arrived, she'd watched Lord Whitley open the safe in the library. The combination had been his son's date of birth minus one year. Figuring out the combination on the safe in Sir John's room had not been as simple. "People tend to use numbers they know, like birthdays or postal addresses, but Sir John clearly considers himself more inventive," she scoffed. "The combination was thinly disguised as a bank account number at the top of each accounting ledger in his desk. I realized the number was important when I saw it at the back of his appointment book."

"How long have you been doing this?"

She told him about Lord Whitley's residence in London and all the times she'd gone there with Charlene under the pretext of planning for this retreat.

The look in Ian's eyes conveyed nothing. In fact, he said nothing at all. Instead, his mouth tightened.

Then she told him about Mrs. Langley, everything spilling out like rain from overburdened clouds, but she wouldn't look at him as she spoke about her mentor's disappearance last September after attending one of Lord Whitley's retreats with Sir John.

"You believe she could have run off and eloped as well."

"I don't know, Bethany. I believe *you* think something happened."

"Whatever happened to Mrs. Langley, Sir John is responsible. I am sure of it. I don't believe she ever left Whitley Court."

"Why?" he asked. "Why does this mean so much to you?"

She slid to her feet. How could she make him understand? Her entire life she'd felt as if she didn't belong anywhere, always a little bit different, always alone in her dreams. Mrs. Langley had picked Bethany up after she'd failed to get into medical school and given her a place to truly belong. "She had no one else. Not another soul who cared whether she lived or died. She was alone. She came to me, Ian. Before she left with Sir John. She came to me flushed with love as if no one could possibly love a vicar's spinster daughter who wore spectacles and loved Plato. I'm the one who told her to go with him to Whitley Court. Now she's gone and no one cares. It's as if she never existed."

A furrow creased Ian's brow. "So, what is it you hope to accomplish?" he said softly.

"I've been gathering information on Sir John for the past five months. I've found evidence that he has altered the accounting books for years. He and Count Verástegui have been embezzling from the workhouse reform funds. He has a wife locked away at an asylum for the insane. . ."

"You've been doing all of *this* alone?"

"I haven't been alone. Mary has been with me."

"Jesus." He rolled his eyes. "That makes me feel so much more relieved. So you are on a vendetta to find Mrs. Langley's murderer. What are you going to do with the evidence? Present it to Whitley?"

Bethany shifted. That was the crux of her dilemma. She could not very well present Lord Whitley with a mountain of stolen evidence without telling him that she had been sneaking about stealing information. Perhaps she could send it to him anonymously—unless of course he really was the anarchist for which Ian was look-ing.

"Do you truly believe Lord Whitley may be guilty of assassinating the Home Secretary?"

"Someone in this organization is. Those papers you've collected could be important. Whitley is searching the rooms in this house. I suggest you hide them well."

"Do you suggest I give everything to you?"

He let the answer hang in the silence. She may not agree with all of her government's policies. She loved her country and would not see her people murdered by anarchists, but giving Ian all of the papers she'd collected was out of the question.

She had found no evidence to connect Lord Whitley to murder. She had not come to Whitley Court to find herself in the position of condemning Charlene and Adam's father to the gallows. Yet, neither was she a partisan who would blindly follow any leader off a cliff.

Sea-washed sunlight suddenly speared the diamond pane glass behind her, dispelling some of the darkness in her room and granting her warmth to replace the chill. "Is your valet even a real valet or is he your partner?" she asked after a moment.

His grin surprised her, the creases deep at his mouth as if he could be at ease with jollity. The smile framed the dimple on his cheek and left her feeling slightly breathless. He settled an elbow against the bedstead and studied her as if attempting to discern her interest in him, but she let her feelings fall behind the wall in her eyes where she placed all unwelcome emotions. If he noted that she no longer wanted to talk about the stolen papers, he said nothing.

"Admittedly, my valet is somewhat rusty since I've only just returned home after a lengthy absence. But he is my real valet. He's been with me since I was out of short pants, and this particular man is special to me."

She lowered her voice. "Are you telling me you really *are* rich as Croesus?"

"Where did you hear that?"

"Gossip from belowstairs." She shrugged. What difference did it make how he knew her source?

Clearly, he didn't take his personal assets seriously, whether they pertained to his looks or financial standing in a community that lived and breathed wealth. The look in his eyes told her he knew her unorthodox inquisitiveness stemmed as much from a desire to know the truth as it did from outright prying.

"My family is not rich as Croesus," he replied. "But neither are we paupers. Before a fever took my brother's life some ten years ago, he built up a profitable sugar plantation in Jamaica."

"Is there a vineyard in France?"

"My sister's husband owns that estate in southern France, which happens to be responsible for a very fine wine. I live in my townhouse in London's West End when I am there. On occasion when life takes an unexpected turn, I come home to visit my mother, who thinks I do not come home enough, and wants no more in life than to coddle me. Are you interrogating me, Bethany Ann?"

Something in the way he said her name like that warmed her. Of course, she was interrogating him. He had hardly been forthright with her. "If you are so well off and from such an old family why do you hold no peerage?"

"Wealth does not equate to aristocracy. In my case, my family has been on the wrong side of every conflict since William invaded England. Somewhere in the past hundred years the royal houses of England quit granting us titles."

Yet she knew he'd achieved the rank of knighthood, a feat that he failed to mention.

Looking away from him, she realized her life was as far away from his as one could possibly go and still be on earth.

She worked as a teacher's assistant at England's Academic Conservatory for Young Ladies. She supported herself, not because her guardian had cut her off—he had not—but out of principle. She was a suffragist and believed in a woman's right to exist separately from a man on all levels.

It had been her involvement in that movement that had brought her to Lord Whitley and the organization that had grown up around the man. She admired him. He was one of the few in parliament who had the daring to sponsor a bill that would give a woman the right to vote. But Ian would understand none of this. If he believed Lord Whitley might be responsible for the murder of the Home Secretary, then he would be as tenacious in his purpose as she was in hers.

"Where have you been these last years that you could not at least write and tell me you were well?" she asked.

Ian leaned against the bedstead at the edge of the wavering light and looked away. "It's not important anymore."

"It is to me."

"The past few years haven't exactly been my greatest moments, Bethany."

"How did she die? How did your wife die?"

Ian held her gaze, clearly not realizing how much that one look revealed to her, and she knew something terrible and dark had happened.

"She committed treason," he said.

"Oh." The single word divined more than shock.

For all the apparent ease with which Ian's voice related that his wife had committed the ultimate crime against her country, his tone confirmed what she suspected. Three years ago, he had been a man in love with his wife.

Ian dropped his arms to his side. "Her memory is dead to me, Bethany. Let it stay that way."

"I'm . . . sorry for prying," she replied. "It is a terrible fault of mine to put my nose where it does not belong."

"Maybe," he said. "At least it is a pretty nose."

Her laughter was unexpected, even to her own ears. She caught it, sucking on her lower lip to stem the sound, for it seemed out of place, yet she was forever guilty of letting her emotions and feelings rule her actions. His eyes moved to her mouth. She wanted him to kiss her, and knew at once the thought betrayed her. She raised her gaze and saw that he recognized her desire because it reflected back from him in the darkening of his eyes. Her breath caught and she watched a frown deepen the shape of his lips.

It took them both a moment to realize neither of them had made any effort to move. "Expect a note from your family needing you to return home," he suddenly said with an abruptness that startled her for all that it was barely a whisper. "I want you to leave Whitley Court. My valet will see that a message gets to you."

Truly he couldn't be seriously considering that he had the right to see her removed. Not after everything she had told him. "My family is in Ireland until the spring, Ian."

"All the better. It is safer for you there."

She folded her arms as if he were some recalcitrant adolescent. "If you're so protective of my welfare, consider taking me home with *you*. I have no doubt my life and virtue would be eternally safe in your capable hands."

One corner of his mouth slowly lifted and she suddenly felt as she did in the passageway, caught out playing a dangerous game.

He stepped toward her. With the intent to do what? Shake her? Kiss her?

She retreated directly into the back of a tall tufted chair.

"Little Miss Bethany Munro. Ever the chameleon."

"Truly, I'm an open book."

His gaze traced the smooth line of her jaw before lifting to assess her eyes. Would he kiss her? For some reason she still felt safe around him. Though she had no idea whatever gave her that erroneous feeling. Ian was the least safe person she had ever known. "Does it amuse you to play the coquette?" he asked.

She tilted her chin. "You make everything I say and do sound so crass, Ian."

"I'm not going to kiss you."

She gasped. "As if I'd want you to."

"Liar," he gently whispered.

It was the absence of malice that allowed her desire to overrule everything else, and Bethany recognized that no matter what her feelings had been about him when he'd found her out in the passageway, they were of little account now. He knew who she was. And she knew who he was, sort of. They had reached an accord. At least she thought they had.

"Not every woman you meet is enamored of you, Ian."

He leaned a palm against the chair, trapping her. "You've thought about kissing me since the moment you laid your eyes on me. You are an impulsive headstrong female, an ungovernable little baggage who deserves exactly what she is asking for."

She sucked in a sharp breath. "I'm not afraid of you, Ian Rockwell."

"Then why are you so nervous?"

"Why are you?" she challenged softly in a voice that equaled his in strength.

His gaze slipped between the delicate arch of her brows to touch her lips, only to lift and find her watching him. A crease formed around his mouth. "How much experience with a man *do* you bloody well have?"

"My grandfather was a doctor, my stepmother a midwife. I know what happens between a man and a woman." She scraped an impetuous strand of loose hair from her brow. "Kissing is practically elementary compared to that."

She thought he smiled. He slid the pad of his thumb against her bottom lip, sending tiny shivers through her nerves. Three years ago, he'd walked away from her. But in the surrounding sunlight pressing against them, three years was a lifetime ago that had no bearing on now, and she no longer cared one way or the other what had gone before. What she did care about suddenly seemed more urgent, more perilous and infinitely more satisfying.

"I could kiss you," he said, lowering his voice and his mouth toward hers. "If I thought you knew how. Imp."

"Oh!" She pushed his fingers from her lips, but his reflexes were quicker and he evaded her whack causing her knuckles to *thump* against the wooden edge of the chair.

"You really should play harder to get."

Nursing her bruised knuckle, she glared at him standing completely at ease as if he knew exactly what he was doing and enjoying it, too. "You are such a coward."

He didn't deny it. A corner of her mouth tilted. "You will thank me later."

She couldn't help admitting to herself that she probably deserved what had just happened. "I've never had a stomach for men who cling to archaic societal standards that place women on pedestals and inside gilded cages where they can never possess desires. Until now, I never considered you that kind of man. But clearly, despite your reputation, you are as conventional as a stone ditch."

He was leaning indifferently with his elbow on the dresser.

She walked to the panel. He stood aside as she edged open the door. "Since we are finished here, you should go," she said.

A cold stream of air flowed from the opening and cooled her flushed face. He took the lamp when she politely offered it, felt the contact of his fingers, and lifted her gaze. Her assumption about him was wrong. He was not indifferent to her. He was amused. "This has been a somewhat interesting afternoon," he said.

"Indeed, it has."

He tilted her chin. The calloused pad of his thumb brushed her lip. "Keep your investigation out of Sir John's chambers and the library. Agreed?"

"Does this mean you'll help me?"

He let his hand fall away from her. "I'll help you."

Bethany felt as if a two-ton boulder had just been lifted off her shoulders. Other than Mary, Ian was the first person who had truly listened to her and agreed to do anything to help her. That he would stand beside her made her heart want to sing. "Thank you," she said.

Yet, for just a moment, before he turned into the passageway, she thought she'd seen him frown. Then he was gone.

It didn't occur until later that she had not asked him what he'd been doing standing outside Sir John's chambers. Had he caught her? Or had she caught him?

Chapter 6

Bethany never returned the guest list or the ledgers she'd taken and copied from Sir John's private study, heeding Ian's advice and staying clear of the room and shadowed corridors. The guest list had been missed, and Bethany did not dare do anything more for now.

In the days that followed her encounter with Ian in the passageway outside Sir John's chamber and then in her own bedroom, Bethany felt the full impact of his presence at Whitley Court. A glimpse at the whist table, an afternoon on the archery fields, her time spent standing at her bedroom window looking across the courtyard at his chambers, wondering why she was behaving like a ninny hammer. Ian had made no attempt to speak to her much less contact her. If they were working together, he certainly had not shown it.

He and the countess were cozy again as if he had not fobbed her off at the treasure hunt. Some women had no sense of pride.

Pushing herself away from the window, Bethany hesitated in front of the long glass mirror. It was a behemoth piece of ironwork framed by painted yellow flowers and dainty scrolls, a perfect rendition of one she'd seen in a

London museum surrounded by the wax figures of Ann Boleyn and her lady in waiting just before she was taken to the chopping block. Bethany remembered feeling saddened as she'd looked at that tableau from England's past for no one had been there to save the young queen.

Bethany focused her gaze on her own image, telling herself she was no longer the romantic idealist she had once been as she adjusted her gown just slightly off her pale shoulders. She only hoped this color green didn't make her look like a cabbage.

A knock sounded on the door and Bethany heard Mary answer the summons. A man's voice startled her out of her cogitations. A moment later Mary brought her a note.

"'Is Lordship wants to see ye before supper, mum," Mary said dropping into cockney, something she always did when she was nervous.

Taking the scrap of fine linen paper from her maid's fingers, Bethany unfolded the note, suddenly feeling very much like that unfortunate queen she'd seen from her past.

Drawing in a deep breath, Bethany knocked on the double-wide mahogany doors, the wooden bastion separating Lord Whitley's private wing from the rest of the manse. With her maid prudently in tow, her final destination was the nursery because that was where Lord Whitley had summoned her. She'd spent much time in this nursery these past few weeks with Lord Whitley's young son, but she had never received an official summons before.

A moment later, a click sounded from the other side and the door creaked open to reveal Adam's nurse. If Bethany's presence in Lord Whitley's private quarters surprised the woman, it didn't show on her face.

Lord Whitley suddenly appeared at the door. "Miss Munro," he said.

She held out the missive in her gloved fingers and disliked that she was nervous. "You wished to speak to me, my lord?"

He held his son, the very image of him down to the blue eyes and the shape of his mouth. Little Adam had been deaf since birth, something very few people knew. He was frail for seven, and looked even more so next to his towering father. The boy liked to see the world from his father's vertical perspective, and Lord Whitley never seemed to mind sharing.

Dressed casually in his shirtsleeves, Lord Whitley looked at ease. "Would you care to come inside?" he politely asked.

Like many of the girls at the conservatory, she had always admired Lord Whitley, believing in his vision of a new world where equality thrived in a society that separated the poor from the rich and laid down a man's destiny before he was ever born. He had been nothing if not always kind to her.

But he must have sensed her hesitation and her lack of want to offend him by declining the invitation, innocent as it may have been.

He chuckled lightly. He turned to the little boy and made a speaking motion with his hand. "Papa has to go now."

The boy made a chopping motion with his hand and fingers. He turned to look at Bethany and smiled impishly.

"Adam says you are pretty," Lord Whitley said.

Bethany looked from one to the other and smiled. "Thank you." Adam always told her that when she saw him. "Tell him he is a flirt. Even if he is only seven."

Lord Whitley laughed. "Tell him yourself. You know how."

Charlene had taught her to speak many of the words in the sign language of her brother. Bethany stepped nearer. She said the words aloud and touched Adam's cheeks with her palms, telling him that he was very pretty, too. This made the boy laugh.

Lord Whitley peered down into his son's face. "Tell Miss Munro that you wish for her to remain and be your teacher," he said and with a motion of his hand added, "Tell her you want her to stay."

This ongoing discussion had begun last year when she'd first learned to sign. At one time, Bethany had been flattered by the respect Lord Whitley had shown her, but she had seen the occasional glance he'd thrown her way when he'd thought she wasn't looking. Now, as she remembered Ian's words about him, she studied the boy and suddenly found herself wondering, how, if Lord Whitley was the monster Ian claimed, he could be such a decent father.

A stooped-over woman appeared in the nursery doorway. She carried a silver tray piled high with two bowls, utensils, and glasses. "That will be all, Agnes," Lord Whitley told the silver-haired servant. "The nurse will stay with my son."

"Yes, my lord." Upon seeing Bethany, the maid shuffled away.

Lord Whitley ruffled the boy's hair. "Now off to nap with you," he said and handed him to the boy's steel-haired nurse standing just out of sight behind him.

After the nurse left, Lord Whitley walked with Bethany into the corridor and shut the door. Mary remained at a discreet distance.

"Is Adam not well?" Bethany asked.

"He had a nightmare last night and was up before dawn today. Sometimes I think what he really wants are bowls and bowls of sorbet. Other times I think he is afraid of this house."

Bethany understood the feeling. Though Adam's perception had to be instinctive for the boy could not hear the creaks and low whistles caused by the wind, he must feel the eyes, as if someone were always watching.

"You concur with my son?" Lord Whitley asked.

"This house is old, my lord. No doubt it has ghosts."

"You know something of its history, then?"

"I know Whitley Court was built around the stones of an old medieval castle and that a great battle was fought here during the time of Henry the II."

"You no doubt already know more than I. It is unfortunate my daughter does not know half what you do. You pay attention to the details, Miss Munro."

Before she could decipher the comment, he glanced at the portraits on the walls around him. "This place has been my family's home for generations," he said without inflection. "I hope to leave my children with a house and a legacy that they will be proud to carry on. Will I, do you think?"

Even now as she looked around her at the world his family had built, she saw things she could respect. His ancestors had been at the frontier of many of the greatest changes that had taken place in England, and he'd taken his birthright and forged onward. He clearly loved his children, and he loved his son enough to learn to speak with him in a way that was foreign to Bethany. She looked away.

The chill in the air suddenly made her shiver.

"You're cold," he said.

"Yes, a little," she admitted, for it was the truth. "I am not sure what it is you are trying to ask of me, my lord."

"My family is everything to me, Miss Munro," he said after a pause. "You and my daughter have been good friends for two years, and I trust you will continue to look after her as you always have."

Bethany didn't understand why he would tell her that, as if she needed prompting. A deep-seated worry began to gnaw at her that whatever was beneath the surface of his concern, he was seeking some sort of information from her.

His hands clasped behind his back, he turned and faced her, his gaze briefly touching on her maid who followed at a discerning pace. "Now tell me about Sir Ian," he said.

Bethany's glance shot to Lord Whitley's face at the same time her heart pitched against her chest in dread. "Sir Ian?"

Lord Whitley looked at her for a long salient moment as if he could read the deepest etches in her soul and ferret out her secrets. "I make it my business to know the people around me, Miss Munro. All of them. I assure you Sir Ian is not unknown to me. I know he once worked with your guardian and that you were once acquainted. Sir Ian was invited because I wanted to meet him."

It was all she could do not to stammer a reply when her tongue had turned to jelly as if she were guilty of something, only because she was thinking of Ian and everything he'd said, wanting to shield and protect him. She wasn't even sure he deserved that protection. But she would throw herself off a rocky cliff before she breathed one word that might harm him.

"We are both aware of my reputation among a certain sect of this government, Miss Munro," Lord Whitley said, and for a moment his smile did put her at ease. "I have nothing to hide."

Yet, Bethany held a suspicion of people who smiled for all the wrong reasons.

"What is it you wish to know, my lord."

"Everything you remember about him, Miss Munro."

Then he opened his arm, inviting her to walk. Reluctantly, she followed.

At first, Bethany didn't think Ian heard the *tat, tat, tat* on the paneled door. She shivered in the icy draft, and the oil lamp fluttered in her hand. Unable to peer through a Judas hole, because one was not present or it was covered, she tapped her knuckles again against the panel door, suddenly anxious that he might not be alone in his room, and her reasons for trekking here in the middle of the night suddenly felt juvenile and suspect even to her mind. Had she come here tonight because Lord Whitley had frightened her or because she was running to Ian?

She heard a *thump* and a scrape as something slid away from the door then it flung open. And Ian appeared in the doorway, knotting the silk sash at his waist. His blond-tipped hair was mussed as if he'd just thrown on the robe. She looked up into a pair of shadowed eyes and felt her pulse accelerate. He did not look pleased to see her.

She held the small lamp in her hand and tentatively asked. "Are you alone?"

Some of the impatience dropped out of his expression. With a quiet oath, he stepped into the passageway. "How did you find this room?" he whispered in clear deference to the possibility their voices would travel. That he might actually be impressed by the feat annoyed her.

She swept past him, her soft muslin wrapper brushing his calf and her slippers slapping against the floor. "It isn't so difficult."

"Do you have any idea what would happen if someone found you in here?"

"You would be compromised and forced to wed me?" She set down the lamp on the table next to the wall, too cold and angry to argue such moot points as she scrubbed at her arms to increase the circulation. "If I thought that trick would have worked on you, I'd have been more diligent to compromise you years ago. Or lied about it. I hope you don't mean to be difficult."

Her eyes went around the crimson bedroom appointed ostentatiously in mahogany and black walnut furniture then back to his face. He made a quick check of the bedroom door to make sure it was locked, then strode to the bed and yanked off the comforter. His robe pulled across the broad width of his back.

"Naturally, to be visited by you at any hour of the day or night makes me fluttery all over. Dying of heart failure is surely more humane than being skewered through that delicate organ by your guardian."

She laughed. She couldn't imagine him afraid of anything.

"Please spare me your angst, Ian. I do not believe you."

He returned to her side, his mouth set in a frown at her observation, and draped the eiderdown around her shoulders, gathering the ends and giving her a small shake.

"What, pray tell, could you possibly want at this hour?"

"When would you prefer I come here? When the entire household is awake? I would have you answer one question."

"Only one?" He observed her more closely. "What happened to you, why are you trembling?"

She buried herself in his comforter. His dressing room door stood ajar, revealing a suit of clothes not yet brushed out as if he had hung them up after dinner last night. His underclothes lay on a rack near the stove. She saw part of what appeared to be a dark seaman's sweater discarded on the floor. Distracted by what she was seeing, she stepped into the room to see more clearly into the dressing room. Ian stepped in front of her.

A dark shadow marked the lines of his jaw. He looked disreputable. Clearly, he'd been out and about doing only heaven knew what.

"You weren't in bed," she accused him.

"Are we going to discuss both of our sleeping habits"—he turned and peered at the small clock on the dresser—"at three-fifteen in the morning? Why are you here, Bethany?"

"Lord Whitley knows that you and my guardian once worked together. He spoke with me about you tonight. Why didn't you tell me that he knew who you were?"

With an oath Ian turned his head away. A lock of his

hair fell over his brow. His jaw tightened, but when he brought his gaze back around, any emotion she'd glimpsed had vanished behind the wall of his eyes. "What did you tell him?"

"The truth. I met you three years ago at Rose Briar when you were working on a case with my guardian. Thank goodness, he thinks you've been relieved of your duty."

"I have been."

"Completely?" she said in shock.

"What other meaning does 'relieved of duty' have for you? I'm no longer in the business of guarding lives."

"Why couldn't you tell me?" Had he not trusted her?

"Why? You're here for your reasons. I'm here for mine. What have you done with the guest list?" he asked after a moment.

"Were you telling me the truth when you told me you would help me?"

"I meant it when I told you to stay out of Sir John's private study and anywhere else you are bound to get caught snooping. I want you to stay away from Sir John."

"We're both after the same thing. Right? Justice. I thought we were going to help each other."

"Help? What is it exactly you think you should be doing for me? You can help me by staying out of my way."

"There are two safes in this house," she offered. "There is another one in the library. You need a map to get around this house."

She set down the comforter on the back of a chair. "I've made a map if you wish to see." She shoved her hand in her pocket and withdrew the paper and brought it to the small secretary desk in the corner of the room. She had drawn corridors that serpentined through the upper wings and marked walls she'd encountered, perfectly detailed to scale.

It was then she saw another map lying on the desk near the panel door. It had been there when she'd entered the room and she was just now seeing it spread over the desktop along with a nib and standish and various objects that belonged on a desk. The lines on the diagram were straight-edged thin, perfect, far superior to hers. Where she'd only needed to find her way to the library and to Sir John's chambers, here she could see there was an entire labyrinth beneath Whitley Court she'd not discovered or explored. What was Ian searching for?

She felt him standing behind her, felt the brush of his silk robe, felt the heat of him warm her through the chill in the room, and knew he was hiding secrets. He had not found for whatever it was he searched, or she suspected he would not be here any longer.

"You're searching the tunnels that lead beneath this house."

She observed the map more closely, noting the different marks he'd peppered over the paper. In her opinion, his map may be larger but hers was still better. "Yes, well it isn't size that counts," she said. "It's the detail."

Ian suddenly laughed. "No, dear. Size does matter. And you're a wee little thing who has gotten herself wrapped up in some very dangerous business, lastly but foremost, at the moment, your presence in my room."

"Obviously you don't consider what I have to offer important." She folded her diagram.

His fingers tilted her chin. "What has lit the fire in your turbines anyway?"

"We both want answers and we both want the truth.

Why were you standing in the corridor outside Sir John's room?"

He lowered his hand. "The same reason you went there."

"I know what you told me. Are you a government informant, then? Is that why Lord Whitley is interested in you?"

"I should hope not." His eyes narrowed. "Nor am I some novice ingénue playing sleuth and putting her nose where she'll most likely find it cut off her face."

Her mouth flattened. "I thought we were at least on the same side," she said.

"Bethany–"

"I can find my way back."

And with that pronouncement, she turned and tripped over the trunk he'd shoved away from the panel door. She'd been so angry with him she hadn't even seen the darned thing sitting at her feet. She stumbled, fell backward over a sharp corner, and hit the ground on her bottom. Her wrapper rucked up around her thighs, revealing her pink lace-edged underdrawers beneath. She felt a rushing sound in her ears, and her throat squeezed, making a gasp stick in her throat. She'd crushed her map, tearing part of it and smearing ink. She'd made a mess of her drawing.

Ian squatted beside her and dangled his wrist from his knee as he set his eyes on her making her think he had divined her real purpose for coming here tonight—to see him. His mouth was tight. His robe opened in a vee at his neck, revealing his throat, and she found her attention drawn to a coarse smattering of hair she saw there. He took her drawing and carefully folded it as if he felt bad that she'd ruined it. "Now what do you suppose I should do with you?" he quietly asked, offering her the map back.

She snatched it from him. "You are not a very nice person."

"I never pretended to be a nice person."

"Why can't you just tell me exactly what you are looking for? Why all the spying?"

"For the same reason I don't take out a notice in the *Post*. And I'd prefer to think of myself as a casual observer of the proceedings here. Spying brings to mind cloaks and daggers and all manner of unpleasant subterfuge. I told you why I am here."

"Then you will vanish, and I will never see you again?"

There was something strange and penetrating in his eyes. "We don't exactly live in the same circle, Bethany."

He'd said the words so casually. "Forgive me if I am not overcome with gratitude for your one small kindness, Ian." She struggled to stand, but he was in her way and she knocked her elbow against his knee. "I don't need your help anyway. I only came to tell you about Lord Whitley."

"Are you sure you really didn't come to see me?"

She gasped at his continued arrogance. She wanted to say something clever and cutting to put him in his place where he deserved. Something witty that would make him think twice about judging her so low. "You're an oaf, Ian."

"Am I?" He held out his hand to help her stand.

She slapped it away. "Don't touch me! I can get up myself!"

He placed his hands beneath her arms and hauled her to her feet. The touch imprinted itself through the thin cloth of her wrapper and she pulled away only to go no further than his arms. His fingers splayed her ribs. She inhaled and her breasts pressed against his thumbs. Then she was staring up into his face, nothing but shadows.

She didn't know if he would kiss her.

She was suddenly hoping he would. His fist tightened in her hair and pulled her face back. The moist heat of his breath touched her lips. "Are you saving yourself for marriage, Bethany Ann?"

His harsh question coming amidst the tremors shivering through her body was like a leaden fishhook on her lips and she found herself wanting to frown. She flipped a finger against his sash. "Then you are curious if I am still a virgin?"

"Bloody hell, it never crossed my mind to ask."

"But you *have* thought about it at least once since the ball."

"Kiss and tell, Bethany?" His hands framed her face. "I doubt you've ever been properly kissed. What is there to tell?"

"You are always so sure of yourself," she said.

He tucked a wayward curl behind her ear. "Tell me I'm wrong." He lowered his long lashes and she felt his eyes briefly touch her lips before resettling with an odd intensity upon her eyes. "What is there to tell? Have you saved yourself for marriage?"

"I have more important things to do with my life than marry. Marriage is about politics, alliances, convenience, and money."

"Or giving a name to a child."

"Which has nothing to do with love or friendship."

His mouth softened. He cupped her jaw. "Being in love doesn't guarantee happiness. You live in a fairytale, Bethany."

"Who was your first lover?"

"She was an expensive Gypsy who thought I had been a virgin too long. I was seventeen, and she was worth every shilling at the time."

"You were fortunate not to have contracted the pox."

"That is an understatement, sweet." He laughed and she felt the heat of it on her face. His voice turned into a breath that was barely her name. "This is insane, Bethany."

Her gaze encompassed his face. "I know you have feelings for me." The pads of his thumbs pressed gently against the corners of her lips as his gaze drifted over her features.

"My feelings at this moment are irrelevant and not the kind you're looking for. What exactly do you think I am looking for?" she asked.

Ian slowly drew back, somehow managing to pull away from the brink, to rein in his hunger. The trust implied in her words anchored him to his conscience. To him, she would always be young and vulnerable. For a moment, he'd forgotten. So much so, he leaned his forehead against hers and shook his head.

"I can't give you what you want, Behany."

"I'm not asking for anything." Her words were infinitely gentle to his ears, as if it were he and not she who needed protection; his jaded view of the world no longer measured within these passing seconds. "I have no want to marry, Ian. Except for the occasional spoutings of troubadours and poets, most intelligent people consider love overvalued."

His hips, which heretofore had only brushed the coarse

fabric of her robe, now touched her more intimately.

His mouth softened. He cupped her jaw. "And you're an intelligent person?"

"I believe I am. Aren't you?"

"No."

Again her quiet laughter was unexpected. He felt the tentative touch of her palms against his chest. Her smile slipping away, she drew in a breath and released it slowly as if she recognized he was making a choice and that choice may not be her. "It's only one kiss," she said on a whisper.

One kiss was not so unmanageable.

A slip of pure electricity burned through him. He *should* kiss her, he realized.

He'd wanted to do something like this since he'd cornered her in the alcove the night of the ball. But he was positive he could commit no bigger crime, unless he murdered Whitley for allowing her to come to this place. He wanted her gone.

But he wanted to taste her lips more.

He drew a deep breath, slid his fingers into her hair and tilted her face toward his. Sin and scandal rolled into one delectable unspoken promise.

Yet a barely perceptible tremor touched the periphery of his senses. For all of her bold talk and progressive attitude toward seduction, she trembled.

"Open your mouth, Bethany," he urged and when her lashes lifted in response, so did her chin. He bent his mouth over hers.

The initial contact was light, exploratory at first as he tested the depth of his own turbulent waters, calmer now as he sought to explore not pillage. He subtly shifted the slant of his mouth. And her lips, softly yielding, parted in response, melding to the shape of his and escalating the hunger inside him, until the taste of her filled his senses. His hands tightened on her head, holding her steady, his mounting assault on her lips heightened by the growing press of her body against his.

She let him press her into the velvet trappings of the canopy bed. He shut his eyes just to breathe. He drew in a deep breath, felt the tentative slide of her tongue against his bottom lip, sending a rush of blood pooling between his legs and taking the initiative from him—or perhaps he merely surrendered it.

He moaned softly, a sound she swallowed, even as he took more from her. She slid her hands beneath his robe and splayed them across his bare chest. He delved his hands more thoroughly into the silken strands of her hair. He couldn't get enough.

And the kiss deepened into something powerful and explosive. His tongue made a sweep of her mouth, dipping along the honeyed underside of her lips.

Pressing her against the velvet and brocade of the canopy bedspread, he bent at the knees and found the natural cradle between her thighs, his inarticulate groan muffled by the catch in her voice. He didn't think he could be thicker or harder than he was now, pressed against her, close enough to absorb her body heat through the black silk of his robe.

He gripped her hair so that he could hold her mouth and he thrust his tongue between her lips. She arched against him. But the groan he heard was his own. He drew back, but not so far that he lost contact with her lips.

Her eyes opened, dark mirrors in the heat and low light

shared between them. Breathing shallowly, her breasts rising and falling against his chest, she held his assessing gaze. "Kissing is new to you," he said against her lips.

"Yes." She traced the shape of his mouth with a sigh.

He shouldn't be doing this, he thought, somewhere in the back of his mind, his lips hovering over hers in an erotic whisper. Determined to set her away from him, he struggled for some semblance of his self-control, even if he held on to it by a thread.

Ian tried to wake up an objection, but his addled libido granted him no quarter. "Bethany," his murmur followed a moan. Hers or his, he didn't know. Frankly, he didn't care.

Ian's thoughts and actions condemned him to the purgatory in which he suddenly found himself.

"Ah hell." He surrendered softly to her lips and floated with her down onto bed.

Chapter 7

In a whisper of silk, Bethany sank into the down comforter within the confines of Ian's massive bed. Only the robe swathing his hips prevented full contact, flesh against flesh. He definitely had a body contoured to fit the valleys and curves of her own body molded against the fabric of her robe. Her legs parted beneath the pressure of his hips. His mouth was warm, his touch hot. Whatever he was doing with his marauding hand across her hip, she didn't want it to stop. He turned with her, rolling her to the center of the bed away from the heating pan. His hands caught her wrists and pressed them into the soft mattress. She trembled as her fingers twined between his. He responded with a husky groan. One of his hands splayed her waist and she felt his thumb glide just beneath the weight of her breast. His teeth grazed her tender earlobe. Then he touched his forehead against hers as they both realigned their thoughts and sought to regain control.

Struggling to catch her breath, she opened her eyes. Her heart was pounding so loud she was surprised he couldn't hear it. The soft lamplight limned his broad shoulders in shiny black but left his face pinned in shadows. "Is this why you came to my room? For this?" he rasped against her lips.

The idea of being done with her virginity was not something she had seriously considered before ten minutes ago when he had kissed her. She only knew that whatever it was she felt, Ian was its source. She burned within its presence.

"Why me, Bethany?"

The query was like asking why does the sun shine. How could she answer him when she didn't know the answers to such eternal questions? Yet, she sensed his question went beyond the physical parameters guiding them. It led in a direction he would not follow with her.

With a quiet oath, he turned on his back and laid his forearm across his brow as if his sigh weighted his thoughts. Pale lamplight manipulated the black silk of his robe, bringing out the silver threads in the cloth and the well-defined shape of the man beneath. Hard and soft in all the right places that were pleasing to the eye.

Her memory of him didn't serve him justice. Certainly it had never included the carnal view displayed before her now. Her tactile senses aroused, she wanted to wrap her fingers around the length of him as much to explore the sensual cravings he aroused as to touch a living part of him and feel his pulse within her palm. But her emotions also made her afraid.

He moved slightly and she raised her gaze. The heavy velvet draperies kept his face in shadows, but she felt his eyes on her, watching her quick study of his person. Heat rose in her cheeks.

He returned to her, seeking purchase with his hands as he slid his palms over hers and turned her on her back.

He braced on his elbows and looked down into her face. A forelock of sun-tipped hair fell over his brow. She could not see the look in his eyes but felt the pad of his thumb trace her lips.

She let the sensations wrap around her, fueled by the deep-down heat that began in the dark pit of her belly and spread through her limbs. She truly wanted to throw caution to the wind and have a scorching affair. She couldn't imagine how it would feel, quite simply because she'd never had an affair. Yet beneath the shivery excitement, she felt something hollow at the base of her thoughts. A sort of growing emptiness that she would never be more than a fling to him. And yet. . . . she found herself in wonder of him, living in the essence of her feelings, sensing the power of response—even as she felt his hesitation.

"You are thinking I could conceive a child," she said, trying to put an explanation to his mood.

"Now that is consideration."

"Aren't there ways to prevent conception?"

"Not reliably. And I doubt you have any of those practiced methods with you. Or do you also study means that prevent conception along with your books on anatomy?" His voice darkened around her and his palm cupped her cheek as if he would read into her thoughts. "What is it you want from me, Bethany?"

The question lingered in her thoughts. "You have always made me curious about that which I do not understand, Ian."

"Then it is your desire to pin my wings on cork and dissect me?"

She laughed at his outrageousness. "It is my desire that you pin *my* wings on cork and dissect *me*, Sir Ian."

The words were out before she could pull them back. Then she was glad she'd said them and her mouth turned up at the corners.

For a moment, she stilled in his dark caressing gaze as something stirred in their depths, and she felt the roughness of his thumbs against lips. "I am not your shining knight, Bethany. Believe me there is nothing shining about me. I'm not what you think I am."

Her mood grew serious. "Perhaps you aren't what you think you are either, Ian."

He laughed and the deep sound of it seemed to resonate in the air like a threat . . . or a promise. She could feel the imprint of his body between her legs. He stroked his thumb along her cheekbone, a frown in his eyes. "Twenty years old and all grown up. What do you really know about me?"

"I know that you are decent. Perhaps that is all I need to know."

"Don't mistake my reluctance to bed you for decency, Bethany."

"Poor, Ian. Thirty-one years old and all confused. You think you want to be alone, but everyone needs someone."

Something unpleasant flickered in his eyes. "Two kisses do not a woman make, Bethany."

Her heart suddenly felt open and much too vulnerable, the enormity of what she had almost done tonight striking her. But Ian hadn't gone further.

"Get off me. Please."

The bed shifted and he moved his body aside in that lackadaisical way she'd seen him sitting that one morning at the dining room table—the way he pulled back inside himself. She slid off the mattress, yanking at the fabric of her wrapper clinging to her, and turned around to face him. He lay on the bed on his side like a rakeshame, resting his head on his hand as he watched her struggle with her clothes, his eyes cloaked in dark secrets just like the rest of him.

He remained on the bed. It was that picture of him she still held in her mind when she left his chambers.

Supper was a magnificent affair with roasted beast, green beans, and something that resembled sweet potatoes. Later, after the music started, Bethany made herself comfortable in various social groups gathered around the green baize faro table. Talk and laughter and jaunty strains of a waltz nearly drowned out conversation. The door remained monitored by liveried footmen, watching who entered and left the ballroom.

She spotted Charlene across the room, turned out nicely in a turquoise silk Worth gown, headed for the lady's sitting room, and frowned.

The last few days had been strained between them. Bethany hadn't known what it was she'd done to offend Charlene, but twice she'd gone to visit her friend in her chambers only to find her unavailable. At meals, Charlene had seemed only distracted and bored with her company.

So Bethany had followed her friend to the orangery yesterday when Charlene was supposed to have been taking part in Lady Thrumble's reading group. Sir John had been inside waiting. Bethany did not have to press her face to the glass to observe what her friend was doing with her father's secretary and bodyguard. Sickened by the discovery, Bethany had turned away, only to find Ian standing near the portico watching her.

He'd known. Even without Bethany saying anything, he'd known what she had seen, and Bethany thought that if he said anything, anything at all, she might burst into tears.

Instead of the disregard she'd expected to glimpse in his eyes, she saw only concern, and he took her inside out of the cold into the dining room, sat her on one of the Chippendale chairs, and gave her hot cocoa to nurse her wounds. Saying nothing, he watched her and she knew how childish she must appear in his eyes.

"Even if the man is not despicable . . . he's married," Bethany had finally said. How could Charlene be such a fool? she'd asked herself a dozen times since. Yet it had been the secrets that hurt the most.

"How long have *you* known?" she asked.

"I've suspected since the morning we had breakfast."

His hand gently moved as he stirred sugar into his coffee, not so rough that he disturbed the drink. She had not spoken to him since that night in his room when he'd kissed her . . . and she'd kissed him back, and fallen willy-nilly on his bed. But for all the darkness and gravity he exuded, his sweet tooth made him a little more vulnerable to her, almost as if it were a chink in his armor, a soft spot in his character that she had not seen before—and something had spilled over inside her and awakened.

He'd waited until she finished her cocoa, then he'd taken his leave of her, and she'd returned to the reading group as if the world had not momentarily stopped rotating.

Turning now to scan the ballroom, she found Ian standing in a circle of men surrounding Lord Whitley.

Dressed much as he'd been the first night she'd seen him here, he was leaning against a white stone pillar, sipping champagne, and listening to the conversation, and she felt that funny hollow feeling in her chest again. He wasn't spending all of his time with the countess tonight.

She suspected if he ever felt deeply about anything or anyone, he would not speak of it, even to himself. Bethany knew he cared about her. He could fight it but the feelings were still there between them.

Glancing hastily away, she sighed at the mystery of him, at what he made her feel, that strange mixture of excitement, fear, and longing. Being with him was like inhaling sunlight after a winter storm. Exhilaratiing and intoxicating. But the invisible wall, the one he erected to force her to keep her distance, was between them again.

But tonight, she'd made up her mind to speak to him about something important. She had only to approach him.

Bethany joined several other guests and waited until Ian was alone. He'd remained at the pillar and watched her over the rim of his champagne glass as she approached. She saw the countess across the glittery ballroom in the arms of another partner. "Has Lady Dermott abandoned you for other entertainment?" she asked when he saw where her gaze had landed.

He quietly laughed. "You don't sound too heartbroken, love."

"Would you care to dance with me?" she asked.

After the briefest hesitation, he deftly set his champagne flute on the table next to a potted fig tree. "And me with so little to do tonight, I thought I should expire from boredom."

Her heart warmed a hundred degrees. She accepted his

arm, and he stepped with her out onto the dance floor.

His arm tightened around her waist, gathering her closer. "You've been standing at that window most of the night looking as if your cat just died."

That he'd been watching her made her smile. "Zeus? That rangy tom is too ornery to die. The big owl encamped in our barn at Rose Briar has been trying to eat him for years. One would think the old owl would just give up."

"Poor owl."

She frowned. "It isn't funny. Who would want to be eaten by an owl?"

"Why don't you just kill the owl?"

"Because that would be heartless, Ian."

"Then Zeus will eventually perish. It is the way of the beasts. You underestimate the cold determination of the hunter, Bethany."

"I underestimate nothing," she whispered, aware of his easy sensuality, conscious of the heat of his hand through her ribbed bodice. *You least of all.*

But she did not say the words aloud.

Taking her firmly in his arms, he quietly laughed as if reading her mind. It was impossible to ignore the feel of his body as he brushed against her, his arm protectively about her, a little snugger than appropriate. She studied a pearl button at eye-level on his silver-threaded waistcoat before looking away. Her head barely reached his shoulder, and his height suddenly made her feel vulnerable. His palm tightened on her waist.

"I want you to ride with me tomorrow," she said. "I had heard Lord Whitley suggested that you see the grounds. I could show them to you myself."

He swept her past lofty windows in the ballroom, reflecting back the sheen of colorful satins and jewels, and the three-quarter time of the graceful waltz faded to the back of her mind. Candlelight from the chandelier glanced off his gold-tipped hair. His hand marked the shape of her waist, his eyes the pale curves of her breasts and everything else about her.

"Tell me something." His voice seemed to hold a smile. "Did you wear that bit of pink froth tonight to distract me and every man here?"

She focused on his face to find him studying her, his eyes neither blank nor masked but unreadable all the same. "Haven't you guessed by now? When a man is looking at a woman and sees only her breasts, he doesn't look into her eyes and see everything else."

He should have been amused by her logic about the male psyche because it was so true, but she found he was not.

"If you quit now you will forever be throwing away the opportunity to know me, Ian." She tried to sound cavalier as if his decision to come riding with her did not matter.

"Are you always so complicated and difficult?"

"I am when I want something. I think I can give you what you want as well. I'm always at the stable just after dawn. Do you still want the guest list?"

The music had stopped. Ian realized he had not even heard the climatic conclusion of the waltz. Neither apparently had she, their presence relegated to the shadows, standing toe to toe at the corner of the ballroom floor, while others were milling toward the punch and cake table.

"How much longer will you be at Whitley Court?" he quietly asked.

"Here you are Sir Ian." The countess sidled next to Ian and peered up at him with her beatific smile. Her dark curls framed a heart-shaped face. "Whatever are you discussing here in the shadows when you could be dancing with me? May I steal you?" she asked, and only then did she turn her head and look toward Bethany.

Ian held out his hand. "Consider me stolen, Lady Dermott." He nodded to Bethany. "Miss Munro."

He took Lady Dermott in hand and swept her into a waltz.

"May I consider you stolen for the night?" Serena purred in a seductive overtone when she sensed Ian's distraction.

He looked down into her face with circumspect attention. She was warm in his arms, her body full, the bright sea green gown a match to her hazel eyes. Their pleasures in each other these last few months had been a diversion for them both, pure and simple. He'd provided her with a distraction from her loneliness since her husband passed away last year; she'd fueled his purpose. But somehow, now, the rules had changed.

Or maybe he didn't want to bed Serena because he was thinking of Bethany.

"Truly, Sir Ian." She tapped his shoulder. "You have turned into a pumpkin at the stroke of midnight all week?"

"A big orange one."

"What would you say if I told you I like big orange pumpkins?"

His breath brushed her ear. "I'd say not at Whitley's house."

She pursed her lower lip, but there was no anger in her eyes. "I thought as much. People change when they come here. My brother does that to a person. Soon he will have you doing his bidding, too."

She was surprisingly serious. "I think it is the air we breathe while here. By the time my brother's guests depart one of his country retreats, everyone will be friends and he will have a new following. Miss Munro is a dedicated convert." She laughed. "I wouldn't trust her with anything less than sterling compliments toward my brother's character."

Ian involuntarily looked over her shoulder to where he'd left Bethany and saw that Whitley had joined her. He glimpsed them standing near the palms in conversation before he lost sight of her in the crowd of dancers. Ian fought the heat spiking through his veins, a feeling so pervasive he forced himself to look away.

"I have overstepped," she said, as he took her in a final sweep of the ballroom floor before the music ended.

Ian bowed gallantly over Serena's delicately gloved hand. "You have not, my lady."

She popped open her fan and fluttered the air between them. "And still you will leave me to find my bed alone again."

But in the end, she didn't seem to mind that he had just made the first overture in ending their short liaison, nor did he attempt to rationalize his logic as he dropped the countess off into the arms of another admirer and retired to the smoking room. Pulling a cheroot from a sterling case withdrawn from his jacket pocket, he searched for and found his quarry, the woman in his thoughts, her blond head easy to spot in the crowd.

Though he'd managed to dismiss Bethany from his conversation, she never completely left his thoughts. And as he looked across the ballroom following that glimpse of pink, he found himself pulled in a direction he didn't want to go. In the midst of his own emotions, he wondered that he could feel anything at all when he had so aptly crushed that part of himself years ago.

No spy provocateur ever truly trusted anyone but himself. He had learned that lesson years ago. And yet, she filled his head to distraction.

Her tenacious persistence reminded him of a three-toed sloth. Ian had seen such a creature once, eight years ago, hanging upside down from a single tree branch for five long hours, then only traveling three feet before resting again and still perfectly content to do so. He'd been working a case in South America at the time when he'd seen that sloth.

His mind suddenly moved thousands of miles and an ocean away to a time he'd tried to forget. South America was where he'd first met Pamela.

His wife.

He didn't know why he'd thought of Pamela just then. Perhaps because he had been thinking of someone else with blue eyes. Someone more innocent and unspoiled by the ugliness of his world.

Pamela had come into his life during a time he'd not been proud of.

In the beginning, he'd been green as they came, a new field agent in the Foreign Service, a man with high ideals born of a desire to give something back to a country that had given his family so much. But by the time he'd met Pamela, those ideals had already begun their slide downward. He'd walked the dark side in his world, taken jobs of the lowest depravity because he'd found himself particularly talented at killing another human being. Most needed killing. Rapists. Murderers. It didn't matter if they were heads of state or religious mullahs. Bethany hadn't known the kind of man he was three years ago when she'd looked at him with youthful love in her eyes and almost made him believe that there was still goodness in this world.

But something had happened to him after that day at Rose Briar when he'd been with Bethany. Something that had struck him deeply. He'd looked at himself and the dark web of deceit that had become his life and he'd taken the first steps toward change—only to end with the assassination of the Home Secretary last fall. He'd lost what had remained of his reputation to a job, to which at any time in the past he would have given his life. It seemed that anything he ever touched in these last three years, he tarnished or killed.

Pulling on the cheroot, he blew out a breath of blue smoke and leaned a shoulder against the jamb, allowing his gaze to go around the crowded room. He spied Sir John at the second door talking to Lady Charlene. A few moments later, they went to different doors and slipped out.

"You're a real son-of-a-bitch, Johnny boy," Ian said to himself, having followed the bastard's trail for the last five months to this place.

It was novel seeing Howard all doe-eyed over a woman.

It didn't fit the picture Ian had of the man, and it gave him an unpleasant new perspective on Lady Charlene, one that bore watching.

When Ian looked toward Bethany again he saw that she'd been watching them, too.

Chapter 8

As dawn spread warming light across a landscape encased in frozen wintry white, Ian, his riding clothes cloaked by a heavy woolen coat, arrived at Whitley's stables. A rare hint of blue for this time of year had already begun to color the sky. The sun would come out today, he decided. He could see the crumbling turrets of an old stone priory in the distance. His breath steamed from his lips. He blew warmth over his gloved hands as he turned to take in the sea.

He'd come early to get a feel for the grounds. The stables were large and well kept, a credit to Whitley. In this part of England where winters were brutal, Ian grudgingly had to admit the stables stood Whitley in good stead. Ian may not trust the man, but he liked the way he cared for his animals.

The sound of a discontented horse drew him around to a paddock adjoining the stable. A groom was attempting to saddle a magnificent black stallion. The horse reared, screaming and thrashing its forelegs in air. Ian watched with interest, absently slapping his quirt against his shiny riding boots. The hapless groomsman seemed neither pleased nor brave enough to be set with saddling the stud that stood at least seventeen hands high. With all four feet on the ground again, the horse pranced to the end of its tether, tossing his head in dramatic fashion, his flowing mane and tail moving in synchronicity with his stride. He was as high-strung as he was splendid. With some coaxing, the groom finally settled him next to the mounting block.

"He is somewhat disagreeable," Ian called to the groom.

"Very disagreeable, sir. Most are afraid of him."

Ian was an excellent rider, but even he had no desire to break his neck riding a temperamental horse over the frozen ground. He considered asking the groom to saddle another horse.

"What is his name?"

"Sampson." The feminine voice came from behind him.

Ian swung around. Bethany stood behind him, a half-grin lifting a corner of her mouth. The morning light warmed the fine features of her face and touched the dark blue woolen serge of a tailored riding habit barely visible beneath her cloak. She wore a matching hat with a blue feather that draped over her shoulder and framed her baby-smooth cheek. She was all of a vision framed by the stark landscape, with a tantalizing glimpse of blue eyes and cheeks colored pink by the cold. She was beautiful.

"He belongs to me." She stepped past him into the corral. "You do not find him striking?"

He leaned on the fence rail and watched her hands stroke Sampson's powerful black neck and purr something that raised the horse's ears. Ian's reaction was a bit more visceral. "Very striking," he said.

"You love me don't you, Sampson." She slipped a cube of sugar from her pocket. The horse ate obediently out of her hand. "Lord Chadwick's Irish thoroughbred sired him." She accepted a leg up from the groom and settled comfortably in the saddle with one leg hitched around the pommel.

Ian looked her mount over from forelock to fetlock catching a tantalizing glimpse of black leather riding boots laced over her ankles. "He's a fine animal."

She ran her palm across Sampson's neck. "Sampson was one of a set of twins born three years ago. The mother died soon afterward." She watched the groom as he reentered the stable to fetch Ian's mount. "I kept both foals alive. Lord Chadwick gave me Sampson and brought him to the conservatory last summer, but Sampson proved too wild to be kept there. Lord Whitley offered this place. Here, when summer comes, Sampson will have open land to run free in exchange for . . ." She actually blushed as if she hadn't come to his room in the middle of the night.

"Stud service?" Ian supplied with unimpaired calm.

"To put it bluntly. Yes."

"Sampson will be one happy horse."

She turned her head, but her bow mouth twitched in a grin. "I imagine he will be very content." She smiled. "You decided to come riding with me. I'm glad."

A half hour later, they were both mounted and riding out of the yard. Ian sat astride a bay gelding, possessed of a comfortable gait and calmer disposition than Sampson, for which he was grateful, though he noted Bethany and her horse were perfectly matched. She urged the horse into a gallop and pulled ahead, her gesture not lost on Ian. She wanted to take the lead. Not that he had a choice, but he didn't care. The brisk wind slipped beneath his coat and he raised his collar, letting her forge ahead. She possessed a fine seat and he remained deceptively content to watch her for now.

They skirted Whitley Court, confronted a shallow stream that bisected the snow-covered terrain, and splashed through ice-encrusted water to the other side. In a distant field, sheep lifted their black snouts and a pheasant startled from the underbrush scurried away. Some minutes later, she crested a hill and turned to wait for him to catch up. He did, slowing alongside her, and silently awaiting an end to her games. And for her to talk to him.

"I've heard the notorious thief Robin Hood is buried somewhere south of here," she said in conversation.

"We're a long way from Sherwood Forest."

"This area was once one of the most active smuggling centers in Britain. Contraband was taken along tunnels under the cottages, eventually to be carried off in wagons. Did you know that?"

He did know it but did not say so.

"But then you are probably aware of the history," she said. "Where is your home from here?"

He pointed north. If she had known him better she'd have recognized his irritation and taken heed. Something was bothering her. "My family's estate is a full day's ride in that direction."

"I thought you were a neighbor?"

"I am. Relatively speaking. We both live on the northeastern coast of England."

She tightened her gloved hand on the reins to swing Sampson around. Ian reached across both horses and stopped her. When he cupped the side of her face, she did not pull away. "Do you want to tell me why you are not worried that Lord Whitley will think I'll do something untoward out here?"

She held his steady, assessing gaze. "Haven't you figured it out yet? He is trying to recruit you. He knows I have a past acquaintance with you. But he also wishes you to see the grounds for yourself."

She nodded at the distant parapets that flanked each end of Whitley Court. He could see movement between the stone merlons. "There are men up there with glasses trained on us as we speak," she said, and waved prettily toward them. "Truthfully, there is nowhere we can go that we cannot be seen from those positions. Except the old priory."

As Ian was distracted, she kicked Sampson into a canter. Then she gave the horse license to run. Ian lost sight of her when she crested the hill and vanished on the other side.

He nudged his bay. Though he suspected she was maintaining appearances for their audience, he would play her game only so long. Watching her ride hell-for-leather across the countryside did not so much test his patience as it did his restraint not to race after her.

He could not have imagined her recklessness before she had sneaked down to his room and practically defied him to kiss her. Now he recognized an identical spark she'd kindled inside him. He had not felt its power in some time. To feel it now when he had felt dead inside for so long was almost like learning to breathe again.

He caught sight of her in the distance and urged the bay into a gallop. When he reached the monastic remains of the priory, she was nowhere in sight.

Ian remained in the saddle and looked around. He spotted Sampson tied to a brass ring imbedded in the nose of a stone gargoyle. A half dozen such statues spread their wings from around the stone structure and sat sentry over the windswept cliffs overlooking the sea. Breakers crashed with a great roar against the shoreline. Dismounting, he looped the reins around a low branch of a lone dead tree gnarled by the wind, and walked up the steps into the Gothic priory.

He looked up at the blue sky visible between granite cross-sections and flying buttresses, probably a twelfth-century structure. The empty structural cavern echoed with silence and the low whistle of the wind. The hammer-beam roof had long ago succumbed to the elements and collapsed. Bethany stood at the other end of the nave beneath a transverse arch, once a main wall but which now framed the sea. She was staring out at the seagulls flying around the rocks below. Ian noted that she had brought them within a protected stone bay away from spying eyes.

"You can't see them now, but there are caves in those cliffs," she said. "If I could climb down there, I would."

Ian peered across the half-moon cove toward Whitley Court anchored on a spit of land bordered on three sides by rocky cliffs. Far below the cliffs, high tide covered the entire beach, waves smashing against the rocks.

"I've come here almost every day," she said. "This spot is the only place that overlooks Whitley Court and the sea."

"He lets you come out here alone?"

She turned her head. "Why shouldn't he?"

"I don't know, Bethany. Maybe you can tell me why he should trust you at all."

She folded her arms and looked away, toward what used to be an old fireplace. Ian placed his hand beneath her chin and returned her gaze to his. His thumb traced the sensitive bow of her mouth. In the darker shadows enfolding them, her face was its own light. A breeze whispered through the ruins and fluttered the faintly blond tendrils of hair curling at her temples. "Did you bring me up here this morning so I would see the cliffs?"

"You know it is more than that," she said without guile.

Every one of his muscles tensed. Her breathing had quickened as well. "Really?" He tilted her chin. His voice was husky and low as he bent over her lips. "Show me."

She didn't pull away but lifted her chin and sealed the kiss between them. His hand fell away from her face and he clasped her shoulders, stepping against her as he held her steady. He let his hands drift downward over the woolen serge of her sleeves, entwining his fingers with hers. He wasn't sure what he was about when he was around her, only that kissing her had become the single focus of his thoughts these past days. He swept his tongue between her parted lips and deepened the kiss. He wanted more of her mouth. He wanted to feel her heat, the hot press of her body. He wanted to inhale her. When he came up for breath, she sucked in air too.

She opened those eyes so dark at the centers, with a slim halo of blue. His breath caught on an edge of anticipation, hot and sharp, no longer a measure of his uncertainty but of something mercenary, as they moved at the same time and she let him back her against the smooth stone wall. The pads of his thumbs pressed into the curves just beneath her jaw. His palms slid over her cheeks and cupped her face. She tasted salty from her exercise, sweet like the morning breeze, and hot, like the humid air they shared, dispelling all the winter's cold surrounding them.

"Bethany . . ." His voice was low and hoarse.

She pulled him back and he kissed her again, open-mouthed and hungry for more. He heard himself whisper her name. Her soft mouth kissed the corner of his and the hollow of his throat. Her breasts pressed to his chest and then into the palm of his hand. Beneath the closely fitted jacket, she wore a laced blouse. He felt its intimate texture, the boning of her stays, and her heartbeat against his palm. His thumb caressed her hardened nipple.

She jerked away, breathing hard. The stone wall stopped her movement. "Say it, Ian," she whispered.

"Say what? That neither of us is thinking clearly?"

"Say that you enjoy kissing me."

The position of her arms around his neck shaped her body against his, and he set her away to look down at the bounty of softness. His struggle was confined to a single glance.

In truth, except for an urgent need to continue touching her, he didn't know what he felt. He wished he hadn't given her the impression they held the same goal or said the words that made her look at him like he was some shining knight, because in the end they were only words, and he was no shining knight. When one had sunk into the depths of depravity, one learned to lose a conscience. Bethany still believed in principles like justice and fair play. They weren't even on the same team.

She leaned her head against his chest and nestled in the

circle of his arms, her warm presence a profound feeling for a man who had not allowed himself to experience tenderness in years. But her warmth and nearness clouded his brain.

She had always done that to him, he realized, had always made him want more than he could have. "How long before the troops are sent out to find us?"

"I've come up here almost every day. No one ever bothers me. But I never stay here long, and I make sure the guards can see me walking along the paths that parallel the cliffs. Though I don't walk too closely." She laughed uncomfortably. "The ground along the cliffs is unstable."

"Which probably means no one watches the cliffs." He dropped his arms from around her, walked to the ledge of the limestone embrasure and peered over the embankment. A sheer hundred-foot drop ended in the foaming surf below. He'd been looking for a way beneath Whitley Court and Bethany had brought him here.

"It would be suicide to attempt to climb down into that cove from here," Bethany said from behind him.

Ian studied the distant terrain. He turned and, seeing her gaze fastened on him in alarm, couldn't help noting she made no effort to join him at the embrasure's edge. "Are you afraid of heights?"

"Of course not. But I was thinking a boat could get into that cove."

"Any ship that set anchor in those waters would be seen. To launch a small boat from anything but a ship is inviting the ignominious trespasser onto the rocks."

"You just want to climb down the cliff," she accused him. "I imagine a sedate life bores you."

Ian laughed. He'd never even attempted to live a sedate life. He studied her. "Why are you interested in the caves?"

"Whatever happened to Mrs. Langley happened here."

He peered at the caves then back at Bethany as if she were insane. "You need my help to get into the caves?"

"Unless you know of another way. I haven't found it. And believe me, I've looked. So have you, I imagine. Why else would you be at Whitley Court, but that you are looking for proof that would connect Lord Whitley to anarchist activities. If he is guilty of anything, you will most likely find the evidence there. If there is no evidence . . . I would like to know that as well."

From the corner of his eyes, Ian glimpsed a distant rider leaving the stables. He swore. "Whitley will be here in twenty minutes," he said. "He's alone."

"We should leave."

"Why? He already knows we're here." Eyeing her pale features, Ian moved away from the embrasure. "Do the cliffs frighten you? Or Whitley?"

"Yes," she said, pressing two fingers against her temple. "No, it isn't the cliffs. I don't know what it is. People respect him, Ian. These country retreats raise enough money to feed an army or an entire village . . ."

"But?"

Ian no longer watched Whitley's approach. Her gaze moved nervously over the stones of the empty priory.

"Bethany?"

She walked out of the wind and into what remained of the nave with half its wall gone. Finally, she stopped beside a stone pillar to mark Lord Whitley's approach.

Still some distance away, his cinnamon-colored Arabian meandered its way down a hill.

"I came here for a reason," she said. "I come here almost every day." She knelt beneath the crumbled edge of the fireplace. She bent and pulled out a packet wrapped in a sheath of oil canvas. "Everything I've collected is here. I don't dare keep anything with me in my room longer than necessary."

Ian took the thick sheath of papers wrapped in parchment. He found a copy of the guest list and a fistful of other papers. If she'd noted his methodical movements as he flipped through every page with near disbelief, she said nothing, wondering how the hell someone so naive had the ability to break into rooms and safes and gather this kind of information: bank ledgers, shipping invoices, contact names, dates . . . She didn't even know what she had accomplished.

"As you said, I can't just present this information to Lord Whitley," she said almost tentatively. "But I'm willing to give it to you if you can help me find Mrs. Langley and the man who murdered her," she said.

Ian knew she had to trust him with her life to give him everything. He wrapped the canvas back over the papers and reinserted the packet beneath the crumpling mortar. "If I do give this to Whitley, do you think Sir John won't know where this came from?" he asked without looking at her.

"It won't matter. After today, he won't be part of Lord Whitley's organization. You will."

Ian raised his gaze. They remained beneath the archway, Ian intensely aware of her nearness, and his own rigid stance.

She'd cleverly manipulated the entire turn of events, he realized, sensing a knot deep down in his gut tighten. "So you told Whitley about Sir John's affair with Lady Charlene."

"I believe Sir John is the murderer we are both looking for."

"Maybe."

"You don't think so?"

"I don't know enough to draw that conclusion," Ian said. "And neither do you."

He watched the color rise in her face. Bethany turned her head as Whitley crested the distant hill still too far to see them in the shadows of the priory. "His lordship is here to talk to you about replacing Sir John."

"To think—" his eyes burned softly into hers. "I used to think you merely idealistic and naive."

"You can't actually be defending Sir John?" she whispered. "You told me you'd overheard him talking about the assassination."

"Even if Sir John *is* guilty of such a heinous crime, and I have no doubts that he is, he could not have committed the act alone. He is an important link to finding the proof needed to convict those involved in such a conspiracy."

"You're important. You can do so much more from inside."

Ian was shaking his head. "Whitley knows who I am, Bethany. He's known from the beginning. No matter what he has told you, he doesn't want me to work for him. He wants me dead."

"You can't honestly believe . . . I thought this would be what you'd want."

"Look at yourself." He took two steps then whirled to face her. "Bloody hell, Bethany. You don't understand . . ."

She flinched.

It wasn't just that he was furious with her. She had courage and initiative but she behaved impulsively and rashly. Yet, even that realization wasn't at the base of his conflict. The root went deeper beneath the surface to a place he had no desire to go. To a place that began in South America all those years ago to another woman who had been Bethany's age when he met her—the real reason why he was at Whitley Court.

"She's alive, Bethany." Shaking his head, he looked at patches of the sky through the rotted beams overhead. "Howard is my bloody link to Whitley. We've been watching him for months."

Bethany adjusted the cloak around her shoulders, pulling it tighter. "What are you talking about?"

"Pamela." He looked away, then, raking a hand through his hair, he turned his head. When he spoke again, his voice came with a dead tone. "My wife is alive."

Stricken, her gaze held on to his. "I . . . I don't understand."

"Until six months ago, she was locked away in an asylum outside Harrogate," he said without inflection. "She has been there for three years. For all intents and purposes, she was dead. Last August, someone helped her escape. Someone high enough in our government to bypass our security protocols and find out that she even existed, the same way he did on me. We discovered Sir John's wife is in that asylum. She's been an invalid for years since a fall down the stairs paralyzed her. He is my one link to my wife."

He made no excuses for himself as if that might make up for his actions. Nor did he say anything more about the woman he'd married. No character assassination. Nothing but a cold, somber acceptance of the facts as they were. "Pamela is somewhere within this organization, Bethany. Whitley's anarchist organization."

"She was never dead to you. Not completely. Was she?"

"Bethany—"

"Don't. Please." She looked away because she could not look at him.

A moment later, Lord Whitley rode into the yard. Bethany turned away to compose herself. Ian walked to the edge of the ruins and waited for Whitley's approach.

He reined in his horse in front of them. The Arabian tossed its head and blew steam from its nose. "You are enjoying the weather?" he asked, pulling his coat collar around his neck. He nodded politely to Ian before focusing his attention on Bethany, who had since turned but did not approach. The white of his shirt emphasized his throat. He wore only a casual shirt beneath his coat, unconventional attire at best. "Have you taken him over the grounds?" Whitley asked Bethany.

"Not yet," Ian replied for her. "We were just deciding which direction to ride."

"I should return to Whitley Court," Bethany said.

Whitley braced a forearm on his knee. The saddle creaked with the movement. "Join us, Miss Munro. I'd like that."

Ian didn't like it. He didn't like Whitley either.

But none of that mattered as he stood aside, inviting Bethany to walk ahead of him. They left the hollowed-out nave. He gave her a foot up into the saddle. With only a curt glance, she thanked him and adjusted her hat. Wisps of butter-colored silky hair he'd dislodged when he'd kissed her clung to her face. He looked away and mounted his own horse. As he swung the bay around, he spied the second horse and rider appearing in silhouette on the rim of the distant hill. Instantly he wondered how long the rider had been there. Even from the distance separating them, he could see a rifle rise to the rider's shoulder.

Ian swerved his eyes to Whitley talking to Bethany.

"Get down! Get down!"

He kicked his horse forward.

His shout turned Whitley in the saddle. Something burned across Ian's ribs. At the same time, he heard the echo of a rifle report in the crisp air. His bay reared in panic, snatching the reins from Ian's grip. Ian hit the ground, trying to suck in enough air to breathe while attempting to avoid the frightened horse's hooves. He rolled once, the pain shocking. He lay there looking dully up at the sky, his back chilled by the cold ground. Somehow he hauled himself to his hands and knees. He could feel a warm dampness at his left side within his shirt.

Whitley's horse lay on the ground, shot. Bethany struggled to bring Sampson under control. She slid out of the saddle and lost her hat as she stumbled to him. His vision blackened.

"Ian!" She dropped beside him.

Whitley was on his feet, shouting to a pair of horsemen

and pointing toward the top of the hill where Ian had seen the gunman. He no longer saw the rider in the distance.

"You saved Lord Whitley's life, Ian," Bethany said frantically, and he heard her voice as if from a great distance.

Dizzy, he touched his lip, then the lump on his head. His hand came away wet with blood. Swearing at the lopsided irony of it all, he slumped into darkness.

Chapter 9

Bethany had never seen Lord Whitley so angry. Still wearing his muddy shirt, trousers, and high boots, he ordered an all-out search for his former secretary and bodyguard. His raised voice underscored his fury.

Charlene sat in a tufted red velvet chair in the drawing room, her face buried in her hands, weeping inconsolably. With Ian upstairs and most of Whitley's men out on the grounds searching for Sir John, the house remained in a state of chaos.

Apparently, there had been quite an argument earlier that morning between Lord Whitley and Sir John—one that the entire house had been privy to, and now Lord Whitley's former secretary was the prime suspect in the shooting.

Bethany turned to look out the window, fighting back the sting of tears. Ian was with a physician. She scraped at the tears on her face. She could see the priory across the cove. Someone was up there walking through the ruins, she realized. Who? One of Lord Whitley's men? She leaned nearer to the window, but when she cleared her vision of the blurry mist of tears, the image had vanished.

"He isn't responsible, Papa," Charlene wailed. "Sir

John left because you ordered it. He would never—"

"Enough, Charlene." Lord Whitley bore down on his daughter. "You've both caused me enough trouble to last a bloody lifetime."

"What happened was never his fault. It was mine."

"Then what did you think I would do to the man if you threw yourself at him? He's married, for Christ's sake."

"He hasn't spoken to her in years, Papa!"

"Do you think that actually changes anything?"

Charlene's bottom lip trembled mutinously.

"Good Lord," he whispered in disbelief. His eyes narrowed. "If he isn't guilty of firing that rifle, then where the bloody hell is he?"

She stood in a rustle of rose silk and faced her father. "I love him, Papa. And I hate what you've done. You've destroyed my life and my happiness. You've destroyed everything!"

Bethany wanted to shrink behind the crimson velvet draperies against which she stood, but Charlene spied her. Her chin snapped up and she slashed away her tears. "You." Her voice trembled with renewed tears. "You did this."

Whitley caught his daughter's arm and spun her around. "Miss Munro did nothing but tell me the truth, which is more than you've done."

Charlene yanked her arm from her father's grip. Her eyes, blazing with hatred, fell on Bethany.

Bethany felt sick to her stomach. "I'm sorry you—"

"Don't you *dare* say you did it for me. I trusted you to be a friend."

"Enough, Charlene!" Lord Whitley commanded. "Go to your room."

"And you!" She whirled on her father, her fists clenched. "I will never forgive you for what you've done today. Never! I'll go. I'll leave this house forever."

"You have no idea what you are saying."

"You are the biggest hypocrite of all. Everyone in this household knows you have a grand fancy for Bethany. I hate you most of all." She advanced a step. "Would that bullet have been better aimed and shot you through the heart instead!"

An animal-like sound came from Lord Whitley. He struck his daughter across the cheek with his open palm.

Bethany gasped.

Speechless, Charlene's trembling hand rose to touch her stinging cheek. Her eyes glistened with tears and shock. But she was no less horrified than Bethany was for wanting to slap her herself, or Whitley was by his appalling actions.

The room had gone deathly still. Lord Whitley plowed a hand through his hair. "Charlene . . ."

Cradling her cheek in her palm, Charlene ran from the room, past Ian who stood in the doorway. Charlene's tears could be heard from the foyer, then faded, until silence fell over the room again. Lord Whitley had not moved from his place in the center of the room. He looked down at his hands. They were trembling.

Bethany's stomach wound in terrible knots. A flood of unbidden tears threatened to spill. Ian had not moved. She looked over at him now. He wore a clean white shirt with his sleeves rolled up his forearms and a bandage around his head, looking like a wounded war hero. His tall black riding boots gave him an extra inch of unneeded height. He had never looked more alert or more capable, despite his injury. His eyes, stark green and entirely enigmatic, fell on her.

Perhaps she had made an error in judgment, perhaps not. But after seeing Lord Whitley strike his daughter when she'd wanted to do the same, doubts of her own righteousness set in.

She had never played God with anyone's life before or intentionally set out to destroy someone. Having done so now did not fill her with a sense of vindication, merely a feeling of remorse and uncertainty. In a pair of hours, her entire life had changed.

Ian stepped into the room, cleared out the servants, and told those standing in the hallway to go back to their chambers.

"Miss Munro?" The distant sound of her name on his lips focused her thoughts more than anything else had. "Bethany."

She had made no effort to move from her place beside the window, not because she was ignoring him but because her mind had scattered into a thousand directions and she couldn't seem to grasp the one path she needed to take. "Go change your clothes," he quietly said.

She stopped in front of Ian, aware of him as she'd never been before, aware of his superfine shirt, of his warmth, the spicy scent of soap he'd used to clean up. Aware that there was nothing about their relationship that had been the truth.

"Are you all right?" he asked.

"What an absurd question when you are the one shot."

Ian had regained consciousness just before reaching Whitley Court and refused to be carried to his room like an invalid. In fact, he'd been so disagreeable, Bethany had remained outside his chambers. Her hands still shook. His blood stained her skirts, but for all the bleeding he'd done on her, his wounds had been relatively minor, requiring stitches only to the back of his head, injured when his horse had reared and tumbled him to the ground. The bullet wound across his ribs had been superficial. Lowering her voice, she asked, "How can you be so calm in the face of everything that has happened this morning?"

Ian's reply came quietly, almost a gentle reassurance. "Do you think I haven't had stitches before? Go wash up."

"You don't need to whisper for my sake," Whitley interrupted in a clear temper. He still had not moved from the center of the room. "Sir Ian, would you come inside and shut the door, please. I would have a word with you before my men return."

"I would seek permission to return to the priory," Ian said.

"Do you think my attempted assassin would return there?"

"I want to find the bullet that struck me."

Lord Whitley shook his head, distracted. "What will that prove?"

"The caliber could possibly tell me the type of rifle used. That shot was fired at over two hundred yards. Was Sir John that manner of marksman, my lord?"

"Are you bloody telling me I was shot at by a sniper?"

"I'll know more when I can determine the rifle."

Lord Whitley dropped into a chair. "Very well. Do what you must."

"I will check on Charlene, my lord," Bethany replied.

"No." He snapped up his head. "Don't mollycoddle her. If she wishes to leave here, let her stay with Serena or go back to the bloody conservatory. I don't know what I might be capable of doing to Charlene if she remains here."

Ian stood aside and waited for her to pass through the doorway. He followed her out. "Bethany."

She didn't want to speak to him, but she froze on the stairway. Her hand on the banister trembled. Clutching the polished oak, she turned.

Ian had been right. She *had* been reckless, as he'd accused her at the priory. Even if Bethany had done the right thing, she had done so for all the wrong reasons.

Worse still, today she may have inadvertently severed her only hope in discovering what had ever happened to Mrs. Langley and bringing her murderers to justice.

But what should she have done? Kept silent about Sir John?

And hadn't Ian told her he'd overheard Sir John talking about details in the assassination no one else should have known? Charlene had no business involved with such a man.

"You don't think Sir John was the shooter?" Bethany said. It was neither question nor fact, merely a rhetorical observation. She already knew the answer.

"It isn't my job to make that decision based on my emotional response or yours."

Sometimes she truly despised the cold sense of logic. She looked down at her wrist when she realized he was holding her arm.

And something inside seemed to break. Despite everything, she felt the hot burn of tears behind her eyes. "Should you be out riding?" she asked without looking at him.

"Probably not." He shrugged a shoulder. Bethany knew he was going back after the packet of papers they'd left in the fireplace of the priory, and he'd risk his life for those, she was sure.

"Besides," he said quietly, "someone needs to make sure Sampson makes it back to the stable."

She'd forgotten all about Sampson in the chaos of getting Ian back to the manse. Her horse had bolted when she'd slipped from the saddle to tend Ian. Now she worried about the horse out there all alone with an assassin on the loose. Her hair had tumbled from its chignon when she'd removed her hat earlier and she scraped her hand through the tangles. Again seeing her skirts stained with Ian's blood, Bethany realized with horror that she had helped bring about this morning's ugly incident.

"Bethany?" He pulled her down a step until they were eye level, until she was close enough to smell his soap, close enough to lean a little nearer and step into his arms.

"What happened today, Ian?"

"Which part?"

She felt his tension, a reflection of hers. Perhaps, like her he was thinking about the kiss rather than everything else that had followed. But what did their feelings for each other matter in a world that held no place for people like them? He was married.

Approaching footsteps sounded from the corridor and pulled Ian's attention away. "Sir," a liveried groomsman said smartly, "we've your horse ready."

He held out a heavy cloak, which Ian took and laid across his shoulders. His woolen coat had been given to his valet earlier to clean, if it was even salvageable. "I'll be out in a moment," Ian told the man.

Working the clasps at his throat, appearing suddenly like a dashing cavalier without the sword strapped to his waist Ian looked up at her.

Bethany swiped at the wetness on her cheeks.

"Were you ever in the service?" she quietly asked.

"Royal marines. A very short stint."

"Short?" There was so much about him she didn't know. "Why?"

His mouth crooked. "Seasickness."

The idea of Ian Rockwell seasick was laughable, but his comment had served to make her smile, if only a little bit.

He scraped a calloused thumb gently across her moist cheek. "Go clean up, Bethany. I'll be back in a few hours."

He turned on his boot heel, sending the cloak swirling around his calves. She remained on the stairs unmoving. Only when the sharp sound of his footsteps on the marble floor faded did she return to the foyer, hoping for a final glimpse of him in the corridor.

Lord Whitley was standing in the drawing room doorway, much where Ian had been standing earlier. His left sleeve was still caked with dried mud. She saw that he was looking drawn and older than she thought him to be, and found herself thinking that he was indeed older. A man in his forties, who suddenly looked very tired.

"You did the correct thing coming to me, Miss Munro."

She nodded, but inside she was no longer sure of anything, least of all the manner of man he was.

"It is only unfortunate that I handled the incident this morning like a father rather than Sir John's employer. I fear . . ."

He paused, but Bethany knew he wanted to say that he feared losing his daughter. Instead of speaking his true emotions, he looked away. "I fear I have given my guests enough fodder to feed the rags for a decade."

"Perhaps you underestimate your friends, my lord."

"Friends?" he asked, with a detachment in his tone that disconcerted Bethany. "Real loyalty is not something money can buy, Miss Munro."

A servant approached Lord Whitley, drawing him away from the doorway. Bethany backed a step, turned, and climbed the stairs. She finally reached her bedroom with every intention of changing her clothes, but for the moment, she locked her door and, after removing her riding jacket and soiled skirt, sank against the down comforter on her bed.

In frustration, she turned on her back and, laying her forearm across her brow, shut her eyes. She had lied to and stolen from this family. She was no friend to anyone. What had she thought would happen today once Lord Whitley learned about his daughter's indiscretions? Charlene should never have said the things she had to her own father.

And Ian should have told her the truth.

The creak of a floorboard awakened Bethany. She opened her eyes and struggled groggily to sit up. A fading wedge of daylight squeezed through a slim crack in the curtains. "Mary?"

She leaned across the mattress to find the clock on her bed stand and realized it was too dark in her room to read its face. She had slept away most of the day.

The sound of a whining dog stilled her movements.

She turned toward the noise. Charlene's little white dog was inside her room scratching on the paneled door as if it had just been shut.

"Charlene?"

Someone was knocking on the main door. Bethany realized now what had awakened her, the knocking. She twisted around on the mattress and looked toward the door. The key was still in the lock.

A sudden chill went over her. The dog barked at the paneled door. Heartbeat pounding in her ears, she scooted off the bed. Nothing looked to have been disturbed until she saw that her trunk at been moved from its place at the end of her canopy bed.

She dropped to her knees, threw open the heavy lid, cutting her palm on a loose piece of the metal rim. She gasped, both from the cut and from seeing that someone had sliced the blue satin lining to ribbons and torn it away from its moorings. Had Charlene been in here?

Why would she have done this?

The knocking on her door grew louder. Bethany shut her trunk. She stood and, dragging a serviette from that morning's breakfast tray, wrapped it around her injured hand as she walked to the door.

"Mum?" Mary called from the other side.

When Bethany swung the door open, her maid was standing in the corridor holding a supper tray. "Lord Whitley told me to bring this up to you," she said.

But Bethany had already turned away and hurried toward her dressing room to don her wrapper. "Is Sir Ian back yet?"

"He was, but he returned to the stable."

Bethany emerged from the dressing room, working the

buttons on her dressing gown as Mary set the tray on a small round table beside the window. "The guests have been leaving, mum," Mary said over the dog's annoying yapping. "Lord Whitley is sending everyone away."

Bethany found a match tin on her vanity but in the darkness knocked her hand against her bottles of oils and the jar of face powder, spilling white dust over her hands and across her sleeves. "Charlene was just in here." Bethany struck a match and lit a lamp. She rewrapped the serviette across her cut palm. She remained in her wrapper, too angry and too tired to change into something presentable enough to appear outside her room. "Find Sir Ian and tell him I've gone into the passageway to Charlene's room."

"But, mum—"

"Do it, Mary."

Bethany picked up the lamp, which could be used as a weapon if need be. Oil and fire could injure a person should someone unwisely try to attack her. She opened her panel door. The barking dog pushed between her feet and ran past her, clearly chasing whoever had been in her room. The trespasser was either Charlene—or someone who had been in Charlene's room and let the dog out into the passageways in the first place. An errant servant perhaps. Who had taken a knife to her trunk?

Bethany hurried through the narrow, winding passageway realizing almost at once that the dog was heading in the opposite direction of Charlene's room. The barking sounds took her through the dank maze and down a stairwell, until she realized she was in a different part of the house than where she'd ever been before. Frustration turning to alarm, she stopped. Her heart was pounding but not so much out of fear as weakness, almost as if she were tipsy. The barking grew more distant.

"Damn."

Bethany turned to look behind herself, vaguely aware as the corridor wavered in front of her eyes. She blinked, trying to clear her head. Then she held the lamp away from her face to see past the darkness in front of her. She might be terrified of heights, but she had no fear of cramped quarters or darkness. Still, she had no idea where she was, and something else was wrong with her. She'd begun to feel dizzy as she started to walk again and almost didn't see the stone stairwell in front of her until it was too late. The gaping maw had appeared from out of nowhere and she would have stepped off the edge and fallen down the stairs had she not seen the dog sitting at the top and heard the low growl emanating from deep within its tiny chest.

Catching her breath, Bethany staggered to a halt and peered down into the stygian blackness yawning before her. Whoever had been in her room had come this way. But she was no longer convinced the intruder had been Charlene. The dog would not growl at Charlene.

Bethany edged a foot onto the first step and hesitated. It wasn't the darkness that stopped her from going down. *Rats!* Dozens down there in the darkness, with more seeming to fall literally out of the stone crevices and woodwork surrounding her.

"What is down there, girl?" she said to the dog.

Besides appearing to be ancient, the place looked dilapidated and dangerous. She picked up a piece of mortar and tossed it down, testing how far it would drop and bounce. It *clinked* over stones quite a distance down.

Bethany didn't particularly like historical houses, this

one least of all, and for a moment, as she focused on the detail of her surroundings, she wondered how old this section of the house might be. This part of Whitley Court had been built around a medieval castle, complete with time-worn grotesques carved into the stone walls . . . and ghosts—for as she felt a gust of icy cold wind crawling around her feet, she knew she was not alone in the stairwell.

"When did she go in?" Ian held a lamp in his hand.

Bent over slightly, he looked from the circle of light in front of him back over his shoulder at Mary, standing behind him and wringing her hands. He still wore his long woolen cloak and riding boots. "Mary!" he prompted, making her jump. "How long ago did she go in?"

Mary shook her head furiously, the brown curls beneath her mobcap bouncing. "Perhaps it has been an hour, sir. I couldn't find you, so I went to Miss Charlene's room."

Ian peered at Miss Dubois, who was pacing and seemed as distressed as Mary. Miss Dubois had been the one who'd finally found him as he was returning with the last search party before dark. Sir John had essentially vanished along with any evidence of the attack on Lord Whitley.

"Tell me this," Ian demanded of the girl. "Do you have any idea why your dog would have been in this room? Who would it have been following?"

"I don't know," she said, wiping the tears from her face with the back of one hand. "A servant must have let her out. I have no other explanation. I swear I don't know."

"You've known where Sir John has been hiding all this time, haven't you?"

Miss Dubois backed another step, as if putting space

between them would possibly protect her if he thought for one instant she was guilty of aiding and abetting her lover. "I don't care what anyone says, he could not have fired that rifle this morning," she said.

"Was he with you?" With growing anger, Ian peered into the passageway waiting for Whitley's signal. But if Sir John were somewhere in these passageways, Ian doubted anyone would ever find him. His only concern was finding Bethany. "Then you don't know what the man did or did not do."

"Papa will kill him," she whispered.

Frankly, Ian had long since decided the entire family should be committed to Bedlam.

A servant, breathless from running, entered the room, followed by two other men covered in cobwebs. "Lord Whitley said she is not downstairs, Sir Ian. He is going into the lower passageways now."

"Sir Ian"—Miss Dubois snagged his sleeve—"My dog . . ."

Ian looked down at her hand clutching the fabric of his shirt. "Are you more worried about your dog or Miss Munro, madam?"

Her eyes wet with tears, she lifted her chin. "My dog, Sir Ian," she said facetiously. "I have no doubt that everyone in this household would risk his neck to rescue Miss Munro. What is one silly little dog to any of you?"

"Let me make one thing bloody clear now. If something has happened to Miss Munro because of your negligence, your father will be the least of your problems." Ian looked over at the servant. "Tell Lord Whitley I'm ready." He returned his attention to Whitley's daughter. "Now show me the way to your room."

Her eyes widened. "But I don't know the way. I swear. I've not ever been in the passageways. Papa has always forbidden it."

One of the servants stepped forward. He carried a lamp. "I'll show you, sir."

After discerning that Bethany had not made it to Charlene's chambers and having met Lord Whitley coming from the opposite direction, everyone backtracked to find other corridors to search. Most had been sealed and led to dead ends. But some had not.

An hour later, Ian found the white poodle listlessly wandering the passageways. He picked it up and his hands came away with something . . . blood. Its underbelly and paws were spotted with blood. The air left Ian's lungs as surely as if he'd been slammed in the gut. As he handed the dog to the servant, he shouted Bethany's name. Then he heard something he would never forget as long as he lived.

At first, it sounded like hundreds of birds—the high-pitched squeaking coming to him from the shadows down the corridor. Rats! He took off toward the noise, blinded by his need to find Bethany.

A few moments later, he found her sitting in an old stone stairwell. His heart tried to pound its way out of his chest. "Bethany?" He stepped down to where she sat.

She was sitting there on the cold, damp stones, like a wisp of cloud, halfway down, her lamp flickering on the step below her. With her forehead pressed to her knees, she didn't move.

"Bethany!"

Her head lifted and his light touched her blue eyes. He recognized shock when he saw it, recognized the pallor of her skin for what it was. Ian removed his cloak and wrapped it around her shoulders, revealing the gun he wore in a holster that clipped to a shoulder strap. "What happened?"

She blinked against the brightness surrounding his lamp. "Did you find what you were looking for at the priory?" she asked, her even voice clearly out of context to the situation.

"No. I didn't find anything."

He'd found no bullets and no casings. Every rifle shot left a casing, which meant the shooter had taken the time to clean up after himself before literally vanishing. "But I found Sampson. He is back at the stable." He smoothed the hair from her face. "Have you fallen?"

She held up her hand. It trembled and he saw blood smeared on her palm. She'd cut herself. Then he saw it congealed on the step below her—the step where he was kneeling and realized it wasn't hers. "I thought if I just remained here . . ."

He looked down into the stygian shadows below him, his gaze following a macabre chorus of frenzied, high-pitched squealing.

Ian stood. Fear sent a chill down his spine. Slowly drawing his revolver with one hand, he held the lamp away from him with the other. He eased down a dozen more damp stone steps, mortar crumbling from his weight. The stairwell was unstable. Above him, he could see a crack in the stone arch holding up the ceiling.

Below him. . .

The squeak of hundreds of rats was deafening, nearly blinding all his senses. Ian froze. Amidst the darkly moving floor, he caught a brief glimpse of wet, dark hair. Then he spied what remained of Sir John, recognizable only by his expensive Italian leather shoes and the signet ring on his finger. From the trail of blood and broken mortar on the stairs, it looked as if he'd slipped and tumbled down the stairwell, possibly hitting his head. If the fall had not killed him instantly, he had not lived long after the rats found him.

Christ!

Ian carefully sidled back up the stairs.

"I would not have wanted this for him," he heard Bethany say, her voice hauntingly ethereal in the stillness. "I swear."

Ian shoved the gun back into its sheath and knelt in front of her. "This isn't your fault."

But she made no reply.

He looked up at the nervous servant, waiting at the top of the stairwell and clutching the dog, his features barely discernable in the shadows. With his own ribs bandaged, Ian didn't think he could carry Bethany out of here. "Can you make it back to Miss Munro's room?" When the man nodded, Ian told him to locate Lord Whitley. "Tell him we found Sir John."

The servant turned away. Ian's eyes hesitated on a darker area of the wall where the servant had been standing. It also appeared to be covered with blood. Ian held up the lamp and brought the light along the rest of the stone stairwell. Holy God, he murmured as the light traced the blood and a piece of what looked like hair on the mortar wall. It was then he felt more than the chill shiver down his spine. A terrible violence had taken place here. This man had not just fallen. He'd been pushed.

And Bethany had been led directly to this place. Hell,

the killer could have been with her the entire time, could still be here somewhere. He wrapped his hand around Bethany's arm.

"We need to go now."

"Did you notice?" he heard her say.

Ian looked down into her eyes, fighting his urge to hold her, thinking only of getting her away from here and from Whitley Court. "Sir John couldn't have been the shooter," she said.

What was she talking about? "Why?" he quietly asked.

"He is still wearing his morning apparel and shoes, not riding boots. He never left this house today, Ian."

Chapter 10

It was the dead of night. Lantern light wavered in the darkness, looking like fireflies flickering amidst the falling snowflakes, swirling around the procession of men carrying Sir John's body, an icy backdrop for a sordid job. The weather had again taken another turn for the worse as a new storm had moved in three days before.

Bethany pulled the hood of her cloak over her head and grasped it tightly at her neck, watching as the corpse was loaded into the black hearse that would transport it to Fountains Abbey for burial. She'd been terribly ill. Even now she could barely stand. She had no business out of bed, but she'd needed to be here as Sir John's body left the house.

She moved beneath an arched trellis out of the way of the drive. Ian, his gloved hands tucked inside his cloak, stood just off the drive as the procession passed. He hadn't seen her standing behind him.

All the time she'd lain in bed these past few days, she had scarcely been able to close her eyes without reliving the scene of horror in the passageways. She tried to tell herself that she was in no way to blame for Sir John's death.

It had taken three days to retrieve what was left of him

from inside the ancient stairwell.

In the end, Lord Whitley had been the one to go back into the passageway with Ian and a small group of volunteers, including the local constable. Once the grisly retrieval was complete, Lord Whitley then met with carpenters and masons and ordered the passageway permanently sealed. All of this Mary had told Bethany while she'd lain in bed barely able to lift her head from her pillow.

Today the constable had finished interviewing those in the house. Bethany suspected Ian did not consider Sir John's death an accident as the constable had—a man who had been hiding and fell—and the more her mind continued to piece together the horror of the scene where she'd found him in the stairwell, the more she saw of why Ian might have felt Sir John's death was far more than an accident. Ian, however, had told no one of his suspicions, and she'd quietly followed his lead.

If what Ian suspected was true, someone at Whitley Court was a murderer and had set her up to take a fall, literally, someone who knew the intricate passageways. Well, silence more than confrontation sometimes had a way of bringing about answers. People made mistakes and became careless when they thought no one watched.

But Ian was watching, and now so was she.

She looked up at the second-story casement that faced the circular drive. Charlene stood at the alcove window, her poodle in her arms. Seemingly without emotion, she stroked the dog as she looked down on the procession. She had not come to visit these past days or, as far as Bethany knew, even inquired about her health. Charlene's lack of concern disturbed Bethany, not because her friend did not appear devastated, but because Bethany was.

Bethany recognized the illogic of her emotions. She chastised herself for putting her emotions before evidence. She had not killed Sir John, but she had judged him in the court of her own mind and found him guilty of sins he might not have committed at all.

Had her supreme confidence in reading people and situations blinded her to what might lie beneath her very nose? Seeing Charlene now, she began to wonder at the subtle signs she might have missed of *Charlene's* character. For someone who had declared herself in love with Sir John, her lack of emotion was frightening.

Bethany remembered the hateful conversation between Charlene and her father in the drawing room.

Hot tears burning the backs of her eyes, Bethany dropped her gaze away from the window. Whether Charlene was capable of murdering Sir John or engaged in a conspiracy to kill her own father, which was unfathomable, Bethany had come to realize one thing. Charlene was not what she seemed, and Bethany feared—for once, truly feared—what she did not know about a woman she had come to regard as a sister. More than that, if Charlene were somehow the one involved in these plots, she couldn't have acted alone. Someone else had killed Sir John and shot at Lord Whitley.

Snow squeaked beneath a pair of heavy boots, then Ian loomed in front of her, his eyes giving her a worried look. Behind him on the drive, the hearse pulled away.

"What are you doing out of bed?"

She patiently endured his hand against her forehead. "I don't have a fever."

"You've had a shock, Bethany. You shouldn't be out here."

Everyone, including the physician Lord Whitley had called in from town, had diagnosed her condition as some form of female histrionics. She didn't tell Ian she'd started feeling poorly shortly after she'd arrived at Whitley Court. But she could not be entirely sure what was wrong with her when she'd been eating the same food as Mary.

She changed the subject. "Did you get what you went after at the priory?"

He'd seized all of her papers and evidence she'd been building against Sir John. "What have you done with everything?" she asked,

His mouth flattened. "It's gone. Away from here."

He'd sent it all away already. So quickly. So perfectly accomplished.

"I have people in London, Bethany."

"I guess it doesn't matter now. Are you remaining with Lord Whitley? Do you still believe he is the anarchist you are looking for?"

He glanced over his shoulder at Lord Whitley, in conversation with the constable as the latter mounted a tall roan to follow the hearse. Without answering her question, he said, "Sir John's steward is missing. Whitley intends to go through the tunnels beneath Whitley Court."

"Is it possible the steward was the shooter?"

"I have my doubts."

"Why?"

His expression betrayed nothing in his thoughts, but there was something else there behind his eyes. "He was missing part of his index finger. It's hard enough to shoot six hundred feet with all ten fingers intact."

She closed her eyes briefly. "I never noticed." When she looked at Ian again, his finely drawn features had become solemn. "You never found the bullet or casing?"

"No—"

"Ian, I thought I saw someone up at the priory that morning after the shooting."

His eyes went over her face. "Why didn't you tell me that earlier?"

"Because I wasn't sure." She pressed a finger to her temple. "I was upset. So much had happened." Her heart raced and she closed her eyes to rein in her spiraling emotions. "Who could make the kind of shot that almost killed Lord Whitley . . . that might have killed you? A well-trained sharpshooter? An assassin? Surely only a handful of people in this country perhaps."

"Maybe a dozen people," he replied.

He said that as if he were an expert on the topic of sharpshooters and assassins. Did he know the mindset of such people because he was one himself?

He smiled gently. "Are you my inquisitor, Bethany?"

She wanted answers to explain the events occurring around her. She wanted to demand why he had not told her his wife was still alive. Or that Sir John was his lead.

She wanted to feel in control again. She didn't like the horrible loss of stamina and underlying panic that seemed to be waiting just to surface. "That day in the stairwell . . ." She paused. She felt as if she were losing her mind. She only hoped the condition *was* no more than the aftereffects of trauma. If only she could rip those hours from her head forever. "I've never seen—"

"Death?"

She laughed on a thread of sound. "Is that what you call it?"

"I call it many things. In the end, it always looks the same. Ugly."

She wondered if he'd ever killed anyone, or why that should suddenly be important for her to know. "Are you an expert on death, Ian?"

He didn't answer her question. But his silence told her as much about him as the question told her about herself. Ian was not unmoved by death—and she was more affected by it than she should have allowed herself to be.

She tentatively touched his hand, not something she'd meant to do in public for all to see. His hand closed and his fingers interlocked with hers. Though their hands were hidden within their cloaks, she knew the moment she'd touched him, the action betrayed more than her feelings. She'd been afraid. Even now with her heart taking flight in her chest, she'd wanted to be braver in front of him, which was why she did not tell him about the nightmares.

Horrible nightmares that had awakened her for the last three nights and sat at the edge of her thoughts, slowly encroaching. *Rats*. If she shut her eyes, she would see them. Rats everywhere. She could not sleep without seeing their red eyes. Or was it blood? A chill seeped through her and she shivered.

A shadow fell over Ian's eyes. "Bethany?"

He didn't remove his hand from hers. But it was his very tolerance of her touch that finally brought her back to her senses. She was no invalid or child to be merely endured.

Releasing his hand, she stepped back and this time he grabbed her hand. "What have you eaten today?" she heard his voice as if she were watching herself from afar.

The back of his gloved hand was suddenly against her chin, turning her face toward him, his eyes searching hers. "I don't know what is wrong with me," she said in a measured tone.

But something was terribly wrong, and, as she stepped around him only to be drawn up short as he stepped in front of her, she couldn't even rally enough strength to tell him to move.

"Answer me," he said. "What have you eaten?"

She tried to remember only because his sharp tone demanded it. She'd had breakfast in her bedroom with Mary. Later, she'd gone to the nursery to see Adam. Whatever was wrong with her did not come from something she'd ingested or others would be ill.

"When the weather clears, I'm going to arrange for you to leave," Ian said. "I mean it. You're going back to the conservatory. This is no place for you."

Mother Mary, spare her from guidance by well-meaning people, even Ian. Especially Ian. "You think I'm a pasty-faced miss who crumbles at the first sign of trouble?" she asked. "I assure you, sir, I am not."

"You don't have to prove anything to me."

"No?" She pressed the tips of her fingers to her throbbing temple. "I think I have more to prove to you than to myself. After all, this is my fault."

He lowered his voice. "Bethany, don't."

They were standing outside in the snow with a dozen men, including the constable and Lord Whitley not a hundred feet away from them. Though in the snowfall, they were barely visible. The weather had worsened in the past half hour, the wind sending a swirl of snow around her cloak.

In the face of his silent regard, she almost looked away. "You can move aside now," she calmly said, making herself as still as the silence surrounding them.

For a moment, she thought he wouldn't.

But then, he did.

She stepped around him, her boots crunching in the snow. Carefully placing one foot in front of the other, she concentrated on making it to the door. Her eye caught movement in the upstairs window and she looked up. Charlene still stood in the alcove overlooking the drive.

As Bethany brushed the hood from her face, her eyes locked with Charlene's and she knew the woman had been watching her and Ian.

"Whatever is making her sick is not coming from the food," Mary replied, her hands clasped in front of her bosom. She was obviously distraught.

Ian had pounded on the bedroom door and the maid had let him inside. Bethany had not gone to her room as he'd expected of someone who looked like warmed-over death.

"I've eaten everything she has, Sir Ian. And look . . ." Mary hurried to Bethany's trunk and opened the lid. He knelt beside her trunk. Someone had taken a knife to its guts and ripped it to shreds.

Ian leveled a probing gaze at the maid. "When did this happen?"

"I found it like this the evening . . . the day Sir John was killed." Mary wrung her hands. "Miss Munro wouldn't let me tell anyone. I think she doesn't know who to trust."

"How long has she been ill?"

"I am not sure. The first few days she did not feel well. But she got better. Then after Sir John . . . I don't know what happened, sir. She awakens with nightmares, seein' things that aren't there. Last night she told me to get the rats off her. There be no rats in here. I'm afraid for her."

Dammit, Bethany. Ian stood, his cloak swirling around him like an angry dark cloud. He walked to the paneled doorway. He'd just come inside and his boots were still wet, leaving tracks on the carpet.

"I've seen to it, no one else can get in through that door," Mary said.

Indeed. Someone had moved a dresser in front of the wall.

"And I've been sleeping on the chair in front of the fireplace," she added, "to make sure no one comes inside. Didn't I tell her from the start she were bein' poisoned?" Mary whispered. "Arsenic, I told her."

He didn't believe arsenic caused hallucinations. "And this began shortly after Sir John's death?" His gaze raked the room. It paused at the dressing table where a half dozen of her tiny Venetian glass scent bottles with ornate toppers sat on a lace doily.

He walked over, lifted the first bottle, and removed the stopper, swiping it carefully beneath his nose. It smelled of rosewater. The third bottle was myrrh and he held it longer to his nose. "Does she use these daily?"

"Yes, but not all of it at once, Sir Ian," Mary replied.

Ian looked at Mary but did not reply to her comment. Instead, he lifted the lid from the powder jar. "Have you used anything on this vanity?"

She shuffled her feet. "On occasion, I take a wee dabble of the colognes. She says I can. Miss Munro makes all the powders and whatnots at the conservatory. This batch was made just afore we come to Whitley Court."

"Pack her things," he said. "We're leaving tonight."

"What are you doing in here?"

Startled, Ian turned toward the voice. Bethany stood in the doorway looking worse than she had an hour ago. She still wore her cloak and gloves. Her skin was the color of chalk. Her blue woolen gown deepened the faint lavender beneath her eyes.

He set the jar of powder on the vanity. "Were you ever going to tell me?"

Bethany slammed the door shut. Where she found the strength, he couldn't guess. Looking from him to Mary, she said, "You aren't packing anything."

Mary turned pleading eyes on him.

"Pack," he said.

"You will not!"

"He says to pack, mum." Ducking her head, Mary swept past Bethany and vanished into the dressing room.

"You have no right, Ian."

She walked past him to her bed, working her gloves off each hand with trembling fingers. Ian stepped in front of her.

"Get out of my way," she snapped.

"How long have you been having hallucinations?"

She looked away.

"Answer me."

Ian tilted her chin and looked into dilated eyes. "Why didn't you tell me what was happening, you little fool?"

Bethany let out a shaky breath and pushed away his hand. "The physician said I was suffering a bout of hysteria. I was trying to handle this on my own, Ian."

"Dammit, you're weaker than a baby."

Her eyes grew wet with tears, and he found himself angry. But not at her. He felt violent enough to strangle whoever had done this.

Her fingers twisted feebly in her cloak. "Don't touch me, please." She tried to back away. "If you do . . ."

"If I do what?" He gently pulled her into his arms and held her against him.

"I might cry. I'm sorry. I don't feel well. Every time I shut my eyes, I see Sir John. There is something terribly evil in this place, Ian."

"Bethany." He kept his voice even and calm, though nothing about him felt composed. He felt more like a caged cat ready to launch himself at the bars. The events at Whitley Court these past days had weighed heavily on him as well. But now was not the time to talk. What needed to be done here, he couldn't do alone.

He stroked the wisps of hair from her temple and forced her to look at him. "Don't carry so much on your shoulders. You didn't wield the rifle that fired at Whitley. You didn't shove—"

"Sir John down that stairwell?" She swiped at the corner of each eye. "I saw him. It isn't easy seeing someone you knew dead like that."

Or to kill a man, he wanted to say. Instead, he sat in the chair next to the bed and pulled her down onto his lap. She was shaking like a leaf. He held her within the confines of his cloak, his mood as turbulent as the weather. He looked down into her face. Dark lashes lay like shadows against her pale skin.

"Someone wanted me to find him."

"Someone is preying on your mind. You are putting your life in danger by remaining here. You bloody well know it."

"What about Adam? What about the countess and . . . Charlene," she whispered. "We can't just leave them."

"Whitley can take care of his own family."

Ian knew he was better off allowing her to think she had a choice in leaving. He had already made up his mind to take her from Whitley Court.

"My mother is skilled with healing herbs," he said.

"You have a mother?"

He smiled against her temple. "Believe it or not, I do. She birthed me."

This served to make Bethany laugh. "Ian—"

He framed his palm around the fragile bones of her jaw. "She nursed me and my siblings through many a mishap. She has a remedy for every imaginable affliction from fixing broken noses to growing hair on one's chest."

"Did it work?" she asked.

"It must have." He pressed his mouth to her brow. "I have hair on my chest."

She eased her palm beneath his waistcoat but he caught her hand. He brought her hand to his lips, holding her gaze over the slim curve of her wrist. "Bethany—"

"I'm not leaving my house. I mean . . ." She shut her eyes. "I meant my horse. I'm not leaving my horse."

She looked confused. She appeared to be getting worse. He turned her hand over in his and saw the swollen cut on her palm. He'd seen the wound on her hand when they were in the stairwell. "Did this injury occur in the stairwell?"

She curled her fingers into her palm. At the mention of the stairwell, she became increasingly agitated. "It is bleeding," she said. "The blood won't stop."

Ian's mouth flattened. "No it isn't, Bethany."

Confusion crinkled her brow. "Yes it is," she rasped. "Can't you see the blood?"

Mary came out of the dressing room. Carrying an armful of gowns, she stopped when she saw Bethany in his lap. "Find my valet," Ian told her. "Tell him we're leaving at once before the storm traps us here. I want the carriage prepared and ready within the hour."

She laid down the gowns. "But it will take me longer than that to pack—"

"What isn't packed remains behind."

Bethany felt an arm slip under her shoulders and another beneath her legs. She felt herself being lifted. Someone had wrapped her in her cloak and warm blankets, but it wasn't enough to keep the cold at bay.

"Will she be all right?" Lord Whitley's worried voice came as if from a faraway tunnel.

"She will be when I get her to a physician," Ian said.

"Good God. Who would do this?" Lord Whitley's voice again. "I don't understand."

"The carriage is ready, Sir Ian," another voice said, one she didn't recognize.

Bethany opened her eyes. Ian wore a heavy fur cap and coat turned up at the collar. She heard a door open and a gust of snow hit her in the face. She turned her face away in protest. But even that simple movement sent shock waves through her head. She groaned.

"The roads will be treacherous." Lord Whitley raised

his voice above the wind. "Let me arrange for my men—"

"Keep your men with you. I suggest you get your family out of here as well."

She let her body relax in the natural cradle of Ian's arms. Minutes passed.

Or maybe it was hours when next she stirred.

Her nightmares awakened her. She could hear crying. A child crying, she thought. She was so exhausted and yet she had a fierce need to save the child.

"Don't you hear it?" Bethany eyes blindly searched the shadows. "The crying. Don't you hear it?"

Someone was shaking her. She stirred restlessly and tried to throw off the heavy blankets that covered her body against the chill. "Mum?" Her maid was kneeling in front of her, a worried frown on her face. "You were talkin' in yer sleep again, mum."

Soft leather squabs framed Bethany's head. She was in a carriage.

"The weather is something fierce, mum," Mary replied. "Sir Ian is on your horse. He rode ahead to find an inn."

A brazier beneath Mary's seat kept her legs warm. Feverish, she studied the red coals within, fascinated by what looked like eyes trapped and burning inside. Her breathing hitched. Her fingers curled into her palms. With a sob of despair, Bethany tucked herself against the corner of the leather seat bench. "They're trying to get out," she said. "Do you hear them?"

"It's only the wind, mum. Please . . ."

It didn't sound like the wind. It sounded like someone in pain. It sounded like someone dying. Bethany shook her head.

"You're lying. Why are you lying?"

"Sir Ian will be back shortly. He will tell you—"

"Make it go away." She covered her ears with her hands. "Make it go away! They're everywhere."

Red eyes.

Or was it blood? She looked down at her hands.

"Blood. Blood. Everywhere."

In the carriage, in her dreams, in her head. Everyone was screaming.

She meant singing. Everyone was singing. Except her.

Her head burned and throbbed behind her eyes. The fire was intense, holding her mind captive to its licking flames. Flames that would consume. She tried to fight the arms restraining her.

"Drink." Ian's voice suddenly came from above her. He held her against him, his long-lashed eyes extraordinarily beautiful in the lamplight of the carriage. "This will help ease your headache."

She obediently drank something that tasted like licorice. Being thirsty, she asked for more. "Thank you, Mother."

She surrendered to laughter. She didn't have a mother. For some reason she thought that was absurdly funny. She *never* remembered having a mother. Who stole her mother?

"She isn't going to die, Sir Ian?" Mary's worried voice sounded from somewhere above her.

Bethany opened her eyes. "Of course I know how to fly," she told the little gosling, then she looked at the big goose with the golden beak and eyes holding her with steady wings. "Tell her," she said snuggling against its warmth. "Tell her I can fly."

* * *

Someone was shouting outside. Ian bent forward and opened the door. Snow swirled in the blowing wind and darkness. His driver stood outside. Ian could see the faint outline of a dwelling ahead. "What the bloody hell is keeping Samuel?"

"'Es coming, Sir Ian."

"Go inside," Ian told Mary, then looked down at Bethany cradled in his lap.

Her eyes were staring at him as if trying to discern what he wore on his head. He gently brushed the tangled hair from Bethany's face. She'd quit fighting him, but he didn't trust her state of mind. "It's only a hat, love."

Lantern light filled the doorway. Samuel stood there with another man who introduced himself as the innkeeper.

Samuel held open the carriage door for Ian. "They only had the *one* room, *my lord.*"

"No worries. We're cleanin' it now," the innkeeper said as Ian's gaze alighted on his valet, wondering what the hell he'd told the man. "Is yer wife all right?"

Samuel inserted himself between the innkeeper and Ian. "She's not sick if that's what's worrying you," he snapped at the innkeeper.

"Just show me the bloody room," Ian said.

The innkeeper held up the lantern. Snow swirled around the pale amber light. "This way, my lord."

Ian stepped out of the carriage with Bethany tucked tightly in his arms. Samuel was suddenly at his back. "Took awhile to get the three men out of the room," he rasped as he forged through the wind and snow slashing at his face. "I had to tell them she was your wife or they wouldn't have done a thing, sir. And seeing as how she is not, you didn't want me to tell them who you really were, did ye?"

"Just see that the horses get tended."

Samuel's eyes fell on Bethany tucked against Ian's shoulder. "Will she be all right?"

Ian didn't know. But he'd be damned if he put his fears to words.

"This way, my lord." The stout innkeeper stood aside as he opened the back door and waited. Ian passed inside, his boots squeaking on the walkway. The innkeeper put his weight against the door and slammed it shut. The sudden silence was deafening. The innkeeper stomped his feet on the ground. One hand held the lantern high. Eyeing Bethany, he wiped the other down his frock coat. "My wife is preparing the room. We've not had guests of your distinction here for some time."

"I'd appreciate it if you'd direct me to my room."

"Yes, my lord. At once. Come this way."

Carrying Bethany, Ian followed the man through the hostelry and up a winding narrow staircase. "We're not called the Wayfarer's Inn for nothin', my lord. Especially on a night like this. Watch her head. This is a narrow passageway."

Ian couldn't have agreed more. The stairs creaked beneath his weight. "Are you close to a town out here? Or a doctor perhaps?"

"We're as far from nowhere as ye can be, my lord. The last doctor expired years ago when he wandered out drunk on the moors and got hisself lost. Never did find him." He cleared his throat. "Your steward didn't tell me where ye be from."

Working his way up the stairs, Ian eyed the man above the fur brim of his hat. "No I imagine he didn't."

The innkeeper ducked his head. "Yes, my lord."

A stout woman stood in the first doorway at the top of the stairs, waiting for them. Mary was already inside pulling down the covers on the bed.

Ian entered the room and walked straight to the bed. The innkeeper's wife waddled after him. "The girl ain't dead is she?"

He placed Bethany on the bed. "Merely exhausted," Ian reassured her, impatient for the woman to leave the room.

The room was small but clean and neatly furnished. A gray woodstove in the corner put out heat. The innkeeper's wife reassured him they had beds for Mary, Samuel, and his driver. Half listening to the woman talk, Ian walked to the window, pulled aside the pale yellow curtains, and peered outside. A crystal-paned inset overlooked the yard. His gaze searched the shadows beyond the stable. Any traveler out on a devil's night like this one was likely to freeze to death on the roads.

"We've an oven full of scones being warmed now."

"Will you see that my servants are served dinner and some tea?" Ian said dropping the edge of the curtain and turning back into the room.

The innkeeper and his wife stood nervously in the doorway. The woman was wearing a mobcap and plain brown wrapper, pitifully threadbare for the cold weather. She looked meaningfully to her husband, nudging him none to gently. He jumped. "Will ye be stayin' with us long, my lord? It's jest that we're not used to guests . . ."

"Of your distinction, my lord," the woman said.

Ian looked past them into the corridor. No doubt this inn catered to a rougher sect of the population and the proprietress worried, whether for his safety or the possibility something would happen to him and she wouldn't be paid, he didn't know. "I'll need more water," he said, walking to the door, edging them out before the pair realized they'd taken a step backward into the corridor.

"It's just been a while since we've had highborn guests, you understand."

"A hot meal and privacy would go a long way toward making me more comfortable," he quietly said.

Later when Samuel and his driver delivered the trunks to the room, Ian dismissed Mary and told her to go to bed. After turning back the single lamp on the dresser, he removed his coat, jacket, and waistcoat. He rolled up his sleeves and sat on the chair next to Bethany. He wrung out a wet rag in the basin next to the bed and wiped down her face. She was pale as death.

Ian turned her on her side and unhooked her dress. He was not unfamiliar with women's apparel, but neither was he an authority. He peeled away her outer and under clothes without too much trouble, and undressed her down to her shift. He covered her then sat in the chair and laid his head in his hands. The lantern's yellowish light cast eerie shadows on the wall. Bethany lay on the bed, tossing her head to and fro.

A knock sounded and Ian opened the door. The innkeeper's wife had truly outdone herself with a meal and he took the tray, politely thanking her. He didn't let her inside the room and shut the door.

After setting the tray down on a chair next to the bed, he seated himself behind Bethany and pulled her back against his chest. The iron bedstead pressed into his shoulder blades, but he managed to settle her where he could get fluids inside her. Ian made her drink, first the broth, then the tea.

All night and into the early morning hours, she drifted in and out of feverish hallucinations, murmuring fractured, incoherent sentences.

He'd seen poisons when he'd worked in the Sudan, hallucinogens used by dervishes to create holy visions. But this was different. He turned her limp hand over in his and studied the cut on her palm.

Whoever was poisoning her clearly was not in a great hurry to end Bethany's life, or they could have the day she'd found Sir John. She'd been alone in that stairwell a long time before he'd found her.

When he discovered the motivation, he'd know the hand behind the act. He knew a hundred different ways to kill a man, all of them too quick for the bastard responsible for hurting Bethany.

Wrapping her in a cocoon of warmth, he smoothed one hand over her hair and held her tightly against him while she shook. Hating her frailty, hating seeing her hurt, he kept her calm with soothing words, telling her the pain would soon be over.

Outside it had quit snowing and as the hours passed, a quiet hush had begun to settle over the inn. Little by little, her breathing grew more regular, she stopped mumbling and her expression softened. Ian continued to hold her. She seemed calmest in his arms, with his heartbeat against her cheek. When she moved slightly, her shift whispered over his forearms like creamy down. It was made of the softest white cotton. He tested it between his thumb and forefinger and lowered his chin against her fragrant hair.

Long sable lashes stirred, and Ian was suddenly looking into Bethany's blue eyes. His pulse stopped if only for a heartbeat.

The corners of her full mouth tilted and he heard her murmur. "I thought you were a dream."

He smoothed the hair off her face. But she was asleep before he could reply, and Ian continued to hold her. It had been years since he'd allowed any woman into his head, but there she remained and there she burned until he could feel nothing but the fire of her in his blood. His uneasiness increased. Not because of her pull on him, but because he recognized his attraction as something more.

"Sleep," he quietly said when she grew restless once again.

And she did.

Chapter 11

Ian focused the field glasses on the cave. He'd left the inn early that morning, while it was still dark. His gloved hands tightened. A few feet from where he lay, the cliff dropped onto another narrow edge, part of the path he'd just descended. Below him, waves crashed over the rocks drowning out the sound of the seagulls flying overhead. He'd been sitting here when the sun awakened the horizon and spread light across a turbulent sky.

Mary sat with Bethany now. Ian intended to be back before nightfall. The inn was only ten miles or so from here. He'd borrowed Sampson and ridden back across the moors to the priory where he and Bethany had stood on the cliff that day overlooking the caverns.

It had quit snowing. A quiet hush had settled over the early morning frigid seascape. He swung the glasses toward Whitley Court to observe any activity. For a moment, the wind was a bludgeon pushing at him. The storm had passed earlier, leaving a white-frozen world in its wake. No one was outside. There were no guards on the roof. There was no sign of life anywhere.

And Ian wanted beneath Whitley's house. He wanted in those caverns. He wanted answers.

He'd initially arrived at Whitley Court weeks ago following Pamela's trail. Sir John had been his only lead. Now he was dead. Someone at Whitley Court murdered him. And someone had tried to kill Bethany.

Ian had been bothered when Bethany told him she'd seen someone up here shortly after the shooting. Whoever had fired that rifle had returned and removed all evidence and trace of the shooting, which meant that person had still been around after the shooting. Tunnels and caverns honeycombed this entire area.

And in his gut, he'd suspected that whoever had fired that rife that day had not been aiming at Lord Whitley. If Ian hadn't moved that morning. . .

Now Ian found himself nestled on the cliff overlooking the cavern beneath Whitley Court, studying the terrain, searching for proof that Whitley harbored criminals, proof to connect him to the events that had transpired these past months. Evidence that would lead him to Pamela and the anarchist group for which half the authorities in England were searching, and to the person who had poisoned Bethany.

Ian strapped the glasses over the bulky coat on his shoulder, lifted his collar, and picking up the light box he'd brought with him from the inn, continued down. The path to the shoreline was not as vertical as he had once thought. The combination of geology, topography, and the various plant communities growing in the crevices made it possible to descend. The tide would remain out for only another few hours, which did not give Ian much time.

After another forty feet, the path dropped away. The upper area was an overhang. He had no belay anchor or rope, so stepped out and grabbed a crevice in the rock and worked his way down to the sand. He was at his most vulnerable in the open as he sprinted the half-moon inlet to reach the cavern. Once inside, Ian fished the tinderbox out of his pocket and lit the lamp.

In the cold darkness beneath the house, the soft sandy soles of his shoes made a raspy noise on the damp stone. He moved away from the frigid draft into the tunnel that eventually opened into a larger cavern with an underlying tang of the sea in the air. Clearly an old smuggling haunt. He walked until he reached a chamber. He held the light away from his face to view the hollowed-out room, his attention piqued. Not by the unordinary, he realized, but by the extraordinary.

He held the lantern high above his head, casting the small illuminating circle another few feet into the darkness. Someone had recently been in this room. The chamber walls and floors had been scrubbed clean. He could smell a faint hint of carbolic acid, sometimes used as a disinfectant or antiseptic.

The chamber was not large. He could feel the stone walls around him. He found a door at the back. Upon further investigation, he discovered the sturdy lock was of recent design molded from heavy cast iron not dissimilar to modern-day shackles. He held the light above the keyhole, but only a cold darkness confronted his curiosity. Setting the lantern on the ground, he knelt and removed his stiletto from a leather sheath strapped to his calf. He slid a long metal pin out of the bone handle of the stiletto and inserted it into the keyhole. Unlike Bethany, he possessed no skill picking locks. He jiggled the latch but soon realized no amount of tinkering would open the door. Whatever was behind the door was meant to remain hidden. With a quiet oath, he returned the stiletto and picklock to their sheath. "To hell with it," he murmured.

Then he raised his boot and kicked in the door.

The room stank. Dead rats littered the floor.

He peered past the circle of light into an old medieval torture chamber resplendent with metal rings that once immobilized chained prisoners. But the room was emptied of whatever used to be inside.

He followed the stones to a dry cistern and squatted on his calves. He rubbed a gloved finger across the grated rim, but the test only confirmed that the gritty substance that came off the stones was nothing he recognized. Whatever the residual chemical, it was probably what killed the rats he found dead on the floor. The room reeked and he covered his nose with a portion of the sweater he wore.

Still kneeling, he braced an elbow on his knee. His small lamp illuminated only a scant circle on the wall. Its moist stones lacked any hint of saltpeter that formed in moist crevices after a time. This room as well had been scrubbed down. Whatever had been in here was gone now and had been for months. Ian withdrew his handkerchief and scraped some of the white crystalline substance off the floor.

He wanted to know what this cavern might have been used for. The bomb that killed the Home Secretary last fall had to have been constructed somewhere and would leave behind poisons. But as he looked around, he knew now that whatever evidence he once had pointing his way to Whitley Court died with Sir John.

Ian reached the inn chilled to the bone and thankful that it was heavy fog he battled and not the sleet, yet by the time he rode into the yard it was nearly too dark to see three feet in front of him. The air was wet and smelled of decaying seaweed. A tarred lantern dimly lit the interior of the stable. No one greeted him at the door, but then he hadn't expected fanfare. A haggardly husband and wife, who could barely keep up with what duties they had, ran the inn. He unsaddled Sampson and gave the horse oats, patting him down and laying a blanket over his damp, shiny coat.

Bethany was still asleep when he climbed the stairs to her room. Mary came to her feet. Folding her hands in front of her, she told Ian that Bethany had awakened once but was now sleeping calmly. "I've been giving her drink like ye said."

Ian draped his heavy coat on the bedstead. He looked at the water pitcher on the dressing table and nodded. "Go get some sleep, Mary."

She lowered her eyes and scurried from the room as if she were a mouse. Ian dropped into the chair next to Bethany's bed. He bent forward with his elbows on his knees and scraped his fingers through his hair. He drew in a deep steadying breath and lifted his head.

Bethany's hand, wrapped in a bandage, looked white and fragile against the down comforter and, as he took it into his own, he was suddenly struck by a sudden deep down weariness that seemed to swallow him.

He'd allowed his emotions to interfere with his mission. He'd allowed personal feelings to outweigh duty. He'd allowed Bethany into his own sacrosanct inner circle that he kept tightly to his chest.

Only one other person had been that close to him.

Now he was hunting her. He had killed men before in

the line of duty. He had committed acts all in the name of his service to the crown, some that left him feeling less than pristine, some that left him filthy. Ian had always done his job, like the mechanical iron beasts that roamed the countryside puffing steam, always dependable, no hill too steep. He'd climbed them all.

And fallen right off the bloody cliff every damn time.

Light pressed against Bethany's eyelids. It was the focal point of her consciousness as she came slowly awake. She stared at the low-beamed ceiling, then at the oak door just at the end of the bed. Her trunk sat near the door. She turned her head toward the light coming through a small dingy window. Late afternoon, she estimated.

A crackling fire in the stove spread radiant heat over the box-size room. Her hair tangled around her. Her body, wrapped in a soft comforter, had been stripped of all garments but her shift.

She spied her clothes strewn on a nearby chair next to Ian's jacket, waistcoat, and heavy coat. Ian himself slouched in the chair on the other side of the bed. He wore a heavy seaman's sweater. His elbow was braced on the chair arm, his cheek rested against his fist. He appeared to be asleep.

With the silence punctuated only by the sound of the fire burning in the stove, she watched him. The sleeves of his sweater were rolled to his forearms, revealing ropey muscular arms, and outlined the muscular lines of his shoulders. His face was bathed in shadows. His jaws looked not to have been shaved in days. He had not been there earlier when she'd awakened.

She moved and winced. Her muscles groaned.

His eyes opened. The faint lines around his mouth deepened.

"Why are you dressed like that?" she asked in a strained voice.

The worry left his face when he realized she was lucid. He sat forward, his elbows propped on his knees. His eyes touched her face with a gentleness she had not seen before. "Have you noticed it's cold outside?"

She didn't notice anything except that he smelled like the sea.

"Would I be remiss if I did not ask how you are feeling?" he asked, his voice husky with sleep.

She frowned and looked around the room. "You've not stuffed me away in some attic at your house have you?"

His mouth crooked at one corner. "My mother would be offended that you'd think she'd put you in a room no bigger than your trunk." He helped her sit up against the pillows then helped her drink a glass of water from the stand. "We're at the only inn between Whitley Court and Queen's Staircase that isn't filled," he said.

Cradling the glass, she pressed the rim against her lips. "Queen's Staircase?"

"A fitting sobriquet for my home and the surrounding village, as christened by some overzealous relative with a perverse sense of the melodramatic."

Despite her wont not to respond to him on a physical level, she smiled, but that mere action made her ache. Their eyes caught and held.

"You've been a lot of trouble, love. You've had us all worried."

She took the moment to study him, unable to look away from his face, until other memories intruded and her momentary peace dissolved into a self-flagellation of mixed guilt, fear, and hurt.

His gaze dropped briefly to his laced fingers. "You're probably hungry."

"Food is the last thing I want."

"Nevertheless you need to eat." He stood.

"Where is Mary?" she asked.

"In the next room." He lifted his coat by his fingertip and slung it over his shoulder. "My valet and driver are upstairs, sharing the attic with five other gentlemen, though Samuel would consider that description generous since they have neither washed themselves nor changed their clothes in the days we've been here. Your horse is in the stable—"

She gasped. "Days?"

"You've been resting for a long time, love."

Wearing a pair of trousers he'd pulled from his trunk and that could benefit from an iron press, Ian peered at himself in the mirror. The room was like ice when he'd awakened that morning. Scraping a palm across his jaw, he knew he needed a shave. He poured water into the porcelain washbowl sitting on the commode, unsure if he wanted to wash or drown himself.

In the days since Bethany had awakened, they had spoken about everything except what was important between them. His feelings were like wrestling shadows. He could not grasp them to throw them out of his head.

He picked up the sponge, and after rinsing it, applied the ice water to the jagged wound healing on his ribs just beneath his left armpit. He was strong and muscular, his body toughened by years of physical activity, but his chest would still carry another scar. He rinsed the sponge and wondered at the one or two invisible ones buried beneath the muscle and the flesh. Dropping the sponge back into the bowl, he braced his palms on the commode and looked over his shoulder at Bethany.

"Would you like me to shave you?"

She was sitting in the middle of the bed, the blankets caught beneath her arms just above her breasts, looking disheveled and willowy soft like someone he'd made love to all night.

He wondered how long she'd been awake and watching him think about her. Inexplicably annoyed with himself, he turned and leaned his hip against the dresser. "Have you ever shaved a man?"

"I've used a knife to scrape the black from burnt toast. Does that count? I'm especially good with crisped muffins." A faint hint of enmity tainted her voice. "Unless you would prefer I not put a razor to your throat."

He reached for a shirt he'd discarded some days ago. "I'll find Samuel. He has my razor and soap. No doubt he has been standing at the window these last few days waiting anxiously for the weather to clear and looking toward home. I need to give him something to do."

"Queen's Staircase?" she asked when he put his palm against her cheek to check for fever. Her eyes suddenly softened. "How is it you said your home was christened with such a name?"

He looked down into her face where his fingers touched the delicate bones of her cheek and felt the oddest fluttering in his chest. "I'll tell you the story sometime when you're feeling better."

She wrapped her fingers around his. "Don't leave," she said. "Tell me now. I don't want to go back to sleep."

"The story is about an ancient Viking ancestor. It will probably bore you to tears."

"Tell me the story," she repeated. "Is your Viking from Denmark or Sweden?"

He had not released her hand, turning it over in his. Then he sat on the edge of the bed, shifting the feather mattress with his weight. "Denmark," he said quietly.

He felt his persona begin to change. The man who now sat in front of Bethany was no longer like an actor in a play, but someone with a heart and a family he loved, a real life that belonged outside the shadow world where he normally lived.

"It seems this errant relative of mine was in love with a beautiful princess of the Royal House of Denmark," he said after a moment, settling into the story. "Perhaps if he hadn't been a famous Viking pirate, his chances with her might have been better. For he was wealthy, after all. Legend has it that he was caught outside the palace gates and thought to be a brigand and was given the choice between banishment or the dungeon. He chose the dungeon. In his mind, he would rather be imprisoned near the woman he loved than free to roam the world with a broken heart."

"What happened?"

He poured her a glass of water from the pitcher on the nightstand. "The princess was so taken by his choice that she went to visit him in the dungeon. It turned out that she had known him as a child. He was the lowly thrall on the estate where she'd been raised and they had once played together before he'd been caught and sold away. When he grew older, he'd escaped to make his fortune, promising to return to her when he was ready to claim her hand. The princess, having loved him since childhood, realized she loved him still and helped him escape. But he wouldn't leave without her."

"Surely he could convince her to go with him?"

"As the youngest of five daughters, she was still a princess, unattainable to him. They might love one another but he knew they could never be together."

"Then he *did* abandon her."

"Not completely. The man returned to England, taking with him a piece of crumbled stone from the steps where they'd last kissed. He then built an exact replica of the palace around that stone to honor his love. Hence the name Queen's Staircase."

"That is a terrible story, Ian. One would think you were Irish for all your blarney."

He slipped the glass from her fingers, then after setting it on the nightstand, he stood and walked to the end of the bed where he'd set his jacket the night before. "You wanted to hear it. I can't help it if the ending isn't perfect."

"I wanted to hear the truth. Was it the truth? Really?"

"Really," he said.

She refrained from commenting. His comment and her reciprocating response had put her back on guard. She knew she wasn't one to cast stones at his integrity. She'd played fast with the truth as well. She'd interfered with Ian's mission—except she hadn't known what that mission had been, and the man who died deserved killing as far as he was concerned. But nothing was ever as it seemed, and he watched the grip she held on her own reality as it became a little more fragile. Ian's dark world was filled with monsters, and now so was hers.

"Thank you," she said when he reached the door.

He shrugged into his jacket. She'd briefly glimpsed the gun in his waistband at his back as he'd turned. "For what?" he asked.

"My head might ache, but my mind is clearer than it has been in days. Thank you for not allowing me to remain at Whitley Court."

"I'll have a bath sent up."

"What about you?"

His glance touched her long hair spread over the pillow then returned to her eyes. "I think it best I take my bath elsewhere."

He hesitated when her gaze went to the gold band on his hand.

Neither one of them had yet spoken what was uppermost on their minds. The real reason Ian had been at Whitley Court.

The presence of that other woman in Ian's life was the current dark cloud raining down upon his head.

Except it was Bethany who was the other woman.

Chapter 12

After ordering a bath to be brought up for Bethany, Ian tended to Sampson. He saddled the stallion and rode the horse past abandoned fields and a world that had seen better days. By late afternoon, another storm forced him back to the inn to seek shelter. He took his ale and settled at an empty table in front of the hearth, away from the other patrons in the common room. A pretty barmaid served him supper. She soon bored of trying to rouse his interest and set her sight on another table.

He wrapped his hands around his ale tankard, staring like some lovelorn Lothario into the flames flickering in the fireplace. He'd spent the last three years running away from his heart, only to have it collide head-on with a train.

And still his thoughts returned to Bethany upstairs naked in a tub, a vision of his hands buried in the silken weight of her hair joining with a desire to invite himself into her bath.

A chorus of rowdy laughter intruded into his musing. He lifted his head and watched as the young barmaid tipped a glass of frothy ale into a man's lap, much to the glee of his cohorts. Reassured that no one was about to commit an act of violence against the girl, Ian let his gaze slip around the room. The stormy night kept the room mostly empty. His eyes stopped on an oaken trestle table crowded close to the far wall where a young woman sat buried in the shadows. He recognized Mary from the brown shawl draped over her head and shoulders.

Ian sipped his ale. Bethany seemed to care for the girl a great deal, but then, with the exception of Sir John, Bethany seemed to be protective of a lot of people.

Another glance at the barmaid told Ian no meal would be forthcoming anytime soon for Mary. The same glance also told him that Mary had drawn the attention of the unruly bunch arguing over the only other woman in the room. It was apparent they'd been drinking longer than he had.

Setting down his empty mug, Ian rose from his chair beside the fire. Mary looked up with startled eyes when his shadow fell across her table.

"Sir Ian . . ."

Her relief at seeing it was he who had approached her was tangible. In her haste to greet him properly, her knee hit the table as she tried to stand and threatened to topple the shiny brass candlestick.

"Stay where you are," he said.

The half-penny in front of her was not enough to buy more than a bowl of soup. He suddenly realized he'd practically abandoned her since their arrival at the inn. "How long have you been down here waiting to be served?"

"Only a bit," she said. "I didn't see you here."

He bade her to stay as he walked over to the table where the barmaid was shuffling a deck of cards. "Find the innkeeper's wife," he said when he had the girl's full attention. "I believe she's in the kitchen with her husband."

"I know me own mother and father," she said.

"Then ask your mother to bring out supper and another plate that I can take upstairs for a guest who is staying here."

The door to the kitchen sprang wide. The harried innkeeper appeared. "Beggin' your pardon guv'nor." He snapped to his daughter, "Get yerself up, Bessie, afore I take a bloomin' switch to yer backside, girl."

The barmaid scampered away leaving Ian facing four unhappy revelers. Two scullery maids, younger versions of Bessie with her dark hair and brown eyes, entered the room. One added more peat to the fire. Another lit more candles to add light to the room. Ian left the men and slid into the seat across from Mary. Hot pea soup and warm bread arrived almost immediately, followed by tea.

"Supper will be out directly," the innkeeper's wife said, gray wisps of hair escaping from beneath her mobcap. "We've roast pork and potatoes tonight."

After the woman left, Mary folded her hands in her lap. "Thank you, my lord," she murmured. Then she gingerly picked up the spoon and began slurping the soup.

The corner of Ian's mouth crooked. "Sir Ian will suffice, Mary."

Her eyes widened at the blunder. He wasn't lord of anything, but he didn't tell her that. Samuel had done an exceptional job convincing the innkeeper and anyone else who dared listen that he was practically in line for the throne.

"How old are you?" he asked.

"Seventeen."

Ian poured her a cup of tea. She stopped chewing and

raised her eyes. She swallowed what was in her mouth.

"How long have you been with Miss Munro?" he asked, stirring sugar into her cup.

Mary tested the tea. "I met Miss Munro at the train depot in Brighton two years ago. I tried to steal her reticule."

Naturally. He wondered why that didn't surprise him. "Indeed. Then she asked you to be her maid?"

Mary laughed. Her shoulders no longer seemed stiff as a twinkle entered her eyes. She tore a piece of bread in half. "No, Sir Ian. She grabbed my hand and told me she'd break my wrist if I so much as moved. I believed her, too." Mary bit into the soft bread. "She could have turned me over to the constable," she said over a full mouth, "but instead she took me to London with her only 'cause I wouldn't allow her to go alone. She taught me to read an' write like a scholar. I've read a book 'bout the entire history of England." She swallowed. After a moment, she folded her hands around the serviette in her lap. "I've been her eyes and ears at Whitley Court. I would never do anything to harm her."

"I would never have left you alone with her the other day had I believed you guilty of anything, Mary."

"She protected me somethin' fierce, always tellin' me to watch what I say." Her lashes slid downward. She listlessly stirred her soup. "I shouldn't be saying anything I'm not supposed to."

"You know I'm not here to hurt her. Tell me about Mrs. Langley."

She set down the spoon. "Mrs. Langley was a foin alchemist always commin' up with special potions and elixirs to make things grow. She kept a beautiful garden.

Then one day last fall she goes off with Sir John to Whitley Court and we never hear from her again," she said in between swallows. "The miss, she feels responsible because she thought Sir John . . . she wanted Mrs. Langley to be happy. One week after her disappearance, Miss Bethany, she tries to get the authorities to help us find her, but they are 'bout as useful as a pond full of croaking frogs."

"Has she always been so bloody stubborn?" The question was rhetorical—he knew Bethany—but Mary's answer spilled forth with enthusiasm.

"Oh, she can take care of herself in most cases. I don't know anyone braver. She can shoot a gun and use a sword as well as—"

"I asked if she has always been so stubborn. Not if she was capable of defending herself."

Mary pressed her lips tightly together. Then she nodded, albeit reluctantly. "You have to understand, Sir Ian," she rushed to say. "The miss is very passionate. If she believes in a thing, she will fight like a pugilist."

"Is Miss Munro ever in contact with her own family?"

"Oh yes." Mary beamed. "She writes them weekly. In fact, she wrote letters before she left the conservatory. When she is away, she has someone post them for her, so her family will think she is at the conservatory."

"Is that so?"

"Last year she and Lady Charlene spent an *entire* four days in a Southampton gaol after a suffrage march turned rowdy and they were arrested. But her family never knew."

"Because they received their weekly letters from the conservatory?"

"She doesn't want anyone to worry about her."

Like hell, he thought. Bethany Anne Munro was clearly talented at subterfuge.

In fact, he'd rarely met anyone more capable. What she lacked in experience she made up for in innovation and passion.

How many years had people in his organization been trying to get close to Whitley? Bethany was fearless.

He frowned. She was fearless when she should be more cautious. She was untrained. A novice. Perhaps that was why he continuously found himself annoyed with her.

Or maybe he found himself irritated because he admired her when he should be approaching her as he would a loaded gun that could shoot him through the heart. Or maybe he just wanted to sleep with her because being with Bethany was like standing in sunlight.

Mary was watching him and, misinterpreting his frown, she'd grown distressed. "Will she be all right, Sir Ian?"

"Here ye be." The landlady returned with dinner and a tray laden with food enough for Wellington's army. "This be fer your wife upstairs. I made her something to drink with me special spices. We only have the best brandy and whiskey to be had. 'Twill ease her aches and pains, my lord."

Ian looked at the bottles lined up smartly behind the bar reflecting the firelight. No doubt the good people in this area were merely engaging in tax-free commerce.

A rowdy cheer suddenly went up in the corner of the room. The four men gathered around the table, all in their thirties and forties, were drinking ale and playing cards, the pretty barmaid all but forgotten when a pile of shillings lay on the table.

He dabbed the serviette over his mouth. "Those men," he asked, "do you know them?"

"They be local folk is all, my lord."

"Local enough to know if there might be tunnels south of here leading to the coast perhaps?"

Tunnels explained how a shooter could simply vanish.

The woman's eyes widened with fear. He slowly set down the serviette and rose to his feet. "I'm not interested in what you do or what you have in this place."

"But that be Lord Whitley's estate." She twisted her hands together and lowered her voice. "Those men will not share such information with ye. It be dangerous to ask."

"Dangerous because they are afraid of his lordship or because I might bring down the revenue collectors?"

"Dangerous because you are alone, my lord," she whispered.

Ian slid the dinner tray in front of Mary. "Take this upstairs. And Mary," he said without taking his eyes off his quarry across the room, "tell her not to wait up."

"Not to wait up for him?" Bethany yanked the down comforter tighter around her shoulders, watching as Mary set the tray on the table near the window.

Water tins littered the narrow space where a hip tub filled with lukewarm water still sat near the stove. Along with herself, Bethany had washed her underclothes and hung them on the back of her bed. "Why would he think I would do such a thing?"

Mary set out the food on the tray. "I don't know, mum. He just got up and told me to tell ye not to wait up for him and walked over to the men playing cards." Her voice lowered to a whisper. "I think those men downstairs are smugglers."

"Smugglers?" The danger Ian was courting downstairs only fueled more anger—and fear.

"He asked the landlady if the men were local enough to know if there might be tunnels in these parts. Then he told me to tell ye not to wait—"

"Yes, yes." Bethany waved her off. "You told me already. What else did you talk about tonight?"

Mary reached across the table and took a roll from Bethany's tray. "We talked about Mrs. Langley. Mostly we talked about you, mum."

Mary slapped butter on the roll. "He asked if ye stayed in contact with your family. I told him you wrote them every week."

Groaning softly, Bethany leaned back in the chair. "Oh, Mary, why would you tell him that?"

Mary dipped the roll into the brown gravy covering Bethany's roast. "Because you need his help."

"He isn't going to help me."

"Suit yourself, mum. But from where I am sitting, it looks like he's been helping ye just fine."

Her curt, no-nonsense tone cut into Bethany. Perhaps not intentionally, but enough for Bethany to feel chastised. She disliked imbalance, but even that was not the source of her current discordant feelings. Soon, Ian would be gone from her life as if he'd never entered it.

"Did you learn anything about *him*?"

Her maid peered at her earnestly. "He cares about you somethin' fierce."

The words cut over the open wound still mending across her heart and for some inexplicable awful reason tightened her throat. "What makes you so certain?"

Mary peered at Bethany's untouched plate until Bethany took the hint behind her maid's meaningful silence and picked up her fork. She stabbed a potato and stuck it in her mouth.

Mary continued eating the roll as if no interruption in the flow of dialogue had occurred. "A woman knows these things," she said in a way that irritated Bethany, especially since Mary was three years younger.

"He just feels responsible for me. Perhaps that is what you see."

"That could be it," her maid agreed, chewing thoughtfully as she considered Bethany over her fork. "Why else would a man spend days at yer bedside worryin' somethin' fierce?"

Looking away, Bethany peered at her sallow reflection in the window. Sleet had begun to form thick crusty ice over the window. Still wearing nothing underneath the comforter, she brought it tighter around her to ward off the growing chill.

"But as you say, he only feels a responsibility to yer welfare, mum."

"You got somethin' more to offer in trade other than drink and all yer quid, m'lord?"

Ian knew the man was referring to Bethany and Mary's presence at the inn. He leaned back in his chair and looked across at the hardened middle-aged smuggler Brian Desmond, a man with dirty brown hair the color of his eyes, shrugging into a heavy woolen coat. He was a tall, heavy-boned man with scarred knuckles and not a single feature one could call kindly. His three companions had left the common room some moments before. Discarded wooden disks still lay scattered over the table among the cards and empty bottles of brandy.

"Quid is all you get, Desmond."

"You are here alone with yer wife," the man said. "What would happen to her if somethin' happened to you, my lord?"

Ignoring the question and the menace of the man who had asked it, Ian tapped the ash from his cheroot and considered more than once how simple the task would be to put a bullet between Desmond's eyes if he tried to touch Bethany.

Ian smiled blandly. "My offer goes to any man who wants to share knowledge about the grounds around here. You can make yourselves rich or not. Either way I'll find what I'm looking for. With or without your help."

Desmond chuckled. "It's a dangerous place and curiosity has killed many the cat, m'lord."

"I'm no cat, Desmond."

A bark of laughter filled the room. "I like you. Oh yes, I surely do." Desmond buttoned his coat. "So, I'll give ye advice, your fancy lordship. Don't ask questions. None of us goes on Whitley land unless invited. Many have been curious and never come back." With that he pulled up the collar of his thick coat, wobbled slightly for all he'd imbibed, and tottered out the door.

Ian stared at the front door where the man had departed. The chill wind settled in the wake of his exodus. A few seconds later, Ian ground out the cheroot in the tray next to his elbow. The room swam around his head.

As a rule, he never drank on the job, but sometime during the course of the last few hours, he'd forgotten to care. It would be dawn in an hour. He'd lost a great deal of his money tonight in cards, but he'd held his drink. Or at least, he was one of the last still sitting upright in his chair at the end of the night, a feat that had earned him a modicum of respect and certainly a reprieve from being robbed outright, he considered.

For his pains, he'd learned more than from where the four hailed. By observing the amount of money they'd gambled tonight, he learned there was no way any of the four had come by that kind of cash honestly. He'd already decided to attempt to follow Desmond's tracks at first light, though the weather could make that task impossible. Desmond would also be alerted to the fact that Ian would try to follow him.

"Reckon we get all sorts here, my lord," the innkeeper said into the silence. The only one left in the room, he stood uneasily behind the bar, a rag in his hand.

Ian had forgotten the man was there.

The rheumy eyes bore into him. "Will ye be needin' help up to your room, my lord?"

"I think I can walk myself," Ian said, subdued by the reality he *was* indeed drunk.

But strangely his mind had moved past the events of the evening and the problem Desmond had presented him and hurried on to thinking about Bethany upstairs in bed. The fire behind him continued to heat the layers of his clothes, and he thought about staying in the common room. He'd been making an excuse to do so for most of the night.

The innkeeper's voice broke into his thoughts. "Count yourself fortunate Desmond refused to take you to the tunnels. He'd be more than likely to leave ye to rot on the moors no matter what ye gave to him, my lord." The innkeeper, suddenly realizing his error, dropped his eyes to the rag crushed in his hand.

"My offer continues to stand for any man," Ian said.

"Then what, my lord? You will remain to protect my family? Sometimes a man doesn't have a choice with what he has to do."

Maybe. Ian tipped back brandy glass and rose. "How long have you lived in these parts?"

"My grandfather built this inn. This road used to be busy. Most of the farms 'ave died off and the tenants gone away. Desmond is right. No one goes onto Whitley land without an invitation. Whitley is real private like that."

Ian finally withdrew a sovereign from his jacket and flipped it on the bar to pay for all the brandy he'd consumed. "We all do what we must to survive," he said.

But a man always had a choice, he wanted to say.

Only he didn't say the words. Sometimes a man's only choice was whether he breathed or not.

Hell, he'd had a choice to stay or leave at Whitley Court. The thought occupied his mind as he climbed the stairs to Bethany's room. He caught his balance on the banister. A single sconce lit the corridor in front of the room where she slept. He had a choice to stay or go.

His hand hesitated a heartbeat around the key in his pocket before it moved forward and unlocked the door. Tomorrow he would trade rooms with Mary. But at the moment, he had nowhere else to go. Bethany would be asleep.

So would he in about five minutes.

Chapter 13

Bethany came awake with a start, the webs of a dream still clinging to her. The lamp burned so low she could see nothing but its pale white globe across the room on the dresser. Momentarily disoriented and frightened, she realized she had fallen asleep on the chair in front of the window. A cold draft sifted around her like unseen fingers. She pulled the comforter tighter around her shoulders and stared out the soot-dusted window at a palette of blackness broken by streamers of melted ice on the glass.

Behind her, the door opened and she turned her head. Ian stepped into the room. As his eyes sought to adjust to the dark, he quietly eased the door shut behind him and turned the key in the lock. He smelled of tobacco and brandy. In fact, his whole personage reeked.

"Ian?"

His foot connected to a water tin on the floor, sending it crashing against the wall. He swore as he hit the corner of the dresser. Glass rattled and he caught the lamp before it tipped, setting the crystal teardrops tinkling. He turned up the light. Bracing one hand against the dresser, he faced her, cocooned like a pale butterfly in the only comforter in the room.

"You're drunk!" she sounded flummoxed, almost comical, even to her own ears.

One of his brows arched and she felt the slide of his eyes over her, nearly stealing her breath. Everything inside her accelerated, her heartbeat, her breathing, her blood pumping through her veins. "Completely drunk," he said as if to say, *Welcome to the real world, Miss Munro.*

He reached behind him and, pulling the small caliber gun from his waistband, set it on the dresser next to the lamp. She had never seen him except in the most sobering light.

"I expected you to be asleep," he said.

As he turned in the small space next to the bed, his foot knocked against the corner of the hip tub. Water splashed on his boot. "Jesus, Bethany. I'd fear for my life less on a minefield."

She stiffened, injured by his tone. "Mary told me not to expect you tonight. I didn't think I'd see you. I would have cleaned up by morning rather than booby trap the floor." Then another thought struck her.

"What did you find out downstairs?" she asked.

For lack of anywhere else to sit, he sank onto the bed with his back to her. "That enough money and drink can go a long way toward not getting my throat cut."

"Then you didn't find what you were searching for?"

His hands pausing on the buttons of his shirt, he twisted around to face her. "No. I did not find what I was looking for."

Abruptly, he finished unbuttoning his shirt and turned his attention to his boots.

He was actually undressing in her presence. "Where are you planning to sleep?"

"Tomorrow I will move Mary in here. But for now, I'll make a bed on the floor. It's warmer by the stove.

She looked doubtfully at the red rope carpet on the floor. "We only have one comforter."

"I've slept in worst places, Bethany. I can use my coat."

She pushed herself out of the chair, restless and no longer aware of the cold. Ian turned abruptly at the sound of her movement, saw her, and she froze in his eyes. The candle flame fluttered in its glass globe. Drafts of damp air swirled around the room and through his hair. His chest was corded and strong. A sprinkling of darker hair started just above his waistband below his navel. He was beautifully cleaved by the shadows. Her eyes snapped to his.

Their gazes locked and held. His face turned dark and brooding. Outside the wind had picked up, and she felt the tempest moving inside her. She wanted him to touch her the same way he'd been looking at her, needful and aware of worldly things she didn't know. She wanted to feel the passion that seemed to spill through her whenever he was near. She wanted him to go away before she did something she would regret forever.

"The floor is cold and hard," she pointed out, lest he perish, and then it would be her fault and something else she'd have on her conscience. "Even for you, Ian."

He yanked off one boot. "Would you prefer I wrestle you for the bed? Or do you suggest we share it? I should warn you, I'm not that much a gentleman."

He had no right to come in here and dictate to her,

and suddenly she resented his banal platitudes. She resented her feelings for him and that he always made her feel young. She resented that she cared about him more than he would ever care about her, and that she really didn't know him at all. He had hidden so much of himself. He still did behind a wall of shadows filled with a life she knew nothing about. "You can take the bed. I'll sleep on the chair," she said.

"Dammit, Bethany. For once will you just bloody cooperate with me? Do you have to argue a different solution for everything?"

"You don't make all the rules, Ian," her voice trailed away into uneasy silence. "Not to me."

His voice softened. "Since when have you let me make the rules?"

He would freeze to death on the floor in his state and she was just in the mood to let him. "You can't even remove your boot," she scoffed.

"I think I can undress myself."

As if to prove his point, Ian yanked harder on the second stubborn boot.

It slid off his foot and out of his hands. The recoil sent the thing across the room to smack against the wall and sent him sliding to the floor with a *thud* and *thunk* to his brains. He lay there momentarily stunned.

"Oh! Ian!"

He groaned. Above him, the mattress sagged and Bethany's head popped over the edge. Her hair spilled over him. "Are you in pain?"

He *was* in pain. Not the kind that killed a man but much worse. He lost himself in her sudden laughter and in the silky cascade of her hair.

When she finished chortling, she stared down at him. The room grew quiet around them as if the rest of the world had gone on ahead leaving them behind frozen in this moment.

He reached up and slid her off the bed and on top of him. Then she struggled in earnest, barely holding on to the comforter for modesty's sake. He rolled with her as he put her beneath him, trapping her arms between them. His hand splayed against her waist. She was naked beneath him. Everywhere she was hot to his touch.

"I *am* in pain," he rasped.

He'd been filled with noble intentions since he'd first spotted Bethany across the ballroom at Whitley Court, practically swimming in honor until he suddenly felt as if he were drowning in it.

His mind spun. And where at first only her gaze had held him, Ian now found himself in a tangible grip of iron, unable or unwilling to move.

She might be bold as brass, but she was still a virgin and no man but him had ever seen her naked. Caught in the flux of air between them, he could barely draw in a breath. Then he brushed the comforter from her breasts to reveal all of her in the golden fire glow of the lamp. He looked down her naked length.

"Let go of me, Ian."

He pulled back to look into her eyes. Caught for a moment without defense, he met her gaze. She lay naked, pinned by his body. His eyes touched hers. And the rest of the world ceased to exist.

He wanted her with a need he did not comprehend except that it was like a hell's fire burning inside him.

Her hands suddenly cupped his whisker-roughened

jaw and he heard her whisper. "Is this the part where you finally tell me who you really are and all of your secrets, Ian Rockwell? Are you serpent, angel, or man?"

He looked into her face, his eyes troubled. "I warned you at Whitley Court I wasn't the man you thought I was."

"I hate this," she whispered furiously and passionately. "I hate you."

"No you don't, Bethany."

Her eyes filled with tears and he kissed them away. They tasted salty and sweet, and he felt her loneliness and her fear, and knew there was nothing he could do to change the future between them or the past that had led to this moment.

He threaded his fingers into her hair. He needed her to know he would never intentionally hurt her. Just then, a gust of windblown sleet rattled against the mullioned window. A storm rained down on the inn, but a different one no less powerful swirled inside the room. He stared down into the depths of her eyes, made nearly black by the deep shadows in the room. His thumb tenderly caressed her bottom lip, in flagrant contradiction to the sober look in his eyes. He needed her physical connection to a world he'd left years ago. His mouth closed over her softly parted lips not so much demanding her surrender as offering his. His tongue came fully against hers.

His palm grazed her flesh, burning lower to linger on her hips and finally between her thighs. And she let him touch her there. She bent her legs and, pressing the soles of her feet into the floor, anchored her movements to move against him with an urgency of her own.

Her hands spread over his shoulders and came up

around his neck. He pressed against her, neither of them consciously taking the lead, yet both seeking the other. "You truly bewitch me, Bethany." The sound of her name caressed her lips.

Still holding her mouth captive to his possessive assault, he pulled her easily to her feet and swung her into his arms, the comforter dragging against his feet. Leaning one knee against the mattress, he laid her atop the bed. The ropes creaked with their weight.

She was no longer a child—as if she had ever been— and she wanted him, wanted him to touch her as he wanted to feel her beneath his hands. Surprised by the slight tremble in his fingers, he shaped his palm to her breast. Her hair spread across the pillows, she opened her eyes when he pulled back to remove his trousers.

Then he was off the bed kicking his pants free. His sex sprang free from the concealing shadows of wool. And he stood naked in front of her. Her gaze widened. Something tightened inside as he waited, vulnerable in his desire to see her pleased. He'd never cared whether a woman found him attractive. No one had ever complained. But he wanted more tonight. He wanted to see himself in her eyes.

Ian leaned a knee against the mattress. She sat up, spilling her flaxen hair in disarray over her shoulders. "Wait."

He froze.

"Wait," she breathed again with less force. "I have never seen a naked man."

Amusement and tenderness at her show of genuine curiosity filled him. "You saw me before. Am I that forgettable?"

"You were wearing your robe. That time didn't count."

Then she was boldly touching him, touching him with all her innocence, her hands a living fire, gliding along his engorged shaft across the broad tip only to encounter his fingers wrapped around her wrist. A bead of moisture formed against her palm.

"Lord, Bethany." He stifled his rasp. "You'll undo me right now."

For an eternity, it seemed that he stared at her bathed in lamplight then her arms came around him pulling up against him and she pressed her mouth to his.

She made him feel so goddamned alive. He slid his hands down the smooth curve of her hip, over her thighs and gently urged her legs farther apart, his palm lingering on that most intimate part of her. "I can barely breathe for want of you," he heard himself whisper.

"Ian . . ." Her restive impulse to feel more stirred her hips against him.

He pushed a finger inside her, opening the hot, wet center of her. His lips moved to her neck. "You are so wet for me."

Then his hands were around hers and he was pressing her back into the pillows. The weight of his body, his sex against her thigh, lay heavy against her. Anticipation swelled between them, and he felt absurdly virginal as if looking at the act for the first time through her eyes, and yet having the experience and wanting to share it all.

His thigh pressed against hers, parting her. Naked flesh pressed against her. He pushed inside her. For a moment, he thought she would not be able to bear the pressure of his entry. Her pain was not unexpected.

He rose above her. Braided tendons and muscle ridged

beneath her palms as she gripped his upper arms. "Look at me," he said against her ear.

His voice lifted her lashes and she was suddenly looking into his face. Clearly she trusted that he would not hurt her on purpose, and that there had to be something more to lovemaking. But he was not moving. "Is it over already?" she asked in such utter disappointment, he nearly laughed.

Braced on his elbows, he smoothed the hair from her face. "We haven't even started." His concerned smile softened on her face. "The first time is never without discomfort."

"Even for men?"

"As you might suspect, it's a little different for men."

She tested the steel of him. He was not quite all the way inside her. "It isn't so bad," she said after a moment, stirring beneath him. "I've . . . felt worse pain."

He laughed softly, a sound that came from the back of his throat. "Your acclamation warms my heart, love."

Her eyes were open and giving, drawing the very breath from his lungs.

She adjusted her bottom and he heard his quiet hiss of indrawn breath. They fit tightly. He placed a palm against her bottom and, lifting her slightly, eased deeper inside her. "Lord," he said on a thread of sound. "I could come now. You feel that good."

Her eyes sliding closed, she stirred her hips against him. His taut muscles relaxed, then his mouth closed over hers once more, tasting her completely, ravishing her lips until she would feel nothing else, think of nothing else but his tender assault. And suddenly his body was fused with hers.

He leaned his hips into her and began to rock. Their palms touched and he laced his fingers, a shared intimacy that she reciprocated, and he loved her with his body. Gently, relentlessly, he moved his hips against her. Her breathing altered. So did his, his breath against her lips no longer tantalizing but needful and demanding, a harsh staccato in the silence. Bethany looked up into Ian's eyes, consuming him with sensations. Her breath broke, and a shudder wracked her body. And when she cried out his mouth caught each remnant of her breath as he continued to rock. His body tightened.

With a rough throttled sound, he rose on his palms, his head thrown back casting his throat muscles in relief. He pulled out of her and spilled his sperm on the sheets. "So there will be no child between us," he rasped.

He collapsed against her. Spent and exhausted, neither of them moved. She held him tightly. Then feeling the icy chill of the night touch his back, he turned with her in his arms and placed his forearm over his brow.

Ever so slowly, awareness returned. And with it came the sound of the wind and the sleet pounding the inn, the whisper of myrrh against nostrils and the soft touch of Bethany's hand against his heart. It was only then that he felt the full import of what he'd done.

Bethany was still not fully aware when Ian pushed out of bed and walked to the washbasin. He returned with a brown pottery bowl filled with chilled water and a sponge. He had not spoken, and she had been too caught up in the awe of what had just transpired to notice anything but her own heartbeat. He sat on the edge of the mattress. It dipped with his weight.

His eyes were tender as they fell on hers watching him. "Open your legs, Bethany."

She did as he told her, letting him wipe away the blood, letting him touch her in the most intimate of ways, not just physically, but deep down into her core. His touch was gentle, unlike the heated passion she had just shared with him. His lashes raised and she was suddenly looking into his eyes.

"What are you thinking?" he asked, and she could only reflect on what she'd glimpsed in his eyes.

A second passed before she spoke. "I have never met anyone like you," she said, when he wrung out the rag.

She slid her fingertip over her hip and touched the milky substance that was his seed. "Why did you do this?"

A frown darkened his eyes. He brought the sponge across her hands and belly, removing himself, but not the scent of musk from her skin in its entirety. Strange that it was all she had left of their passion, that and an indelible tenderness between her legs.

"Unless it is your wont to sire a bastard, Bethany." His quiet voice pulled up her chin. "You understand that would not be wise . . . for either of us."

One of his hands wrapped itself in her spilled hair smoothing the tangles. "But nothing is a hundred percent."

"Do you have a passel of children someplace, Ian?"

"I can honestly say to my knowledge, I do not."

"Do you want children?"

His hands stilled in their tender ministrations. "I am not blind to the fact that I would make a poor showing for father. I have children enough through my sister's family."

"Are you close to your family?"

His lopsided smile opened his expression and made her heart beat faster. She suddenly found herself wanting to own a part of that smile. "My family is the most generous, giving, domineering, and simply nosy bunch you will ever meet. My mother and sister have only my best interest at heart after all." His eyes twinkled. "I love them all, most of the time."

Love. He said the word so easily.

Yet, Bethany had forever struggled with the notion of family and love her entire life. Truly, she loved. She'd always been someone of great passions, but owning the ability to open her heart did not mean the world accepted her or that she felt any more wanted, like that silly big-eyed puppy she once saw caged behind a sooty glass window in London Town, watching and waiting for that perfect someone to notice it was even alive.

She'd never belonged to anyone or any one place, anchored like the deep-rooted trees that withstood passing storms. She'd never known a real mother. Her father had abandoned her to his duties in India rather than remain home with a scrawny, rambunctious three-year-old girl who forever had her nose where it did not belong, a trait that endeared her to few . . . except her grandfather. Grandpapa had nurtured that god-given curiosity inside her and given her a passion for life. Her stepfamily loved her, but they had a family of their own. So Bethany continued to follow that slice of sunlight like the leprechaun follows the rainbow in search of the elusive pot of gold. But always the treasure is just beyond the next hill, never quite within her reach.

Until now.

And yet . . . that precious nugget of gold had never been farther from her hold. She didn't even know where or how to grasp it with her hands.

She only knew that Ian was the only person alive who made her *feel* truly alive. How could someone so perfect be so imperfect and unattainable? Maybe it would be enough just to be wanted.

She must have slept. Some time later, before the sun had greeted the frozen world, Ian made love to her a second time, laying siege to her with his hands, his mouth, and his body, letting his strength surround her. He made love slow and easy, and she surrendered her doubts, feeling safe within the sheltered promise of his arms. Then she felt him lay the comforter over her shoulders, but as Bethany settled in the warm little mecca he'd created for her beneath the blankets another part of her was aware that Ian did not sleep.

Chapter 14

Ian dressed in the silence, his eyes on the bed. He couldn't bring himself to commit any sort of guilt or anger over what had happened between them.

In fact, he'd never felt more alive. Every ache and pain in his body only confirmed that feeling. He turned to the mirror. When he finished shaving, Bethany was awake and watching him.

After tucking his shirt into his waistband, he sat on the edge of the bed. "I have to admit there are worse places we could have been stranded during a storm. I will order you a hot bath. It will help with the . . . soreness."

Despite her outwardly bold demeanor, a blush stained her cheeks. "I enjoyed last night," she said, and he found himself wanting to give in to the rush of pleasure filling him.

"I hope you are taking it all in because your next view will be from your back if you keep looking at me that way."

His first inclination was not to kiss her, but he did anyway. He settled his mouth on hers and felt her lips part on a soft, lush breath and the concept of casual foreplay gave way to real hunger. He slipped one hand to the back of her neck and kissed her passionately. Her mouth, hot and ardent, fused with his. Her arms wrapped about his neck and she took him back down to the bed. He caught himself above her.

"Are you finished talking, then?" she asked against his lips.

He pulled back to look into her face. "I have to get breakfast," he rasped, feeling ridiculously adolescent.

"That's good," she said, "because I don't want you leaving this inn without me."

He gave a curt laugh. "Did I tell you I was leaving this inn?"

"You don't have to tell me anything, Ian," she said, sliding out of bed. "If those men you talked to last night weren't very cooperative, you'll want to follow their tracks. You aren't leaving me here alone." She proceeded to root around for her clothes. "You took my evidence from the priory and Mary said she told you everything about me. That makes us partners as far as I'm concerned."

The statement gave him pause. "Does it?" He pulled on his boots, reached for the gun he'd set on the dresser last night, and shoved it in his waistband at his back, deciding against wearing his leather shoulder holster.

He walked to where she was kneeling on the floor looking for her drawers, which she found at once, and with a soft exclamation stood. She almost collided with him. His eyes narrowed. "Have you considered that you and I might not be on the same side?"

Bethany stared at him in stunned amazement.

"Have you considered that with all of your evidence you collected that you may not only have already set Whitley up on charges of treason but the entire organization? Many of whom are your friends? Nothing about this case has changed, except Howard is dead."

"I . . . know that."

"I am not on some romantic crusade to right the wrongs of the world and avenge the death of your friend. I'm sorry that she is gone, but what happened to her or how it happened is not my concern at this moment."

Her hurt gaze dropped to the ring on his finger, and she looked away. A forbidding silence fell between them. Conscious of the chasm suddenly growing between them again, he shoved his hands in his pockets and feeling the weight of her confusion settle on his chest like an iron anvil, he stepped past her to peer out the window. "Or have you forgotten, Bethany?"

"Who are you?" Her quiet voice touched him. "Are you some sort of policeman? Foreign Service? A spy? I don't even know what it is you really do."

He stood at the window like a statue, aware of the frozen world stretched out in front of him, obscenely barren of life and beauty. The sound of squealing pigs filtered through the background of his thoughts, a riot of fertile discontent. The innkeeper's wife was outside, dumping a slop bucket in a trough.

Bethany wanted his reassurance as if he had the power to make the world right itself again in her eyes. He didn't even know how to begin to explain the black pit of his life.

"Are you still in love with your wife?" he heard her ask.

Feeling Bethany's eyes on him, he turned. "Do you think I could have done all the things I did with you last night if I was in love with another woman?"

She turned her face away from him.

"We were married a year," he said. "She was my partner."

Bethany would never understand the complex, dark web that was his marriage when he had been no worse than Pamela. But he had loved her.

His love for her had been his weakness. His downfall. And nearly cost him his life.

The revelation was never a welcome one and Ian found he didn't want to discuss a woman he'd purged from his mind and his soul years before. Yet he owed Bethany the truth.

"We were working a mission together when I met you. Her betrayal nearly cost us the mission and my life." His voice paused and for a moment he shut his eyes. "In the end, I couldn't see her hang, so I agreed to put her in a ten-by-twelve cell at an asylum that catered to invalids and the insane for the rest of her life. Last August, she escaped. Her trail led back to John Howard or more exactly to an account that fronts Whitley's organization."

Bethany walked to the window to where he stood. "Did she have something to do with the assassination of the Home Secretary? Is that why you are so hell-bent on hunting her yourself? Or is it something else?"

"What is that supposed to mean?"

"I know a little of betrayal," she said, her voice punctuated with pain.

Several curls had tumbled over her temple and he tucked them behind her ear. "Has your life been impossibly difficult, Bethany?"

"I think Charlene was the one poisoning me."

Ian narrowed his eyes. "Why do you say that?"

Bethany shook her head and looked away. But Ian placed the back of his hand along her jaw and forced her to look at him. He was not rough, but neither was he gentle. Merely persistent. She had just made a huge conjecture to cower from the subject now. "I'm interested in knowing why you think that."

"It was the way she looked that day in the window when the hearse was leaving with Sir John's body. She loved him. I know she did, yet . . . It was as if she were watching the procession as a spectator, the way one watches a parade. How could she have endured what happened to Sir John? Then there was her dog in my room that night I went into the passageway. That poodle follows no one but her. I'm sure that dog was deliberately put into my room so that I would find that body. If she was capable of doing that, then she is capable of murder, which makes her capable of poisoning me."

"Have you considered that Whitley killed Howard before he even came to the priory that day?"

If, God forbid, Pamela had been there at Whitley Court, he thought to himself, he doubted she would be working for a scatterbrain like Charlene Dubois.

"I was so convinced Sir John was behind everything, Ian."

"Do you still think Lord Whitley may be innocent?"

Her chest rose and fell with her breath. "I believe he is an idealist."

"Idealists historically have been responsible for starting wars and genocide, Bethany. They're as dangerous as religious zealots."

"I know that."

Ian moved close enough that his breath stirred strands

of her hair against her temple. "Does your instinct really tell you he could be innocent, Bethany?"

She stared at him. Tension made her body rigid and transferred itself to him. But he wanted to know her answer, needed to know, perhaps because he still didn't know if he could fully trust her. "Lord Whitley has a little boy," she said. "He's deaf. But Lord Whitley wanted to make sure that little boy would not be alone and taught him to communicate to the world with his hands. He has fought to bring work reform to the coal mines and other factories. There is no greater voice for the working people in this country. You have asked me to believe he is a cold-blooded murderer when you truly have only proof that Sir John committed those crimes. How could he be the man you portray?"

"The Home Secretary stood in the way of his reform bill," he said without inflection. "Anarchy is about striking fear in others, Bethany. It's a bully's power over others. Sir John was under his domain."

A knock sounded on the door. Bethany startled. Ian looked at the door and hesitated. He might have expected Mary. But the knock had come high on the door from someone taller than five feet.

"Maybe it's your valet," Bethany offered in a low voice.

"Sir Ian," Samuel's hushed voice came from the other side.

Ian strode across the room, turned the key in the lock, and opened the door. His valet stood in the corridor. "Someone is downstairs asking for you. Or was. We were eating breakfast in the common room and heard the chap talking to the innkeeper. But seeing as only a few of us know your real name, the innkeeper couldn't say he knew you."

Ian took his eyes off the corridor and looked at Samuel. "Just the one man? Where is he now?"

"I couldn't say for sure. I believe the chap left."

Nodding, Ian told his valet to go back downstairs, then shut the door.

"Who could it be?" Bethany asked.

"Get dressed." Ian walked four steps and snatched up his coat where it had fallen on the floor last night. He shrugged into the sleeves, turning to look at her. "I need you to stay up here."

"No. Wait." She placed herself in front of the door, blocking his exit. "It could be a trap. Someone should be with you."

He adjusted his collar as his eyes went over her. The comforter she'd wrapped around her appeared like some oversized wedding gown, without sleeves and looking a thousand times more carnal. "I hope you aren't suggesting you should accompany me looking like that?"

"Don't mock me, Ian." She struggled with the comforter in an effort to retain some modesty as she looked around for her clothes. "You can use my help."

Ian let his gaze wander over her face, tumbled hair, and lips before he took in all of her standing before him like a vengeful Valkyrie. "As my second, can you raise a gun and shoot a man between the eyes if you had to?"

"I . . . maybe."

"Well, maybe isn't good enough, Bethany, which is why you are remaining up here, and in case I didn't make myself crystal clear . . ." And because he didn't trust her not to follow him, he took the key from the door and slid it into his pocket. "Get dressed."

When she grasped his meaning, her eyes widened. "Don't even *think* about locking me in this room."

He squeezed past her into the corridor. "I won't."

"I mean it—"

"I'm not thinking about it at all," he promised.

"Ian!"

Then he locked her in the room.

"Bastard!"

Bethany slammed her palm against the door. Hearing voices outside in the yard, she ran to the window. She scrubbed a circle in the frost that layered the inside panes of glass, obliterating the crystalline patterns that looked like snowflakes. Ian was talking to a woman carrying a slop bucket in one hand and a broom in the other. The snow had stopped. She rubbed the glass again and saw that Ian, with his hands shoved into his pockets and his head bent forward against the cold, was already striding toward the tall thatch-roofed stable. After a few deep breaths to calm her thoughts, anger left her and she realized she wasn't incapable of escaping from this room and following him.

Temper thus cooled, curiosity revived. She spun back to face the room. Shrugging off the comforter, she stepped into the hip tub, gritted her teeth, and sank into the icy chill of yesterday's water to wash between her legs. Her tender flesh made her gasp, and, closing her eyes, she waited for the shock to pass.

The scented water mingled briefly with heated memories of last night and she opened her eyes. Her gaze fell on the tousled bed and the bloodstained muslin sheets. Even now, she felt a blush warm her body.

Ian had taken far more than her virginity last night. Some of her independence had gone with it. So had her will and certainly much of her self-control. From afar, she had been in love with the idea of being in love with him. He was handsome and mysterious, with that extra dash of danger—the perfect man in her mind. Nothing about last night had changed her physical perception of him. Yet something inside her was different today, and she wasn't at all sure she liked it.

In fact, as she splashed water over her body, she realized she didn't like these new emotions. They made her feel needy and exposed, not at all like herself. And if Ian Rockwell thought to lock her in a room while he gallivanted about exposing himself to danger, he had a lot to learn about her. He *needed* her.

She rose and stepped out of tub, sloshing water over the floor. Twenty minutes later, she was dressed in a warm woolen gown, stockings, and heavy cloak, her hair plaited in a single braid down her back. Mary had told her last night that many of her belongings and toiletries had been left behind in the rush to leave Whitley Court but at least she had a warm cloak.

Bethany knelt beside her trunk and threw open the lid, looking for the case containing her hairpins, then set to work on unlocking the door.

Some minutes later, the lock clicked. Bethany rose to her feet and opened the door—only to stop.

Ian's valet was sitting in a spindle-back chair in front of the door.

At her appearance, he rose to his feet. "Mum."

She looked past him at the stairway landing. "Are you supposed to be my guard?"

"No, mum." He swallowed visibly and held up a key. "Sir Ian told me to give this to you when you got out."

"When I got out—?" Bethany snatched the key from his hand. "Did he?" Then locking her away was merely a delaying tactic. "Where is he going?"

"He didn't say, mum. Except you should remain here, and Mary and me were to see to your needs until he returned. The innkeeper reassured him we would be safe as no one comes to this place until after dark."

Bethany stepped past him and, holding her skirts up, took the stairs two at time. She burst out the front door into the bright light of the day, a rare bout of sunlight making the snow sparkle like glittering fairy dust and blinding her. She tented a hand over her eyes and toward the stable just in time to see Ian stealing Sampson.

Bethany ran into the yard. "Ian!"

Her call caused him to saw back on Sampson's reins. With leather gloves on his hands and a flowing dark coat swinging around his legs, he cut a commanding figure. He didn't look happy to see her. And then Sampson, impatient to be gone, reared, his forelegs pawing the air.

"No wonder you locked me in the room," she shouted. "You wanted my horse!"

Laughing, he wheeled the horse, the flash of his white teeth startling against his face and sending her senses into a warm reel. "Go back inside. I won't be gone long."

His grin always did that to her, she thought, irritation shoring up her resolve.

She waited until he reached the outer yard then put two

fingers between her lips. A shrill sound pierced the air. Sampson set back on his haunches and stopped abruptly. Before Ian could turn him, the stallion bowed his back and dumped his rider into a tall snowbank at the edge of a ditch. Then, tossing his head and dragging reins, Sampson cantered happily toward her.

"That's my good boy," she cooed to him, tying his reins to the paddock fence. Then she ran to where Ian lay supine.

His eyes opened when she reached him. They turned on her and narrowed. "Are you bloody trying to kill me?" His voice seemed drained of breath.

Her heart skipped in panic, but before she could step out of his reach, he grabbed her ankle, and, with a yank, dropped her on her back in the snow. For a second, he still appeared too winded to react, then he was suddenly on his knees dragging her toward him, his coat whipping around him. She kicked out and flailed at his chest with her fists.

They scuffled together in a tangle of limbs and clothing, rolling through the snowbank. He ended up on top of her, straddling her hips and pinning her hands to the ground next to her head. Snowflakes dusted his hair and his eyelashes, his hot breath steamed and mingled with hers. Despite herself, a thrill ran through her blood, which further concentrated her anger.

"Are you finished fighting?" he calmly asked, yet with a grating edge of steel to his voice.

Breathing hard, she glared at him sitting comfortably atop her, then managed to wrestle her emotions into some semblance of calm. "You're not riding my horse," she announced as one who had just been responsible for unseating him from Sampson.

"Yours is the only available horse I can ride," he countered softly. "Unless you would rather hook Sampson up to the carriage when I get back. I have to go."

"Why? Who is the man you are following?"

"He's my contact."

For a moment, she couldn't speak and wanted to think she'd misunderstood. "Your contact? And you couldn't tell me that?" An indrawn breath filled her lungs. "Whether you like it or not, we made a deal at the priory. I don't care what you've said. I've given . . . you've *stolen* all my information. Now you're just going to leave me? Get off me! You . . . you four-flushing imposter."

Ian gave a crack of laughter. "Isn't that somewhat redundant?"

Feeling hurt by the high-handed way he'd disregarded his behavior, her jaw clenched. She suddenly wanted to slap him.

He must have sensed the violent turn of her emotions, for his demeanor softened.

His eyes grew serious. "Bethany, listen to me." He caught her chin between his thumb and forefinger. "I'm not in a position to tell you more at the moment."

"More deceit, Ian?"

"We'll talk more when I get back. But I have to go after my contact. My people have been looking for me."

The fight drained out of her.

"I have no intention of leaving you here alone," he murmured against her ear in a lazy drawl. "I'm telling you the truth."

Semantics not withstanding, he hadn't told her the truth since she'd met him. But this time when his gloved fingertips grazed her chin and turned her to face him, she only wanted him to kiss her.

And he did.

Chapter 15

Ian crested a hill roughly five miles from the inn and assessed his surroundings. Thatched houses dotted the horizon, smoke curling from their stone chimneys. A cemetery lay in its cold silence to his right. A strong afternoon wind swept across the moors carrying the scent of snow, sunlight, and smoldering peat.

A closer look revealed a single cloaked rider, astride a black-and-white mare, waiting beneath the barren limbs of a tree. Behind him, the crumbled structure of an ancient church served as a windbreak. Rory Jameson, part Gypsy bastard with Scot's aristocratic blood swimming through his veins, looked more like a highwayman than one of the most efficient members of an elite organization of which Ian, by happenstance, was also a member. Considering he had a relative in his distant past hanged for selling secrets to the colonials, Ian lacked the usual pedigree required for elite service to the Crown. Yet, Lord Ware, the leader of this corps, had trusted and believed in him.

Ian reined Sampson to a walk. As he approached the church, Jameson tipped back his hat. His silver eyes looked back at him from beneath the sweep of dark hair across his brow. Like his face, Jameson's eyes held no expression.

Ian and Jameson had been more than associates with a common mission. They were friends. Greeting him, Ian felt a sharp renewal of edginess that something else had gone wrong. He would have been the first to admit he deserved a dressing down for deviating from his mission at Whitley Court, as if he had a choice, but he had a feeling that wasn't why Jameson had come. Even if the man was of a mind to deliver a reprimand, he wouldn't.

"Congratulations on your recent nuptials," Jameson quipped when Ian pulled Sampson next to the mare. "The innkeeper was gushing about his important guest on his honeymoon. You look like hell, Rockwell."

Ian crossed one hand over the other and leaned on the pommel. "And here I was thinking kind thoughts about you. I know Lord Ware hasn't had time to go over all the dossiers and ledgers I sent."

"There you are wrong. Ware is interested in talking to the young woman who brought out those papers you sent us. He was very interested when he learned she was Lord Chadwick's ward. What happened at Whitley Court?"

"I fucked up my job." Ian's breath steamed in the cold. "The caverns beneath Whitley Court were empty," he said after a moment. "If there was ever anything there, it's gone now. Has Sir John's secretary been found?"

"No, he has not. And Whitley left to return to London last night."

"Did his daughter go with him?"

"I was told his entire family left with him." A gust of wind whipped at Jameson's coat. He ducked his head into his collar.

"We have another problem at the moment, Rockwell."

"Hell, when is that new?"

Jameson pulled an ivory-and-gold embossed envelope from his pocket. "This was delivered to the London office three days ago, addressed to you."

Ian slid the letter from Jameson's fingers. Neither wafer nor wax sealed the folds of the deckle-edged sheet. An object was inside and he funneled it into his palm.

His blood turned to ice. The light glimpsed off a conical-shaped piece of lead, the kind fired from an old issue Enfield rifle.

Ian moved the letter to his side, out of the wind.

My dearest,

A love like ours will always survive. Remember we are both alive today because of each other.

P

He lowered the letter, but his pulse was pounding so loudly in his ears he barely heard his own thoughts. He wondered how he did not crush the letter. But somehow, he did not.

The horse shifted beneath Ian. And if for nothing else but his own unwillingness to sink into a vat of pitch-dark anger where he could drown, Ian looked out across the icy flats. He thought of Bethany alone at the inn and felt a palpable need to wheel Sampson around.

Then his thoughts hung suspended and harkened back to something Bethany had told him about Miss Dubois—even though she may not have realized its importance. "I want Sir John's body exhumed," he said. "Especially since Meacham is still missing."

Jameson's brows converged in a frown. "Even Ware needs permission to do that."

"He could have an order inside a week. The body was taken to be interred at Sir John's estate near Fountains Abbey. It would be simple enough to confirm if Meacham was the man we found in that stairwell. He was missing a finger on one hand. An anthropologist could tell us within moments."

Jameson leaned forward in the saddle. "Can I ask what brought on this sudden epiphany?"

Ian thought about saying nothing and waiting for the results of the exhumation. The last thing he wanted was to bring Bethany's name in as the source for his information especially when Ware's curiosity was already piqued about her, but Jameson needed to know the truth. "Miss Munro told me something about Miss Dubois that made me think we may not be taking into account every angle in this case."

The sound of a carriage approaching on the road from the direction of the inn drew Ian from his thoughts. At once, he recognized his own carriage as it slowed.

Jameson dismounted. "Then you won't mind if Ware talks with Miss Munro."

Ian's gaze cut back to Jameson, who had taken hold of Sampson's bridle. The carriage came to a jangling halt on the road. "What is this?"

"Lord Ware is escorting Miss Munro to Queen's Staircase himself. He has sent you your own carriage. You'll meet her later."

"Go to the devil, Jameson. I'm not sending her off alone with Ware."

There would be only one reason Lord Ware had made

the trip from London, one reason he'd separated Ian from
Bethany.

Jameson's uncompromising gray eyes fixed on him. "If
you try to ride out after her, you'll only injure this horse
when I stop you."

Half-Gypsy bastard that Jameson was, he could break
every rule ever carved in stone and commit all seven
deadly sins on a weekly basis, but when it came to following Ware's orders, the man was a saint. He would do
exactly as Lord Ware bid.

"She isn't trained to do what he'll ask of her. People
are disappearing and dying all around Whitley. For God's
sake, she isn't Pamela."

"Are you speaking from the head or the heart, Rockwell?"

He forced himself to calm. "Let loose the goddamned
bridle."

Standing just out of range of Ian's boot, Jameson tightened his grip on Sampson. "Let her make the choice herself, Rockwell."

Ian told himself to disconnect from his emotions, told
himself repeatedly and failed. He'd been poised to set out
after a quartet of smugglers in search of the tunnels beneath Whitley Court that morning; now he thought only
of Bethany.

But in the end, it was because Ian didn't want to injure Bethany's beloved horse that he finally loosened his
grip on the reins and swung from Sampson's back. His
boots sank into the wet snow. He and Jameson stood eye
to eye.

"Ware telegraphed ahead to your mother to let her
know you invited guests home and should be there before

nightfall. Be grateful Ware is so considerate of the people who work for him."

Ian handed over the reins. "Be *grateful* I haven't shot you between the eyes, Jameson."

Sitting in the carriage on its soft leathery seats, Bethany kept her hands folded beneath her cloak and her eyes averted out the window, watching the quaint inn fade from her sight.

Silence reigned loudly. Across from her, Lord Ware, once the formidable Minister of Foreign Affairs, clutched his walking stick, his gloved hands resting just beneath the silver lion's head. His silence terrified her, though she would never let him know it.

Not thirty minutes after Ian had ridden away from the inn, another carriage rolled into the yard. Bethany had been dining near the hearth in the common room when the door opened and Lord Ware walked inside, pinned her with his steely gaze, and approached. Nearly choking on her toddy, she'd recognized him at once.

A year ago when she'd been in Westminster attending a workhouse protest gathering, the leaders of the rally had burned all the cabinet ministers in effigy. Lord Ware had been one. Of course, the leaders had been promptly arrested and made martyrs to the cause of government work reform. What better way to unite the troops, of which she had been one, than to watch her leaders go to jail for a passionate cause. A year ago, she had believed in something good. But somewhere along the way, her life had changed dramatically.

Maybe that moment had come the day her teacher and her friend had vanished, or when those same leaders she'd so admired became suspect to her murder. Or perhaps the moment of change had come just recently when she'd learned a select few in Lord Whitley's organization may have taken it upon themselves to blow up the Home Secretary and destroy a popular cause with violence. She'd once believed Lord Whitley could be innocent. Now Bethany no longer knew what or in whom she believed.

"Why haven't you asked if you are under arrest?" Lord Ware inquired.

"You haven't come all this way to personally arrest me," she answered, her voice as flat as the countryside. She turned her head to face him. Gold-rimmed spectacles rested on the bridge of his nose, his features framed with gray hair and coarse mutton-chop whiskers. "You could have sent your minions to do that. Clearly, I have something you want."

Though she couldn't imagine what, when Ian had already given him everything she'd taken from Whitley Court.

Lord Ware's hawkish attention turned to Mary, who, seated silently next to her, raised her chin in her Joan of Arc stance, practically daring him to burn her at the stake.

He surprised Bethany by chuckling, and when his frown softened he didn't look nearly so formidable. He was tall, his silhouette formed by the same sunlight that spilled through the carriage window and engulfed her. He looked almost grandfatherly, as far from what he really was as could be.

Holding his sharp eyes directly, she said, "You're the man for whom Ian Rockwell is working."

She waited for him to confirm or deny the question. He did neither.

"Did he tell you why he came to Whitley Court, Miss Munro?"

She didn't know how much of what Ian had told her was the truth or what he may have left out. But despite everything, she still felt loyalty toward him and chose vagueness over the possibility that she may betray him. "He said his reasons were personal."

"I see."

"Will I see him again?" She hated that her voice sounded so small in the confines of the carriage.

"That is up to him, Miss Munro."

"Perhaps if you wish any more answers from me, you should repay the favor by answering questions I have, my lord.

"It was not a facetious statement, Miss Munro." Removing a silver watch from his brown woolen vest pocket, he popped open the lid. "In fact, he is probably at this moment being escorted to his own carriage. He will be meeting us at Queen's Staircase."

"We are traveling to his home?"

"Yes." He slipped the watch back into his pocket. "It is closer and more seclusive than returning to London."

Everything had grown far more complicated in her mind and in her heart. Ian wasn't just a man hired to protect people, she'd already figured out that much. Working for Lord Ware made him one of the highest-level government operatives in this country, higher than the Foreign Service. She'd heard rumors that Lord Ware commanded a highly trained elite team of men who served Britain's national security interests here and abroad. Mrs. Langley had once told her she'd heard rumors such an organization existed.

Bethany almost laughed aloud. Ian had never needed her help at Whitley Court. He had never needed her at all, only further cementing the reality that her presence had merely jeopardized his life.

The carriage bumped and jostled her so she caught her hand on the window. "You must know Sir Ian left Whitley Court because he thought I was in danger. If that is why you are—"

"Your defense of him is admirable, Miss Munro, but unnecessary. Leave no doubt, he and I are still on the same side."

She steadied herself against the carriage's rocky movements. "Yet you've kidnapped me, a mere peasant of no consequence. Since when does one of your distinction play fetch and carry, your lordship? You don't think your action piques my curiosity?"

He settled against the squabs. "*You* pique my curiosity, Miss Munro. I know who you are. I know your family. A fine bowl of Irish stew this is, too," he mumbled over his own irate sniff, clearly referring to the fact that her guardian was black Irish with an Irish temper to go with his dark looks.

He reached inside the leather satchel sitting innocuously against his thigh and pulled out the thick sheaf of papers Ian had taken from her hiding place in the priory. Her mouth opened in disbelief, but he spoke over her shock. "You are a thief," he said. "An excellent one, if I may say so. Is safe-cracking a skill you acquired at home or at that conservatory that passes itself off for a proper women's university?"

"It is a progressive school for young women."

"Balderdash, young lady. Just where did you learn to crack a safe?"

Her fingers twined in her lap. She had learned early in life how to get around most doors and locks. She used to pick the cabinets in her grandfather's surgery just to peer through the microscopes and read his patients' records, not out of any malicious desire to hurt others, but because learning about the lives of those around her had been an enormous source of fascination.

"I didn't crack the safe at Whitley Court," she finally replied. "I merely watched others open it first. Then figured out the combination on the other."

"Others as in . . . ?"

"Lord Whitley and Miss Dubois."

"You are close to Miss Dubois and her father?"

"I was," she whispered.

"Then you have no trouble betraying those who are close to you?"

Tears burned at the backs of her eyes.

"Answer the question, Miss Munro."

"I do what I must, my lord."

"Out of loyalty to yourself or to the Crown?"

To Charlene, she'd wanted to say, but did not. The only thing she'd truly accomplished these past weeks was to get Sir John murdered and to lose herself in the nightmares for the rest of her life. "To me," she whispered.

His brows met over the bridge of his nose. "Because you wanted to avenge the death of a friend?"

Bethany no longer found her reasons so noble. Looking back at her actions, she wondered how she'd managed them at all.

He chuckled quietly. Leaning on his heavy walking stick, he peered at her as if he were studying her beneath a magnifying glass. "Sir Ian is one of my best people. It took meeting you to destroy his mission entirely."

Bethany opened her mouth to reply, but no sound came out. She still didn't understand exactly what Ian did for Lord Ware. It worried her that she did not.

Lord Ware had turned his head and was looking out the window at the rolling countryside, and she studied his hawkish profile. Did Lord Ware know something of Ian's character that she didn't? Did he know something of hers?

Her hands did not relax their grip in her lap. She wasn't normally so nervous. But Lord Ware hadn't asked her anything, not about Lord Whitley or why she was with Ian at a remote inn in the middle of nowhere. Everyone was governed by self-interests. She had only to figure out his.

Provoked by doubt, a renewed desire to see Ian pounded inside her, for she was suddenly as anxious about what she didn't understand of the events surrounding her as she was about what she did. But the result of her unhappy meditations was she didn't care why Lord Ware whisked her from the inn.

Turning her gaze from the countryside, she asked, "Will you tell me what happened to him? Why is this case so important to him? This is about more than him finding his wife."

Lord Ware pondered her. The carriage hit a rut and jolted. Beside her Mary was asleep against the window, her hat tipped to one side and bobbed to the movement of the carriage. Bethany pulled the blanket higher over Mary's lap where it had slipped.

Lord Ware frowned thoughtfully. He adjusted his spectacles. "It is an unpleasant thing," he said, finally with a gruff sniff. His gloved hands clutched his walking stick. "Sir Ian was the man in charge of the detail served to protect the Home Secretary and his family. That family included Lord Densmore's wife and daughters aged fifteen, thirteen, and twelve."

"They were all killed," she whispered.

"Sir Ian would have been killed had a telegram not arrived that took him out of the room. The message had been sent from his wife. It wasn't a message really, except for the part that thanked him for saving her life and her name. Until that moment, we hadn't even known she'd escaped from Harrogate. There had been an abrupt change in staff at the same time and records disappeared along with the warden. She had already been missing a month by then."

Bethany turned her head to look out the window.

"Because of that message sent to Sir Ian, some accused him of complicity in Lord Densmore's assassination. I can assure you those members of our government did a grave disservice in their treatment of him. The lead came after a record search turned up Sir John's invalid wife at the same asylum and we had a connection to Whitley."

Bethany realized Ian was fortunate to have this man at his back. She lowered her gaze to her hands folded in her lap.

"Why are *you* involved with people of Whitley's ilk, Miss Munro?"

Because she'd wanted to believe in something good, something that had the power to touch people's lives. She'd wanted to make a difference to someone. But ever since leaving Whitley Court she'd been running away scared, her confidence shattered into a thousand tiny pieces.

Then suddenly everything made more sense. She knew why Lord Ware had found her, what he wanted of her. He'd been studying her, watching her. "You're going to ask me to go back to the organization, aren't you? You've been observing me, testing me. To see if I pass. It won't work. He knows of my past acquaintance with Sir Ian. I left Whitley Court with him. Whatever advantage you think I had with Lord Whitley is gone."

"Only if he thought you were hiding something."

"You wouldn't care if I told him everything I know about you?"

"He knows far more about us than you do, Miss Munro. You can tell him we threatened you with sedition. No one would ask you to do anything you haven't done already."

"That was different," she said quietly, her heart pounding because she was afraid. "Before, I was after Sir John."

"It's unfortunate you didn't exercise the same zeal toward his boss."

Her first glimpse of Ian's home came as the carriage crested a hill just outside a seaside town and she looked down across the dale and saw Queen's Staircase sitting on the distant rise, framed by the sky and the sea. The winds coming off the North Sea had pushed the clouds across the sun, but there was a warmth present that even the cold weather could not cool.

Bethany continued to gaze out the window at the wild, unkempt field where she imagined butterflies lilting idly about in the summer months. This was the world where Ian had grown up, with an older brother and sister. For a moment, the house vanished behind the rise, then came into sight again, closer, as the carriage rumbled across a stone bridge.

An impressive stone structure with two wings, Queen's Staircase was by no means small, but neither was it so huge that a person could get lost within its rooms and corridors. Candlelight burning in the mullioned glass windows welcomed the visitor.

Ian was standing at the bottom of the stately stairs sans heavy coat, his wheat-colored hair visible against the amber orange skies. He stood with one foot braced above the other on the steps, the wind tugging at his hair and sleeves, a restless silhouette embraced by the warm splendor of Queen's Staircase. As the carriage rolled onto the circular drive and slowed, she watched him, hugging her cloak to her shoulders until the carriage rolled to a stop, bouncing on its springs. Ian found her in the glass. Her heartbeat raced with childish abandon.

Perhaps it was only because she'd been so worried that her relief was so great.

A footman opened the door. Mary climbed out first, followed by Lord Ware. Her eyes on Ian, Bethany moved forward only to be drawn up short as Lord Ware set the tip of his walking stick against the doorway.

She turned her head. His somber expression was a perfect match to the churning clouds outside. "He cannot give you what you want, Miss Munro."

She resented his observation. She didn't even know

what she wanted. "I don't know what you're talking about, my lord."

"You may not. But he does."

Lord Ware waited for her to step down. Ian approached. When she didn't move, Lord Ware stepped out ahead of her. She heard him say something to Ian, then her heart warmed as Ian suddenly filled the doorway.

He dismissed the footman and when his eyes came back around to hers, she felt the intensity inside him equal hers. She wanted to hold him and not let go.

"You are well?" he asked.

She folded her hands in her lap. "I am. And my horse?"

"Sampson is in the stable."

"Am I a prisoner here?"

"You're no prisoner."

"That is fortunate for you. I do not make a very sedate prisoner."

They could have been two strangers talking about the weather if not for the tenuous current of electricity flowing between them. "I really want to kiss you," he whispered softly.

"How do you do that?" she asked, her eyes focused on his face, questioning and confused.

"Do what?"

"Make everything feel as if it is all right."

A corner of his mouth turned down. "Do you mind a walk with me?"

Without awaiting her answer, he stepped back and spoke to the driver, then climbed in and shut the door. "We'll ride to the carriage house and walk back."

As the carriage jolted forward, he intertwined his fingers with hers. "Won't your guests be waiting for us?" she asked.

"Probably." He tugged her into his lap. His voice rose as a warm breath to fan her hair, a soft husky prelude to the slant of his mouth across hers. "Let them."

A thrill ran through her that started in her abdomen and spread through her veins. She shivered as he kissed her deeply and raised her arms to curl around his neck, craving only to touch the source of her pleasure.

They lingered over the kiss a moment longer before he pulled back, drawing her closer against his chest.

Nothing else mattered to her at that moment. This was how she remembered him from her girlish fantasies, strong and protective. She felt absurdly clingy, wanting to curl up inside him and remain.

"Why couldn't you have told me more about Pamela?" she asked. "Lord Ware spoke about the note she'd sent you. I'm sorry, Ian. I understand now that there was so much more that happened. Lord Densmore's death and that of his family must have been horrible to endure. Then to be accused of complicity?"

His arms held her but not as snugly as a moment before. She rested her head against his shoulder. "He is not such a terrible man," she said quietly. "Lord Ware, I mean. He supports and believes in you."

Ian pressed his chin against her temple. "He would have to, wouldn't he?"

"He isn't the type to waste time on idle frippery."

Sensing a quiet change in him, she pulled back to better survey him. He regarded her through half-lowered lids. "What are you thinking?" she asked when she glimpsed an off look in his eyes.

The rattle of carriage wheels enjoined her from truly reading his mood. "I'm thinking I like looking at you." His palm cupped her cheek. He tucked a wayward curl behind her ear. "I'm thinking you're too young to be caught up in this business. You should be attending balls or back in your classroom teaching. You should have a dozen beaux courting you."

She assessed his gaze. "I don't want a dozen beaux."

"With all the men of the world at your disposal? You should be married some day with children."

She'd never felt truly beautiful in any man's eyes until last night when Ian had loved her—when he'd been intoxicated—but for that moment she'd felt like sunlight.

Looking away, she thought of only one man she'd ever wanted to be with forever, and knowing it would not happen.

"I shall never marry," she said.

He played with a strand of her hair. "I suppose you have broken perfectly good hearts with that philosophy."

"To break a man's heart would mean he had to have been in love with me. I'm not so easy to love. Anybody who knows me can attest to that."

He pulled back and looked down at her. "Are you so unlovable, Bethany Ann?"

All this time thinking only of herself, she had assumed she knew what she'd wanted. Yet, anxiety fluttered in her stomach. "I told you before I wasn't interested in marriage."

His fingers splayed the back of her head. "What *are* you interested in?"

That was the very crux of her problem. Since leaving Whitley Court, it was as if she'd left part of herself in the rat-infested tunnels. She wanted Ian. He made her less careless. He was warm and passionate and made her feel safe inside. She wanted shelter. She wanted him to feel her worthy of him.

"I'm interested in you. I want *you*," she said.

Tension ran through his body and infused itself into her mood. "Because you're running away from something else and you think I'm safe and comfortable?"

"I am in love with you."

He smoothed the hair from her cheek. "Why haven't you asked me how I feel about you?"

"Ian—"

"You are in love with me. What does that mean exactly?"

"It means I want to be with you."

His arms loosened. Leaning back against the squabs, he touched the back of his hand to her cheek. "That is not love, Bethany."

The very tenderness she felt in his touch belied the subtle mockery in his eyes and made her sit up. An eddy of cold air rose between them. "And you know all about the trials of love."

His eyes narrowed. "I know what it's like to have your bloody entrails ripped out by it."

Bethany was at once ashamed by her heartless comment and hurt that he would consider her feelings for him less important or insubstantial than his feelings for his wife.

After a moment, he said, "We should return to the house."

"I want to be your partner, Ian."

Shaking his head, he looked away.

"Is that so awful? We could work together."

Ian scowled at her. With an odd sense of shock, she realized he was angry. At her?

"It won't happen."

"But we would make excellent partners."

"We'll never be partners, Bethany. I don't know what Ware told you . . ."

Ware hadn't actually told her anything at all. They'd talked. He'd asked her questions. But all of the conjectures had come from her. "Why else would he bring me out here?"

"Did you consider you had information he wanted?"

"What is it with you people? You answer questions with questions." She removed herself from his lap and sat across from him. "Stop being Mr. Spy for a moment and be the man you were at the inn."

Ian leaned forward with his elbows against his knees. One hand brushed hers and she withdrew from his touch. "Bethany—"

"Don't. Please." Conscious only of the unbearable silence swallowing her, she looked away because she could not look at him. She certainly did not want to look inside herself, for whatever Ian had felt when he'd stepped into the carriage and kissed her passionately had now vanished.

He leaned sideways and lifted the edge of the curtain. The carriage had stopped. Neither one of them had noticed that they'd already pulled into the carriage yard. The driver and footmen were nowhere to be seen. Snow had started to fall.

"What is it you want from me, Bethany?"

She suddenly doubted he admired her on any level,

certainly not in the same way she looked at him, couldn't help looking at him. She doubted a lot of things, mostly elements in herself. She had failed miserably at Whitley Court, and in doing so she'd failed Ian.

"You don't think I'm good enough."

"I think you are young."

Scathing resentment boiled her thoughts, yet the internal voice shouting inside her pointed that arrow of anger, not toward Ian but someone else, and most of her fury found no fuel to remain burning inside. She was about to lose him. But then she'd never really had him to lose. One night in bed did not a relationship make.

Tears welled and she swiped angrily at them, glaring at Ian. "It's your fault I've come to this pass." Because in her heart he was to blame for everything. "I was doing something right for once at Whitley Court. Something decent. You shouldn't have been there to ruin everything!"

She'd been on a goodwill mission, convinced on the rightness of her cause, convinced she knew what she was doing when she'd struck out to find justice with all the nobility of a dead saint, wanting in her heart only to avenge the murder of one friend and save another. "But I didn't really know anything, did I? You tried to tell me. I ruined a case and got someone killed. You were almost killed by a bullet."

Her logic was skewed and irrational on every front; a part of her knew that, the part that loved Ian and didn't want to loose him.

"You didn't shoot me, Bethany."

Without cognizant thought, she took his hands into her own and held them against her cheek. Her chest hurt and it was difficult to draw breath.

Had this been what Charlene felt then toward Sir John, a married man? The thought did nothing to lighten her heart, but, in the end, her heart was too blind to care.

Though her mouth opened, no words formed to deny what was clearly in her heart for him to see. A tremor went through her. She leaned forward and placed his mouth on hers. He didn't stop her. In fact, she wished that he had.

Emotion surged, partially eclipsed by apprehension. She felt trapped by a wall of longing. Beyond her will, her hands raised to his shoulders. The pressure on her lips increased. His tongue penetrated deeply. The white-hot heat of his mouth melded with hers in a warm communion of mutual desire.

Drunk on sensation, she heard the soft sound of her name against her lips. Tiny shivers skipped across her nerves. Pleasure surrounded pleasure and spun into need. His arm slipped under her knees and lifted her legs across his, the palm of his hand against her back pressing her hard against him. She felt his strength through layers of wool.

He kept her off balance, aware of nothing but his arms surrounding her, holding her tightly as if it were he that needed her and not the other way around.

Nothing had changed, yet everything was different.

She splayed her palms across his chest, feeling the beat of his heart surge through her. She tore her mouth away. He stopped readily. For the longest moment, her eyes were trapped by his.

"Bethany . . ."

"It would be better if I hated you," she quietly said, stirred by panic she could not explain but that grabbed hold of her like a vise around her chest and refused to let go.

"You're not like me, Bethany. You don't belong in this part of my life."

She scrambled to escape. In a burst of energy, she flung open the carriage door, climbing out without benefit of a step, and, in her haste, nearly stumbling to her knees. But she kept walking heedless of the cold and the snow, leaving only the imprint of her feet to mark her flight to the house.

She wasn't like Ian because she was a coward.

Chapter 16

A slender butler with large ears confronted Bethany at the door. She stepped inside out of the cold and, without removing her cloak or gloves, walked in the direction from which she heard voices. In a pale yellow and blue salon, Lord Ware sat comfortably, warmed by a crackling fire. An older woman perched beside him on the settee, pouring tea and chatting amiably. She wore black in the way of a housekeeper, but her camaraderie with his lordship confused Bethany. Her gaze traveled to the other two men standing near the hearth talking, one of whom was Lord Ware's owl-eyed secretary.

No one noticed Bethany's presence until she moved beneath the archway of the salon. The stranger next to the fireplace turned his head, saw her, and straightened. The stark white cloth of his shirt tucked into the waistband of his trousers pulled at his shoulders. His dark hair touched just below his nape. But it was his silver eyes behind a fringe of dark lashes that held her rooted in place. Instinctively, she knew this was the man Ian had left her at the inn to meet. His contact. Partner. Another self-important man in the elite club of spies.

Clutching the cloak tighter against her chest, she forced her attention back to Lord Ware.

"I wish to leave here. As soon as possible," she told him.

For a moment, she didn't think he heard her. Then his head dipped briefly. "I can arrange for you to leave as soon as the weather clears, Miss Munro."

The wind left her sails. She had not expected such easy capitulation. She had expected . . . what? A plea for her to stay because her services were important and needed? Because *she* was important? Why did he even bring her here, then, if he was only going to allow her to leave so easily.

She glanced past him at the liverish colored skies framed by the windows. "How long do storms usually last around here?"

He watched her from behind his spectacles then brushed a piece of lint from his sleeve. "A week," he said. "At the very least."

"A *week*?" Bethany narrowed her eyes. "I will arrange for my own way out. I have a horse for which I also must secure transportation."

"It will be difficult getting him to London," he said. "Do you have the funds?"

"I . . ." Bethany realized with shock that she had no funds at all. She'd arrived at Whitley Court accompanying Charlene in her father's carriage. Sampson had already been moved from London this summer past.

Aware that she'd betrayed herself foolishly in the presence of these people, she drew her spine erect. "Surely the means to that end will be provided from what was" —*stolen from me and handed over to you?* she'd wanted to say, feeling brassy and frustrated with the old states-man—"given over to you from Sir Ian, my lord."

His disquieting eyes did not coincide with the subtle lift of his mouth. He braced both hands on the curved handle of his walking stick, then rose. "That can be arranged," he said. "When the weather clears."

Knowing she would get no further, Bethany finally turned to the woman who had been openly appraising her. She'd set down the teapot. Bethany wasn't in the mood to digest the look in the green eyes of the housekeeper. Still not fully recovered from her illness, she was suddenly very tired, wanting only solitude. And she was slightly fearful she'd been hasty in her decision to return to the conservatory alone when she was not yet confident that she could handle any meeting with Charlene or her father.

"May I please be shown to my chambers? I . . . I am exhausted and wish to rest."

The older woman rose in a rustle of black taffeta that moved like a whisper as she approached. "Of course, dear."

Her grace and carriage told Bethany this was no house-keeper.

The front door suddenly blew opened, and Bethany pulled around as Ian stepped inside. He stamped snow from his feet, saw her standing in the corridor, and stopped. The wind had whipped strands of his golden hair across his brow. Bethany's heart skittered. His gaze moved to the woman she'd spoken to in the drawing room. She'd stopped beneath the archway.

"Ian, dear." The woman smiled. "You are neglecting your guests."

He stamped more snow from his feet. "I doubt they are being neglected, Mother."

Bethany turned to Mrs. Rockwell, her face aflame. She and Ian's mother had stepped into the corridor out of sight of the room. "Mrs. Rockwell," she said the name over a deep breath, "I'm terribly sorry for my impertinence earlier—"

"We had not been formally introduced, child," Ian's mother said graciously, with a twinkle in her eyes as Ian approached. "The fault is my son's."

Bethany snapped her gaze back to Ian, who clearly wasn't amused, yet neither was he angry. "Thank you, Mother, for pointing that out. Now she can add poor manners to her growing list of my sins."

"Nonsense." Mrs. Rockwell patted Ian's cheek with motherly fondness. "You have clearly had a tiff is all. Is that why you are running about outside with no overcoat?" She lowered her voice and spoke to Bethany. "Whatever he has done, understand that my son has *never* brought a woman into this house. You are the first."

Bethany thought Ian actually blushed. "Do you wonder why that is, Mother?" His attention shifted to Bethany. "Forgive her. She knows not of what she speaks."

"For the last hour, he paces like a lion in his cage, waiting for Lord Ware's carriage to arrive. I have not seen him like this since he and his sister were to perform a duet for his father's friends at our annual Yule gathering. He couldn't sing a note, mind you, because there was a young girl in the audience on whom he had a crush."

Looking harassed, Ian shoved his hands into his pockets. "I was ten years old, and I'm sure Miss—"

"He has always been a timid sort," Mrs. Rockwell said.

"But he can sing like an angel. Oh, can he sing. If his sister were present, she could always get him in front of a crowd. She could charm a sugar teat from a baby. Perhaps you can sing for us tonight, dear?" she said to her son.

"I'm not going to sing, Mother."

A feeling verging on maternal, Bethany's gaze softened on Ian's face. His eyes held hers and, for a heartbeat, neither of them looked away. She liked this house. And she liked his mother. She reminded Bethany a little of her own beloved grandfather.

"I'm sure Miss Munro is exhausted and would like to be shown her room," Ian said.

"She has asked to leave as soon as the weather clears."

Ian's green eyes remained hooded. "He is letting you go?"

Avoiding the keen edge of pain building inside her, Bethany said, "I only need to make arrangements for Sampson."

His tone brooked no argument, but his eyes no longer held an edge. "Do you have a place to keep Sampson once you are settled?" he quietly asked.

She nodded. It was a lie. The conservatory may have its own stables, but they weren't made for a horse like Sampson.

"You should get him back to Rose Briar as soon as you can."

Rose Briar had once been her home, the place where she had first met Ian.

And all at once, she didn't want to be furious at him or wade through oceans of hurt. She wanted back that precious spark that had ignited between them at the inn. She wanted Ian.

But he wasn't hers to hold. He had never been hers. And clearly he wanted nothing else to do with her.

"If you will excuse me, Ian." She turned to his mother. "I'd like to go to my room."

Ian's hand shot out to the wall and barred her way. "Bethany?"

"What are you doing?" she rasped, horrified and incensed at the same time. What would his mother think about such behavior?

Carrying the quiet certainty of authority, Ian raised his gaze and politely peered over Bethany's shoulder at his mother. "Will you give us a minute alone?"

Then he pulled Bethany into the parlor across the hallway.

Before Bethany could open her mouth to protest his high-handed actions, Ian hauled her across the room and through the pocket doors into the formal dining area, where he was sure no one would bother them. The room was chilled and dark, the draperies drawn against the cold. He pressed his palms against the wall at her back, trapping her between his arms. His eyes met hers for a fraction of a second before he regained some modicum of control. Then he said, with softness and regret. "I'm not proud of what I've done to you. I've been an ass. But I won't have you leave here thinking the bloody worst about me. You deserve more than that from me."

Her eyes wet with unshed tears stared back at him with accusation. "I have been abused, kidnapped, tricked, lied to by you, manipulated . . ."

"And?"

"And what?" she snapped. "How much more is there?"

"Aren't you going to add rape to your list of crimes?"

"Rape?" she gasped. "You didn't rape me."

Some of the tension left his body. "Seduced?"

"Please give me more credit than that. I wasn't *that* naive—either time. I take full responsibility for my part in what happened between us. A mere tryst for me as well."

Their eyes held. Hers huge and wet. Sensation clouded everything, the scent of her hair, the warmth of her skin, her breath rough against his cheek. "We shared no tryst," he said, his mouth hovering above hers.

"Of course we did. Please don't make it more than what it was."

His eyes dropped to her mouth. His tone softened. "Look at me," he said.

"Don't you dare kiss me." She lowered her voice and didn't look at him. "You have guests waiting to talk to you. They can probably hear every word we're saying."

"Not unless they have ears pressed to the dining room door behind me."

"They're all a pack of spies. Why wouldn't they have ears pressed to the door?"

Shaking his head, he quietly laughed. His thumbs stroked her cheeks. "No one can hear us unless we shout."

She leveled a censuring look at him. "What do you want from me, Ian?"

He dropped his hands from her face. "Not this." Her face was half in shadow. A wedge of light spilled into the dining room from the pocket door he had not shut completely. "I don't want you to leave like this," he said.

He didn't want her to leave at all. Hell, he didn't know what he wanted.

"Why?" she asked.

He took a step back. Not because she demanded it, but because he found he did not like himself as a bully. She stepped out of his reach. "You told your mother one minute," she said. "I've given you five more than you deserve."

Anger surged within him. God in heaven, he congratulated himself on his restraint. "I'm flattered," he managed with less sarcasm than he felt, and more than he realized she deserved. She had a right to hate him. "You did say you enjoyed last night. That should have earned me the extra five minutes to say *bonsoir*. Have a nice life—"

"You pompous a—!"

"Un-unh." He lifted a finger in front of her nose. "Don't say it, my love."

She gasped, then whirled on her heel, a flurry of fragrant wool and petticoats.

He furrowed his brow. He tensed and wanted to stop her from flinging opened the pocket door. He didn't. His temper had worn as thin as it could without snapping. Folding his arms, he rolled his eyes and leaned against the doorjamb. With Bethany gone, the scent of lemon oil now dominated the room.

"Perfect," he murmured. "Bloody perfect."

He knocked his head three times against the wall. One. Two. Three. Twice for being an idiot and the third time for good measure to keep himself from chasing her.

A voice coming from the darkness saved him. "Miss Munro is an impressive piece of baggage." Jameson settled against the edge of the dining table.

"You aren't standing so far away I can't give you a

facer you'll feel into next week," Ian said without turning his head.

"Ware wants her on this case."

"She doesn't belong on this case. She's rash and impulsive. And at the moment very confused." The rigid set of Ian's shoulders conveyed more than his temperament. He folded his arms and turned to face Jameson. "She just went through hell and doesn't know what she wants. She isn't like you or me. She's different, Jameson."

"You actually care about the girl."

"She's no girl."

"She's no man."

"You know what I mean."

"What did you think you would do with her when you left that inn, Rockwell?"

"I didn't think." He strode past Jameson in the darkness to the breakfront and withdrew a crystal decanter. Without asking Jameson if he wanted a drink, Ian sloshed brandy into a glass. "Someone at Whitley Court poisoned her," he said, changing the topic to something he could work with. "I also found a strange substance in the caverns beneath Whitley Court I want analyzed. Whatever was stored there is gone now. At the very least we can know what it was."

"Ware is sending a request to London for the order to exhume Sir John's remains."

"There is a man named Desmond who was at the inn. I was about to follow him this morning when you arrived and ruined a perfectly productive day." Ian tossed back the drink and poured another.

"Are you asking me to find him?" Jameson quipped.

Ian turned and leaned his backside against the breakfront. His mouth quirked. "You're frightening demeanor should terrify the locals enough not to try to kill you the first night."

Jameson took the insult in stride. He picked up a crystal ornament off the table centerpiece and seemed to study it. "What do you intend to do about Pamela?"

A week from now would be soon enough to realize the truth of that answer. Ian threw back the brandy, then set down the glass and braced both hands on the breakfront. Pamela had to know he would find her. She had to know what would happen when he did.

"She is my responsibility, Jameson. I should have dealt with her years ago."

"I agree. Why didn't you?"

He shook his head and let the chill in the room steal up on him. He made a wan laugh. "I don't know. Maybe I couldn't stomach watching a woman executed. So much for noblesse oblige."

Ian didn't hear Jameson leave the room, but knew when he was alone again.

He should be glad Bethany had walked away from him. He didn't want her here. She had no business caught in the muck of his life or in this bloody case. She didn't belong in it anymore than she belonged to Ware or to the organization Ian served.

But he had long since begun to feel the strain of his work, and long since begun to want more than the clandestine life he led, the lies that had become his existence. The shine of the world in which he'd once thrived had dulled, the excitement dimmed, leaving only a tarnished memory of his endeavors.

For the first time since joining the service a decade

ago, Ian considered retiring to France to live near his sister and take up the wine business.

"No one should live in the shadows as you do, son."

Still braced against his palms, he turned his head and looked past the polished dining room table. Backlit by the light in the salon, his mother stood in the pocket doorway.

Some of the tightness in his chest loosened. Ian hadn't seen her wearing anything but black since his brother's death a decade earlier. She looked like a wraith, and he knew she had not been in the best of health this past year.

"Is Miss Munro in her room?" he asked.

"I've settled her in." His mother sighed. "I'm not going to ask what happened between you both that you would allow her to leave angry," his mother forged on, "but even a blind person can see the two of you are in love. Surely you can apologize for whatever it is you did."

Ian shook his head amused by the insult his mother had just paid him and his current discontent. They had always been close and he was used to her speaking her mind. "Thank you for your vote of confidence on my character, Mother." He shoved away from the breakfront. "You should be lying down."

"Pah." She waved her hand at his concerned tone. "I have shown your other guests to their rooms as well. How long will everyone be staying?"

"I don't know. Until this storm passes. You know the weather can close down on us for days." Worried about her, Ian stopped in front of her. "I told you to go to the south of France and visit Emily and the grandchildren. This is no place for you in the winter. It's too cold."

"Is that why you are never here? Why you leave and never come back? What is the former Minister of Foreign Affairs doing at this house? Are you working for him, the same way you were working for the Home Secretary last fall?"

He let out a breath and looked away.

"Why do you never tell me anything? And why haven't you told me about her?"

Half the time Ian never understood his mother's direction of thought. He'd always respected her Spartan approach to their family's small business empire, which had instilled responsibility for others in her children. So he knew from experience there was a road she followed in her thinking that led to her conclusions. A person had only to find that road. He just didn't have the stamina to find it now.

"What do you want to know?" he asked.

"Why haven't you told me that you've married again?"

"*What* are you talking about?"

"Your driver confirmed you've spent the past week at an inn with your wife. Nor did Samuel dispute the driver. In fact, he just coughed and went to find a glass of libation."

With a silent oath, Ian developed a sudden urge to throttle Samuel *and* his driver.

"Well, is she not the woman with whom you spent the week?"

Ian felt awkwardly snagged on a topic he had no wish to hash out with his mother, of all people. "Miss Munro was seriously ill when we left Whitley Court," he said. "I cared for her health. That is all."

"Indeed," his mother sniffed and lifted her chin. "You more than care for her health, Ian. Where is your decency? Have you no shame you may have injured her reputation?"

Nothing about Bethany Munro made him feel shame. "Even if I wanted, she wouldn't marry me, Mother."

"Why ever not?" his mother replied, scandalized. "Is something wrong with you?"

Ian laughed. "At the moment, you could grant Miss Munro the throne of England and she would not take it to marry me."

And Ian's life was complicated enough without introducing that possibility into the already unpleasant equation.

"Supper is at eight, son," his mother sniffed before he could escape. "If you won't sing for us tonight, at least dress properly for the occasion."

He felt perpetually eight years old whenever he was home. "I'll try to find something suitable," he said.

As he strode from the room, he could only hope the storm inside him would die a merciful death long before the one outside.

"Sometimes weather like this lasts for weeks," Ian's mother replied to something Lord Ware had said.

Ian half listened to the drone of voices about the table, the clink of silverware, the musical sound of warm feminine laughter.

Paying little heed to his grand surroundings, Ian sprawled leisurely in his chair at the end of the table, his gaze resting on the empty claret glass in his hand. His finger traced the diamond design cut into the crystal stem. His body movements pulled against the fabric of his cutaway coat and black trousers. The red carpet that lined the dining room floor captured most of the noise in the room. But another bout of laughter raised his gaze.

He pinpointed the source of merriment at the other end of the table as Jameson regaled Bethany with the heroic exploits of a long-dead hound named King George. Jameson was Scots after all; he could get away with the slight of naming a dog after an English monarch.

Ian didn't know how Jameson did it, idling down memory lane as easily as one took a forest at sunrise or admired a crest of snow on a mountain peak. Adorned in forest green velvet, with upswept hair free of distracting ribbons or jewels, Bethany could have been that verdant forest at sunrise. A frisson of awareness raked over him, even before she looked up and intercepted his stare. A healthy blush warmed her cheeks. She peered at him over the rim of her glass and drank.

The fact that he did not leap down the table and tear Jameson away from her was a point in his favor and cooled a temper that had been brewing inside him since a weather system had sent them all to shelter for the last pair of nights. He'd been encamped at Queen's Staircase as ice and snow pounded the house.

"Ian dear, you really should try to pay more attention," his mother said from beside him. "I just told these fine gentleman and lady that I have decided to take your advice and go to France."

Ian knew that. He and his mother, who was sitting next

to him, had talked extensively on the topic over the last pair of hours. He'd gone to her room earlier and asked her to go visit Emily. He didn't want to have to be worrying about her. There weren't enough men in England to protect her if someone wanted to harm her to get to him. More than that, she had her health to consider.

"You will give Emily my love?" Ian asked, a perfunctory comment he hoped didn't sound too dismissive.

"I thought perhaps you would want to come with me and visit your sister," his mother said.

"She'll be glad to see you, Mother."

"But what do I tell her of why I am visiting?"

Ian smiled over the lip of his glass. "You are perfectly capable of telling the devil to go to hell, Mother. I'm sure something will come to mind."

"Ian!" She smacked his arm with the tip of her fan. "You know better than to speak that way with a young lady present at this table. Don't pay attention to him, Miss Munro. He's been in a snit since this weather system moved in. He never did like to be caged."

Ian gave Bethany a short charged glance.

"Most people don't," she replied.

"My apologies if I offended you, Miss Munro."

Bethany patted the serviette over her lips. "Apology accepted, Sir Ian."

Their eyes held. She was still angry with him.

She suddenly stood, bringing her male audience to its feet. "I have enjoyed supper," she said graciously to his mother. "But I am sure the gentlemen here would like this particular *young* lady to retire so that they may enjoy a glass of port or cigars"—she waved at the air around coiffed hair—"or a game of dominoes. Whatever it is gentlemen do at this late hour."

Dinner adjourned like the fall of a gavel in court.

After her departure, his mother kissed him on the cheek and retired to begin packing for her trip.

"I'll be on my way to Sir John's estate near Fountains Abbey in the morning," Lord Ware said. "Miss Munro has agreed to await our findings before attempting to leave here."

Ian wondered if he shouldn't have been more upset by that announcement. Lord Ware's secretary trailed after him.

Jameson sauntered up and clapped him in a brotherly fashion on the shoulder. "We should postpone our game of dominoes, old chap. My bed calls."

"As long as it is calling only to *you, old* chap."

Jameson's chuckles followed him out of the dining room. Then the room was suddenly empty and Ian was alone.

He walked to the breakfront, removed a crystal decanter and tumbler and took both with him to the drawing room, where a fire warmed the air. He made himself comfortable next to the window.

Movement reflecting from the doorway lifted his gaze in the glass. Lord Ware stood behind him. Ian knew why he had come. The reason why Ware had manipulated Bethany into staying.

"I don't want her on this team," Ian said. "Not for this job or any other."

"She has the makings to be one of the best," Ware said in the answering silence. "You and I both know it."

"She's too young."

"No younger than you were when you first came to us. She's a natural and you know it."

Ian found no solace in that truth. "She isn't emotionally prepared for anything the council may ask her to do."

"She only needs a mentor, Rockwell."

"Mentor?" The rigid set of Ian's shoulders conveyed more than his temperament. He folded his arms and leaned against the casement. "You're asking that I mentor her?" He stopped short of telling his superior he was cracked in the head to consider Ian qualified for that job.

Lord Ware looked over the rim of his spectacles. "I wouldn't presume to tell you who you can or cannot sleep with, Rockwell. Nor would I presume to instruct you on how best to accomplish your mission. I only trust that you will, and before anyone else is killed. If she can help us, then she is of value to the council."

Ian eyed the decanter he'd set on the window seat and considered pouring himself another glass. "Like Pamela was of value to the council?"

The thought roused him enough to push away from the window. Finally, he faced his superior. "I won't execute her," he said when Ware gave him his full regard. "Not for the council. Not for God or Queen. We put Pamela away without benefit of a tribunal the first time. I won't carry out a sentence a second time."

Something in Ware's usual hawklike gaze was surprisingly paternal. "She has always been your weakness. If you won't consider yourself then consider the safety of your family, should such a tribunal go public. We deal with our own, Rockwell."

Ian raked a hand through his hair. He knew Lord Ware was right. A tribunal would bring Pamela's existence into the public arena and do more than shame his family. Her knowledge of him and many of his peers made her a danger to them all.

He'd made powerful enemies in his past. Ian had never regretted his actions or questioned the morality of the orders he carried out. His actions had always had purpose, a higher cause to which he answered. He did his job well. He went in. He went out. He went up the hill. He went down. . .

Last fall something had happened to change all that. He hadn't just been in charge of the Home Secretary's security. He'd been the person charged to protect the man's life and that of his family. Lord Densmore had a kindly wife and three young girls on the brink of womanhood who would never grow up because Ian had failed. Pamela was involved with the anarchist group that had planted the bomb that killed Lord Densmore and his family, and Ian had one more reason to see her pay for her sins.

"Do I need to be concerned about your ability to do your job, Rockwell?"

"Which one? The one where I execute my wife or the one where I attempt to seduce Miss Munro into our organization, now that she has gotten it into her craw that she wants to go back to the conservatory and never set her eyes on us again. Try asking her yourself, my lord."

Lord Ware snorted. "I want her on this team, Rockwell."

After Ware left, Ian glared at the empty place in the

doorway where Ware had been standing. With an oath, he looked away.

These cerebral glitches were a necessary encumbrance these days as he traveled over the bumps in his conscience to arrive at the destination where he needed to be. He preferred having no conscience at all.

Chapter 17

Bethany's descent downstairs brought her into a flurry of activity as servants flitted about the corridors and chambers helping Mrs. Rockwell depart for her trip.

No one bothered with Bethany or seemed concerned that she should be wandering the hallways. She hadn't seen Ian for days. Alone and left to her own devices, she found herself trapped by the walls in her room, broken only occasionally over tea with Ian's mother. But Mrs. Rockwell was leaving for France. Today Bethany had come out of hiding and gone exploring. Ian had grown up in this house, and despite her current opinion about his character, she still found herself drawn by her curiosity to explore something so intimately his.

Already she'd discovered a fencing studio and had even spent yesterday working with the foils. Her guardian, Lord Chadwick, was a master swordsman and had trained her himself.

He had taught her to take care of herself. He'd tried to teach her self-confidence and independence. Lessons that eluded her now.

Bethany stopped just inside the first larger drawing room just past the grand staircase. A roaring fire crackled in the hearth, spreading radiant heat throughout, making the multitude of faces staring down at her from the portraits lining the wall feel a little more welcoming. She heard the sound of voices outside, and walked to the wide crystal-paned window overlooking the circular drive and drew back the heavy green brocade draperies. Her heart gave a familiar *thump* and she leaned into the glass.

She had found Ian. Dressed warmly in a heavy woolen coat that seemed to broaden his wide shoulders and would have given him that dashing flavor of a highwayman she'd come to love—if not for the civilized hat he wore—he was speaking to the carriage driver. The carriage itself was an elegantly appointed conveyance with a fresh coat of black lacquer to hide what once looked to be the family crest on the doors. The driver would be taking Ian's mother to Dover, where a packet to France was scheduled to leave three nights hence. Two of Lord Ware's men would be accompanying Mrs. Rockwell and the host of footmen and servants.

Bethany glanced about at the fluffy clouds burrowing through the morning sky. She folded her arms and turned back into the room. Portraits lined the oaken-paneled walls. This vintage room and the gallery upstairs shared the Rockwell ancestors. The tall portrait above the hearth pulled the focus of her attention and Bethany found herself standing at the foot of the painting, gazing up at the white-haired childlike sprite, wondering whom she was, but not surprised to see a little of Ian in her eyes.

"The old duke married her and brought her to this country," Ian's mother said from the doorway, startling a gasp from Bethany as she turned and held her hand against her wildly beating heart.

Mrs. Rockwell, dressed in black bombazine traveling attire with a white lace scarf across her bosom, came across the carpeted floor to stand shoulder to shoulder with Bethany in front of the portrait. Her gaze fastened on the elfin face of the woman staring down at them from an age long past. "This is the only portrait our family has left of her. She was a Danish princess."

Bethany felt her heart trip with a moment's awe. "A Danish princess? Then the story is true?"

"I don't know to which story you are referring, dear. There are many."

Bethany gazed at the beautiful woman in the portrait. "The one where the Viking thrall had been imprisoned in the king's castle and the princess freed him."

Mrs. Rockwell laughed. "Good heavens, child. Where did you hear such a thing? Theirs was a political marriage. The man was an English duke and the Royal House of Denmark had the wealth. That is the way of such marriages."

And Ian was such a liar, Bethany thought, remembering the story he'd told her about his errant Viking thrall in love with a princess. Yet, there had been something so romantic about the story and the way Ian had told it to her.

"Ian's sister used to tell her two brothers that tale," Mrs. Rockwell said, her pensive eyes no longer on the portrait. "Emily would have her brothers hanging on her every word and believing in white knights and dragons. All three of my children were very close. He had a difficult time of it when his brother passed," Ian's mother said after a moment, and it took Bethany only a second to figure out Mrs. Rockwell was talking about Ian and his brother.

The woman turned toward Bethany. "Ian is not as tough as people think."

Clearly, Mrs. Rockwell had no grasp of what Ian did for the Crown.

"He would not appreciate my comment. But I love him, you see. He is my only son left to me. You cannot fault my desire to see him happy."

Bethany didn't understand why Ian's mother was telling her this. Because she had no place else to look, Bethany gazed once again at Ian's ancestors.

"The lot of them were scapegrace noblemen," Mrs. Rockwell sniffed. "The last man who held the ducal title was caught spying for the colonists. King George had him executed. Ian's grandfather was born a commoner."

"What's this about my grandfather?" Ian asked from the doorway.

Bethany turned. His hat no longer covered his head. His heavy coat opened to reveal a careless necktie and tall riding boots. Looking wholesomely virile, he held her gaze and seemed to let the silence settle between them.

"Did I miss something?"

"Only your family history lesson," Bethany said.

Leaning a shoulder against the archway, he folded his arms. "Ahh," he said with no remorse for making up that absurd fairytale he'd told her at the inn. "Mother isn't fond of the old duke." He flicked his eyes to his mother as she approached in a swish of fabric. "Did you tell Miss Munro what happened to the first Queen's Staircase?"

"Yes, well that one burnt to the ground during a drunken house party. Ian's grandfather is responsible for rebuilding everything that we have." Mrs. Rockwell leaned forward and kissed her son on the cheek. "It is a shame you have no son or daughter to inherit."

"Then it is fortunate you have other grandchildren who will inherit, Mother."

She sniffed. Some moments later, Samuel joined them. Taking Mrs. Rockwell's elbow, he escorted her out the door. Ian remained leaning against the doorjamb as he watched Samuel and his mother leave. He brought his gaze back around to Bethany.

"You lied to me about the thrall in love with the Viking princess. Your mother told me about the duke."

"You wanted to hear a fairytale, Bethany. I told you what you wanted to hear."

He was right of course, she realized, and it was that truth that hurt. Her belief in shining knights and a happy-ever-after made her young in his eyes. But it also made her an optimist.

"Life isn't just about the cold hard facts, Ian. You should take the time to look at an occasional sunset, walk barefoot in the sand, visit the zoo and pet the bunnies. Gaze at an occasional rainbow."

He shook his head in an exaggerated motion. "Rainbows and sunsets?"

"There is nothing wrong with a little bit of sky gazing," she quietly said. "Hopes and dreams define who we are."

She brushed past him only to have him take her arm. The sleeve of his greatcoat brushed her hand. The air vibrated between them. "*Will* there be a child in our future?"

The heat climbed high into her face. She looked down at his palm on her arm. He followed her gaze. He lowered his hand. "As I said, nothing is ever a hundred percent."

"Thank you for your concern. But no, there will be no children."

She hadn't meant to use the plural, but her intent was still clear. They had had their fling and it was over. And, all at once, a sadness pervaded her. It crept into her malleable veins, spreading like a toxin in her blood and suddenly she couldn't imagine her life without Ian—any more than she could imagine him with her. And so she stood struggling for balance.

She waited, wondering if he would say anything else. Then he stepped back but not so far that his cloak did not brush her rose-silk skirts. "Lord Ware should be back by the end of the week."

She stared at the place where his coat touched her skirts then back at him, at the frown she saw in his eyes.

"Do you really believe Sir John might be alive?" she asked.

"It's a possibility we have to confirm or refute before we can continue."

And then what? she wondered.

After a moment, he turned on his heel. Her hand went to the wall where he'd been leaning and she remained there as she listened to his footstep fade. The front door shut.

Bethany came awake with a cry.

Heart racing, she sat straight up in bed spilling the covers around her. A sob rose in her throat, before she realized she was not at Whitley Court.

Oblivious to the cold, she stared around her in the darkness. The lamp by the door had gone out. A white-faced clock sat on her nightstand. She turned it into the moonlight and saw it was just midnight. Then she heard a masculine voice in the corridor.

Ian talking to someone. Broken words, low, yet distinctly his.

Bethany flung off the covers. With the floor cold against her bare feet, she hurried across the room and eased the door open. A draft fluttered the hem of her white cotton nightdress. She peered into the dimly lit corridor.

She followed the voices as far as the landing.

Ian stood at the bottom of the stairs, wearing a heavy coat and removing his gloves, speaking to someone just out of her line of sight. Their voices carried in the hush. "You only have to observe. Jameson has been looking for one of the smugglers named Desmond . . ." Something about tunnels, gold exchanging hands, and the inn where he had stayed.

"I'll leave in the morning. Good night, sir," the other voice replied, surprising Bethany because the voice belonged to one of the men who had left over a week ago with Lord Ware.

Lord Ware had returned to Queen's Staircase, she realized.

Bethany walked back to her bed, but in the end, her inability to sleep had her moving from the bed to the window bench. Pulling her knees to her chest, she rested her chin on them and peered outside. The uneven terrain was brilliant bathed in moonlight. It was as if the entire world had frozen in a white tableau caught in a moment of time. She could see the carriage house's distant roof and the stables framed against a velvet sky. Nothing stirred.

Over the course of the past few days, others had arrived at the house. Sometimes at night when she could not sleep, she would hear the sound of horses on the drive. She knew Ian came and went, even when she had been told travel was impossible.

And he'd left her alone.

Turning away from the night, she drew on a pale pink wrapper and worked the tiny buttons as she stepped into her slippers and went to her door. She moved down the stairway past generations of Rockwells in a house as silent as a graveyard.

A fire lit within one of the rooms down the corridor showed her the way. She found Ian in the drawing room with the Danish princess.

Bethany stopped on the threshold.

The fireplace provided the only illumination. Ian occupied a chair in front of the large stone hearth, his cravat loosened, his long legs stretched in front of him and crossed at the ankles. His eyes closed, he held a cheroot in one hand and a glass of brandy in the other.

Bethany stepped into the drawing room and eased the double-wide doors shut.

He still did not move. Her feet made no sound on the carpet as she crossed the room and came to stand in front of him.

"I'll be upstairs in a moment, Samuel," he said.

When no reply followed, Ian's eyes opened.

Nothing outwardly suggested he was taken aback at seeing her, but she sensed his surprise nonetheless. She stared at his face, marked by the flickering shadows in the room.

He set the glass down on the table beside the chair. His loosened cravat made him look appealing even as it made him vulnerable. He looked tired. "I wasn't expecting anyone to be awake at this hour," he said. "I apologize if I awakened you."

"I heard voices in the corridor."

He ground out the cheroot in a tray, but still did not stand. "Why am I not surprised to see you running about in the middle of the night?"

She looked down at herself. "I am completely covered." Even down to the furry slippers on her feet.

His silence sobering her, she straightened.

It would be a lie to deny her physical need to be with him. She wasn't noble or righteous and she had done things in her life of which she was not proud. Perhaps Ian was not noble either, but her heart didn't particularly care when she was with him. Lord Ware was here and her time with Ian would soon be at end.

She looked at the cut-crystal decanter on the bric-a-brac table beside him. He didn't offer to pour her a glass, so she took his own.

"You aren't going to like that," he warned, a mix of amusement and something watchful in his eyes.

"I know how to drink, Ian." Yet instead of proving her point, she found herself cradling the glass and said instead, "I heard you speaking to one of Lord Ware's men. He was returned then?"

"An hour ago." He peered at her over steepled fingers. "He just went to bed."

"What has he discovered about Sir John?"

"No conclusive evidence could be reached."

"I don't understand. I thought an anthropologist could make the distinction. I thought . . ."

Ian rubbed a point between his brows. "There wasn't much left of him to examine."

Dawning poured over her. "He was in the stairwell . . . with the . . . rats."

Something horrible and cold swept over her. She pressed a hand to her brow. Bethany thought she might throw up.

Ian was suddenly standing before her. He grabbed her arms and held her steady with both hands. "You wanted to know," he said without sympathy in his voice.

His superior tone made her angry. Her temper flared. She stepped away from him. "I don't need you to coddle me." And took a huge sip of what remained in the brandy glass.

Hell-fire burned down her throat and stole her breath. Tears welled. She gasped for breath.

He took the glass from her and set it aside. "Clearly your tippling does not extend to hard-core Irish whiskey, love."

"You are insane," she rasped. "How can you drink that stuff?"

But she was still too woozy to put up any reputable defense and her temper had been effectively doused in the fires of hell. His hands splayed her waist, strong and entirely masculine, and she didn't recover her senses until he'd sat with her on the chair straddling his lap. "Put me down, Ian. I am not some princess who needs to be rescued."

He stared at her with pitch-black eyes in the darkness. "Does it look like I'm rescuing you?" Then he gave a throaty chuckle. "More like I need rescuing from you. And me being so well-behaved all week."

"Like a choirboy to be sure," she snapped in a rasp.

He lifted the whiskey bottle from the table beside the

chair. The air wafted with heavy spirits. "Here, try it again. Tippling is always smoother the second time."

"Get it away from me."

His green eyes glittered with mirth. He set down the bottle. Drawing in her first normal breath, she was suddenly conscious of the heat in her blood and the fact her hair was undone and a mess about her shoulders. She was aware of his eyes on hers.

"Did you come in here just so you can drink my whiskey?" he asked.

"I heard you talking—"

"And here I thought we'd developed a certain modicum of honesty between us?"

She scoffed at the notion. Then her eyes grew serious. "With Sir John dead, you have an unsolved death and nothing but circumstantial evidence that links Whitley to any crimes of treason," she said. "But I may be able to do something. At least that's what Lord Ware thinks, doesn't he? He thinks Whitley has a *tendre* toward me and wants me to use that as an advantage."

Ian didn't reply, but his expression took on a hint of steel.

"He's right, you know." Bethany pushed, not so naive she didn't recognize her worth as a special commodity to Lord Ware. "I could explain away my relationship to you and tell him that Lord Ware approached me. Tell him everything, and that he is under investigation. It is something he must already know, so I'm telling him nothing new."

"I don't give a toad's horn if Ware thinks you are the next Miss Jenny," he whispered. "You have no bloody business going near Whitley or any of his family again."

Bethany drew in a deep breath. Miss Jenny had been an infamous British spy during England's war with the colonies a century before and a much-revered person among the more enlightened women at the conservatory.

Pushing his fingers into her hair, Ian forced her to look at him. "Listen to me, Beth—"

"Don't be high-handed with me, Ian."

"Is that what you think I am doing?"

"I think you cannot help yourself." She pressed her lips against Ian's throat, and he closed his eyes. "Let me into your life, Ian."

A surge of emotion closed around Ian's chest. She *was* a "valuable commodity," as Bethany had phrased it, and it sickened him that he understood exactly what Ware saw in her. She was beautiful, vivacious, and so completely alive, drawn by the same idealism that Ian once had.

He'd recognized it in her from the beginning. Now all he felt was disgust with Ware and this whole damned business.

And yet, the firelight lent a magical essence to the equation, spilling across his hand, dark in contrast to her hair. The spell wavered and wobbled like a child's top and seemed to become fragile.

He slipped his fingers through the cool softness of her hair. She had not moved from his lap. His eyes held hers. He could taste the whiskey on her breath. "Are you trying to seduce me, Bethany?"

His gaze dropped to her slim fingers resting on his chest, then rose back to her eyes. In the dim light, her widened pupils made her eyes nearly black.

Straddled as she was across his thighs, her knees

pressed against the back of the chair, he knew it would be no difficult feat to guide himself inside her.

"Are you afraid?" she asked him.

The question stopped him. Not because he had a conscience, but because she had touched the very crux of something deep down, brought it out of hiding and into the light.

Ian *was* afraid. But of what, he didn't know.

A momentary question reflected in her eyes, its answer neither of them willing to face, not now, maybe not even tomorrow. But it was there between them sharing the simmering passion that even now burned and stirred the air surrounding them.

Smoothing the strands of hair away from her mouth as if she were made of glass, and with no pretext behind his actions he reached to the buttons of his trousers to free himself. She watched his hands:

"If I were decent, I would never have allowed you to remain at this house," he said, his mood no longer biddable as he pulled himself from his trousers, wanting inside her.

But she didn't stop him. She was liquid. He eased into her, stretching her. He held his hands on her shoulders so he could watch her eyes as he took her. She pressed her thighs against his, sucking him deep, and the breath left him. His hands splaying her bottom almost lifted her off him, then he drove into her again, impaling her so completely he had to stop himself or come inside her. His head fell back against the chair.

She pressed her forehead against his, and said in the barest of breaths. "I think I might scream."

His mouth twisting in rueful amusement, he held it to her temple. "Is that right?"

Her voice held a small edge. "Love me, Ian."

And she pulled him into a kiss.

His heartbeat pounded and, sliding his hands into her tumbled curls, he kissed her hard until she gentled him with her own brand of need, merging her passion with his as they began to move.

Her hands stole beneath his shirt and up his back, hesitating on the fine ridges of his spine, drawing his mind to her palms. His tongue slid past her parted lips. Moaning she arched against him. The fire blazed hot at her back and her breath caressed his face. Wrapping his palms around her hips, he shifted his hips and spread her legs wider. Then he was using her weight to pleasure him and loving her in earnest, holding her to the kiss, the only sounds in the room the breathing between them.

She crested, coming apart around him, and, moments later, he joined her, gripping her with his hands as he drew in short panting breaths, aware as he did that she watched him. He didn't pull out of her, but gave her his seed. How long had it been since he'd come inside a woman?

With no words between them, he laid her on the floor in front of the fireplace. He wanted to make love to her, lying against her body, and to savor her like fine whiskey. She stared at him for several moments, her eyes solemn as he worked the buttons on her wrapper. Then he was sliding his hands over her breasts, touching her and needing her all over again. When she'd finally fallen asleep, he carried her out of the room and to his bed upstairs.

After stirring the fire in the stove back to life, he lit a cheroot. He turned and peered through the haze of blue smoke at Bethany lying asleep in his bed. Then he was standing over her. He could watch her for hours, he realized, and might have been amused if that insight wasn't so damn pitiable.

He walked to the window where he drew aside the heavy draperies and looked out across moonlit fields toward the road that led away from Queen's Staircase, an endless terrain broken by patches of heavy mist forming near the ground and finally sat on the bench. He plowed his hands through his hair then held out his hands.

His eyes dropped to the wedding ring, burning a hole into his soul, and for the first time in four years slid it from his hand.

He had forgotten more in the past three years than he'd remembered in a decade. Somewhere he had lost himself. Not for the first time did he consider retiring from the service.

He'd even considered walking away from this job. The seductive thought passed through his mind like the scent of myrrh, as did the thought of a future with Bethany.

He did not understand what it was he felt for her or what it was she felt for him. Love was too vague, too opportune a word, too convenient and overused by poets and white knights. She most certainly saw him as part of a world painted in vivid colors when he saw only the shades of gray. It wasn't that he felt hopeless; it was only that he was not hopeful.

Sensing Bethany watching him, he turned and felt the strange impact of her gaze. For a long time neither spoke, then she raised the covers, inviting him to bed. It was not so very long before Morpheus finally claimed him in Bethany's arms.

* * *

The tall clock in the entryway had just struck eight times when Bethany entered the smaller dining salon. Even with the sky still in the throes of a winter sunrise, the salon was a sunny room that exuded springtime warmth made pleasant by walls painted bright yellow with crocuses. Lord Ware sat at the breakfast table, eating a hot croissant and sipping a cup of tea as he perused a two-day-old broadsheet.

"You're late," Ware said, looked up and visibly paused.

Lord Ware was an imposing man, merging into old age, but still handsome in a calculating way. Observing her over the rim of his cup, he casually drank as if he hadn't just been caught by surprise. His eyes landed on her hair. She'd tied it back with ribbon and suddenly felt absurdly young, which made her push her chin a notch higher.

"Tell me about Sir Ian's wife," she asked.

He set the cup down on the table. "Why would I tell you anything at all, Miss Munro?"

"Because you want my help and I won't help you unless you tell me the truth."

Amusement and something like respect flashed momentarily in his eyes. "That's something I appreciate about you, Miss Munro. You have no ladylike qualms about hitting below the shoulder." After a moment, Lord Ware folded the newspaper and set it aside. "The wind has stopped. Would you care to take a morning constitutional with an old man?"

Old man, my toe, she thought. He was every bit as sharp as a well-honed blade and just as perilous. Still, there was something about him that challenged her to stroll along that edge of steel she saw in his eyes just to prove to him she could. She had been thinking all morning how best to approach him, not only about Ian but about this entire case against Lord Whitley. She'd suddenly found herself unable to walk away.

A half hour later dressed in her woolen cloak and wearing gloves and a bonnet, she and Lord Ware strolled along the garden pathway that led to the sea. The stark blue sky stretched for miles. A seagull sat on a white fence post undisturbed as they passed out of the yard. The air was crisp and smelled like brine.

"You are considering joining my team?" Lord Ware said. "Do you want to know our professional mission? Or are you only interested in Sir Ian's part?"

Lord Ware's question inched up her chin. "I want to help Ian."

"If you choose to join the league council, Miss Munro, you best be doing this for yourself, and yourself alone. Sir Ian doesn't want you here. If he'd had his way he would have shipped you back to the conservatory your first night here."

"Why didn't he send me back?"

Lord Ware sniffed. "I ordered him to keep you here while I attended to the business at Fountains Abbey." Something that sounded like a sigh followed. "Sir Ian is conflicted, Miss Munro."

She knew Lord Ware spoke to the existence of Pamela. Ian may not love Pamela but he had feelings. She wondered if there was something inside him that still felt honor bound to try to protect and save her.

"Shall we?" He motioned the way down the path. "Our team has one mission at the moment," Lord Ware said as they started walking. "Hunt and prosecute the anarchists responsible for the Home Secretary's murder. Find where they are making their bombs and destroy their supplier. Do you know what makes these bombs special, Miss Munro?"

Bethany knew something of chemistry.

"The incendiary explosion that caused the fire that killed Lord Densmore and his family wasn't dynamite," Lord Ware said. "It was a very volatile and powerful explosive device capable of tremendous damage, with a new manner of detonator. One requiring a great deal of sophistication. Traces of phenyl and mercury were found at the scene. The chemicals used are extremely lethal. The detonator allows the device to be activated by a timing mechanism. The one that killed the Home Secretary and his family was believed to have been brought into the room with the tea service."

"Count Verástegui is an arms manufacturer," she murmured.

"We knew the count would be attending the function at Whitley Court."

"Surely the council takes into consideration the fact that someone tried to assassinate Lord Whitley when considering his guilt or innocence as a leader of the anarchist group. Why would someone try to kill him?"

"Consider that the only person shot that day was Sir Ian. Pamela Rockwell can take an apple off a fence post at three hundred yards."

Bethany stopped walking. "Do you believe the shooter was Sir Ian's wife?"

Lord Ware studied the shiny lion's head atop his walking stick. "I have no doubt Sir Ian does."

Yet Ian had said nothing at all.

His silence concerning Pamela hurt more than she would have thought possible. Not because he had once loved that woman, but because he would forever exclude Bethany from that part of his life.

"What happens after he finds his wife?"

"Sir Ian knows what has to be done. He understood the rules when he accepted responsibility for her incarceration three years ago."

"But you can't ask him . . . it's inhumane. He loved her."

"Oh, to be sure, he did. She tried to kill him once. She tried to kill your stepmother as well. You didn't know that, did you? That mission Sir Ian was on three years ago when you met him involved her. Your guardian now—Lord Chadwick—Sir Ian, and Pamela were the three sent to your tidewater town to flush out a killer and a fortune in stolen jewels.

"Unbeknownst to us, Pamela had turned. If not for Sir Ian, she would have killed your stepmother and gotten away with a fortune."

Bethany folded her arms beneath her cloak as if that would keep the warmth close to her body. "No one ever told me exactly what had happened to my stepmother. No one talked about it. Sir Ian left before I could say goodbye." Her shoulders rose in tandem to her words. "I never expected to see him again."

"No doubt he was more surprised to see you." Lord Ware studied her with interest. The wind pushed at his collar. "Now you are standing before me ready to throw down your life, for what exactly? For Sir Ian?"

Bethany didn't know how to reply to that statement because a part of her did want to be what Ian was. But not because she was in love with him and saw his life as some romantic fantasy. It was because he did something important, something that was greater and bigger than himself. His life held purpose.

"If I believe in the cause, I can do anything." Passion infused her voice. "I'm not afraid of dying."

Lord Ware observed her with a reserved curiosity. "The council is not about fighting or dying for a cause, Miss Munro."

Bethany did not miss the gibe in his remark and recognized her mistake. She should have been more circumspect in revealing her emotions, especially when they suddenly felt childish and fraught with melodrama.

"Could you kill another human being, Miss Munro? Could you place the mission above your own life? Your principles?"

Ian had asked her once if she could kill a man. Her response was the same now, which was no response at all. She didn't have an answer because she didn't know.

Lord Ware proceeded to walk again. Her shoes squeaked in the snow as she followed him. "When one sets out to do a job, he checks his personal life at the door. He does what it takes to finish the job and get his team out alive. If you can't do that, then you will die your first time out—or worse, you will get your partners killed. There is no place for misplaced idealism or childish emotion in this business. The stakes are too high."

The wind had pushed her hood to her shoulders, and the sunlight suddenly seemed too bright. "You make it all sound so heartless and . . ."

"Cold-blooded?"

She had no idea how to reconcile what she knew of Ian and the kind of man Lord Ware held up as a shining example of a dedicated operative. The man Lord Ware portrayed was not the Ian she knew. Or was he?

She pulled the cloak tighter around her torso and drew herself up. "I don't even know what she looks like."

"As a matter of fact, she looks a lot like you, Miss Munro."

Bethany gripped the hilt of the thin fencing foil with the finesse of a true swordsman. She lunged and retreated, then began the dance again, the long blade made only a little less dangerous by the protective cap on its tip.

Earlier this afternoon, on her way back from the cliffs, she'd remembered this fencing studio. After her talk with Lord Ware, she'd needed to go somewhere to be alone. The studio had suited her purpose perfectly, the exertion her state of mind.

She wore now the red sleeveless woven top and breeches her guardian had made for her years before. Clothes she carried with her whenever she traveled that had always sat at the bottom of her trunk. She had not spent enough time practicing since she'd left Rose Briar.

The setting sun shining through the glass doors that framed two sides of the room was her only partner.

She dimmed the lamps and, closing her eyes, allowed the dark cadence of her mood to replace the shadows. She willed herself not think of Ian and had almost succeeded in banishing him from her thoughts and finally finding her rhythm. She didn't expect him back from town until supper.

So when she opened her eyes and saw him standing with his back against the door, she was momentarily struck still. He looked sinfully beautiful, bathed in what remained of the golden sunset and wearing a stark white shirt that contrasted with the surrounding light and shadows. The shadows somehow made him seem to tower even higher over her. No one had ever made her feel as small and helpless as he did.

She didn't like that he'd sneaked up on her. In fact, she didn't like *him* at the moment.

She lowered the foil and straightened. "Go away, Ian."

She set her feet and resumed her practice.

"I talked to Ware."

She ignored him. What would she say anyway?

"He said you came to him. He has put you on this team."

When she didn't reply, he pushed off the door. "You couldn't just decide to go back to your family like a good girl. You have to push, don't you? Push until something breaks."

She raised her foil and stopped him. "It's in my nature to break things."

She sensed his anger and something more. Resentment. What right did he have to rancor anyway? Certainly, he did not own her. Nor was Bethany Pamela. Ignoring his statement, she swished the foil in front of his nose. "Would you care to challenge me?" She dared him to try. She was finished trying to salvage her honor with him.

He folded his arms across his chest. Despite his lazy posture, his eyes were intent. "What are we fighting for? Your honor or mine?"

"Don't presume to think this is about more than a simple competition, Ian. Though I would not wish to humiliate you."

"You aren't capable of beating me."

"What are you so afraid of, that you will fail or I'll succeed?"

His boots thudded across the wooden floor to where fencing equipment and foils lined the wall. Lowering her guard, she watched as he tested each one for weight and balance, then tossed her a protective leather vest and a mesh mask. "No doubt there is much we can learn from each other about swordplay."

"Is there?" She set aside the foil and settled the vest over her head. "I would have thought, grand spy that you are, you're well trained in all manner of blood sport."

He flashed a smile she could only call dangerous, then slipped the mask on his face. "Not the virginal kind, love. You're the first."

Bethany knew he wasn't ready. He'd only just tied the laces on his vest and barely set the mask on his head. Deftly and quickly, she went on the attack. But his reflexes were quick.

He raised his foil and parried her lunge. Still she drove him back two steps, then three. He feinted, but she led the dance across the floor. She smiled behind her mask. "This is the best you can do?" she asked.

"Reckless gets you killed, Bethany. I thought you would have learned that by now."

She didn't want a lecture when she very well knew her weaknesses. Her eyes met and clashed with his through the mesh of their masks. "Never trust that you are in control. Isn't that what you are always trying to tell me?"

Their clicking foils eclipsed the sound of their breathing in the studio as they crossed the floor. "You're good, but you aren't that good, love. Yet."

A skein of doubt filtered from his words into her gut. She wished she could see his eyes through the mask to know his thoughts, and she didn't like that she'd started the fight before she'd made him remove his boots. His height gave him an unfair advantage. But she didn't fight by the rules, and, stepping out of their circle, she parried, then lunged and easily scored the first point with a jab to his heart, right across the leather vest that covered his white shirt. One more and she would win.

She swished her foil with two cutting strokes to the air. "I won't let you best me, Ian Rockwell."

He tore off his mask sending a lock of damp hair across his brow. Clearly, he'd not anticipated that she'd cheat. But winning was winning. She could be as merciless as he and she would prove it.

"Your anger makes you careless, Bethany."

"Call it what you will, but I can do anything you can. I'm not afraid."

A smile twisted his handsome features. He settled the mask back over his face. "You want no rules, love? Then we shall have no rules between us."

His words sent an odd shiver down her spine. Bethany realized at once that her mistake had not been in underestimating Ian's expertise but in giving away her level of skill too early.

"The first thing you must learn in this business is to separate fact from illusion. But then we both know I'm no novice at deceit."

Their foils clicked and they circled one another.

He sensed her every step. The clack of their foils increased in intensity as he relentlessly took more ground and she fought harder not to concede. She suspected she was miles below his level of proficiency, but he didn't strike the point. Instead, he worked to wear out her defenses. She wanted to feel challenged by his aptitude. Instead she felt cheated.

"Get used to it, Bethany," he said, reading her mind. "Nothing is as it seems or as it should be. You want to be part of this team, learn that now because it will get bloody."

"Strike your point, then," Bethany rasped. "Isn't that what you want to do? To prove I'm not capable of being here? That you don't want me as a partner . . . And now you want me gone?" she said, lowering her defenses. All of them.

Ian waggled the foil tip in front of her nose. "Is it your intent to let me win so easily?"

She straightened. "Strike the bloody point. And prove that I'm not good enough to fight with you, to stand beside you."

"En garde, Bethany. This is what you want? Finish it."

She parried to knock aside Ian's foil and missed as he easily danced aside, toying with her. He was hell-bent on teaching her a lesson, but the more he thought she couldn't beat him the more determined she was to do so. "I know what you're doing."

She could see his smile behind the mask. "Do you? You're a mind reader now? Then read this."

She ducked and rolled beneath his foil and was suddenly behind him, coming to her feet, panting as he swirled on his boot heel to counter her attack. Her ribs ached. Her lungs burned. Her arm began to feel like lead.

He backed her against the windows and she got caught in the velvet draperies. She swung her left fist but he captured her wrist, shoving her against the wall. His other hand grabbed her foil arm and pressed like an unforgiving vice against the draperies.

"Are you so easily defeated, Bethany? How long do you think you'd last in my world?"

Her eyes locked on his face. They were both breathing hard.

"I'm not like her, Ian. I'm not Pamela."

His eyes narrowed. "Don't presume to know what I'm thinking. Don't you goddamn dare to presume anything!"

She struggled again to free herself from his grip of steel. But he pressed her against the wall, holding her there, leaving her to manage only to straddle one of his hard thighs. She stilled. So did he.

"I am not she, Ian." Her voice whispered. "No matter what I look like."

His expression changed, a mix of fatalistic forbearance and incredulity on his face behind the mesh of his mask. "Am I supposed to know what that means?"

"Lord Ware said I looked like *her.* I look like Pamela."

He reined in his initial reaction. Then he stepped away. He released her and stripped off his mask. Damp strands of his wild hair pasted themselves to his forehead. She tore her mask away as well. They faced each other, both hot and sweaty, like two rams ready to butt horns to the death. She felt a sharp unexpected pain in her chest.

"No, Bethany, you do not look like her," he said quietly. "Not to me."

"Why would Lord Ware say that?"

"Why do you think? He knows there is something between us. I imagine he wants us to have this conversation sooner rather than later. Considering my history, can you blame him?"

"Will there be a later, then?"

"Whatever I think isn't important," he said, his eyes dark and troubled. "You and I are on the same team because Ware wants it that way."

"What do *you* want?"

He peered down at her. He actually had the audacity to laugh. "Take one goddamn guess what it is I want?"

Bethany tipped her foil toward the ground. She no longer wanted to fight him. He had become her center again, and, in her focus, she regained her equilibrium. Despite everything, she trusted him. She respected his judgment. "I don't want you as my protector, Ian. I want you as my partner." She wanted *him* to see her as his peer.

He took her foil and mask and returned them both to the wall. Then he stilled and placed both hands on the wall, leaning against his weight. Bethany came to stand behind him. They remained like that, neither speaking.

Tears burned at the back of her lids. He'd put her at a crossroads.

"This is what I need to do, Ian. What I want to be. Like you, this is who I am."

"Who you bloody are?" He turned. "You don't even know who you are. You're idealistic and young."

She reddened, for the barb struck directly at the truth of the matter. But it was her emotions for him, not her age that made her feel inexperienced. "And sometimes I forget you are old. All of one and thirty to be exact."

Something flashed briefly from behind the fringe of his dark lashes, then his eyes softened and some of his anger fell away. "You are also passionate, warm, and loyal."

"Then why are you so afraid?"

He emitted a ragged laugh. "Because passionate, warm, and loyal isn't enough. No, let me rephrase. It is just enough to get you killed or me killed worrying about you or trying to watch your back. Hell—" Raking a hand through his hair, he shook his head and glared at the plaster cornices on the ceiling.

"I am leaving tonight to see Jameson," he said. "He is looking for a smuggler named Desmond, the man I had a conversation with when we were at the inn. Lord Ware is on his way to London where I will be meeting him. I have been ordered to report to the council. Ware has left two of his men here tonight. They will take you and Mary to the depot tomorrow afternoon. Ware has already arranged for someone to be waiting for you when you disembark in Old Bedford Park to escort you to the conservatory. He will be your contact until you hear word from Lord Ware. He will assign you a handler."

She started to protest. Her mouth tasted dry like burned paper and her heart raced. An awful remoteness had fallen over her.

"Lord Whitley is in London," he said misreading her response. "You can't exactly go knocking on his door. You are returning to your life. You will soon learn most of this business is about waiting."

"What about Sampson?" Bethany asked. "Will he be able to remain here?"

"Sampson should stay here . . . at least until you know where you will be in a few months."

She nodded. Behind her the sun had left the sky.

"Are you going to be my mentor?"

"No, Bethany. I am not."

Chapter 18

The conservatory was a day's carriage ride from London, nestled in the middle of the virgin, serene countryside, untouched by the hustle of England's most crowded city. After arriving at the Old Bedford Park depot earlier that morning, Bethany waited for hours before finally renting a hack. No one had met her and Mary at the depot. Perhaps Ian should have been more specific about a way to make contact with her associate waiting so she could have at least known how to leave a message behind.

Her chest tightened. Neither she nor Ian had spoken since he walked out of the fencing studio. He'd ridden away last night. No goodbyes. No promises. That morning she had left Queen's Staircase, feeling right where they had begun and ended three years ago. He was still married. And she'd been a fool.

Feeling the sunlight on her face through the carriage window, Bethany opened her eyes and peered outside. The rolling parkland was bathed in a crystalline white after a late afternoon dusting of snow, and she tried to concentrate on its solemn beauty.

She could see the great stone halls of the conservatory through the trees. Classes would not be in session for another few weeks, and for the most part their arrival went unheralded except by the few deer in the park.

The academic year was divided into three terms of eight weeks. During sessions, women of all ages lived in the wings of the manor, which once belonged to the Dowager Duchess of Bedford and had been endowed to the founders of the conservatory two decades ago. And while women still were not admitted to the University of London for degrees, and where Cambridge and Oxford was more traditional and catered to men, this university offered a place for young women of all backgrounds. Since graduating to a teacher's assistant, Bethany lived in one of the more private cottages that housed the staff across the park. For some, like her, this school was home year-round.

"It's good to be home, mum." Mary turned to her, bright-eyed and eager. "Aren't ye excited? We'll be among friends again."

Mary had slept the early morning hours away on the train, while Bethany had listened to the relentless *clack, clack* of the wheels, marking the miles. "Mmmmm," she murmured halfheartedly.

"Do ye think Miss Charlene is in residence, yet, mum?"

Bethany leaned her head against the squabs. "I don't know, Mary."

"I don't think she has ever cared for it here, mum. Not like you and some of the others."

"Why do you believe that?"

"You both began university together, mum. You have graduated to a teacher's assistant. She has barely passed her exams."

Charlene still had another year to attend before she

graduated. Lord Whitley sat at the head of the Board of Governors. He expected her to be a shining example of feminine academia. Not because he adhered to his daughter's intellectual achievements, but because he would not tolerate embarrassment if she failed him. Strange that Bethany recognized that about Lord Whitley now.

She thought then of little Adam and wondered what would become of him if his father turned out to be the monster Lord Ware and the league council thought he was.

Bethany turned her attention to the outside as the carriage pulled onto the main drive. She bid the driver to pull up to the main building that housed the headmistress, Mrs. Harriet Filburt, who arrived only last fall.

Told by the receptionist that the headmistress was in her office, Bethany proceeded up the stairs to the second floor. Mrs. Filburt appeared in her late forties, though pretty if one looked past her solemn personality, especially when she removed her spectacles. But the woman had a way of looking at a person and reading one's thoughts, which made most students uncomfortable.

She was sitting at her desk when Bethany entered the small, cluttered chamber filled with dusty books and wooden filing cabinets overflowing with students' records. Bethany was surprised by how little the office had changed in the months since Mrs. Filburt's arrival. In fact, the room remained impersonal and cold, looking as if she never spent time here at all.

Mrs. Filburt looked up from her work, and surprise flashed across her face before she carefully schooled her features to a polite blankness. "Miss Munro." She set down her pen. Not a single strand of her gunmetal gray hair strayed from the harsh chignon resting above her nape. "We did not receive word of your pending arrival."

"I have been out of touch, Mrs. Filburt. I thought I should let you know I've returned." She was unfamiliar with Mrs. Filburt's mood. Her old headmistress at least knew how to smile. This one did not.

Bethany's gaze homed in on the cabinet behind the desk. "If you don't mind, I will take the keys to the science laboratory. With classes starting in a few weeks, I thought perhaps I could begin preparing the classroom. Has a new teacher been hired to replace Mrs. Langley yet?"

Mrs. Filburt remained seated. "We've candidates interviewing, Miss Munro. We should have a new instructor by the time we finish renovating the lab. It is currently closed."

Closed? "I don't understand."

"The foundation has granted us a significant increase in our funds this year. The Board of Governors has approved extensive updates to our facilities. The work will be completed before the new session begins."

"I didn't know," Bethany said. "I wasn't told."

Mrs. Filburt's mouth turned up in a stiff, social smile. "Are you told about everything that goes on in this school, Miss Munro?"

Heat flooded Bethany's cheeks. "I apologize if I seemed impertinent, ma'am. It is only that Mrs. Langley—"

"Mrs. Langley is no longer with us. I will be hiring a new science instructor and if she chooses, she may keep you on as her assistant. But until that time, you might wish to occupy yourself elsewhere—read, attend chapel, visit your family. Session does not begin here for another few weeks. Now, please, be a good girl, will you?" she said dismissively, returning to the papers in front of her. "And close the door on your way out."

Bethany remained standing in the doorway. Her fingers wrapped themselves in her velvet skirt, and she rued that she hadn't thought to remove her traveling cloak. Its presence only highlighted her ability to leave as easily as she'd arrived "Has Miss Dubois arrived yet?"

"She returned some days ago," Mrs. Filburt replied, busily scrabbling notes on the tablet in front of her. After a moment, the pen stopped and she looked up. "She said you left Whitley Court with a man."

Accusation flavored the statement. Students and teachers lost their positions for far less. Bethany always behaved in an exemplary fashion . . . most of the time when others were looking. "I had gotten ill," she found herself explaining, the half-truth not as fluid sounding as she'd hoped. "I was quite, well—chaperoned, Mrs. Filburt. My maid can attest to that."

Mrs. Filburt thrummed her fingers. "Is there a problem, Miss Munro?"

"No." Bethany turned and shut the door, her skirts rasping at the swift motion. She felt as if she'd just been spanked.

The hall was dark and quiet, nearly as cold inside as it was out. *This used to be a friendly place.* She walked outside into the chill air. She had sent the hack on to the cottage across the park and proceeded on the path. In the springtime, tulips and crocuses would bloom here. Right now, the grounds were an ugly brown covered with patches of snow. She walked toward the outer buildings and noted the dispensary and commissary closed. Just beyond the thatched rooftops sat a large unpretentious building of whitewashed stone shielded by an evergreen hedge. The laboratory and science building. She stole a glance over her shoulder back at Mrs. Filburt's office and saw her standing in the window just before the blinds snapped shut.

Bethany kept walking. A shiver went over her. She pulled her cloak tighter, still feeling that probing look aimed between her shoulder blades. Mary stood out front of the cottage. "This place gives me the creepies, mum," she said as Bethany swept past her into her cottage.

"I couldn't agree with you more."

Five minutes later, Bethany stood in the middle of her chambers, breathing in the familiar scents of frankincense and myrrh and letting her gaze touch the portraits of her family sitting atop her dresser.

Only this place no longer felt like home, she realized, as she removed her bonnet and cloak and looked around her quarters where she and Mary had lived comfortably for the past six months. She noted none of the trunks she'd left behind at Whitley Court had been delivered yet. At the very least, she would have to make a new batch of toiletries.

She sighed. When the new session began two other teacher's assistants would be living in this cottage. Charlene had clearly moved out, Bethany realized as she walked into the cozy parlor and found most of the bric-a-brac gone and the walls bare. She pulled aside the draperies and stared out across the parkland. A thin ribbon of smoke visible above the trees came from another cottage beyond the trees. It was the only one that exhibited signs of human inhabitation. If that was where Charlene lived now, she had not moved far.

Bethany would have to confront her. Eventually.

Ian would be in London perhaps by tomorrow. She didn't know.

"I feel as if I'm living in a blind," she said as Mary placed coal into the stove. "We need a newspaper. We also have to locate the man sent to meet us. The town is not that big and there are only two hostelries. I don't understand why he wasn't at the depot."

"I can return to the depot when I go in for supplies tomorrow, mum. Perhaps he was not properly informed of our arrival."

"Perhaps."

Bethany dropped the edge of the curtain. She hadn't thought about supplies. For all of her independence she'd always been living with or traveling with someone who managed the particulars of day-to-day survival. She had never truly *been* on her own. "Do we *have* anything to eat?"

Bethany waited until the next afternoon after a decent night's sleep and breakfast before finally gathering her nerves into one forceful bout of determination and making the trek to see Charlene. The path was damp with melted snow and thick humus from the dead leaves of fall still littering the grounds. The tangy scent of woods and foliage tickled her nose. Ducking her head against the frigid wind, she quickened her pace. Mary had taken one of the grooms from the stable and gone into town some hours ago.

Charlene's maid answered Bethany's knock at the door, but only after Bethany had knocked four times. The door squeaked open and Charlene's moon-face servant peered out at her. Her eyes widened. "Mum," she whispered almost in relief. The door opened wider and she filled the entryway. "You've returned. All of a piece, you have. We weren't sure where you had disappeared, or if you would be with us again. But here you are."

Mrs. Pembroke had been with Charlene for as long as Bethany remembered and in all that time, Bethany had never seen her so gaunt. She wore no cap. Her short white hair was spiked as if she'd run her fingers through it a thousand times.

"I'm in good health, Mrs. Pembroke. I arrived back yesterday."

"Oh, mum." The woman twisted her soiled apron in her hands. "Miss Charlene is upstairs. She has been asking for you."

"Is she ill?"

"Somethin' terrible. I should warn ye, she is . . . she's been distressed. Just after lunch, I finally sent for Mrs. Filburt."

Bethany brushed past the older woman and hurried up the narrow stairs to the cottage's upper rooms. Drawn curtains shut out the daylight. She found Charlene in her room, lying in the center of her large bed. Plump white lace pillows surrounded her, making her look small and insignificant. When her friend turned her head, her sunken cheeks and hollow eyes shocked Bethany. For a moment Bethany couldn't speak.

"Charlene?"

She was looking at Bethany as if she didn't know her, then recognition clicked behind the soft brown eyes and tears welled.

"You came," Charlene whispered. "I didn't think you would."

Bethany sat on the edge of the mattress and pressed a palm to Charlene's brow. A vicious bruise marred her pale skin. Bethany turned Charlene's cheek into the light. She had been trying to conceal the bruise and a cut below her eye with face powder. This was a recent injury. "What *happened* to you, Charlene?"

Charlene turned her face away and stared vacantly at the wall. The room smelled sour, indicting she must not have bathed in days. Anger rose inside Bethany. Why hadn't someone changed the sheets or been in here to air the room? There was another scent present as well, but Bethany could not place it. Antiseptic?

She turned to the maid who had not stepped into the room as if whatever ailment affected her mistress would touch her. "This is not something caused by distress," Bethany snapped, stripping off her gloves. "Who hit her?"

"She fell, mum. She come down with the queazies two days ago. She fainted and hit her head on the banister. Dr. Goodman said it was merely a stomach ailment making her ill and that she should recover."

"Where is her dog?"

"The little nipper died, mum." Again the apron twisting.

She pointed to Charlene's dressing table. Perfume bottles lay scattered over the top as if swept aside by an angry hand. Powder sprinkled the wall and floor. "Her ladyship found him on the rug. Two days ago, mum."

Bethany rose and walked over to the dressing table. She drew open the draperies for more light and unlatched the window to let in air. "What happened over here?"

"Lady Charlene's been distressed. After she and her father come to blows, he sent her here, and she doesn't like it, throwing things around."

Bethany's gaze stopped on the familiar palm-size container holding face powder. The one identical to the one

Bethany had left behind at Whitley Court. She looked at the powder dust on the floor. "And the dog died after . . . ?" Her heart pounding, she started to lift the amber jar and paused. The smell stopped her The powder was the source of the antiseptic smell. She suddenly remembered the way her own powder had smelled.

She folded her fingers into her palm and stepped away from the table. She and Charlene had made that powder from the same batch of mica and iron oxides Bethany used to make her own powders just before she'd gone to Whitley Court.

Charlene had left her own jar here at the conservatory. Bethany had not. Powder was all over the dressing table.

If Charlene had just returned to the conservatory . . . and now, she was ill.

Bethany's panicked thoughts flew further back. When had *she* begun feeling unwell? She hadn't started using the toiletries until after she'd arrived at Whitley Court. But she had been queasy those first nights.

A knock sounded downstairs. Mrs. Pembroke mumbled something and skittered away.

"Am I going to die?"

Charlene's whisper shot through her, whirling Bethany around.

"No." Bethany returned to Charlene's bedside. "You aren't going to die."

Charlene grabbed onto Bethany's hand. "I didn't think I would see you again." Her weak voice trembled.

"Why ever not?" Bethany tried to keep her voice light. Unafraid. Someone was coming up the stairs. "I live at the conservatory, after all."

"No one ever comes back."

A chill crawled down her spine. "Why would you say that?"

Confusion touched Charlene's eyes. "I'm going to have a baby, Bethany."

"What?"

The rustle of fabric in the doorway turned Bethany's head. Still wearing her cloak, Mrs. Filburt stood next to Mrs. Pembroke. Gloved hands rose to remove the hood. "How long has she been like this?" Mrs. Filburt demanded of the older woman.

"She come down worse last night, mum."

Suddenly pushing herself onto one elbow, Charlene pointed a trembling finger at Mrs. Filburt standing just inside the room. "Get out of here!"

Bethany gasped, "Charlene—"

"I want her out." Charlene clasped Bethany's hand. "Make her leave, Bethany. Make her go away. I don't want her here. She'll bring Father back." Her voice lowered to a desperate rasp. "Don't let her bring my father."

Mrs. Filburt turned to the maid and, stripping off her gloves, snapped, "Get Dr. Goodman here now."

The gray head bobbed. "Yes, mum."

Charlene gave a hysterical sob. "They should hang him, hang him by his neck for everything he has done to me, but they won't."

Mrs. Filburt stood beside the bed and grabbed Charlene's chin. "Charlene? Look at me. Have you taken something again?"

But Charlene turned pleading eyes on Bethany. Her tears welled and poured hotly against Bethany's sleeve and she wrapped her fingers around Charlene's. "I won't leave you, Charlene."

The physician arrived a half hour later. Bethany backed away. Unnoticed and helpless as she watched her friend's struggle and listened to her sobs, she stood against the wall as Mrs. Filburt held Charlene down while Dr. Goodman injected her with morphine.

Bethany knew enough about medicine to understand that morphine was a powerful sedative. If the doctor thought that was what Charlene needed then she would have to trust him. She did not know Dr. Goodman well. He'd come to work at the conservatory nearly the same time as did Mrs. Filburt. He was in his sixties, balding with gray muttonchop whiskers and deep lines that marked his mouth, the kind of lines that came from smiling a lot.

She'd never seen him less than cheerful when he'd treated the various ails he'd been called upon to fix. But a shadow marked his eyes now, and, looking at Charlene, Bethany was suddenly afraid for Charlene's life.

"She should sleep for a while," Dr. Goodman said as he stood and scraped his hand through his hair, but he'd spoken to Mrs. Filburt. "We'll need to contact his lordship. Do you want to be the one to give him the news?"

"You knew she was suicidal. Someone should have been here."

As if sensing her presence, they both suddenly turned.

A knot of dread tightened around her chest. "I'm staying," Bethany said flatly, as if they had a right to look at her as if she were an intruder.

They could *try* to drag her out of here.

But suddenly she was truly afraid, as much for herself as she was for Charlene. She didn't really know Mrs. Filburt or Dr. Goodman. Neither of them had made an effort to get close to the students since their arrival.

Mrs. Filburt dragged up her cloak and swept it around her shoulders. "Let her stay. Someone needs to remain here in case Miss Dubois's condition changes. I'll send for Lord Whitley. Mrs. Pembroke is downstairs. I suggest you interview the woman and find out what the girl may have ingested."

After Mrs. Filburt left. Dr. Goodman snapped shut his bag and looked at Bethany. "I'll have Mrs. Pembroke bring up water."

He strode past Bethany and into the corridor. A moment later, she heard him talking to Mrs. Pembroke and her distressed replies.

"They'll bring Papa," Charlene whispered from the bed.

Bethany turned her head. She dropped to the mattress beside Charlene and brushed the matted hair from her face. "Did you take something to hurt yourself?"

Charlene's velvet brown eyes welled with tears. "No."

"Does your father know about the baby?"

Charlene's dark head shook. "I didn't know where else to go." The hands Bethany held tightened. "I'm so sorry. I'm so sorry for everything."

Bethany's eyes grew liquid. "You'll be fine, you'll see."

"None of it matters anymore."

"Of course it does. I'm here. You aren't alone."

A smile cracked her friend's sallow face. "Always the crusader," she whispered, "trying to save the world. I never could be that strong."

Bethany shook her head. She was the least strong person in the world. "You're wrong, Charlene. You are stronger than you think you are."

The fire crackled in the hearth, warmth and silence blending into an odd sort of truce between them.

Bethany remained with Charlene for the rest of the afternoon as she lay in bed going in and out of sleep, always waking if Bethany moved her hand from hers, so Bethany stayed close to her friend. She helped her eat and drink.

"I can see them," Charlene whispered. "They're here."

"No one is here but us."

Dr. Goodman had been by an hour before. But no one was here now.

"When I close my eyes, I see them. Can't you hear them?"

A shudder ran through her. "Hear what?" Nothing Charlene said made sense. "Charlene—"

"Tick. Tock. The mouse ran up the clock." Charlene giggled. *"Listen!"* Wild-eyed, she suddenly peered at the door, her face growing more ashen. "Can't you hear them?"

Bethany twisted around, but the room remained empty. Her friend was seeing shadows that weren't there, hearing voices that existed only in her head.

"The rats," Charlene whispered. *"The rats!"*

Bethany's voice paused in the catch of her breath. "Rats?"

"How can you not hear them?" Charlene pressed the heels of her hands against her head. "Make them go away. I can't bear the noise. I can't bear it. Please make them go away."

But Bethany was too shocked to respond. Charlene tossed her head back and forth, murmuring incoherently about rats and blood. Familiar and horrifying.

Had they both seen the same vision in the stairwell at Whitley Court? Bethany gripped Charlene's shoulders. "Look at me. You were there, weren't you?" Bethany gave Charlene's shoulders a shake as she tried to get Charlene's attention. "Weren't you?"

"No. No. I wasn't. I wasn't anywhere."

"I followed *your* dog, Charlene."

"No! Sir John didn't mean to do it. He didn't mean it. It wasn't he. I swear."

Bethany pulled away but Charlene's hand wrapped around her wrist. "Papa will kill him if he finds him."

"Is Sir John alive, Charlene?" she whispered.

"You have to help me. Oh, God . . ." Charlene clutched Bethany's hand, her wide eyes filled with panic. "Make them stop," she cried, her sobs reminiscent of Bethany's own nightmarish fight that night in the carriage when Ian had taken her and left Whitley Court.

Everything was *exactly* as it had been that awful night in the carriage. The hallucinations mixed with terrible memories that would never go away.

A chill sliding down her spine, Bethany dropped her gaze to the clawed hand wrapped around her wrist, then to the powder traces beneath Charlene's fingernails. In a panic, she nearly tore Charlene's hand away as she sprang to her feet.

Bethany swiped her palms on the counterpane as if she were on fire and burning, then backed quickly away from the bed. But . . . she had already touched the stuff, she realized in horror, looking down at her hands.

Bethany returned to the dresser. For a moment, she was afraid. Then she withdrew a handkerchief from her pocket and wrapped it around the jar. She had to get this to someone who would know what to do, an alchemist, anyone outside the walls of this school.

She knotted the handkerchief to contain the powder.

Bethany turned, only to be drawn up short as she nearly collided with Charlene. She stepped back. Charlene had a maniacal air, with her hair uncombed and wearing only her thin batiste shift. "That's mine. Give it back."

For a moment, Bethany could not breathe. "You need help, Charlene."

"You don't like me, do you?"

"That's not—"

"You're just like *her*. You do Papa's bidding."

"Charlene . . . listen to me."

"Everyone *says* you are in love with my father.

Bethany stumbled backward and caught her hand on the vanity, knocking a bottle of cologne to the floor, where it shattered and filled the room with heady scent. "I'm not in love with your father."

She struggled not to be desperate, but Charlene was driven by madness, a madness of which Bethany knew something herself. Nor was she eager to wrestle over this jar of powder. A memory of herself hovering in a corner of the carriage, tearing at her own hair, danced across Bethany's panicked mind.

"Give it back!" Charlene launched herself at Bethany.

The collision sent Bethany crashing against the window she'd opened earlier. She grabbed for the draperies. Fabric ripped from the moorings on the ceiling at the same instant she and Charlene fell against the casement. The windows slammed opened and together, Bethany and Charlene tumbled out.

Chapter 19

Dying never felt this good, encased in soft down and warmth like a swaddled babe in her mother's arms.

But the pain in her ribs and head had not slackened, and, presently, Bethany heard herself groan and opened her eyes.

A face appeared making her blink at the sudden apparition. That was when it hit her all over again. Throbbing pain. The light pounding into her skull came from the lamp he was holding and set beside her bed. Darkness lay beyond the amber circle.

"Miss Munro," said the scowling man peering into her eyes. "You have a concussion."

Pressing her fingers to her temples, Bethany knew she would never have to feign a headache again. Her head throbbed in waves. She shut her eyes. "Is that all?"

Dr. Goodman suddenly chuckled. "Why? Are you disappointed you did not break your neck?"

His bedside manner brought her gaze back to bear on him. She could actually understand him. The thought startled her. She was not hallucinating. She had not drifted off into madness, as she'd feared. She was lying in her own bed.

She pressed a hand to her temple. "How long have I been unconscious?"

"Most of the night. You're a very fortunate young woman, Miss Munro. The shrubbery beneath the window cushioned your fall." He held up a syringe.

The jolt of panic that seized her told her she was indeed conscious. A new wave of anxiety spilled through her. What had happened to the jar of face powder she'd been holding?

"I do not need an injection."

"It's only morphine." Dr. Goodman looked over the terrible-looking needle at her, speaking as if morphine was not a powerful medicine. "Believe it or not, I am doing you a favor. It is best that you sleep tonight. You will feel better in the morning."

"Where is Charlene?"

"She is currently in the infirmary," he said without lowering the syringe. "She's better off there. Mrs. Filburt is with her right now. Her father is on his way."

But as Bethany waited for the room to stop spinning, she couldn't throw off the horrible feeling that if Charlene were taken off these school grounds, no one would see her again. Just like Mrs. Langley.

"You need to sleep, Miss Munro."

Bethany wrapped her hand around the wrist holding the syringe, taking him by surprise. The only person she trusted completely with her life was not in this room.

"An injection is not necessary." She didn't fake the tremble in her voice. But clearly, it was not in her best interest to appear too healthy. "I couldn't get out of bed if I tried."

She must have looked or at least sounded weak enough. The tension left his arm. She remained alert, prepared to scream her lungs out if necessary, though she doubted she could reach the pitch and volume it would take to be effective. Or if there were anyone around who would hear or care that she was in distress. She suddenly realized how very much alone she was.

"Very well, Miss Munro." Dr. Goodman stood and opened his black leather bag. "But you need to sleep. Stay in bed. I will check on your progress in the morning."

Relief made her weak. "Where is my maid?"

"She was quite hysterical after your fall. I gave her something to help her sleep. She is lying on the settee in the salon. She'll be fine in a few hours when she awakens."

Would she? Bethany's heart raced but somehow she kept the apprehension from her voice as she thanked him for help.

Dr. Goodman turned down the lamp until the light snuffed out and only the smell of oil remained in the air. Bethany waited a few minutes, listening to the sound of the man's footsteps in the corridor and finally to the front door of the cottage shutting. She managed to pull herself out of bed, noticing for the first time that she wore only her shift. Someone had undressed her and put her to bed.

Yanking a blanket over her shoulders, she sat up and waited for the dizziness to pass. She made her way to the window and carefully pulled up the edge of the drapery to peer outside. A mist hovered over the conservatory grounds, but she heard the crunch of footsteps in gravel and snow and she looked past the drive to see Dr. Goodman's form in the darkness.

He had not even asked her why Charlene would push her out a window. He had asked her nothing about the incident.

Her eyes continued to track him in the darkness. He hadn't taken the path back to the infirmary, but had headed into the woods. It wasn't until he vanished into the trees that Bethany realized someone else was there in the darkness. A moment later, the shadow became more distinct as moonlight touched the cloaked shape of a man. Then it too vanished and Bethany was left wondering if she had imagined the entire scene. She tried to keep her eyes opened and focused. Finally, she lowered the edge of the curtain.

She found Mary asleep on the settee in the salon just as Dr. Goodman said she would be and knelt beside her. Bethany found the glass Mary drank from on the floor and sniffed the rim, smelling opiates. Bethany put a hand on her shoulder. Mary's eyes fluttered open. "Mum." She smiled groggily.

Bethany was so relieved to discover her merely asleep, she almost wept.

"Is it already time to rise for breakfast?"

"No, it isn't yet dawn." Bethany smoothed the hair from Mary's brow. "Did you find the man Lord Ware sent to meet us when you went to town today?"

"No, mum." Her eyes fluttered closed.

Bethany fought to keep her own eyes opened and to stay alert. "Mary? Do you remember if anyone ever talked about where Mrs. Filburt or Dr. Goodman came from?"

Mary smiled dreamily. "He is very nice. Don't you think?"

Nice like a spider, Bethany thought. "Mary?" When Mary didn't respond, Bethany gave her shoulders a gentle shake. It would be useless to ask Mary if anyone had found anything outside the window where she'd fallen.

Bethany sat back on her heels. What had happened to the powder? And why hadn't she gotten ill again?

Her mind went back to when she had been at Whitley Court.

Bethany had quit using her own powder after the first few days at Whitley Court because it had had a strange odor. Except the day Sir John had died. She'd knocked her hand against the jar while she'd been grabbing for a serviette and spilled it on her injured palm. Within hours, the poison had gotten into her blood. That was the key!

Charlene had had an open wound on her face.

The poison became lethal when it entered by way of an open wound.

Bethany walked to the window and looked out across the mist-shrouded parkland. And whatever was in the powder must have come from the laboratory . . . a laboratory closed again for a second renovation in six months.

Dawn broke through ominous black clouds. Even before the scullery maids in the main hall rose and stoked the breakfast fires to life for the few residents living within the halls of the school, Bethany dressed warmly and set out to find Dr. Goodman's tracks in the woods. She had no difficulty finding the place where he had disappeared into the woods last night. The weather had grown colder since yesterday and, looking up at the dark sky, she picked up her pace.

More than one set of footprints merged beneath the trees where she'd seen him vanish into the darkness. So she *had* seen someone else. But she was not a tracker and could not tell if the one set had followed or joined the other.

Sleet had started to fall and pebbled against the tree branches, reducing visibility. She pulled back the hood of her cloak to better observe the footprints. Both sets led to the science laboratory. Backing away, she returned to Charlene's cottage and rooted around the area where she'd plummeted out the window the day before, looking for the powder jar. Her heart raced so fast her hands trembled. The snow had compacted to chunks of ice in places where the wind had blown it against the cottage. After awhile, with her lungs and fingers burning from the cold, Bethany wanted to beat her fists on the ground, frustrated because she couldn't spend anymore time looking. She was already reckless for being outside at all.

The rattle of an approaching carriage drew her up.

Pushing to her feet, she stumbled to the corner of the cottage and peered around the thick hedges. The winds whipped wet and cold around her, and she pulled her cloak tighter about her shoulders. Lord Whitley's stately carriage, pulled by six black horses, thundered beneath the stone archway, wending its way through the sprawling parkland toward the conservatory.

Her heartbeat faltered for a frozen moment. He was here.

She whirled away in a swish of petticoats and starched poplin, her foot bumped an object, knocking it into the hedge.

Bethany dropped to her knees. The powder jar!

But while her heart raced, her smile froze on her face. For a dragging moment, she stared incredulous at a pair of muddy black Italian shoes that had suddenly appeared on the other side of the hedge. Shoes she'd last seen on a dead person.

Sir John knelt and picked up the jar. "Is this what you were looking for, Miss Munro?

Chapter 20

Ian reined in his horse just at the edge of the woodland copse beside a lazy stream journeying over rocks and ice. The moon had climbed high into a cloudless black sky spangled with stars, but a chill breeze sifted through the branches. Where was Jameson?

He braced a boot, dulled by the dirt of travel, on the low stone wall, which demarcated the beginning of the conservatory's property. A west wind at his back whipped at his dark woolen cloak. All around him, the naked branches clicked, then settled as the gust died.

He looked east toward the lights of the conservatory, its mullioned windows reflecting the warmth from the lamps within. Clustered about the great wing were the low-roofed outbuildings, surrounded by elms and maples, their branches now barren for the season. When he'd finally arrived at the inn outside of town, he'd received Jameson's message to meet him at the low stone wall.

A match flared, and Ian saw the glow of a cheroot. Jameson sat on the ridge of rocks on the other side of the wildwood hedge. "It took you long enough to get here."

Ian dismounted. He wrapped the reins of the horse

around the lower branch of a birch. "Where is Bethany?"

Jameson handed Ian the pair of field glasses sitting next to him on the rock. He pointed to the small thatched-roof abode sitting two hundred yards east of the main school wing. "She lives in the corner chambers."

Ian shifted the glasses to the outer buildings. He stood beneath a barren oak branch to keep the moonlight from sky-lighting him. "I received your message yesterday," he said wryly. "'*I miss you? I can't live without you?*'"

Jameson exhaled a cloud of smoke and reached inside his vest pocket. His teeth flashed white in the darkness, like the wolf Ian had trapped one winter near Queen's Staircase. "Would you rather she have said, 'Help, help, we're all going to die'?" Jameson tapped the ash from his cheroot.

Ian frowned. "When did she send this? How?"

"It seems your man never showed at the depot."

"Bloody hell," he said between his teeth. "And we're just now finding out?"

"She somehow managed to send this telegram via Queen's Staircase three days ago," Jameson said. "Knowing every man jack between here and there was privy to the message, she was rather innovative, don't you think? Your man at Queen's Staircase knew where I was and brought the missive to me at the Wayfarer's Inn. I knew where you were. A nice progressive chain of events." He returned his attention to the main hall. "I've been here since this afternoon. From what I heard in town, Miss Dubois isn't expected to live out the week."

Ian narrowed his eyes. "What happened?"

"Some form of poisoning. Then she had an accident

and never regained consciousness. Whitley hasn't moved her." Jameson inhaled from the cheroot and said thoughtfully, "For a bastard, who may be responsible for killing the Home Secretary and the man's family, Whitley has the grieving father routine down pat.

"This also came to you." Jameson handed him a sheaf of paper. "From your Alchemist at Queen's Staircase. It seems he has been in a hospital for the past week and only just returned to his shop. The crystalline powder you found in the cavern at Whitley Court nearly killed him."

Ian held the letter against a shard of moonlight.

"It's a mixture of mercury and phenol," Jameson said. "The compound used to make an antiseptic and disinfectant better known as carbolic acid . . . and more egregiously it is used in making explosives. Clearly, whatever was being made in those caverns was moved somewhere else." After a moment, Jameson said, "Whitley sits at the head of the Board of Governors at this school. This university has a stellar science laboratory."

Ian shoved both notes into his pocket, his stomach twisting. "Mercury can cause hallucinations."

"If it doesn't kill you first."

Ian locked the field glasses on the infirmary, but he struggled against the urge to swing the glasses toward the cottage. "Bethany had been at Whitley Court following the trail of someone she believed was murdered there," he said. "Mrs. Langley was the science instructor here until her disappearance last fall."

"Then we bloody may have found our connection, Rockwell."

Christ. He needed to reach Bethany. The instinct was bone deep and pulled at his legs like some godless puppet master pulling at him. He was so engrossed by his thoughts and his need to find Bethany, he wasn't aware of Jameson's hand on his shoulder until he tried to move.

"She's a brave thing, to be sure," Jameson said. "When this is over, I'd like to get to know her better, boy-o."

"Go to hell, Rory."

"She knows what she's doing, Rockwell. I got a note to that little maid of hers today. Miss Munro knows I'm here."

Ian's eyes dropped to Jameson's hand. Ian was willing to allow reason to change his mind, but he would not be backed into a corner to see it done. Not this time. This time he would not let Jameson snatch him away from Bethany. Jameson released him. They remained at a standoff for all of the next ten seconds.

Ian felt sick to his stomach. Yesterday, he'd received Jameson's message just before he was due to appear before the council. He'd turned around, walked away from responsibilities, and ridden directly here, nearly killing his horse in the process. Now he had to rein in those same emotions. He knew he had to pull himself together. He was behaving exactly like some bloody novice. He was behaving like a man who was in love not a man on a mission.

Goddammit. He tore at his anger. He didn't need this.

He clawed a hand through his hair. He was behaving like a man who'd been a bloody idiot, walking away from her the way he had. He'd tied up his heart in the past with so many knots, he strangled himself on his own rope.

Jameson began telling Ian in more detail what had happened since Bethany arrived at the conservatory. That Miss Dubois suffered the ill effects of some hallucinogen brought home the reality that Bethany was fortunate to be alive.

Ian raised the field glasses to his eyes, panning the grounds, then froze on what looked like the main hall, as the front door suddenly swung open and a woman—not Bethany—stepped out from beneath its gabled roof. "I don't know why I let you provoke me . . ." he said, his voice trailing.

Jameson chuckled. "You've turned into a cream puff, Rockwell. You've been playing too safe for years now. You used to like women who took risks."

Ian restrained himself from saying what he was thinking as he continued to watch the woman. Wrapped in a gray cloak and prim bonnet, she was undistinguishable, yet something familiar touched him and he felt his hands tighten on the field glasses. Maybe it was the way she paused on the porch and looked across the parkland, marking every change in her surroundings, committing every detail to memory. Such an action was something Ian did as a habit.

"Did you inform Ware you were coming here?" Jameson asked, but Ian didn't lower the glasses. "What's wrong?"

Ian lost the woman in the mist. But before his mind could wrap around the conclusion he'd just come to, Jameson rasped, "Someone's coming."

A rustling came from the hawthorn scrub. But Ian had already melted into the shadows, a knife in his hand, kept low so as not to pick up a glint of moonlight on the blade.

Another twig snapped.

"Mr. Jameson?" Bethany's quiet rasp came from Ian's

left. In the darkness beneath the trees, no one could see the other. "If I knew how to whistle in code, I *would*."

Jameson appeared almost as a conjuring act in front of her and then froze in the frosty stillness of the glade. He and Ian saw Sir John at the same time.

"Wait!" Bethany rasped too late.

Sir John, suddenly seeming to panic, brandished a gun at the same time Jameson's gun appeared.

"Get away from me, both of you." Sir John grabbed Bethany. "I told you—"

"*Put* your weapon down, Sir John," she hissed.

"Do as she says, Howard," Ian said from the shadows beside Bethany. "Bloody, now!"

Sir John whirled with her in his arms and aimed the gun at Ian. "Bastards," He backed a step, swinging the gun from Ian to Jameson.

"I knew I shouldn't have trusted her."

"Now that's harsh, Howard," Ian said, "coming from you."

"Do what he says, Sir John!" Bethany rasped.

"Who died in the stairwell?" Ian asked. "Your steward, Meacham? Or some other unlucky bastard?"

"I didn't murder Meacham. It was an accident—"

"Stop it! All of you!" Bethany's voice broke a little. She swung her gaze from Jameson to Ian. "I don't like this any better than the two of you!" She looked up at Sir John, holding her against him. The weaseling coward. Bethany wanted to strike him like she had when he'd come crying to her for help. His unkempt appearance bordered on wild. He had sworn on a bible he'd not murdered Mrs. Langley, sworn he'd not poisoned anyone. He'd begged her help to contact the authorities. "Put that gun away or you *will* be dead," she warned. "I didn't bring you out here to start a gunfight and get us all killed."

To Ian, who looked as lethal to Bethany as he sounded, she said, "I promised him safety."

Only then did Ian's eyes shift to hers. Moonlight found the curve of his jaw and touched his mouth. Awareness of him slammed against her.

She had not expected to see him and her heart raced. Unexpectedly, emotion swamped her.

Unlike Sir John, who looked weak and disheveled with his unshaven jaw half washed in moon shadow, Ian looked dangerous and capable of leaping the distance separating them and crushing the man's neck. "Let her go, Howard," his voice lashed out.

Then he turned the knife in his hand away and carefully dropped it on the ground. His cloak opened to reveal a careless necktie over a white shirt, dark gray trousers, and tall riding boots that hugged his calves, not something one would wear to a clandestine meeting in the dark. But in that brief instance when he'd spread his arms, she glimpsed the leather sheath beneath his jacket and knew he had a gun in his possession.

"She promised she knew someone who would listen to me." Sir John's voice began to fade along with his fight. The gun in his hand trembled. "I didn't know it would be you, Rockwell."

"Seeing as how we have such a fond history, I don't see why not."

"Put the gun away, Sir John," Bethany said on a quieter note. She knew Jameson had come up behind him. "Unless you *want* to die."

He exhaled a pent-up breath and held out his hands,

palms up in surrender. Jameson eased the weapon from Sir John's grip. "I suggest you sit," he said, pointing to the rocks a safer distance from Ian.

Sir John did as Jameson said, leaving Bethany facing Ian. He took a step toward her then seemed to stop himself. Silence bore down on the moment. She couldn't go to him, certainly not in front of the others.

"Jameson's note didn't tell me you were here," she said.

Ian moved into the same moonlight bathing her. "Is that supposed to make me feel better?"

She gave him a thin smile. "Sir John came to *me*. What was I supposed to do? Faint?"

Ian shot a murderous look behind her. Sir John struggled back to his feet from his place on the rocks. "Don't you understand? You have to help me. I'm not safe anywhere."

"You aren't safe here either," Ian said, clearly unmoved. "You're lucky I don't break your bloody neck where you stand. Who died in the stairwell?"

"Tell them everything you told me," Bethany said.

Moonlight flickered on the hard set of Sir John's mouth. "It was Meacham. He may have been my steward, but he worked for Whitley. He would have just left me in that stairwell. That's what they do. They take you into the tunnels . . . Charlene saved my life." His eyes pleaded with Ian as if he knew Ian was the one he had to convince. "He was a bloody assassin. That's what the bastard did. He took people down into the passageways. No one ever comes back."

Bethany knuckled away a tear. "That's what happened to Mrs. Langley, Ian," she whispered.

Ian moved nearer to her, his warmth shrouding her back like a protective cloak. "That dog wasn't left in Miss Munro's room by accident, Howard."

"That was Charlene's idea." Sir John turned accusing eyes on Bethany. "Someone had to find the body. Since she was the one who bloody destroyed my life in the first place, it only seemed fitting that person should be Miss Munro."

Bethany could feel tension invade Ian's muscles. "She's the only truly innocent person in all this, Howard," he said in a quiet dangerous voice. "If you weren't fucking Whitley's nineteen-year-old daughter, you'd still be one big happy family sitting around the table making plans to blow up the world. Instead, Whitley discovered the truth and decided to end your affair with his daughter his own way."

"What exactly do you want from us, Howard?" Jameson asked.

"I *want* Whitley's head on a platter. I want him to bloody pay for what he's done to my life. He won't rest until I'm dead. Whitley ordered you killed, too, Rockwell. It was supposed to look like an attempt on Whitley's life. Only the assassin missed."

"Did he poison Miss Munro and his own daughter?" Jameson asked.

"His lordship may have no problem murdering an opponent or eliminating a threat to his family, but he'd kill the man who harmed his own children. Whoever did this to Charlene best be counting his days."

"Then if Whitley didn't poison his daughter or Miss Munro and you didn't, who the bloody hell did?"

Bethany was no longer listening. She had her theory

where the poison had come from. She dropped to the spongy trunk of a felled tree. Her body was still sore from the fall out the window days before. A sudden icy gust fluttered the barren tree branches overhead and whipped Ian's cloak against her legs. He sat down beside her. "How are you doing?"

How could she explain? No matter what had happened or who they were, she had lived with these people, loved these people. "Charlene might die. I'm sure I know how it happened. I just don't know why."

Ian slid his gaze back to Jameson. "Take Howard to the inn and contact Ware. Take my horse. I'm remaining here."

Jameson pulled Sir John around by the arm.

Sir John stopped in front of Bethany. "I love her," he said. "Whitley told Charlene if she resumed her place and came back here, he would let me live. She agreed. She did that for me. And now she is going to die." He wiped the back of his hand across his nose. "You promised me justice, Miss Munro."

They came through her bedroom window. It bothered Ian that he could break into Bethany's chambers so easily. But Bethany only had eyes for the powder jar she had just rooted beneath her dresser for. And while he sat watching her, wondering how to begin talking to her, she rose and carefully set it on the small round table in front of the stove.

"Charlene left her jar here, at the conservatory, when we departed originally for Whitley Court," Bethany spoke in low tones as she turned up the lamp. "Whatever was in the powder had to have come from this conservatory."

From his place against the desk, he listened to her conjectures and theories regarding what she now called Whitley's treasonous brotherhood of murdering assassins. Ian watched her remove her cloak and gloves, noting her stiffness with a frown, and the tightness growing in his chest. He had not allowed enough for her intelligence when it had been her passions that had drawn him to her.

Her dark woolen dress seemed dour and out of place in the surroundings of her chambers where cheerful yellow walls complimented lacy doilies. He had never been in her private chambers before—a place belonging solely to her—and found his attention diverted to the row of miniature family portraits lining her dresser. The room smelled like her, a touch of myrrh, just enough to tickle his senses.

"Are you even listening to me?"

Folding his arms beneath his cloak, he gave her his full attention. "You scare the hell out of me."

"Why?" she asked crossly, then with hurt. "You think my ideas are foolish?"

"Just the opposite."

His words caused her to pause. He abandoned his sprawl against the desk, walked past her to the door and peered into the corridor. A light burned in the salon. He was angry and he was shaking, and he didn't know quite how to fix the problem. "Who is out there?"

"Mary, making tea," Bethany said confidently.

"Who is the woman I saw leaving the main hall tonight?" He shut the door and snicked the lock.

"I don't know. Mrs. Filburt, perhaps, the headmistress."

He walked to the dresser where the powder jar sat.

"When will the majority of students return to school?"

"The new session is supposed to begin next week. But when all of this gets out . . . Lord Whitley sits at the head of the Board of Governors. Even an institution that has served a community and two generations of girls will not be exempt from the kind of political fallout that is already beginning with news of Charlene's accident."

Ian folded his arms and leaned a hip against the dresser. He thought of his gut-wrenching fear when he'd seen her walk into the glade tonight with Sir John. He found himself restless and it was difficult to treat Bethany as he would someone on his team when all he wanted to do at that moment was protect her.

He knew she was hurting—even if she didn't recognize it. Charlene had been her friend. She had believed in Whitley's cause once. Mrs. Langley had most likely died a horrible death at his orders.

But Ian had also been around the world a time or two with men like Sir John, liars and manipulators of the mass murdering sort and had little faith in mankind. "You understand Sir John can't be trusted."

She turned her face away.

"Do you want to talk?" he asked.

"Do you coddle Mr. Jameson?" she challenged. "If you can't work with me, maybe he should be my handler."

"I am not one to split hairs over a woman, love, but should he *handle* you in the slightest way, I would split his skull."

She laughed but the sound died in her throat and she looked away from him. "I left the council with their breeches in a twist yesterday" he said. "How could I not respond to a message that says, '*I miss you. I can't live without you*?' It just pulls at my baser male instincts."

A slip of her buttercream hair spilled over her shoulder and she edged the piece behind her ear. "I feel as if I failed her, Ian."

"Don't." The single word harshly spoken snapped up her head. "I am not going to allow you to think you could have saved her. She was responsible for taking you into that passageway. Never forget that."

She cast him a glance of dislike but he didn't care. Let her snarl at him.

Then he was standing in front of her, wanting to do more than wrap his arms around her.

"But don't you ever feel that if you could have just said or done something differently that it may have saved someone's life, made them make a different choice?"

"Every damn day, Bethany. Every damn day of my life."

She raised her chin and pressed herself against him. His arms came around her. She belonged in his arms, he realized, aware of her heartbeat against his.

Perhaps the only person who had ever needed protecting had been him. Not from Bethany, but his own fool guilt over a past that he'd tried and failed to bury, his anger, the horror of failure, and watching a dream die. All of this he thought about as he held Bethany.

He drew in his breath, dragged his hands through her hair and cupped her face, spanning his fingers across the delicate bones of her cheeks. He looked into her eyes with all of his heart shining in his. "I love you, Bethany." His voice was a harsh rasp, and they were not words he spoke easily. "I think about you in the morning when I awaken and you're the last thought before I close my eyes." She filled his every waking thought. "I don't know quite how to handle myself around you."

Her voice came all soft and wet from the pale linen lapel of his shirt. "I'd say you are doing well, Sir Ian."

He pressed his lips to her hair and felt a smile against his chest as she tightened her arms, content to hold him locked against her, and he didn't mind the cage she'd formed around him. They shared the silence.

"What are we going to do now, Ian?"

He knew the question reached to all facets of their life. The only one he had an answer for was the one in front of them. The reason why they were both here. The job.

After a long moment, he finally asked. "Are you informed beyond the basics of chemistry to assess what is in the powder yourself?" He told her about the missive that had arrived from the alchemist and which Jameson brought to him. "I want a look at the laboratory. Is it possible the powder picked up some kind of contamination? Phenol or mercury?"

Her eyes widened. She realized he wasn't asking her if she could establish the contents in the jar, but if she would, even knowing how dangerous it could be. She lowered her arms, though she did not step away. Then she raised her chin and he was suddenly looking into her eyes. "Unless I am testing for something specific I can only tell you what it is not. We can go just before dawn. Right now a light would give us away."

He smoothed the hair from her face. "Will you have to steal a key to get us inside?"

"I don't need a key to get into a locked room," she whispered against his lips. "And you're not going inside with me."

"Like hell."

He resisted being pulled into a kiss and set his hands on her waist.

She stretched her body against him, wrapping her arms around his neck and tracing the shape of his mouth with a sigh. "I don't know what I am dealing with. I don't want you in the laboratory. You are going to have to trust my judgment on this and find a way to watch the building from the outside."

He edged her against the bed. Even as hard as he was on the outside, he was feeling softer and far more tender inside. He felt her smile against his lips. "You're enjoying this, aren't you?" he asked.

She pulled him down to the bed and into a warm kiss that lingered and deepened into something hungry and alive, then she climbed over him and pressed his hands into her mattress. "We're partners, then?"

A smile touched his lips. He loved her more than he could express. "We're partners."

Chapter 21

The next morning, Bethany found the science laboratory door locked. A quick glance over her shoulder revealed Ian crouched just at edge of the yard next to a wildwood hedge. A ground mist concealed most of him.

Naturally, this wouldn't be simple, she thought.

Pulling two long hairpins from the back of her chignon, she knelt and inserted them into the lock. Daylight had begun to spread and warm the air, burning away the last remnants of dawn. A *click* finally followed, and Bethany quickly turned the latch and stepped inside.

She shut the door and turned into the room. Silence surrounded her. And Bethany felt a chill go over her.

Tall windows and a host of wall charts broke up the monotonous hospital gray walls. Twelve rows of parallel draft tables formed a half-moon around a large black chalkboard. Not a stick of furniture in the classroom was out of place. A lamp hung from a hook in the windowsill, a contradiction to the methodically organized room. There were no renovations taking place.

She walked toward the window, careful not to be seen from it. The room overlooked the parkland. She wondered if this lamp was some sort of signal. She stood just left of the casement. The light would be visible from across the park.

She moved away from the window and looked into the room. A sense of sadness touched her when she realized this would probably be the last time she'd step in here.

The powder jar weighed like an iron anvil in her clutch purse. She walked to the back wall that also led down into the herbal.

She removed her cloak, hung it on a hook outside the door, and replaced it with an apron. This laboratory had been Mrs. Langley's brainchild. She'd even acquired microscopes, an optical instrumentlike scope that magnified even the tiniest particle. There were no windows in this room. She lit the lamp inside and let the welcoming light chase away most of the darkness. Raising the lamp, she assessed the chamber.

Bethany's gaze took in the chemical cutting boards and various bins, pausing suddenly as the light caught a glint of liquid silver on the floor beneath one of the cutting tables. She walked over to the spot and brought the lamp closer, bending as she scraped the tip of one gloved finger across the floor, surprised to discern the substance was mercury.

She detected a faint hint of carbolic acid. Except for this missed, telltale spill, the walls and floors had been scrubbed clean.

Normally, she would've thought nothing of the scent, especially since the room had obviously just been cleaned. But phenol was used to make carbolic acid, an antiseptic. Phenol had also been found in the caverns beneath Whitley Court and was quite possibly the unwanted element in the powder. Phenol and mercury were two ingredients that did not belong in a school laboratory, the two ingredients she remembered Lord Ware had spoken to her about when describing the incendiary device that had killed the Home Secretary.

Heart racing, Bethany moved the lamp away and hung it on the hook against the wall. She set the jar of powder on one of the cutting tables and quickly pulled her gloves over each of her long sleeves. She wrapped a thin scarf over her mouth and tied it at the back so that she looked like a bandit.

After retrieving a magnifying glass from a shelf, she began a visual dissection of the table where she had made her powder and studied the pores and crevices etched on the stone cutting boards. Even in small amounts, phenol was highly toxic. As for mercury, everyone suspected that many in the hat industry had gone insane from breathing mercury fumes. Had traces of those two chemicals and others been present on this table when she'd mixed something as innocuous as face powder? She studied the powder beneath a microscope, finally confirming the truth.

Bethany had always been so careful, but no amount of cleaning could entirely rid a surface of that kind of contamination. When she had made her powder and used these tables she had somehow picked up trace elements of these foreign chemicals.

Bethany straightened and looked at the shelves behind her.

Had the anarchist group Lord Ware had been searching the breadth of England for been beneath her nose the entire time?

For what did such a group have at their disposal here at

the conservatory but a large science laboratory in which to play? In her heart and soul, Bethany now knew this was the reason Mrs. Langley had been killed.

Ian lay on his stomach beneath a wildwood hedge, the field glasses propped against his nose, trained on the infirmary where another carriage had arrived in the past hour. He lay about fifty yards from the white stone building where Bethany had yet to emerge. A cold mist layered the air with moisture, and he had to wipe the lenses on the glasses. He'd chosen the thicket, which overlooked both the laboratory building and the parkland, so he could watch the infirmary and the front door of this building as well.

More horse's hooves passed barely a dozen yards from his nose as other riders approached. But that wasn't where he'd trained the glasses.

The mysterious Mrs. Filburt had once again appeared outside and was now speaking to the newest arrival, a man carrying a black leather bag, similar to a physician's case. All morning people had been going in and out of the building as if their heels were on fire. All morning he'd been watching her.

After a moment, he reached beneath his cloak and pulled out his watch. Bethany had been in the laboratory for two hours. Another glance at the drive told him she was about to have company. He swore. The man with whom Mrs. Filburt had been speaking had turned and was headed toward the laboratory, picking up three men along the way who had just ridden up. Ian recognized one of the men from the inn where he and Bethany had stayed some weeks ago. *Desmond.*

He slipped the fob back into his pocket and was about to back out from beneath the hedge when Bethany suddenly sidled up beside him and nearly made him jump out of his boots. "Bloody hell!" he hissed. "Don't do that again."

"I love you, too," she spoke breathlessly in the silence then kissed him soundly, and only then did his heart stop racing. There was something about her touch that always both excited and calmed. He also knew her well enough to sense her troubled mood.

"I had to lock the front door so I came out a window," she said against his lips. "We have to go. Now."

He noted she wore no gloves and started to ask what she'd learned when a small commotion broke from the direction of the infirmary. Lord Whitley had burst outside the doorway, visibly upset, waving away two black-clad nurses who had come down the stairs after him. Ian turned the glasses on the approaching carriage with its lone horse. His stomach twisted.

"What is happening?" Bethany asked.

He handed Bethany the glasses and watched as she raised them to her eyes. Then he felt her stiffen, and sensed more than heard the quiet sound from her lips. The second carriage slowing to a stop behind the first was an undertaker's conveyance. There was only one patient currently in the infirmary.

Ian held no fondness for the dark-haired, brown-eyed Charlene Dubois, Viscount Whitley's daughter, except he knew that Bethany had cared for her. "I know she was your friend."

Her hands tightened around the glasses. He refrained from further conversation as the three men approached the front door of the laboratory, but his eyes remained on her profile and the patch of shadow cast from the wild-wood hedge brushing against her hair.

"They've been using the laboratory to make explosives, Ian," he heard her whisper. "Phenol and mercury and arsenic leave residue poisons on any surface the chemicals touch: countertops, mortars, pestles, brass, glass . . ."

He narrowed his eyes. "And you made powder on the same countertops and used the same utensils? Then no one intentionally put poison in the jar—"

"Intentional! They contaminated the lab. They are making bombs, Ian. The entire building could blow up."

"Whitley must have moved everything here months ago.

A sudden shout drew his head around. One of the men had walked back to the path, followed almost at once by the other two as they argued about something. Ian ducked his head. "What did you do?" he asked in low voice.

"I put pine resin in all the locks," she said defiantly, edging out from beneath the hedge. "Their keys no longer fit any of the doors."

He reached for her cloak. "Where are you go—?"

"I know how to get to the cottage without being seen."

The hedge abutted the woods. With a muttered oath, he looked back at the men running back to the infirmary, then he followed her, keeping low to the ground.

She took him deeper into the woods and over the low stone wall where he and Jameson had met her the night before. When he was sure they were out of sight, he grabbed her arm and spun her around. "Do you want to tell me what you are doing?" He kept his voice just above a growl.

She flinched as though he'd struck her. "Getting us back to the cottage. I need to change my clothes if we're going to follow Lord Whitley—"

"Bethany . . ." He looked around him. The urgency of the situation pressed down on him, and he crouched with her out of sight behind the stone wall.

She snatched away from his grasp. "Let go of me."

"Look at me."

Her jaw tightened. "I *had* to foul the locks." Tears brightened her eyes. "There are no windows in that laboratory. That door is made of solid oak. It will take a battering ram to knock it down. This will give us time to rally."

"Bethany—"

"You don't understand." Her hand clutched the velvet reticule where she'd put the powder jar. A pull string closed the clutch and tied to her wrist. "I made ordinary face powder from simple mica and iron oxides. I've been doing it for years, usually as a lesson in basic science for some of the older girls. By the grace of God, Charlene and I are the only two who used this batch.

"I can only assume I'm still alive because the concentration of trace chemicals was less in mine or there was less contamination in my jar. I don't know. I have no answer. The irony of it all is that Whitley's actions murdered his own daughter and he doesn't even know it. He's a monster, Ian. They are all monsters. I want to be looking in his eyes when you tell him what killed his daughter."

He thought he heard the nicker of a horse and peered over the wall. The sky that had been pearl gray when they had left the cottage hours ago had grown brighter as the clouds moved away from the sun. The edge of the winter parkland was visible through the trees. Most of the snow had melted, leaving the ground wet and soft. He could see the silhouettes of men on horseback. There was no reason to suppose the riders were out for a breath of fresh air. They'd probably followed their tracks, he realized.

Bethany ducked her head and pressed against the wall. "Are they looking for us?"

They both heard the faint jangle of a bridle. Harried shouts could now be heard as the riders combed the woods. "Stay down," he spoke softly and pulled her along the wall.

He stopped just before they reached a clearing that divided the woods from the stable. Two men stood outside the main paddock in the back. "Damn." He turned to look behind him. There was nowhere else to go but out into the open. He saw that Bethany also recognized they were in trouble.

"If Mr. Jameson got the telegram out last night to Lord Ware, he should be here with more men tonight. Right?" she whispered. "We just have to remain hidden un—"

"Listen to me." Tilting her chin, Ian splayed his palm over her pale cheek. "Sir John is the only man alive who can tie Whitley to anything. Jameson needs to be warned. Can you get to the inn where he took Sir John last night?"

She was shaking her head. "I'm sorry, Ian."

He felt only wrenching tenderness. "You did the right thing with the locks."

"No." She faced him with white-lipped calm. The hood of her cloak fell around her shoulders, leaving the sunlight to touch her crown of cream-colored hair. "I mean,

I'm sorry, but I'm the one who must stay. You can find Mr. Jameson far quicker than I can."

She backed away. He grabbed her arm. Her shocked eyes slammed against his. A horse was approaching just the other side of the wall. He couldn't allow her to risk her life in that way—not when there was another reason he'd needed to be the one to stay. One he didn't have time to explain. "Just trust me on this. There is another reason I have to stay."

She wrapped her fingers in his sleeve. "Don't you *dare* do this to me, Ian. We're partners."

He removed his revolver from its sheath beneath his shoulders and placed it in her hand. "*Go*," he mouthed the single word and rose to his feet, almost in front of the startled horse and rider.

Before the hapless rider could bring his mount under control, Ian braced a hand on the wall and leapt the barrier. Someone saw him and shouted from the woods. At the same time, he yanked the rider off the horse by his shirtfront and stepped into the tread himself as he bent low for the reins, then sat in the saddle. Ian whirled the horse and set out toward open ground only when the other riders crashed through the woods after him. His only intent was to provide a diversion for Bethany to escape, not him.

But a rabbit hole in the middle of the clearing cut short his noble plans. The horse stumbled to its front knees before regaining its balance. Ian barely managed to maintain his seat. Holding the reins in one hand, he bent over to calm the distraught horse. Speaking soothingly while gently patting the mare, he brought the horse under control. A half-dozen horses and riders crashed through the trees toward him. Unable to run, Ian merely crossed one hand over the other as if waiting to invite them to tea.

"Gentlemen." He allowed the generous word to roll off his tongue.

The horses snorted and stomped in a circle around him. "Your *lordship*," the burly man beside him tore off his brown woolen hat. "Remember me?"

It was Desmond from the Wayfarer's Inn, heavy-boned and pelted like a bear, not a single feature behind his beard that a person would consider friendly. Yes, Ian remembered him well.

"Where is she?" Desmond asked.

"Where is who?" Ian politely inquired.

Desmond's quirt slashed across Ian's chest and cut into the horse. The mare screamed and reared, tearing the reins from Ian's hand and throwing him backward off the saddle. He hit the ground hard, barely avoiding being trampled.

Goddamned Desmond.

A pair of muddy boots appeared in front of Ian's nose. Struggling for breath, he braced himself on his elbow and peered up at Desmond's ugly face.

"We followed two sets of tracks, yer fancy lordship." Desmond crouched. "And the other wee bitty tracks didn't belong to no man. Unless you've taken a fancy to boys."

Ian leaned on one elbow. "I guess I don't need to ask whose side you are on." He smiled recklessly and spat blood on the man's arm.

This time Desmond hit him, and Ian did not get up.

Chapter 22

"Damn you, Ian."

Bethany dropped behind the prickly hedge that pressed against the infirmary walls. Mud caked her soft leather half-boots. Her feet and hands were wet and cold, the cast metal of the pocket colt Ian had given her like ice in her palm. Cloak wrapped around her, she crouched as best as her stays allowed, watching the front door where most of the activity seemed to be taking place all afternoon. She'd been outside too long in the cold. Her cloak no longer kept out the chill, but it wasn't until she'd stopped moving and the sun had dipped below the trees that she'd begun to shiver and her teeth to chatter.

Think, think, think.

The undertaker's hearse no longer remained in the drive. She had not seen Ian since two men dragged him into the building some hours ago.

After glaring at the darkening sky, she scanned the infirmary's exterior, a former eighteenth-century carriage house with round-topped upper windows and a low-beamed dark interior that made it difficult to see inside.

Lord Whitley's voice came from the direction of a corner chamber almost directly above where she huddled.

He was yelling at someone, throwing the man's incompetence into his face for taking too long to get into the laboratory.

Until this moment, she'd still held out the minutest hope he had not been part of any plot to assassinate the Home Secretary, that he knew nothing of the laboratory's nefarious use, that he mourned the loss of his daughter and would not have ordered Mrs. Langley killed.

"We've been through the laboratory twice—"

"Then have your men make another *bloody* sweep!" Whitley said in a low dangerous voice. "If we are not on that train and gone in the next hour, it's over. I will not *allow* this to be over. Do you understand that concept, Desmond? Find my detonators!"

The window was not more than a pair of feet off the ground and Bethany glimpsed a man's broad back. He held a quirt in his gloved hand. Other men stood around him. Mumbles sounded and two left the room. A moment later, the front door opened and they descended the steps grumbling. "Is Goodman still with Rockwell?" Whitley asked the bastard whom she'd seen strike Ian, his reply lost in the sound of approaching horse and riders as the men who had been combing the grounds for her drew near.

". . . if you can't find Miss Munro then find that maid of hers and bring the chit to me."

Pulling her hood over her hair, Bethany eased around the building to the back. She had already found Mary and sent her to get anyone present out of the main hall, instructing her to deliver a message to Jameson. That had been hours ago. Mary knew the intricacies of the school grounds far better than Bethany did. She would find a way to escape and get to the inn unseen. Bethany's mission remained here. Not only because Ian was here, but because Whitley was—and no matter what, she couldn't allow him to leave.

Bethany looked at the gun in her palm then at her reticule. With her pulse thundering in her ears, she knew what had to be done. She didn't know much about pistols, but she did know about chemicals and poisons.

She set down the gun and using all of her strength smashed the velvet clutch against the brick wall, looking around her to make sure the muffled *thud* didn't carry. The first strike did not break the jar. The second did.

Careful not to let the glass cut her she shook up the contents and, adding soil, bits of tree bark, and rocks, made it an effective lethal weapon. Mesh and beading reinforced the velvet but it wasn't enough to prevent a small tear in the fabric. No powder seemed to be leaking, and Bethany realized the handkerchief wrapped around the jar probably helped contain its contents.

She let herself inside into the postern. Brick and flint walls, reminiscent of a bygone age, shielded her. Lord Whitley's voice now came from the direction of an upstairs room. Bethany eased her foot on the stairs and ascended one slow step at a time until the hallway was visible from where she hid.

She could see four rooms. Whitley's voice came from the other end where a man stood guard outside a door.

Too late, Bethany heard someone coming inside the back door. She couldn't run upstairs without being seen. She knew she was trapped in the stairwell. Then Mrs. Filburt suddenly appeared in the postern. She shut the door and came to an abrupt stop. Shock flashed briefly across the other woman's face, transforming into patient surprise when Bethany pointed the gun at her.

"I only came here for Ian Rockwell," she said, her voice remarkably composed considering how fast her heart raced.

"Miss Munro." The woman removed the hood of her cloak and let it fall around her shoulders. "I am hardly worthy of your noble sacrifice should you shoot me."

Her gun hand trembled, but Bethany kept the barrel level on her target. "What do you know of nobility, Mrs. . . . ?"

Bethany couldn't say the name. Because she suddenly knew exactly whom she faced. Perhaps it was the color of the woman's blue eyes, or something Ian had said when he'd told her he had another reason he'd needed to stay.

The woman slowly removed her spectacles. "So. You know who I am." She peeled away the stern gray wig. Blond hair spilled over her shoulders and down her back. "I know nothing of nobility, Miss Munro. But I used to know something of passion. I suggest if you want to save Ian, you try to live."

A man's running footsteps sounded upstairs. Bethany turned her head as Lord Whitley came to a halt on the landing. His height more substantial in the confines of the low ceiling, his presence filled the stairwell like a harbinger of doom.

"I told you she would come after him," Mrs. Filburt—Pamela—said.

If he was surprised to see her, it didn't show. "Miss Munro, how nice of you to finally join us." He stepped onto the stairs and held out his gloved hand for her weapon.

Bethany could have panicked and dissembled, or tried to shoot him. She knew she'd be dead before she turned the weapon on him. She was in Ian's world now, where living and dying were all part of the game. She wanted to live. Ian needed her alive. And there was the powder in her reticule.

Whitley took the gun. "Did you deal with our little problem at the inn?" Whitley asked Pamela, his eyes still on Bethany, and his tone told her that whatever wrath he harbored for Desmond and the rest of his men extended to Pamela Rockwell as well. His anger held no favorites.

"I did. A telegraph *did* go out to Ware last night. But Jameson was not at the inn."

Doubt wavered through Bethany. They had Sir John. She'd sent Mary to the inn to warn Jameson.

Too late.

Please let Mary be safe.

"See to our other guest. The train leaves in an hour. Are my daughter's remains on board?"

"Yes, my lord," she said without expression.

Something flickered in his eyes. A hint of anguish that vanished as quickly as it came.

Bethany turned her face away. Pamela squeezed up the stairs past Bethany and Whitley. "I will see to your other guest now."

Lord Whitley's gaze followed her departure, until she disappeared around the corner. When he'd turned back to Bethany, she saw only loathing in his eyes.

"Where is Adam?" She found herself asking.

"Don't you *ever* say my boy's name. You've lost the right to speak his name again to me."

He moved in front then below her on the stairway as

if to block her escape. A day's growth of beard covered his jaw. He looked menacing, no longer the vulnerable or heroic leader she'd once thought him to be. He *looked* like a man who had committed murder and would do so again. Bethany's hand tightened over the string attaching the reticule to her wrist.

"I'm disappointed in you," he finally said.

"As I am with you, my lord. Do you think we'll be as easily made to disappear as the others? How many have you already killed in your political cause?"

"How many has men like Rockwell killed? I doubt you even know the manner of men who work for the league council. Is my cause any less worthy because the Crown does not sanction it? I can guarantee I am far more passionate in my beliefs than Rockwell is in his."

"Tell *that* to your daughter."

Fury blighted Whitley's smug expression. "Oh, I have my ideas about who poisoned my daughter, never you worry, Miss Munro."

"You don't know anything."

"And you think you do?" His bark of laughter turned his mouth into a sneer. "You're just a naive little girl playing at big-people games. Where are my detonators?"

The question coming out of nowhere served to betray her into a response. Bethany backed up a step.

"You'll make it easier on Rockwell if you answer my questions, Miss Munro. Where are my bloody detonators?"

She shook her head, unaware that she was doing so more as a response to his approach and the absolute fear that he was about to snap her neck. "I don't know what you're talking about!"

"Dammit, do not lie to me. *Where are my detonators?*"

She swung the reticule but he was fast and caught her wrist, pushing her backward against the stairs as he barely missed being hit by the purse. With an enraged growl, he came at her. Bethany struggled to get her footing, but he grabbed her ankles. She thrashed out with her sharp heels, driven by blinding panic until he furiously backhanded her across the face.

No one had ever hit her before, and she was appalled and shocked by the utter humiliation and helplessness as she braced herself.

She did not fight him when he tore the tassel string off her hand and in the process of ripping it away the glass pressing against the sides of the purse sliced his palm open. "*Bloody hell!*"

He glared at the blood welling on his hand. He narrowed his eyes on hers. "What is this?" He dumped the fine particles of powder, rocks, twigs, and pieces of glass onto the floor, letting it filter through his splayed and bloody fingers. Bethany wondered if she was evil not to stop him.

She wondered if she was killing herself in the process. She wondered a lot of things as her eyes went to his face, and she reminded herself that he had killed Mrs. Langley.

She prayed for the strength not to collapse into a blubbering idiot. "It makes an effective weapon," she whispered past her throbbing lip.

Footsteps approached and a man appeared at the bottom of the stairs, startled into stopping when his eyes came to rest on the violence taking place in the stairwell.

Bethany recognized the new arrival as the bastard who had beaten Ian. "What is it, Desmond?" Whitley snapped without taking his eyes off her.

"The detonators are not in the laboratory, my lord."

Whitley glared at her in sharpened rage. His fist crushed the reticule and he threw it against the wall at the bottom of the stairway, where a small mushroom cloud of grit and granules exploded over the man who stood in the postern.

Removing a handkerchief from his pocket, Whitley spun on his heel and strode past her up the stairs.

"Bring her."

Against a wall with hands tied behind his back, Ian drifted in and out of consciousness, after being dragged into this god-awful room that smelled of urine and sickness. Someone was shouting in some distant part of his head. He opened his eyes. He'd been aware of voices in the room with him for some time and though he cherished a consuming dislike for all those present, his eyes now focused on a woman standing at the periphery of his vision, her small frame concealed by the nondescript cloak she wore over a steel gray gown. A ghost in the shadows.

Pamela stood less than three feet from where he sat on the filthy floor. He observed her as a connoisseur would the finest art, for beneath the pasty makeup and spinster clothes lay the face of an angel with the heart of a serpent.

"The makeup does wonders for your new look," he said.

Nothing in her passive expression moved. "Hello, Ian."

He hadn't shot her dead three years ago when he'd had

the chance. She'd interpreted his inaction as cowardice. But, then, she had always considered him weak. He was surprised to feel only a moderate abhorrence for her.

The thought brought a grim flicker of amusement to his mouth, as the room swam in currents around his head. "What have you done to me?"

He turned his head, to see the supposed doctor Goodman leaning over him, his expression passive as he observed Ian stirring. During his so-called interrogation, Ian had discovered Goodman was the resident bomb builder, the *genius* chemist who left poisons behind to contaminate an entire laboratory that would eventually kill his employer's daughter. The irony would have been too beautiful if it was not so damn tragic. No one here even knew what they'd done.

"Do you feel more inclined to talk with us now, Rockwell?"

"Go to hell."

"Tell them what they want to know, Ian."

Pamela's sweet voice drew him around like the drug in his veins. He smiled. "You should have stayed where you were."

"And waste all of her god-given talent in an asylum cell?"

Whitley's voice forced Ian to shift his focus, and he wanted badly to smash a fist into the man's face . . . except his hands were tied. His head fell back against the stone wall.

"That morphine our fine doctor gave you will take away all your worries and pains, Rockwell," Whitley said. "Traveling is simpler if you're cooperative. Right now I need you cooperative."

The words Ian had been about to say died in his throat as Bethany was dragged forward through the door.

Jesus Christ.

That Whitley had Bethany was enough to temporarily counteract the morphine.

Ian's instincts immediately went on alert. But the drug seemed to absorb the jolt like ripples in a lake.

"He doesn't know anything," Bethany said.

Whitley waggled the gun in his hand, Ian's own gun, he realized, as if it were a dinner fork and he was about to indulge in desert. "We'll make this simple, Miss Munro," he said. "I ask questions. You supply answers. We all live for a few more hours."

Ian tore his gaze from Bethany. Fury aimed directly at Whitley boiled from his innards all the way to his brain. "Goddamn you—"

"God?" Whitley laughed. "What God? God wouldn't have killed my wife in the most unbearable way and cursed my only son with a defect that makes him a virtual outcast in society. He wouldn't have taken my daughter the way he did. There would be no disease, and no one would lack the basic sustenance needed for survival. God doesn't exist, Rockwell, so damn him all you want."

Christ . . . the man was insane. "Society is filled with people who have problems that affect their entire lives and they don't murder people."

"We all pay a price, whether that is for change or for one's silence. Do you work for Ware, Miss Munro?"

Ian looked at her.

"Ware came to her after she was ill. He wanted her to help attain information against you." He shut his eyes.

"She wouldn't agree to it but he threatened her with sedition if she didn't cooperate."

Whitley flashed a reptilian grin. "See how simple this process is, Rockwell? How quickly we get things done? Did you steal my detonators, Miss Munro?"

"She doesn't know anything about detonators."

Whitley pondered him. "She doesn't know. You don't know. Yet they are gone. Are you trying to protect her, Rockwell? Are you in love with her perhaps?"

The question lashed out at him.

"He's only my partner," Ian heard her say and the taint of desperation behind the words as she sought to shield him.

She was far more than his partner. She was his heart and the air that he breathed. She had become the very thing he had feared. "No, she is not my partner," he rasped. She is not part of the council league."

With a deft movement of his hand, Whitley grabbed Bethany by the back of the neck and Ian watched with impotent rage as he pressed the barrel of the colt against her temple. "I didn't ask if she is part of the council league. I asked if you are in love with her."

"Let her go, Whitley."

"Are you the one who stole my guest list, Miss Munro? Were you the little spider in my house? Did you steal my detonators, too?"

Whitley tightened his hand in her hair and cocked the trigger. A tear squeezed from Bethany's eyes. Finally, she nodded. "Ian had nothing to do with any of it. He didn't know."

"Christ . . ." Ian managed to get out but it was barely a whisper. He swore this world wasn't big enough for Whit-

ley to hide in if he hurt her. "Let her go, Whitley."

"Where are they, Miss Munro?"

"I destroyed them," she rasped. "All of them."

A terrible silence descended on the room.

"Who else was with Sir John at the inn, Rockwell?" Whitley's low voice growled. "We got past one guard. How many more of you are here? Answer me, Rockwell. Her life depends on it."

When Bethany looked at him, all he could do was look away. The argument was a moot point, he told himself. If Whitley's gossoons had been to the inn, they wouldn't have killed Sir John without first making sure they knew everything. In fact, Ian now wondered if Whitley even would have killed Sir John at all. Having a prime witness disappear completely would be a lot more circumspect than murdering one outright and leaving evidence lying all over the place. Better to make it look like he ran away. They were all going to be taken somewhere no one would see them again and executed.

"And to think I could have spared you Dr. Goodman's company for a few more hours," Whitley said.

Ian leaned his head against the wall. "And deprive him of such fine entertainment?"

Whitley shoved Bethany from him. "It looks like he would have let you die, Miss Munro." He spoke to Desmond. "Put her in the carriage."

Ian shut his eyes. With his hands bound behind him, the rough, gritty surface of the rope burned his wrists. The pain at least kept him conscious. "You've got me," he said as Bethany was dragged from the room. "Just let her go, Whitley."

He knelt in front of Ian. "Is this the drug speaking

perhaps or is it something more, Rockwell?" Perching an elbow on his knee, Whitley peered up at the petite woman standing like a ghost beside Ian. "Do you hear that, Mrs. Filburt? Our boy has feelings."

Whitley then rose to his feet. "This one may have the heart of a viper, Rockwell, but she has a streak of sentimentality a mile wide when it comes to you." He thought this amusing. "Give him another dose, Goodman," Whitley said. "We're leaving in five minutes. We should make his final hours happy."

Ian didn't fight the injection. He continued to look at Pamela who had not left the room.

"What does he have on you?" He leaned his head against the wall as Goodman packed up his little brown bag. "This isn't about his cause or money, or vengeance against our own government."

Her passive silence echoed falsely in the room. "I'm not here because he forced me."

"No? He doesn't trust you," Ian said, closing his eyes. "Perhaps deep down inside his black heart, he thinks the same person who poisoned Miss Munro poisoned his daughter. Were you at Whitley Court? Ooops," he slurred the word. "Of course you were. You tried to kill me."

"Can you help me go someplace where no one will find me again?" she asked. "And live in the style in which I used to be accustomed? This business is *always* about the money."

"That's really good, sweetheart." A faint smile appeared on his lips, the merest hint of movement. "You'll need all the wealth you have. Because the devil will expect his due on your way to hell."

* * *

Bethany came awake with a start. Her head leaned against the window. A southbound train rolled past her on the other tracks, its passing cloaking her in silence as her eyes adjusted to the darkness. She'd been brought to the depot and loaded in a private rail car. Somehow she'd slept. Deep sapphire watered silk draped the windows of the rail car, matching the sofas and chairs. The colors seemed to meld with the shadows. She knew the train was headed north, most likely she was being taken back to Whitley Court, only to vanish in the tunnels beneath the house. Was this Mrs. Langley's last route before she'd disappeared forever? Would it also be Ian's?

She realized she wasn't alone. Pamela stood in front of the window at the other end of the car. Her head turned when she heard Bethany stirring.

Pamela had not spoken to Bethany since their party had left the conservatory hours ago. She hadn't even searched Bethany, as if Bethany were of no consequence. With her hair and blue eyes uncovered, and the aging makeup sponged off her face, Ian's wife was truly as beautiful as a snow angel.

Bethany shivered in the cold, but rather than ask for a blanket she turned her face away. A moment later, a blanket dropped in her lap. Pamela stood beside her. Though Bethany knew there was nothing kind and good about Pamela Rockwell, the woman had kept Desmond from striking her in the carriage, not out of any fondness but because—Pamela claimed—she couldn't abide a man beating a woman. "Are you hungry?" she asked.

Bethany shook her head. "No."

The pocket doors dividing the railcars suddenly opened and Lord Whitley stepped into the darkened car. He es-pied Pamela then walked to where Bethany came to her feet, clutching the blanket.

He started to place a gloved hand against her cheek, but she jerked her face away. He looked at the blanket in her hands. "Don't let Pamela fool you, Miss Munro. She'll cut your heart out if it serves her purpose, or mine."

"Leave her alone," Bethany whispered.

His eyes narrowed. "Let me explain something to you, my dear. She and I have a business arrangement. She doesn't feel. She doesn't think. She doesn't do anything except what I tell her." He gentled his voice. "Do you, *Mrs*. Rockwell? If you'd done her job in the first place, none of us would be in this situation and my daughter would not be dead."

"I had nothing to do with what happened to your daughter."

"Just like you had nothing to do with what happened to my detonators or any of the other failures that have led us to this point. You *promised* to watch over her. You couldn't even do that right." His glance touched Bethany. "Do you want to know what else she couldn't do?" Lord Whitley tipped Pamela's chin with the walking stick. "She couldn't kill her husband. One simple shot that day at the priory, and our bloody worries would have ended on that cliff. And she couldn't do it. But we're in this together, aren't we, my dear. All the way to the end. You've killed women and children in the name of my cause. There is no escaping."

Pamela shoved aside the walking stick. "Where is he?"

"In the livestock car, chained to a stall with the horses. Goodman isn't finished with him yet." He held Pamela's stare with a cold one of his own and laughed. "Don't go all soft on me, love. Rockwell will kill you if given half the chance, and I've half a mind to let him."

He turned away and left Bethany caught in a maelstrom of fury and doubt. She stared openly at Pamela as the other woman stared back, emotions briefly unveiled behind her blue gaze. And in the back of her mind, Bethany thought about the shot that could have killed Ian at the priory.

"Sit down, both of you." Lord Whitley poured himself a drink from a crystal decanter behind the small bar. His hands trembled. Without asking if anyone else wanted libation, he took his glass, sat next to the window, and stared out at the passing countryside, glimpsed briefly in spurts of lamplight and moonlight. "We'll detrain in a few hours."

Bethany and Pamela each reluctantly took seats across from the other. Even without the plain gown and remnants of makeup, Pamela's new disguise vanished within the icy persona Bethany saw now. Like the chameleon, eerily invisible, the woman became her surroundings. And yet Bethany already sensed the flaw, the potentially fatal crack in the diamond. He was currently chained to a stall in the livestock car.

They were both in love with the same man.

Chapter 23

Ian lay with his face pressed against the floor of a carriage, having been stuffed into its interior after being removed from the train. He didn't know for sure how much time had lapsed as he came fully awake. His hands were bound behind him and his ribs hurt like hell. The carriage had stopped, he realized. That must have been what had awakened him. He turned his head to see Goodman sitting on the leather bench seat bending over him.

"You've been uncooperative, Rockwell. I'm afraid it will not go well for you here on out."

"Be afraid. When I get loose, you're the first I'm going to kill."

The sadistic bastard. Goodman looked like a nice old man, a grandfatherly type, capable of no more violence than swatting at flies.

Hands grabbed Ian and pulled him from the carriage. He heard a struggle and sobbing, as Sir John was also dragged bound, gagged, and beaten from a nearby carriage. Ian had had the displeasure of sharing the same stall with him for the last few hours along with the crates of swine and chickens, listening to him weep.

Dawn sat on the horizon and blanketed the ground in

soft glittery white as the first glimpse of light touched the layer of frost. More than one carriage had been parked in the clearing. Ian counted eight or ten men standing in a half circle in front of him.

Bracketing Whitley, he saw three others. Pamela was there. And Bethany who was looking at him with fear in her eyes. He didn't like that there was nothing he could do for that now.

Distant waves crashed against rocks. They could not be far from the cliffs. From the amount of time they'd been traveling, they had to be near Whitley Court.

Sir John was dragged and dropped to his knees in front of Whitley. He sobbed and trembled.

Someone shoved Ian toward Whitley. He stumbled but he didn't fall. Whitley stepped forward, his shoes making no noise on the soil. His breath steamed out in the cold. "You've had a comfortable trip thus far?" Whitley inquired.

Unshaven and not smelling his best, Ian still wore his heavy frock cloak over a loose-fitting shirt stained with blood from a gash above his brow where Desmond had hit him yesterday. "The company was lacking. But I've traveled in worse accommodations."

Whitley chuckled. "Ever the humorist, Rockwell. Don't untie him, you fool," he shouted at the man who had dragged Ian from the carriage.

"Because you know I'll break your neck?"

He earned a blow to the back of his knees for his belligerence, staggering and dropping him to his knees beside Sir John.

The man holding Bethany moved forward. "Desmond

ain't come back from yonder tree, m'lord. Somethin' is wrong with him."

"It doesn't matter," Whitley said, not looking very well himself, Ian realized. "Pamela is going to do the honors for us all today."

Pamela, who'd been standing just to Whitley's left looking ethereal wrapped in the first breath of dawn, momentarily startled at Whitley's order.

Whitley removed the pocket colt from inside his coat. "Pamela?" Whitley prompted when she hadn't moved. "This time you will not miss, my dear."

A moment of tense silence ensued. Then she took the pistol and walked over to Ian. Her face passive, she raised the gun to his head, but he saw something flash in the back of her eyes as she made the mistake of meeting his gaze.

"No!" Bethany struggled against the hands restraining her. "You're not going to do it! Let go of me!" She kicked and fought.

"You asked where my son is, Miss Munro? He's on his way to France with my sister. I know that Ware has been apprised of my alleged involvement in certain anarchist activities. But I am going home to bury my daughter and that is where he will find me when he arrives at my doorstep this afternoon. He will attempt to arrest me but without physical evidence or anyone's testimony, Ware can hold me on nothing, which is why today I have decided to resort to doing my own housecleaning. When all else fails . . . ?"

Sir John's gag was ripped from his face and he sobbed, crawling forward until his face was inches from Whitley's shoes as he begged for mercy. "You can't do this, my lord, I have done nothing. Please . . ."

"You were not easy to find, Howard," Whitley said. "You cost me a lot of time and resources."

The man very nearly wet himself in prostrated fear, but while he wept and blubbered for his life, Ian felt something drop beside his calf. "He's going to have me execute you," came the softest of whispers in his ear, and he realized Pamela had, under cover of her skirts, dropped a knife. "You don't have much time."

He didn't waste time questioning her purpose. He grabbed the knife and began sawing through the ropes. "The entrance to the tunnel is a hundred yards north." Her lips barely moved as she kept her eyes trained on Whitley. "If you try to run anywhere else they'll catch you on horseback and kill you."

"No, no, god no," Sir John continued blubbering, swearing he'd never tell anyone anything, promising loyalty, allegiance, and fealty to his dying day, which by the looks of it was about to end in a few minutes. "I don't want to die," he pleaded.

"Tell Miss Munro what you did with Mrs. Langley, Howard."

Sir John's panicked gaze flung to Bethany.

"Tell her, Howard."

"I took her into the tunnels and left her," he blurted out.

"You took her down without light and left her to the rats. Why did you do that, Howard?"

He bowed his head. "Because she was going to betray us, my lord."

"Would you like for me to show you what we do with traitors, Howard?" Whitley quietly asked, then raised the gun in his hand and pointed it at Pamela. "Maybe we should ask Pamela about fealty. Did you poison my daughter?"

"You know I did not."

The gun wavered in Whitley's unsteady hand. "You warned me she was going to be a problem and now she is dead." He stepped over Sir John's prostrate form. "Show me your allegiance. Pull the trigger. Do what you should have done the last time I told you to kill Rockwell."

"You arrogant fool!" Bethany had fought herself away from the men restraining her and stepped into the line of Whitley's fire. "She didn't poison your daughter. *You* did! You killed her with your poisons and your contamination in your lab. Mrs. Langley knew something wasn't right. She suspected what you were doing in the laboratory."

Ian sawed desperately at his binding ropes, his aching hands suddenly free. He nodded to Pamela.

He could barely grip the knife hilt.

"Bethany!"

Ian's voice turned her around.

"Drop!" Ian yelled.

To her credit, she dropped to the ground as Ian rose to his feet, lethal blade in hand. At the same time, Pamela took aim at Whitley. Ian swung around toward Goodman and dropped to one knee, the forward momentum propelling his arm out as he let the knife fly directly at the doctor. But he hit the bastard in the shoulder instead of the chest where it would kill him. Everyone else leapt for cover. Pamela fired the gun at Whitley.

Ian heard the gun click on an empty chamber. Pamela fired again in desperation. Two more empty chambers.

"You think I'm fool enough to give you a loaded gun?" Whitley raised his gun as Bethany leaped at him and grabbed his arm.

Her panic and fury propelled him off balance, then Ian, his breath coming icy fast, was beside her, emotion pouring through him as he grabbed Whitley's gun hand and wrapped his forearm around Whitley's throat. "Tell your men to stand down." Ian pulled Whitley backward. "Now."

"Like bloody hell." He started laughing. "You're dead. You're all dead."

Pamela had already taken off running toward the tunnel. Bethany saw her, too. "Ian . . ."

He was hesitant to send Bethany after her. Facing down eight armed men seemed fraught with less danger than dealing with Pamela. But Bethany was going anyway. "Dammit." He hadn't even been able to give her the gun Whitley had been holding. "I'm right behind you."

Maybe. Depending on how much Whitley's men wanted Whitley to live, he thought as he began pulling the man back with him.

Something told Bethany Pamela knew where she was going. Even wearing skirts, Bethany covered the distance, keeping Pamela's shadow in sight. Her path descended into a ravine. A mist covered the ground and settled in the still air like the grounds of a cemetery in an old church-yard. Bethany leaped a slow moving creak, slipping on moss as she gained the bank on the other side. She caught up to Pamela at the entrance of a half-hidden tunnel barely discernable between the rocks and the thickening mist.

Pamela spun around. For a moment neither moved. Behind Bethany, the crack of gunfire and shouts echoed.

"Push," she heard Pamela hiss.

Together they put their backs into shoving aside what looked like a dead tree wedge between rocks.

"You saved my life," Pamela said.

"You saved Ian's."

Their eyes met in momentary accord. A truce both knew would not last but one nonetheless. Pamela may not own much honor, but she did seem to possess a strange sense of fair play. For the moment, anyway, they were on the same team.

More shots followed the last. Pamela's voice came from inside the tunnel. "He's on his way. Hurry."

Bethany pushed inside the tunnel. Looking past the other woman into the pitch-black corridor inspired no confidence. "How do you know he's coming?"

"The shots are moving."

Another crack of gunfire proved Pamela's observation. "Hurry." Bethany heard the strike hiss of a match. Then Pamela returned to the entrance. She handed Bethany a lantern. "We have to go."

"Not without Ian."

Pamela glared at Bethany. "Oh bother," she said like a curse. "Finish in here. Make sure the lanterns are filled and dump the rest of the oil over the floor just outside the entrance."

"Why are you helping us?"

Pamela propped a foot on a rock and shoveled up the hem of her skirt. "Ian is the only person who ever cared about what happened to me." When she came up again, she held a gun. "Even with everything I did to him, he protected me these past three years. That just makes a woman go shivery all over, I guess." Her facetious remark narrowed Bethany's eyes.

"You have a strange sense of duty," she called out in a loud whisper as she worked hastily to fill the lanterns.

Pamela took up position next to the rocks. "What killed Charlene?" she heard Pamela ask.

Bethany quickly told her about the laboratory and the powder as she turned to finish dragging the barrel of oil to the tunnel entrance. "Whitley got a dose of his own poison. Desmond was a bystander." She dusted the grit from her hands. "I don't know if either will die, but they *will* suffer."

"Not bad for a neophyte, Miss Munro. You and I aren't that different after all. Are we?"

Bethany sucked in a deep breath. "You and I are nothing alike."

Were they?

A loud *crack* sounded. "There!" Pamela pointed to movement below them in the ravine. The hill crawled with men and the smoke fluttering off their torches. "He's overshot us."

Pamela stepped out and fired twice, sending Ian's pursuers to ground. "Cowards," she whispered.

A moment later, Ian reached the tunnel. Breathing hard, he saw Pamela. His gaze jumped past her to Bethany. "Are you all right?"

"This is all very sweet, but do you mind?" Pamela waltzed past them and kicked over the oil. A thin line of liquid spilled toward the lantern they'd left out front of the tunnel. Any moment now, a fire would explode and the tunnel entrance would be blocked for a while.

Ian picked up two lanterns, and handed one to Bethany. Pamela was already running ahead of them, her skirt swishing with her pace. They made it fifty yards and rounded a corner when the kerosene barrel exploded and shook the walls. Even as wounded as he was, Ian pressed his body against Bethany, shielding her. The horrific noise reverberated through the walls, sending rocks crashing down on them. They struck Bethany's arms as a dust cloud rushed through the tunnel, leaving her coughing. Silence followed, filled only by the sound of their breathing and the quiet hiss of lanterns.

Bethany lowered her arms. Ian remained standing next to her but in his hand he'd drawn his gun and now pointed it at Pamela as she raised hers at the same time in a sudden standoff. Neither moved.

His hair caked with dust and debris, his clothes beneath his cloak bloody and torn, Ian's appearance only amplified the dangerous threat in his eyes, extending to the gun he held. He didn't conceal his intent behind any façade. "Because I don't bloody trust you not to put a bullet in the back of my head."

Pamela's eyes flashed. "I could have done that already, Rockwell."

"You needed my help to escape Whitley. I didn't see you waiting around afterward."

"You need my help now."

"I can find my own bloody way out of here. We aren't that far from the caverns beneath Whitley Court."

She tossed back her hair. "People have been lost in these tunnels for days."

"Sometimes forever. Isn't that right?"

Something dropped from a crack in the wall above Bethany's head and plopped to her feet, skittering off with a harried squeak. *Rats!*

Bethany slowly raised her gaze to the rock ceiling. "Can we continue this discussion *after* we get out of here?" she suggested when neither Pamela nor Ian seemed inclined to move from their dogged position. But they had both seen what Bethany saw, and Ian surely remembered the last time they'd come up against rats.

"A truce, Pamela?"

"Until we get out of here." She lowered her gun.

He lowered his gun.

"You're injured," Bethany said.

Almost as an afterthought, he looked down at his side. Blood dripped to the ground from a wound at his side. "I must have been hit outside."

She stepped forward to check the severity. His fingers wrapped around her wrist. "It can wait," he said quietly, his eyes going to the walls and cracks in the ceiling as another rat dropped from the wall with a squeak.

"How many bullets do you have in that thing?" he asked Pamela.

She backed away, her eyes round. Pamela would also know about the rats. "Not nearly enough." She whirled on her heel. "But then I'm not the one ringing their dinner bell."

Bethany put her shoulder beneath Ian's, accepting his weight. "You've chosen a bad time to get injured."

He held a lantern and so did she. Their shadows wobbled on the walls. Pamela had stopped at the fork ahead to await them. "Tell me about it," he said.

Chapter 24

"**T**hey sound just like birds," Pamela whispered from her place against the wall.

The tunnel's acoustics were ripe for amplifying sound. The noise that seemed to emanate from all directions and in the walls had been building over the last few hours.

Ian had marked the passing time by the amount of oil the lanterns had burned. All of them were exhausted.

"How lost are we?" Bethany asked, easing Ian to a place where he could rest his weight.

"Isn't this just bloody ripe!" Pamela raised the lantern looking back the way they'd just come.

Ian could go no farther, he realized without doing something about his leaking side. There wasn't an inch on his body that didn't hurt and he was nauseous with the aftereffects of the morphine. "We took a wrong turn somewhere at one of those forks we passed," he said. "We have to go back."

"I don't *take* wrong turns," Pamela said. "And I'm not going back."

Ian worked the buttons on his shirt. "You've been taking wrong turns your entire bloody life, Pamela."

Bethany started to pull away, something he'd been

seeing too much of in the last few hours and he grabbed her hand. "Stay." He almost grimaced at his imperious sounding command. "Please."

"We can't remain here long," she said, but her eyes told him she knew what he was doing, even if he hadn't recognized it yet.

He couldn't continue to keep her between him and Pamela indefinitely. She wasn't there physically, of course, but she was a barrier nonetheless, like a glass wall where Ian could see out but not feel.

Yet, he kept his gun at the ready beside him. He didn't trust Pamela, and he knew he could no more permit her to go unfettered back out into the world than he could allow a black widow spider to escape his boot heel.

"How did you two ever end up married to one another?" Bethany asked.

Ian looked across at Pamela who was watching him. She smiled, but some of her impudence had faded. "A woman just has to look at him to know that answer."

Ian felt Bethany tense and he tightened his hand on her arm. *She's pulling your chain*, he'd wanted to say, but instead he asked her to help him sit. Pamela told them she was going to check the tunnel ahead.

"I'm only slowing us down," he said.

"No, you aren't."

He let Bethany examine his side. *Damn.*

Ian grimaced against the pain shooting through his entire body. "Do you think you can be a little gentler?"

"You've lost a lot of blood," Bethany said. "We need water. You aren't going to last much longer on your feet."

He looked down the narrow corridor for Pamela as she moved off into another branch of the tunnel.

"Do you think she'll be back?" Bethany asked some minutes later.

"She doesn't have more than ten minutes of light left." At the moment, Ian didn't care if she got herself lost in the tunnels forever. His main concern was getting him and Bethany out. Bethany was holding up remarkably well, considering their current circumstances.

"Quit worrying about me." Her hushed voice fell over him and he opened his eyes.

She was bent over his bandage, tying what he hoped was the last knot. Her petticoat lay in shreds around them. They'd been sitting no more than the ten minutes it had taken for her to slice up her lovely undergarments.

He scraped his fingers into her tangled hair, forcing her head up and looking into the shine of her eyes. He loved her so much. The emotions ate through him into the core of who he was—and who he wasn't. He was not a man who would ever have a "normal" life, who could ever do anything else than what he did. Yet, he'd never felt so disjointed.

"Why didn't you tell me about the detonators?" he asked. When she didn't reply, he knew she was bothered by the fact she'd told Whitley she'd stolen them. "It doesn't matter what you said back at the conservatory, Bethany. You did what you had to do."

"The same way you left me at the stone wall? It should have been me who remained behind at the conservatory," she countered. "You were better able to hike the miles to the inn. In trying to protect me you broke your own rules."

"There was more to it than that."

"We are a team," she quietly accused him. "Our mission is to find the anarchists and get that information to Ware first. We should have been there for each other."

He bit back an oath as Bethany tied a knot in the bandage she'd wrapped around his waist. "Am I being too forceful?" she demanded in an angry tone he knew he probably deserved, for waiting so long before he finally tended to his wounds and because she was correct on all accounts.

"Tyrannical." His gaze softened on her.

He closed his eyes as she finished working on the bandage. The wound was just above his hip and made it difficult to move.

Pamela's voice came to him. "The first mission together is always the most difficult." She sat just beyond the light. He wondered how long she'd been there listening and watching Bethany doctor him. "But you aren't partners yet."

A rustle of movement followed and Pamela appeared, her hair nearly white in the light and uncombed and wild around her shoulders. "He should know about the human character. I taught him everything he knows."

Bethany looked at Ian. "She was your mentor?"

"He didn't tell you?"

"Why don't you come into the light, Pamela," Ian said tiredly. "You don't have to stand out there and be afraid."

She glanced at Bethany then moved a little closer and sat against the wall, folding herself into her cloak. "How can you stand the darkness? The noise?"

"We're about to be down to one lamp," he said. "It's going to get a lot darker and more unpleasant if we don't find our way out of here."

Ian picked up the second lamp and struggled to stand,

then Bethany was there to save him from falling. He didn't like it that he could barely stand.

"What happens when we get out of here?" Pamela asked.

He couldn't save her this time. And he was sorry, he realized.

Sorry, that she had made her own foolish choices and couldn't see beyond the right and the wrong of any matter, and now the consequences of her actions were at hand.

The noise around them grew more deafening. Without a word, she reached down and took the second lamp. He'd been prepared for her to pull her gun, but she didn't. Her fear of dying alone in these tunnels and what would follow was currently greater than her fear of him. And for some reason, she'd continued to honor their truce. Until another hour had passed and Ian had stopped to rest and let Bethany tighten the bandage on his waist, only to open his eyes and find her gone.

"Stop." Ian's voice barely registered above a rasp and he bent over his knees for breath.

Bethany tried to tamp down the panic as she braced her shoulder beneath Ian's and stumbled along the narrow passageway, heading blindly into the darkness. Pamela had long since abandoned them with the other lamp and taken her gun, leaving them with Ian's one pistol with its one bullet in the chamber. Bethany had checked.

This couldn't be happening, Bethany thought over and over to herself. Her heart sank and icy blades of fear sliced into her chest, but somehow despite exhaustion, hunger, and thirst she kept her mind focused on walking. The fact that Ian desperately needed her kept her focused.

"Tracks." He pointed to the ground.

Bethany stopped. "Pamela came in this direction."

"My tracks," Ian said. "Yours. Pamela's. We've all been here before. That's my boot print."

"You mean we've been going in circles?"

Bethany took the lamp from Ian's hand. She walked twenty feet and found other prints where the bottom of the cave was soft with earth.

Bethany almost laughed at the macabre irony of it all, especially since they were about to loose the last of their light. She tried to read the direction of the footprints.

"It looks as if we've passed here twice," Ian said.

He seemed to put everything into perspective, and his quiet laughter drew her back to his side. Bethany could see him leaning heavily against the stone wall. "We could be returning to the entrance," he said. "But which way?"

Bethany held up the lantern and saw the flame flutter. The lamp was about to go out. "Ian?"

"Have I told you how much I love you?" his voice came to her in the quasi shadow just before the flame extinguished.

She felt his arm go around her shoulder and pull her against him. "You could have left me," he said into her hair as she shared the warmth of her cloak with him. "I'm only slowing us down."

"I'll never leave you, Ian."

"If you ever thought . . . if you ever thought I considered you anything like Pamela . . ." He shaped his palm to her waist and she let its warmth sift through the fabric to her flesh.

"You don't have to explain to me anything anymore, Ian."

They no longer heard the rats. It had helped that Ian had left his cloak and blood-soaked bandages back in the passageway before they'd found the last fork. That had been at least an hour ago. She drew in a deep breath and felt the growing chill in the air. After a moment, she opened her eyes. "It doesn't feel as dark as it should."

Ian's body shifted. "No, it doesn't."

They both looked down the passageway. Bethany settled beneath his shoulder and they felt their way another hundred feet, slowing as they worked their steps around the corner and for the first time in hours saw a hint of light at the end of the tunnel.

A few moments later, they stood at the entrance. Much of the tunnel though not all had been destroyed and rendered impassable by the fire and explosion. Their steps stirred loose rocks and gravel. Someone had been here before them and dug out a space between the debris and the rock wall where an opening had remained. That someone had only made it wider.

"Pamela was here," Bethany said, too happy at the moment to care for the implications.

If she had been here then she may still be around.

She helped Ian out into the sunlight and they both stood with their faces pressed to the rare bout of warmth peaking through the clouds in the sky. They made it to the stream and drank thirstily. But Ian wouldn't last long without care and shelter.

"I need to check the glade," she said, worried about stragglers from Whitley's group.

No one had met them coming out of the cave. Indeed the world was silent, almost expectant in the soft hush of the breeze.

Ian realized he'd slept.

He came awake with a start. He hadn't been out for much more than a few minutes. He sat with his back against the shelter of a rock with his knees pulled up and his feet braced in the dirt. A shadow had passed across his body. Even as his hand reached for the gun he kept beside him, he opened his eyes. The gun was gone. Bethany must have taken it when she'd left. He hadn't remembered taking it out.

Pamela stood braced in front of him. The sun reflected in his eyes and he couldn't see her face. She held a gun.

"I'm sorry, Ian," she said, and he thought for once in her life, she truly might be sorry about something. He was sorry, too, but only because he wasn't in the mood to die.

"It doesn't have to be this way, Pamela." He was surprised how calm his voice sounded.

"I won't go back to face a tribunal," she said.

"I know."

She cocked the trigger, her hand remarkably unsteady. "Even if they do decide to give me one, I'm dead. If I leave, you won't quit hunting me until I'm dead. Tell me this isn't true. Tell me anything. Lie. Make me believe in something."

He thought of the Home Secretary, his wife and daughters who would never grow up, and knew Pamela would probably kill again. It was what she was trained to do. It was what he had been trained to do and yet . . . he knew he was not like her. "Are you going to murder Bethany, too?"

"I'm sorry, Ian. I truly am."

"No sorrier than I am, Pamela." Bethany's voice stopped Pamela from pulling the trigger.

It was Bethany's voice that kept Ian from leaping across the short distance separating him from the gun and making one final futile effort to save himself. Bethany who stood behind Pamela her hands clutched around the revolver ready to defend his life.

Bethany who pulled the trigger.

Chapter 25

Bethany didn't see Ian for weeks after the incident near the tunnel. She'd made the trek that day across the moors with Ian terribly injured. Rory Jameson had found them on the road and Bethany had never been happier to see anyone in her life. Lord Ware and reinforcements had arrived and Lord Ware had gone to Whitley Court, only to find Lord Whitley gone.

Ian had been mostly unconscious during those first few days. Lord Ware took her back to London while he'd sent Ian to a safe place to recover. Because of her knowledge of Whitley's organization and everything that had happened at the conservatory, she served as witness against Lord Whitley. Her deposition was in the warrant for his arrest. He had been found days later ill in a failed attempt to get across the channel to France. Sir John had also survived his ordeal, but soon found he would be granted no immunity for the crimes he'd committed. Five weeks later, the tribunal sentenced him to hang along with Whitley and the rest of the anarchists, including Desmond and Goodman. The conservatory remained closed and the laboratory torn down.

She had not seen Ian. She knew he'd been recovering

from his injuries, and that later he'd taken Pamela's remains to be interred somewhere near where she had been born in southern England.

Bethany had never killed another human being. That she had not felt more remorse frightened her in the beginning, but she had been unable to allow Pamela to kill Ian and knew she would do the same thing again. And as the weeks passed, that small token of remorse vanished and she no longer wondered fearfully if she were not more like Pamela than she realized.

She went to Ireland to visit her family, whom she had not seen in so long. It felt good to touch their smiles again and know they loved her without question or judgment. She began to understand the strength of family and recognized the source of Ian's own moral courage.

There was a fine line between good and evil. She had seen the murky gray, felt its power, and recognized its danger. It was a line Ian walked every day and yet he never lost that which made him good and decent.

She returned briefly to Queen's Staircase, but Ian had not yet returned, so Bethany took Sampson and went home to Rose Briar where it had all begun for her three years before, when he had walked into her life. Lord Ware let her go home, but made it clear he wanted her back and, when she was ready, to find him.

Bethany had been at Rose Briar two days when she looked up from brushing out Sampson's shiny coat to see Ian standing in the doorway of the barn. New springtime leaves rustled. Sunlight and shadow danced at his feet. Wearing a frock coat, his hands in his pockets, he was dressed much as he had been when she'd first set eyes on him and decided that he was the one—the only one in the world for her, remarkable, intense, larger than life.

A lock of hair blew across her cheek.

"I thought I might find you here," he said as if he hadn't been out of her life for the last eight weeks. "I missed you in London and again at Queen's Staircase. It must be a sign of the times to come that I am already chasing you across the breadth of England."

She felt herself smile. Strange that she'd been waiting for him, and now she couldn't seem to move. They both stood in the barn surrounded by the smell of straw with dust moats dancing in the air, no longer quite so sure of the future, yet feeling its power pulling them.

They'd been together under the direst of circumstances and been apart as the world healed itself. The last few months had not altered who they were deep inside, except to convince her that they were far stronger together than apart. The pull was there between them. It had not gone away, and now Bethany realized it would not. Everything would be all right.

She continued brushing Sampson as if her heart were not racing and every inch of her body not aware of Ian's presence. As if she did not want to fly into his arms and ravish him where he stood. Anticipation warred with patience.

"When I was a little girl, I wanted to be a horse doctor," she said conversationally. "That desire goes with my want to fix things, I suppose. I've always been somewhat unconventional. Not like other girls my age." She stroked and smoothed Sampson's coat until it began to glisten. "I felt out of place and awkward, always looking back toward the sunset and wondering if I was missing something. When all along I should have been looking at the sunrise and the entire world that lay before me. Do you ever feel that way? Like you were lost? But now you are found?"

His eyes had locked on her face, and the corners of his mouth warmed into a smile. "Until you."

"My grandfather once told me a man's true measure is not found in the girth of his chest but the weight of his heart." She smiled at the memory. "But I believe I like your chest as much as I do your heart."

Satisfied that Sampson's coat could not shine more without actually glowing, she set down the currycomb on a shelf next to the stall and locked the gate. When she turned, Ian stood behind her, not quite touching her, yet close enough that his presence stirred the air with warmth.

"I've been—"

She put a finger on his lips. He didn't need to explain where he'd been these past weeks. She already knew and understood, and told him so as she slid her arms around his neck. "I've missed you."

"I love you," he said. "But then you've known that for some time."

Her fingertips feathered over his eyebrows and traced the shape of his beautiful mouth. "What story shall we tell everyone about us, my errant knight?"

"We met at a grand ball." Backing her against the stall, he began, "Where once upon a time a knight fell in love with the beautiful princess from the Royal House of Munro." He slid his hands beneath her hair and trapped her head in place as his breath brushed hers. "Perhaps if he hadn't been a spy, his chances with her in the beginning might have been better. For he was wealthy, after all, and very nice-looking, or so all the ladies of the court had told him. But he took one look at the princess and fell in love, breaking all those other hearts."

She sniffed.

"He married his princess and sired . . . ?"

"Three."

"Three dozen children, all beautiful and fair like their mother, but not until their father had taken her to see the world."

She laughed and nuzzled her mouth against his throat.

"Ware has an assignment for us," he said.

"I know."

A question mark filled the sudden silence in her heart, but his hands went to her face and he held her between his palms with searching tenderness. "There is no one in this world I want at my side more than I want you, Bethany Ann. I want you in my bed, my heart, and in my life. I don't want to be alone anymore."

"Are you asking me to be your partner or your wife, Sir Ian?"

His lashes lowered over those sensuous green eyes as her mouth became his sole ardent focus. "Is there a difference?"

Bethany twined her arms around his neck. "Does our fairy tale have a happy ending?" she breathed.

"I want a big wedding," he said against her hair, her temple, her throat. "In a church with our families present. I want you in ivory lace with a veil, and afterward, I want you in nothing at all but a contented smile on your face." He brushed the hair from her face and his eyes smiled into hers. "I can't promise that we'll always be safe or we won't throw an occasional cooking pan at each other, but

I can promise that I will be faithful and our life will be an adventure."

She too would remain faithful. There were some lines she would not cross even for love of country and duty. "Will I have to behave?"

His mouth twitched into a smile. "Only in public, my love. Only in public."

They remained looking into one another's eyes like two adolescents in the throes of first love.

"What do we do now?" she asked in anticipation.

He looked up at the lofty ceiling spun in silvery webs moving in the afternoon breeze. They'd stood in this exact same spot once when she'd thrown her arms around him and vowed undying love. A wicked gleam entered his green eyes. "Finish that kiss you wanted all those years ago," he said softly.

"I wanted more than a kiss, my lord knight," she whispered.

A hot shiver went through her body as he lifted her against him until she suddenly didn't know where he ended and she began. "You were very naughty, love."

Then she captured his mouth and kissed him passionately with all the love in her heart, three long years crumbling into a mere memory at her feet and suddenly being naughty held new promise. And somewhere between the sunset and the sunrise, her life truly began. Unconventional perhaps. Daring certainly. But perfect in every way. The future belonged to them.